monsoonbooks

OLIVIA & SOPHIA

Rosie Milne lives in Singap— ... she runs Asian Books Blog (*AsianBooksBlog.com*). Her two previous novels are *How To Change Your Life* and *Holding The Baby*.

Also by Rosie Milne

How To Change Your Life
Holding The Baby

Olivia & Sophia

ROSIE MILNE

monsoon

monsoonbooks

Published in 2016
by Monsoon Books Pte Ltd
www.monsoonbooks.com.sg

Editorial / Sales:
No.1 Duke of Windsor Suite, Burrough Court,
Burrough on the Hill, Leics. LE14 2QS, UK

Registered office:
150 Orchard Road #07-02, Singapore 238841

First edition.

ISBN (paperback): 978-981-4625-27-2
ISBN (ebook): 978-981-4625-28-9

Cover design by Sarah & Schooling.
Cover watercolour of Government House, Buitenzorg, Java©The British
Library Board.

National Library Board, Singapore Cataloguing-in-Publication Data
Milne, Rosie, author.
Olivia & Sophia / Rosie Milne. – First edition. – Singapore : Monsoon Books
Pte Ltd, 2016.
pages cm
ISBN : 978-981-4625-27-2 (paperback)
1. Raffles, Thomas Stamford, Sir, 1781-1826 – Fiction. 2. Raffles,
Olivia Mariamne, 1771-1814 – Diaries – Fiction. 3. Raffles, Sophia, Lady,
1786-1858 – Diaries – Fiction. 4. Colonial administrators – Great Britain
– Fiction. 5. Colonial administrators' spouses – Great Britain – Diaries –
Fiction. 6. Singapore – History – 1819-1867 – Fiction. I. Title.
PR6113
823.92 -- dc23   OCN921310201

Printed in Singapore
18 17 16   1 2 3 4 5

For Aurelia

PROLOGUE

PROLOGUE

The inscription on the pedestal below the life-size white marble statue of Raffles in the north choir aisle of Westminster Abbey:

To the memory of Sir Thomas Stamford Raffles. Lieutenant-Governor of Java and first President of the Zoological Society of London. Born 1781 Died 1826. Selected at an early age to conduct the government of the British conquests in the Indian Ocean, by wisdom, vigour, and philanthropy, he raised Java to happiness and prosperity unknown under former rulers. After the surrender of that island to the Dutch, and during his government in Sumatra he founded an emporium at Singapore, where in establishing freedom of person as the right of the soil, and freedom of trade as the right of the port, he secured to the British flag the maritime superiority of the Eastern Seas. Ardently attached to science, he laboured successfully to add to the knowledge and enrich the museums of his native land, in promoting the welfare of the people committed to his charge, he sought the good of his country, and the glory of God.

Part One

OLIVIA

March 1805, Golden Square, Bloomsbury

And so I am honourably married again. 'Tis all most satisfactory; for sure my new husband pleases me far more than did my first one, tho' whether he pleases me more than did Jack I will not say … O Jack, I think it must be very wrong of me to remember you, now that I am wife to Thomas Raffles. So be it: a dead lover ain't a thing too easily forgot.

'Twas only yesterday, Thursday, March 14, that I acquired Tom as my new husband, and Mrs. Raffles as my new name. But who is she this new-born Mrs. Raffles? Who is she and what will be her story? This diary I plan sh'd be the answering of those questions, and if they interest none but me no matter, for my diary will have none but me as reader.

My happy acquisitions – husband, name – were made possible thanks to Tom's sudden and unexpected advancement through the ranks of The Company, an advancement in turn made possible through the kind efforts of his chief, Mr. Ramsay.

This good Mr. Ramsay is more like a father to Tom than the pitiable wreck that sired him, and much more able to promote his interests, being Secretary to The Company, an exalted and an influential position. Aye, 'twas thanks to Mr. Ramsay's kind intercession on behalf of his most capable, ambitious and adventurous Junior Clerk that 'twas last Friday announced Tom is now appointed Assistant Secretary in Penang.

I confess I'd never hitherto heard mention of this place Penang, but I now know 'tis an island we have in East India, more distant even than Madras. By all accounts 'tis but a small and insignificant settlement, nevertheless 'tis grown suddenly important to The Company; I follow not the reasons why, except to understand they are all in a knotty tangle: fears about Napoleon, and his wars in Europe intertwined with alarm for the China trade. But what care I for Boney and his vast ambitions? And what know I of trade? It matters to me only that The Company has decided Penang must now have a new government to replace the little one at present runs it. Hence a draft of recruits is soon to be sent half across the globe from Leadenhall St., and Tom is to be of its number.

O, what a boon! Tom's salary is henceforth to be one thousand, five hundred pounds a year! One thousand, five hundred pounds to he that until now was earning but seventy! That is sufficient funds to enable any man to marry, and when he is about to quit all other ties and affections 'tis only natural he sh'd secure for himself one bosom friend, one companion on his journey to sooth the adverse blasts of misfortune, and to gladden the sunshine of prosperity. Or so Tom pressed me, ardent, when he proposed. He added, less feeling, that since I'd once lived in Madras I must have much to teach him about life in the Eastward, if only I'd agree to sail with him. I said I didn't want things between us to stand as teacher and pupil, but I hoped the sunshine of prosperity w'd burn away the blasts of misfortune, if, indeed, blasts c'd be burned away, and yes please, how quickly c'd we do it?

So now here I am: Tom's wife, and have a husband in my lodgings that were until yesterday mine, and are now *ours*. From gratitude for his patronage, and for want of other candidates, I w'd have asked good Mr. Ramsay to give me away yesterday, had we ever met. But we never have, and Tom objected 'twere a terrible idea to introduce us now; he said he knows too well the ways of clerks at India House to allow such familiarity. No, he said, there is swirling about him in the office such jealous resentment of his great and rapid advancement that he dare not now mingle too much or too obvious with Mr. Ramsay for fear of malicious tongues murmuring against them both, and rumouring God knows what.

No, 'twas not Mr. Ramsay gave me away yesterday, but Mother's Mr. Etherington. The old sot limped clumsily by my side, on account of his gout, and clung to my arm against the risk of stumbling, and wobbled his jowls whenever he spoke. Still, he is a kind man – as he must be to tolerate Mother.

I wore my pink silk woven with a design of small silver leaves to be married in, and I'll say without embarrassment that I looked very well in it; let sharp-beaked, crook-toothed women whisper that I'm vain, but I want nothing to do with false modesty.

Alas, my parish church, St. George's, Bloomsbury, ain't renowned a pretty place – indeed, 'tis renowned perhaps the most hideous ecclesiastical building in all London. Yesterday, 'twas as chilly and echoing as ever, and even as I walked the aisle a bride I thought it had something about it of a mausoleum. Then again, I do not approve Our Rev'd; his charity seems to me as thin as his bony frame. As he tied the knot, he said he'd be sure to make it a tight one, which is I suppose what he always says, but he did not smile as he spoke, and I swear he looked at me as if I were a bolt of cloth, and him a cloth merchant, appraising how to price his goods.

He looked the exact same way at Mother, who behaved most decorous, tho' her bonnet was somewhat fantastical, and caused Tom's mother to stare. Mrs. Raffles, whose own bonnet was plain, cried as we took our vows, and this perhaps less for the sweet sadness of a mother's mingled loss and joy to see her only son wed, than on account of the bride he'd chosen. Aye, poor Mrs. Raffles has had to toil so hard to cling to a life respectable she values respectability most high. Tom has, in consequence, told her little about me; nevertheless I think she suspects my history ain't as crisp as newly laundered sheets.

Mothers and Mr. Etherington aside, our party was small.

Tom's three younger sisters were there, fluttering and sighing as maidens do at weddings, all dreamy with their own hopes. My dear Maria stood as a witness, and so did Tom's amiable lawyer friend, Richard Taylor, who is to protect our interests whilst we are in the Eastward. Our final witness was Tom's Uncle Charles, a tea merchant just as nondescript as a dish of the cheapest of his wares. The same ain't true of his son, Elton, who was also our guest. This Elton, Tom's cousin, is handsome, charming, witty, and mad. He's writing his autobiography in hopes 'twill be published. When asked why, pray, the world sh'd be interested in his story, he says, with confidence, 'tis 'cause he has the secret to perfecting mankind, which secret he will not tell until the day he announces it in his book.

As to who was *not* at St. George's to see me marry? Well, there was one that weren't invited, and I don't mean Tom's wastrel father, who I ain't never met and did not miss. No, I mean Harriet. I mean my daughter, and Jack's, who, living, haunts me always and everywhere, as if she, like her father, were naught but the glassy-eyed absence of a ghost.

March 1805, Golden Square, Bloomsbury

What joy! 'Tis confirmed what I hardly dared to hope: I am to see Harriet again before I sail for the Eastward. I wrote to her in Scotland, telling her of my marriage and of my impending voyage, and now I have her reply, saying she travels to London post-haste, in order that she and me may have our portraits painted in miniature, these portraits to stand as our mementoes to each other, lest death gather one or other of us whilst I am abroad. Alas, she adds that I must not be disappointed if she sees me only at our sitting, as she will be much occupied with society whilst she is in town.

Mother happened to call just as I was reading my letter. Tho' she caught me with it in my hand, I resolved to pretend it did not exist, and this out of sensibility for her feelings, for she cannot read, and it chafes her that she can't, and I can, and in any case I did not think she'd like its contents. So I slid my letter under some sewing lying by me on a side table, and I began to prattle of the purchases I'm making, in preparation for my coming journey. But Mother is sharp, and nosy, and, through insistent questioning, she soon wormed from me the news I wished to hide.

When I said 'twas Harriet who wrote me my letter, Mother sighed in a suffering way, to remind me she ain't once laid eyes on her granddaughter – her only grandchild – since she was but a slip of six. And at news of our portraits, she narrowed her eyes and she sniffed I'd have my big head that was already turned enough turned further by having it immortalised in a portrait, just as if I were a duchess, or a great lady, and what's more I'd be a fool if I allowed a fashionable daub of paint to lead me to think I'd grown as grand as my daughter.

Aye, my vain and jealous Mother thinks me vain, and prone to put on airs. Since I c'd think of no response to her carping, I said nothing at all. After some moments of silence, Mother disparaged she supposed it must be William w'd pay for this luxurious extravagance of miniatures, since with my load of debt I c'd never afford to commission one portrait, let alone two, and with his load of female relatives to support, nor c'd Tom.

Well! I was offended, tho' Mother spoke the truth: I *am* too poor to afford to commission my portrait, and what with so many other calls on his funds, Tom c'd not agree to it neither. No, 'tis indeed Harriet's husband, William, will meet the artist's fee.

I met this William but once, and thought him a stiff prig. Tho' his manners c'd not be faulted his politeness seemed to me acted, as if he wished to congratulate himself: look how polite I'm being toward this woman that don't merit my attention. I confess I pitied my poor Harriet, thinking that her marriage to him was as mine to Fancourt: contracted as a thing of household management, and destined never to deepen to anything richer.

But now I'm hoping I read everything wrong, as women are so wont to do – and men, too, for that matter. William cannot be such a cold fish if he thinks to provide Harriet with a portrait of me at just that moment I am about to quit these shores, and 'tis most generous of him to think of furnishing me with a portrait of her, before we take leave of each other, possibly for the last time. He is to accompany Harriet on her journey southwards, and when I meet him a second time I intend to thank him so profuse our former chilliness will be replaced by warmest friendship.

I said none of this to Mother. No, I met her tartness with tartness of my own, saying that rather than speculate who was paying for *my* portrait, she sh'd ask Mr. Etherington to commission *hers*. In spite of his kindness he is as tight as he is gouty, so this is something won't never happen. Mother was so much put out by my insolence she flounced home, after roundly scolding me for sauce.

March 1805, Golden Square, Bloomsbury

I've scarce seen Tom these past few days, my good and loving husband is also a good and loving son, so if he ain't at India House being flogged by The Company, he's out urgent busy trying to raise sufficient funds against his future salary to ensure that in the years when we are absent his mother and his sisters ain't distressed by want of money.

Tom's harassed looks when he considers his accounts make me remember that I too am now added to the female weight that he must carry – and I am an especial heavy burden, worse than most wives. Aye, instead of a dowry, I bring him debts, and large ones too – this in consequence of living high so long on lowest income, which living high is terrible hard not to do, even if a woman can't afford a candle, to light her way to bed.

Still, my sweet Tom lies he's grateful for my debts since they were my path to him. And this they were, thanks to Maria. Worried, perhaps, I c'd never repay the monies I owed her – for my friend had become also my creditor – worried, I am sure, for her own purse, 'twas she who first suggested I sh'd investigate whether The Company had a Compassionate Fund I c'd petition for support, for nobody, she said, nobody c'd deny Fancourt died my husband, in The Company's service in India, even if I had long since fled both man and Madras for a chancy life in London.

And so it was that one warm day early last September I dressed myself very drab and seemly, and then, with eyes cast down, presented myself at India House, that drear pile on Leadenhall St. Here 'twas an efficient clerk called Tom Raffles who arranged for me to receive a sum of twenty-five guineas, and a pension of one shilling and eight pence a day – and who, when he glanced up from his ledger and first beheld my face, bestowed upon me from across his desk such longing looks, both tender and passionate, that I c'd not help myself winking him a smile in return. And never mind my pension, as it happens that one thing leads to another, and sometimes not to calamity, so it is that six months later that same Tom is responsible for paying off my debts that he pretends to regard with such great gratitude.

March 1805, Golden Square, Bloomsbury

Mary Ann, Tom's youngest sister, is sixteen, and accounted a beauty. So 'tis decided we are to take her to the Eastward, to find a husband. This was my idea; I lit upon it from pondering the incidents of my own life, and also of Harriet's: did we not each, mother and daughter, through casting in the teeming Eastern Seas, land for ourselves a husband-fish? And if neither fish c'd be called a jewel enamelled of the ocean so be it: a poor fish is better than no fish, for who w'd be an Old Maid? Who w'd be fated to worry, ridicule, trouble, and as often as not naught to eat but destitution?

No. We want none of that for Mary Ann. And if women seeking marriage in India can overcome such scandal as riddle me and Harriet, then surely 'twill matter not that Mary Ann has neither family money, nor family connections as she casts her net. Or so I argued to Tom. I told him there are so many fair men in the settlements, and so few fair women, that with her face, and her youth, Mary Ann may yet land herself a whale. Well, he said, w'd be of considerable relief to him to have one sister at least off his hands, and thus he gave his blessing to my plan.

March 1805, Golden Square, Bloomsbury

Harriet and me have sat for our portraits, at the studio of Mr. Nathaniel Plimer, no less. This Mr. Plimer is the most sought-after miniature portraitist in London, tho' Tom's cousin Elton sneers he don't know why, the man's miniatures are very pretty, but they ain't *paintings*. When asked pray what are they instead, he waves his hand and dismisses they are naught but baubles and flattery.

For myself, I can't see the use of a portrait that *don't* flatter, and I'm in equal parts glad mine and Harriet's are to be set in pearls – big as peas, I hope – and distressed we'll never be able to flaunt them at our throats or bosoms, as necklaces or as broaches. Alas, they were only ever intended as private mementoes, which fact is now more than ever *pikant*, as I shall soon explain.

Harriet and me were dressed similar. We'd both piled our hair on our heads, and curled it short around the face – the face we share, that she got from me – and we both wore dresses of white muslin, *daycolletay*, with puffed sleeves, and gathered under the bosom – the latest style, a pretty one, I think, notwithstanding Mother says it makes every girl look pregnant. I had expected to see William, too, and I had prepared a speech to thank him for what so recently seemed his great generosity in enabling an exchange of portraits between my daughter and me, but the coward did not come, and my thanks went unuttered, for which I'm now most glad.

Mr. Plimer's studio is on New Bond St., a most good and fashionable *melyer*, where great ladies and gentlemen come and go. A boy served us a dish of tea in an anteroom, and then Our Artist himself came in to greet us. He is a plump man, with wild hair, and staring eyes, somewhat comic in his gait. He led us through to his studio, which was neat and clean but smelled peculiar, from the inks and paints he uses. Here he posed us together on a dainty sofa placed before a great window, for the best light, he said.

Absorbed, Our Artist spoke little as he made his deft sketches, and I was mostly silent too, on account of listening to Harriet, uncommon self-possessed, who spoke at me much, and quietly, tho' not softly. No, her words were, to me, as harsh as whips: their lashes caused me to judge I'd been wrong ever to think her tender, and to reverse once more my opinion of William.

Aye, from cold, to considerate, I now think William cold again, and this 'cause it transpires he commissioned my portrait, to be given to Harriet, not that she may take comfort from it whilst we are separated by half the globe, but as some kind of proof or record she ever had any mother at all. And hers he commissioned not as a generous and feeling gift for me, but as some kind of sop, or bribe, or indulgence, or I don't know what, from shame for his behaviour.

O, 'tis hard to write it, but the words Harriet this morning stung me on Mr. Plimer's sofa were in gist this: William has decreed that since I am in any case quitting England, he and Harriet may as well seize the opportunity to be rid of me entirely, and what's more the shabby girl has agreed to this. Aye, that lordly pair have decided they will henceforth have nothing no more to do with me. In consequence, Harriet this morning commanded she w'd prefer me not to write from the Eastward, and warned I must likewise expect no letters from her. For shame! But my daughter, unblushing, said she thought it best for her shiny new family name if 'twere not sullied by raffish connections. She said she and William must think of future children: 'twould be best for their little ones, when they come, if 'twere not widely known their mother was born out of wedlock, and that a woman with my reputation was their grandmother.

My own dearest girl! She may as well have accused to my face I was a bawd, which is the thanks I get for gambling all for love with Jack that glittering summer when I was young.

From pride, I did not wish to speak, but however hard I grit them, I c'd not make of my teeth iron bars, and bitterest rebukes escaped me. I says, all withering, and meaning the opposite of my outward words: in the face of your great and welcome elevation, 'twould of course be selfish if I were to protest your husband's decision that I am henceforth to be denied. I says: I understand that to be born out of wedlock is a stain – tho', I adds, 'tis a stain I have lived with well enough, as did your father.

To this my faithless daughter replied 'twas not Jack's parentage, nor mine, at issue, but hers. I agreed that aye, 'twas so – and being so demanded how, pray, she w'd in future account for her origin, if she c'd not mention me?

Ye gods! It seems obscuring rumours are already being put about in distant Scotland: one, that Harriet is Jack's legitimate daughter by that wife he never loved, and another, that she is the daughter of some fictional second wife he never had. I asked, all haughty, if a name had been assigned to this fantastical second wife? Harriet, blushing at last, told me 'twas being whispered she was one Miss. Thompson, which is a name so dull none w'd question it, I suppose.

When I heard my daughter w'd pass herself off as some false

Miss. Thompson's child, rather than acknowledge me, I twitched my skirts away from hers, and I rose half an inch from the sofa, preparing to quit Mr. Plimer's studio. But without looking up from his work, Our Artist asked me please not to break my pose. The few moments of this little intervention were all the time I needed to realise that I badly, badly wanted to carry my daughter's portrait to Penang, however inconstant is that daughter. So I sank back onto the cushions, and I resettled my limbs, and I told Harriet, stiffly, it seemed I had no choice but to accept my erasure from her biography. I said I'd do it gracefully; that I'd not embarrass her by bringing to general attention the threadbare nature of that fictional creature, Miss. Thompson. I reminded her that for seventeen years I've been discrete she is my daughter, and I said 'twas but a small step from discretion to silence.

Harriet and me now looked at each other long and significant, and I thought her eyes were clogged like reedy pools with meanings I c'd not decipher, and I thought her eyes must be a mirror of mine, and I felt the hovering presence of my own absent mother, she who bequeathed to me my eyes – the dark Circassian eyes which I, in turn, bequeathed to Harriet – and I felt too the hovering presence of the daughters Harriet may one day bear, daughters that with their histories cleansed of any trace of me will grow up thinking themselves cloaked almost in nobility and I thought: I can expect nothing now except to be forgot.

Still, now I've had time to gather my calm it occurs to me I was too gloomy on Mr. Plimer's sofa. Harriet and William ain't the only ones thinking of children; Tom and me likewise have our hopes, and if we are blessed with chicks, 'twould be bad luck indeed if they as well as my firstborn chose to forget me.

April 1805, Golden Square, Bloomsbury

The cost of sea passage to Penang is shocking. Shocking! Tom will have to pay one hundred and fifty pounds for passage for himself, and the same for me; for Mary Ann he will have to pay one hundred and ten pounds, the amount charged for single ladies.

But the bare cost of passage ain't the half of it. We must also find money for the food we will be served on ship, even if most of it be lost to seasickness, or never touched at all, from the same cause. Then there is the beer and wine we must purchase, all the porter, sherry, gin, rum, &c, for when the supply of fresh water runs out between ports. Then there is all the business of beds and bedding, washbasins, ewers, chamber pots, desks, chairs. Aye, all the things of daily life we must provide ourselves, or suffer for it.

Of course, my Tom also wants a bookcase. Alas, for want of money, he had but two years at school, which is two more than me or any girl I ever knew growing up, but then he was a boy and 'tis sad for him his family c'd not provide him with a gentleman's education. He now feels as a great lack and sorrow, and also as an impediment to his advancement, all the lessons he never had, so he is teaching himself the knowledge he never got from no doctors of divinity. He is interested in everything, inquiring about everything, and his studies, snatched in stolen moments, include French, Hebrew, Greek, and every branch of natural philosophy, in particular botany and zoology. So 'tis no surprise he says he must bring all his books to the Eastward, nor that he has been buying yet more books to add to his collection – he says there ain't no circulating libraries where we're going, so what is he to do?

I that am barely educated in a formal way am all for learning. Nevertheless, I have had to remind Tom that if he is to bring all these big, heavy vols. to the Eastward, we will need trunks in which to transport them, which trunks we must buy, and trunks, good wooden trunks bound with brass, cost money.

Likewise we will need trunks for our clothes: warm clothes for the earlier weeks of the sea passage, and light ones for the heat of India, which, I have warned both Tom and Mary Ann, is a seething heat, and stinking. I have told Mary Ann to pack only the lightest and loosest of her muslin dresses, and to bring only calico under things: she will need neither wool nor flannel, tho' I encountered in India a strange belief amongst the English ladies there that flannel ought to be worn next to the skin, to ward off the many diseases that stalk that killing land. This belief I ignored during my time in Madras, and I have told Mary Ann to ignore it, too. Tom, meanwhile, is ordering things by the four-dozen: four-dozen calico shirts; four-dozen undershirts; four-dozen long drawers, &c.

'Tis all dizzying expensive. Between paying off my debts, supporting his family, paying for sea passage, and equipping three people both for a long voyage, and also for the life that will follow it, if said people are spared shipwreck, disease, or other disaster, between all this Tom reckons he must borrow around two thousand pounds from The Company's agents before we even take the stage coach to Plymouth.

Two thousand pounds! But tho' I am alarmed, my cool husband claims to be unworried. He reports he will be given at least four years to pay back whatever loan he takes out, and he shrugs 'tis certain we will avoid the debtors' prison – which airy nonchalance maddens me.

April 1805, Golden Square, Bloomsbury

There is something I have been keeping from this diary, in vain hopes I c'd keep it also from myself: the man who will be Tom's chief in Penang, the new Lieutenant-Governor of the settlement, is none other than Jack's Philip Dundas.

Philip Dundas ain't an outlandish name, and The Company is large. Until yesterday I had been trying to believe there was some slight chance there c'd be two men called *Philip Dundas* on the establishment, and that Tom's new chief was not the same man as

Jack's good friend, last heard of in Bombay. Even if the same man, I further tried to believe, 'twas possible neither Jack nor Harriet had told him that her mother was Olivia Fancourt. And even if he knew of this Olivia Fancourt, I argued, there was no reason he sh'd realise his new Assistant Secretary's wife, Olivia Raffles, was that same Olivia, now living under a different name.

O you fool, Olivia, you fool! Of course the Philip Dundas Jack held dear is Tom's chief! Of course this Philip Dundas knows full well who I am, and who was my lover, and who is my daughter!

My foolishness revealed itself last night, when my poor husband returned late to our lodgings most agitated, and with his foxy colour even higher than usual – his hair is as russet as mine is dark, and his complexion as ruddy as mine is clear. He wasn't barely through the door before he was calling for Madeira, and when I asked why so thirsty, he said he'd come direct from an interview with Philip Dundas, and why the deuce hadn't I warned him his new chief knew my whole history?

Shamed, I flushed and told the truth. I says: I *don't* know the man, I know only his name. And I don't know why I kept from you I know his name except for longing I do not. What? Says Tom, you closed your eyes deliberate against something you did not wish to see? I says: aye, you've caught my meaning well enough. I went on I was sorry for my willed blindness, and even sorrier for keeping from him information I sh'd have shared, which keeping from was not a nice way for any wife to behave, and especially not one who had a husband as gentle and loving as *mine*.

Tom was less angry than he had right to be. He threw himself on the sofa and said 'twas all damnation awkward and c'd worse disaster ever have befallen a man newly elevated in The Company? I sat by him, took his hand, and asked him to tell me what had happened.

It seems that just as Tom was leaving India House for the day, Dundas approached him and asked him to walk with him along

Leadenhall St. This was a most irregular request, and Tom was much alarmed. They walked a few moments through the damp chill rising from the river: two silent men amongst all the noise of the tinkers and the street sellers crying for business and all the clatter and jingle of horses; two grey-dressed men slipping like fog through the muddle of thieving urchins, pimps, pouncers, whores, dollymops, mudlarks, ladies, aldermen, clergymen, all the riot of male, female, tall, short, fat, thin, old, young, virtuous, and vicious that is London.

Dundas stopped at last, and turned to Tom. He is apparently a blushing sort of man; he cleared his throat, and hummed and hawed, and then he cleared his throat again, and finally he got it out that since he'd approved Tom's appointment as his Assistant Secretary, it had come to his attention that he'd taken a wife, and that his bride was a widow named Olivia Fancourt, and tho' he supposed there c'd be several Mrs. Fancourts running around London, had Tom's by any chance had a husband in Madras, one Joseph Fancourt, until his death Assistant Surgeon in The Company's service in that settlement?

Tom told me he suspected now what was coming, and that it took great effort not to let horror flit across his face. But, mastering himself, he nodded and confirmed this was indeed the very Mrs. Fancourt he'd so recently had the great joy to wed.

Now Dundas hummed and hawed some more, and then he jittered that alas he was privy to information about this Mrs. Fancourt of which Tom may be ignorant, and such was the gravity of this information he felt 'twas his duty, as a man and as Tom's chief, to make him aware of the truth.

Tom said that at these words it seemed to him the buildings of Leadenhall St. lurched like drunken men. He said again he struggled not to reveal by his outward expression his inner uproar, but again he mastered himself and his voice was steady as he challenges, courageous and direct: Dundas, do you mean to ask whether I know that before she wed Fancourt my wife already had a daughter?

Dundas now blushed fierce enough to combust, and cleared his throat not once but several times. Eventually he agreed that this was the fact he'd wished to impart, and that he'd known this daughter in Bombay, and he'd known her late father, too. As an afterthought he adds: the girl is a good girl, and her late father was a good man.

Poor Tom confessed he thought it probable this was Dundas' roundabout way of saying by omission that I, the girl's mother, and the father's lover, was not a good woman. He said there followed a long silence that he felt as stifling. He said he felt sicker and sicker as this silence stretched, until finally he asked, very nervous, what he felt he must: did the fact he'd married a woman whose name c'd be bandied mean The Company had lost confidence in his judgement? Did the fact he'd married me mean his appointment as Dundas' Assistant Secretary w'd be revoked?

Dundas now became flustered and says: good heavens no, no, no, not at all, not at all. He gabbled that now he knew Tom had married not in ignorance of his wife's natural daughter but in full knowledge of all that, he felt the affair was none of his business, and, rest assured, he intended to say no more about it, but to treat Mrs. Raffles as he w'd any other wife going out to Penang; indeed the only person who'd henceforth have whisper of this scandal, at least from his lips, was his own dear wife.

Here I jibs: Dundas' *wife*? No, Tom, Dundas' wife drowned with Jack, when the *Earl Talbot* was broke on rocks in the South China Sea.

Even as I spoke I realised Dundas must have remarried. Rather than comment on the obvious, Tom directed his gaze to my shoes, where the buckles poked from my skirts. Without lifting his eyes he takes a deep breath, and he trembles: Dundas says not to worry, his wife can be trusted with any secret, she's a veritable sphinx.

All the members of the new government for Penang, and their dependants, are to sail to the settlement on one ship, ergo I will be cooped with the new Mrs. Dundas for all the long months of the voyage, and never mind inscrutable sphinxes, I understood Tom's nervousness. Aye, I know too well the ways of ships. Such close confines the passengers endure. Such lack of privacy. Nothing for women to do for weeks and months on end but backbite and gossip, and pass on tittle-tattle when they can, and invent it when they can't and in all ways chatter, and squabble, and intrigue.

Tom and me looked at each other, very meaningful. Neither of us said what was surely in both our minds: on the coming voyage, Mrs. Dundas' silence seems too much to hope.

April 1805, Golden Square, Bloomsbury

Mr. Plimer promised me he'd hurry with Harriet's portrait, that I may have it before I sailed, and he has been as good as his word: his boy delivered it today; I have it by me now. And my portrait is, I assume, now bound for Scotland, to be kept close by Harriet, if she chooses, to be handed down, perhaps, as a hidden heirloom, through the women of her family far into the future, along with whisperings of me, for tho' I think I'll be forgot by that line, I hope I won't be; 'tis my comforting fancy that one day some distant granddaughter may speak aloud my name.

The pearls ringing Harriet's miniature gleam like tiny moons, and my new jewel has become at once my most treasured possession, notwithstanding 'tis a token of betrayal. 'Tis a most excellent likeness of my daughter Mr. Plimer has caught. She wears on her face a dreaming expression, and in her eyes is such a wistful quality it further pains my aching heart to see it. O! If only Tom and me are blessed with children, I will show them Harriet's likeness, and I will tell them: this is your sister.

April 1805, Golden Square Bloomsbury

'Tis only a week now until we sail, and last night Tom and me gathered a party about us here at our lodgings, so we might bid our loved ones *adjoo*. I provided cake and wine but the mood was funereal. Mother's Mr. Etherington, morose in his cups, rambled a speech which dwelled long on the likelihood one, or more, or all of our party may be dead before we can meet again. Mother wept, and enjoyed her weeping, tho' her sadness was genuine: she is convinced she will die before ever I return to London, and she don't seem much consoled when I tell her far more likely *I* will die, from some swift mysterious disease of the tropics. Tom's mother was more restrained, but his sisters sobbed at the coming separation – Mary Ann hardest of all. Tom's Uncle Charles gave us a sack of tea to take with us, and as he presented his gift he said he hoped it shouldn't be lost to shipwreck. In his speech of thanks Tom reminded the company that in the event of his death, his will was with Richard Taylor, who alas c'd not attend last night. Cousin Elton promised to send us a copy of his autobiography, if ever it finds a publisher, and if we live to receive it, and if we don't to make of it, to us, a posthumous dedication. Maria said she wouldn't write since letters take so long to travel to the Eastward 'twould waste her ink. I said little; I was thinking of Harriet: her absence pricked me, tho' I knew it w'd have been impossible to have had her there to bid me farewell, even had she not renounced me.

April 1805, The Bell Inn, Plymouth

I am all rattled about and cold: for the past three days Tom, and Mary Ann and me have been jolting and jouncing by draughty stage coach from London to Plymouth, where today all is shades of grey – if I hadn't seen India for myself, then in this drab and rainy city I sh'd find it hard to believe that distant exotic land exists in fact, as well as in fantasy and fable.

'Tis here in Plymouth, beneath massing clouds and drizzle, that we are to spend our last night in England, and on firm ground, for who knows how long: come the morning we'll join the East Indiaman the *Ganges*, and commence the horrors of a long voyage; we'll be rocked for many nights in the heaving cradle of the ocean, until we reach Madras – there we'll rest a while, and change ships for the last leg of our journey through the seas of East-Insular India, to Penang.

The ways of destiny are ever obscure, but tonight we can at least foresee that our lives are about to change in ways we cannot foresee, and our mood is strange as we prepare to quit these shores of home.

Mary Ann one moment wails for her mother and her sisters, but the next she chatters excitedly of all she hopes to see in India – fakirs, and maharajas, and elephants, and rubies. And then she remembers she rides the trade winds to a husband, and she sets to girlish giggling.

Tom is in a fever of excitement. Even to his liver he shivers to be off; he is eager to pursue the great chance he's been offered, he is hungry for adventure, and hungry also to stretch himself against whatever boundaries threaten to contain him. He pants for fame. This he says is easier for bold men to win in the freedom of the Eastward, than in London, where all is rigidity and rules – well, if fame comes to anyone, I feel it must come to the swarm of restless, striving, driven energy that is him.

As for me, tonight, when the distance between us is about to become decisively geographic, I think it likely I will miss even my mother, and I am filled with sorrow to think of my daughter. I gaze on Harriet's portrait, and I remember the softness of her skin, when she was but a babe, and the smell of her that I wished to bottle, and her infant prattle – and I remember, too, her saying last month I was not good enough for her now, I w'd not do.

But this sorrow of loss mingles in me with greedy optimism, and with hope. I want everything the East has to offer. I want its sights, sounds, textures, smells, tastes. I want its fruits. I want money. I hope the backwater Penang will soon blossom into as fine a place in which to shake the money tree as anywhere else in India.

Aye, I dream that when eventually Tom and me return to England we can live in a fine house, and keep four prancing greys and a carriage, and have many servants, and costly foods, and costlier wines, and that thanks to that fame he longs for, by then, with luck, accrued to him, we can move in the highest circles of the land.

April 1805, the *Ganges*, The English Channel

So, I am aboard an East Indiaman again, and the *Ganges* is as horrid as any other ship I have been on, including the *Rose*, which, tho' Jack was on it, I cannot say was a rose to me since it stank as high as rotting meat.

I ain't got the vocabulary of ships. I know not how to name all the masts, sails, ropes, knots that make our little wooden world, that seems littler than she even is against the vastness of the ocean, and nor can I say her tonnage, displacement and so on. But this I do know: she is very well armed against pirates, thank God, as are all the other ships in our convoy, which is a big one, for our safety. The morning we departed Plymouth was fine, and as we sailed out of the harbour I think we must have made a splendid spectacle of billowing white sail, and flags and pennants fluttering and flapping from every masthead and yardarm, some bearing the red-on-white Cross of St. George, some The Company's striped ensign, some naught but cheerful bunting. Still, most of us on board had our eyes fixed not on waving flags, but on people waving from the quay – waving and twirling their hats – our fellow countrymen that we were leaving – and on the receding shoreline, the long ribbon of coast unspooling between us and the home that's our refuge, or that we're fleeing, but which in any case we'll most of us not be seeing no more these next few years.

We are now three days out into The English Channel, bouncing along under a brisk wind, with half the passengers prostrate with seasickness, and me most grateful I am a good sailor, and have already my sea legs. 'Tis very different for Tom and Mary Ann, they were both too queasy to eat last night, and the same at breakfast, and they do not so much walk about the ship as stagger, clutching whatever they can for support.

Tom is a nervous sailor, and this fear of his seems to me amiss: I think he sh'd be unconcerned by waves however monstrous, for he was born upon the sea. His father that is now a husk was in his prime a seafaring man, and master of a West Indiaman. Captain Raffles sometimes had Mrs. Raffles with him when he went to trade his cargoes of sugar and slaves, and so it was that Tom was born on a ship, off the coast of Jamaica. But he ain't been back to sea since he arrived in England a babe, and he blanches like any other landsman when the *Ganges* happens to lurch a little. He did not even smile when I remarked last night I trusted it a good omen for our forthcoming voyage to the *East* Indies that he survived so young the hardships of seafaring in the *West* Indies; he said East Indies, West Indies, 'twas all the same to him, the ocean was everywhere deep and cold and indifferent who it drowned.

This landsman of mine is now in Dundas' cabin, consulting with his chief – of which Chief Dundas more in a moment. Mary Ann complains already of boredom, and tho' Tom advises her to take up study of history, or languages, she seems averse to such self-improvement. Instead of sitting with some worthy book she has taken her sewing to the cuddy, that social space on the quarterdeck that serves as dining room, and as games room for cards, and will some evenings serve as venue for dances, and other evenings as playhouse for theatricals. She hopes there to find companions to help her while away all the yawning empty mornings ahead.

As for me, I have this diary to entertain me. Aye, it now occurs to me a diary is an excellent answer to the question of what a woman is to do with her day. I am writing now in our cabin, at Tom's slope I've set upon his desk, and the motion of the sea causes me here and there to blot the page. My hand ain't the best, but not so poor it don't vex me to see my letters sometimes jumbled by the jumbling of the sea – but I can't command the waves be still to suit me, so I must be content.

I wish I c'd be content with our cabin, but 'tis a miserable little dirty hole, even with our furnishings in place, and damp as a cellar. 'Tis some relief the partitions between it and the two to either side are of wood, and not of loosely slung canvas, as w'd allow for no shyness at all, but we have no window, and 'tis as dark as a crevice: tho' 'tis mid-morning, I am forced to light a candle, which is always a risk on a ship, notwithstanding the water everywhere surrounds it, but the danger of my candle's tiny flame becoming the leaping flames of a general conflagration is one I must run, if I am to see what I write.

Worse even than our cabin's lack of light is the lack of fresh air. Already I feel half-poisoned by a variety of stinks: the chamber pot effluvia and vomit from seasick passengers; the drifting smells of that detestable tar the sailors use; the emanations from that odious galley, which I suspect will produce only ill-concocted soups, queer-looking ragouts, and jellies the colour of saltwater.

Then again there is the stink of the animals. The fore lower deck is as usual a crowded manger: sheep, goats, pigs, rabbits, and a cow are all in pens, shuffling and bleating in hay already malodorous. I think even Tom, who loves all animals, must regret that in order we may have meat and milk to sustain us between ports, we must have a smelly farmyard floating with us as we sail.

Likewise the poop is stacked with chickens, ducks, and turkeys in coops. I enjoy a fresh egg to eat, but that poultry makes such a noise I hope the coops are swept away in a storm; the blow of loss to the table w'd be so much softened by the peace of silence – a silence I sh'd say broke every moment by the cries of the sailors, the thud of activity on deck, the creaking of the ship's sides, the wind in the rigging, the lapping of water, and all the ceaseless din of a ship.

But I stray. I was coming to write of Tom's Chief Dundas. Our introduction is now behind me, thank God – and perhaps Dundas thinks the same? He did not say in so many words he'd be happy to see the back seams of our meeting's hose, but the very hour we quit Plymouth he sent a note (ahem) inviting me and Tom to his cabin, writing he desired the pleasure of meeting for himself and at once the new Mrs. Raffles, whom he felt sure w'd be an ornament to the little shipboard society of his new government sailing for Penang.

'Tis well known Dundas gave the money tree a great shaking when he was in Bombay. I've heard it whispered that when he was Master Attendant of the Marine Board there he had ten thousand pounds a year, and further accumulated seventy or eighty thousand pounds with which to return to England. He has thus faced no need to stint on his accommodation, and has taken a cabin in the roundhouse beneath the poop deck – the best part of the ship where the cabins are large, and each has a window high enough out of the water to be rarely closed, even in rough weather, and these windows hung with lace curtains.

The circumstances of our meeting were so awkward and embarrassing I confess I was uncommon nervous, and so was Tom. But Dundas put us at ease, and him I liked – I thought him kind, tho' somewhat ponderous. At our introduction he hummed and hawed just as Tom had described, and then he glanced from me to Tom, and back, and then he took my hand and he said he knew I'd lived in India, and then, with great emphasis, that this was all he knew about me, and please to tell him more.

Tho' his manner was more significant than I'd have liked, I was most grateful for his decent, friendly deceit that he was ignorant of my history. I kept my own tone as light as I was able. Yes, I trilled, I'd been married in Madras, to the surgeon there, now dead these five years, and had only recently wed Tom and was most happy to be sailing with my new husband to Penang. Excellent, excellent, says Dundas, now come and meet my ladies.

His ladies are two, his wife and her sister, Miss. Wedderburn, that I suspect, like Mary Ann, is travelling to the Eastward to find a husband, for she's too ugly to have much hopes of one in England. These two were sitting together on an upholstered sofa that looked more comfortable than any other piece of furniture I've yet seen on the *Ganges*. There w'd have been room for me, had they resettled their skirts, but they did not. I said my how d'you do, and how d'you do, but they said nothing, and, in silence, Mrs. Dundas indicated a stool – a hard stool, with no cushion. Here I sat. Dundas now turned to talk to Tom, abandoning us three women to each other.

'Twas clear as gin one sister had whispered to the other the scandal she'd had from her husband – I mean I knew at once Mrs. D had whispered to Miss. W about Jack and Harriet. What's more, they knew that I knew that they knew. All this was clear from the telling glances we now exchanged – theirs glittery as icicles. Nothing was said, of course; these were well-bred ladies that knew they must say nothing of my past.

At least to my face. But what about behind my back? Aye, I set to worrying again whether Mrs. D w'd be able to resist the temptation to tell all about the *Ganges* what it is she knows of me – and likewise her sister.

Since I c'd not speak what was on my mind, I offered a few

compliments to Mrs. D on her dress, which was a hideous thing of mustard silk. The rules of society now forced from her a reply, but she all but gagged on her small talk, and her frost-patterned eyes told me she considered it an absolute insult that a disreputable low baggage such as me sh'd talk to a fine, respectable, high personage such as her.

As I recall this now I cannot but regret anew that having his chief's women set against his wife can be neither pleasant nor advantageous for Tom. I regret even more the likelihood that this voyage 'tis me will spice the women passengers' gossip, for tho' I'm glad to be of service, I wish 'twere in some other way.

Sometime, someplace on the ocean

I remain confident the year is 1805, and I am aboard the *Ganges*, but I write as my heading *sometime, someplace on the ocean* 'cause sailing across the nothing, nothing, nothing, and yet more nothing of the sea has addled me about both calendar and map.

The map I have quite lost track of. At dinner I say my daily toast to happy sight of the next land, and I think: where is that next land? Which is to say: where are we? With no landmarks to watch for by day, and, by night, not being able to read the stars, I am as ignorant now of place as must be the fishes swimming in the waters beneath me.

The calendar too, is becoming hazy to me. The tyranny of breakfast at eight, dinner at two, tea at six, and supper at nine keeps me abreast of the hours, but when I think of day and date 'tis as if one of our chilly sea fogs has reached its fingers into my mind, so I no more know whether 'tis Monday, Saturday, Wednesday, or Sunday, than I c'd say our position on the globe.

Sometime, someplace on the ocean

Was ever a ship so filled with ill-wishing people as this one? I grant Mrs. D and Miss W seem to have kept their mouths shut, but they have all but ostracised me, which makes things terrible trying in the cuddy.

Mary Ann knows no more of my history than does her mother, and yet I think she smells a rat. She sighs often and pointed that she cannot understand why the great ladies of Dundas' party refuse to be civil to me, unless it be 'cause I am of Circassian blood? Either from loyalty, or from a desire to stir things up, she even threatened if Mrs. D and Miss W c'd not be polite she w'd in turn cut them dead. But Tom forbade her to do any such thing, saying whatever quarrel those two chose to pick with me, she had no part in it, and she must mind her manners, even if they c'd not. Furthermore, he cautioned, we'll all continue living close as bedbugs even once we've reached Penang. Mary Ann, he says, w'd be best for you if you c'd survive at least the journey without making enemies in our small society.

But not even Mrs. D and Miss W mark the end of my troubles. There is also a man of our party called Robert Ibbetson. He ain't yet twenty, and he w'd be handsome were it not for a mouthful of crooked, tawny teeth, and his haughty eyebrows, which when he looks at me he raises in such a way to tell me plain I ain't worth looking at.

Even before we sailed Tom warned me of this Ibbetson, saying he was one of those at India House who most resented his steep advancement from Junior Clerk in Mr. Ramsay's office to the heights he has now attained, and that from envy Ibbetson kicked him one afternoon from a lighted fire at which he was warming himself. When I asked: why did you not kick him back? Tom replied 'twas better revenge to remember that he was to be Assistant Secretary in Penang, whereas Ibbetson was to be but a clerk.

Is not my husband's equanimity endearing? And also infuriating. Even now, when Ibbetson each meal snubs him in the cuddy, and when Mrs. D and Miss W refuse even to say good day to me, Tom affects to disregard their hostility, and tells me I must disregard it too. He says he will ignore both the man's petty jealousies and the women's rudeness, in favour of studying his Malay grammars – Malay being the language of Penang, and him eager to perform his duties all the better once we reach there. Aye, Tom is using the months of this voyage to learn the rudiments of the tongue – which tongue nobody else on the ship knows nor has any intention of learning.

But I stray. What I am coming to say is that Ibbetson has joined Mrs. D and Miss W in ostracising me. He wants to ingratiate himself with his chief's inner circle, I suppose. Worse, and I can think only for envy, he is slandering Tom. This I know from eavesdropping, which is a silly, shameful thing to do, that never has a good result, but the self is very fascinating to itself, is it not, and what woman w'd not tarry to listen, if she heard her name being bandied, not to say blackened?

Yesterday morning was cold and rough, with a heavy swell, and I hoped the chill of the wind and the lurching of the ship might together keep most to their cabins, thus allowing me to enjoy a few moments of blessed privacy on an empty deck, and to breathe air so clean 'twould shock my lungs, so I headed for the fo'c's'le. At just the moment I was about to step out onto it, from the shadow of the hatchway that leads to it from the lower decks, I spied Ibbetson, as hardy as me, standing with three or four of the *Ganges*' officers. All the men were wearing greatcoats, and stamping, and each sucked on a pipe: the steam of their breath mingled briefly with the smoke from the bowls, before the wind whipped both breath and smoke away.

This company of fellows was laughing together. Nosy, I admit, I pressed myself further into the shadows, and strained my ears against the sounds of wind, slapping water, flapping canvas, groaning timbers, &c, to try to catch their joke.

Well! What seemed funny to them did not seem so to me. Lucky we are to have a Circassian beauty aboard, leers one, in the horrid, licking tone men sometimes use when they speak of women. I knew he meant me – I am like as not the only Circassian this side of Circassia. The sly officer continued: I sh'd like to see her dancing, singing, playing music – all the skills of the high-class whore, was what I knew he meant to say, tho' God knows not the most important, and all his whoring was surely done in the gutter, where if they make music 'tis only drink singing.

Now another speaks up, an old sea dog from the look of him, which was mostly a shaggy mass of beard. He takes his pipe from his mouth and: I was in Istanbul once, he says, with my ship, you know. There's a slave market there where they sell them all: Georgians, Russians, Abyssinians. I saw a Circassian auctioned. Sweet girl, warranted virgin, beautiful as heaven. 'Twas the sultan himself what won her. I'll never forget the price; he had her in the end, boys, for one thousand five hundred dollars.

Ibbetson at this story looks down that long nose of his, and makes a disdainful moue. Tom Raffles ain't no sultan, he scoffs, and no more is Mrs. Raffles warranted virgin, nor has been since some year last century.

The men all laugh again, more raucously even than before. The youngest pipes up: how much older than him is she, d'you think? Old enough to dandle her bonny little boy, says Shaggy Sea Dog, and two inches taller than him, as even an oyster c'd see.

This cur! My Tom, tho' happily youthful in his appetites and ardour, is much older in attitudes, feeling, and good sense than many men twice his age, yet it cannot be denied: I *am* ten years older than him. And I *do* top him by an inch or two. But if I noticed these things when first he looked at me with such yearning from across his ledger at India House, then I do not notice them *now*, and I am proud of my Tom for his social irreverence, and proud of myself for it, too.

Still, I have had to teach myself to pretend to ignore the smirk in unkind peoples' eyes as they register my age, Tom's age, my height, Tom's height – a hard lesson only imperfectly learned.

I was still smarting from the sailors' banter, when Ibbetson says a most extraordinary thing, in equal parts puzzling and defamatory. He says: I'd pity any man such a bride, even Raffles, if I didn't know he'd had his pockets stuffed with gold to wed her.

At this it seemed to me the pitching ship stopped pitching and slammed to stillness. What? My Tom paid to wed me? My Tom who all he had from me of money was debt? What was this? What silly, wicked rumour? Who w'd pay him? And why? I was minded to walk boldly onto deck, slap Ibbetson's haughty sneer from his face and tell him to watch his filthy mouth, except that w'd have given him the satisfaction of running back to Mrs. D and Miss W to tell I'd behaved as a fishwife.

No, tho' I was on all sides umbraged and affronted, I kept my dignity and I retreated to the lower deck. I have since acted to everybody as if I heard on the fo'c's'le only the wind – but it ain't easy, this acting. O, I c'd cry to think I have months and months more of being outcast, being mocked with no one to support me but Mary Ann, who ain't much use for it – for all she's sixteen she remains in many ways a child – and Tom. But I can't tell my husband this nonsense he was bribed to wed me; his pride is as fierce as his heart is loving, and pride, heart, I will see neither wounded.

Later, a postscript: it occurs to me now that other people's diaries, if found, always so irresistibly demand to be read. And since I don't want Tom reading what I wrote earlier I will henceforth lock mine away when I ain't at it. If Tom frowns and asks why so shifty I'll trust inspiration for an answer at that moment strikes me.

Sometime, someplace on the ocean

So now I know why Ibbetson makes of my name and Tom's two links in a tawdry golden chain. Now I know what stinking rumour that villain is spreading, and I wish I had a man on hand to wallop him, which even if I c'd bring myself to tell Tom why walloping were required is something my husband c'd never do, being so slight and short of stature, and meek as a maiden.

'Twas Mary Ann enlightened me. She flew to me yesterday, all in an excited, breathless tizz. I thought perhaps 'twas some business of the heart – there is one among our party called Mr. Thompson and 'tis clear he and Mary Ann have caught each other's eyes. But 'twas not Mr. Thompson had put her in a commotion, but Ibbetson.

She'd come direct from the cuddy, where I don't go now, except to take my meals. Here she'd been sitting alone, darning stockings and thinking of this and that and humming little snatches of song to herself, and hoping *someone* w'd arrive to offer her companionship – by her arch way of saying *someone* I knew she meant Mr. Thompson. 'Twas not for deliberate choice, but where she sat, by a window, for the light, it happened she was obscured by the wooden screen used to hide that place where the servers pile the dirty dishes they have removed from the table: somebody, or else some action of the sea, had shifted it so it hid her chair.

Soon, she heard the clatter of others coming in from the roundhouse. Happy at the prospect of conversation, she w'd have stood up and called out a greeting, but from their voices she recognised at once Mrs. D, Miss W, and Ibbetson and she had no wish to be friendly to that lot. No, she kept hidden and quiet, not meaning to spy on them, but not averse to listening-in to their conversation, neither. Mary Ann now looks at me, her eyes shining with excitement, here's a thing, she purrs, soon enough the three of them are filleting a sordid scandal as tho' 'tis a fish.

I flinched, for I was sure Mrs. D and Miss W had yielded to temptation and spilled my secrets. O Jack, I thought, O Jack, our secrets told?

Mary Ann it seems did not notice the dread in my eyes. Sorry she says, as blithe as you like, sorry, sorry, I can't hardly say it, tho' I know I have to. Say what? I obliges. What Ibbetson was saying in the cuddy, she replies, 'twas terrible calumny, both on you, Olivia, and on Tom. I gathered myself. Me? I says, with studied nonchalance, Tom? They were discussing us? Aye, says Mary Ann, and Mr. Ramsay too.

This took me unawares. Mr. Ramsay? I echoes, in some confusion. Mr. Ramsay that is Secretary to The Company, and Tom's patron? Mary Ann nods and, o, 'tis horrible to say, she says, with relish, the horriblest thing I ever heard. Spit it out, child, I snaps, spit it out.

Mary Ann paused a moment longer for the drama of it, and then she told me they all seemed to know it in the cuddy, to know it for a certain fact, that I was until recently Mr. Ramsay's mistress, and what they called my otherwise incredible marriage to Tom, and also his otherwise incredible promotion from Junior Clerk to Assistant Secretary, were varieties of hoax; that our marriage was nothing to do with affection and all to do with his insatiable ambition and my desperation; that his rise was nothing to do with his superior talents, and all to do with corruption. She said Ibbetson said Tom had been favoured 'cause he'd been prepared to take me off Mr. Ramsay's hands, once I'd become an embarrassment to that sly old dog, and what he wanted of the match was the chance to win money and fame in Penang.

And why pray had I wed Tom? Why, 'twas clear as gin I'd had no choice! Aye, it seems 'tis agreed in the cuddy I acted for despair that Mr. Ramsay had grown tired of me, and wanted to be rid of me, and no other man but Tom was depraved enough to have me.

In short, they were saying in the cuddy Tom and me have no feeling for each other, that we wed merely for pure calculation of interest, 'cause we were useful to each other – which useful sort of marriage, tho' it be the commonest sort, I want never again no part of. No, I put the loneliness of that kind of contract quite behind me when I fled Fancourt.

At the end of her rattling Mary Ann looked at me with indecent hunger for my response, but I was in too much shock to speak. Me. Tom. Mr. Ramsay. Did they think in the cuddy we all three dwelled in the brothel?

Amidst my turmoil I was remembering Tom telling me, when he was appointed Assistant Secretary to Penang, that he knew well the ways of clerks at India House; that he expected resentment of his advancement. Now I guessed this canard about me and Mr. Ramsay must be the result of clerks' tongues jealously flicking. I remembered, too, Ibbetson coveted for himself Tom's office of Assistant Secretary. I knit these thoughts together, and concluded Ibbetson had picked up a bucket of nonsense at India House and that he was now dipping from it to spread lies about the *Ganges* in hopes of injuring Tom's reputation, and of lessening the portion of honour and moral principle to which my husband can by rights lay claim.

When I regained control of my tongue I says this. I says: well here's a fine story, worthy even of our splendid novelists Ann Radcliffe and Frances Burney. I says: for sure it makes sense of Tom's recent history, and the plot hangs together well with no holes, there is but one problem with it; it ain't true; not a word of it; 'tis all lies, spiteful lies.

I let that soak through, and then I told Mary Ann that Ibbetson has a heart full of rancour against Tom. I said he must be repeating this canard out of emotions as mean as those had concocted it: resentment, envy, false indignation – false 'cause no injury or insult was done him or any man by Tom's elevation. I spoke firmly the truth: I ain't never met Mr. Ramsay; Tom gained nothing from our marriage, but affection and nor did I, excepting only that Tom was paying off my debts.

Mary Ann cries: 'tis vile, 'tis vile! She then added, happily, she'd never for a moment believed Mr. Ramsay c'd be a philanderer – Mr. Ramsay that she knew Tom highly esteemed, just as she knew he esteemed me as a husband sh'd esteem his wife, and tho' it w'd be understandable if a widow turned of thirty took a man without love, 'twas plain from my manner to Tom I had not wed trusting love to come later, if it ever came at all.

Here I shot my sister a look sh'd have shamed her, tho' it seemed it didn't, since she prattles on, all bright and eager: what sh'd we do now? Sh'd we tell Mr. Dundas his wife is scandal mongering all about the ship?

This time I was sharp. Child! I says, 'twould be strange indeed if Mr. Dundas, that is a competent and clever man, were unaware of these wicked rumours; it must be that knowing the truth that Tom won his chance on fair merit, not from sinister advantage, he chooses to ignore the chatter, which is noble, sensible behaviour that you'd do well to take as your model.

Mary Ann looked disappointed, tho' she did concede, all regretful, 'twere true running to Dundas to tell tales on his wife c'd not promote harmony – indeed must make the bad atmosphere on this small ship even worse. And then she says: well then, never mind Dundas, ought we not tell Tom what is whispered against him?

I was aghast. Tom w'd feel flayed to learn they cast him in the cuddy as one who'd save another man's reputation by trading his life, almost, for his advancement, and they cast me as one who'd trade her life, almost, for marriage, and that poor blameless Mr. Ramsay, that he looks upon as a father, a man towards whom he feels the most grateful sense for his friendship and protection, they cast as a scoundrel. And why subject him to such anguish?

To what end? 'Tis is enough one of us sh'd suffer it.

No, no, no, I says, no, Mary Ann, Tom need not know this trash, the weight of which may bend him down to hunchback – he stoops very bad from all that drudging over his writing desk at India House. I said if her proud and loving brother were to know what was said of him, and me, and Mr. Ramsay, it w'd be as disagreeable to his feelings as 'twas discreditable to his character, and if she loved him as a sister, then she sh'd do all she c'd to help me protect him from the pain, the bitter pain, of learning of it.

I can feel no guilt for this blackmail; 'tis with relief, not shame, I report Mary Ann agreed, all sorrowful, that she w'd indeed be a kind sister to Tom, and hold her tongue.

Sometime, someplace on the ocean

Last night, in the hour before candles must be extinguished – which is ten o'clock, for fear of fire consuming us all we are allowed no candles after that – in the hour before ten Tom and me were as usual sitting together in our cabin. Mary Ann w'd have been with us but we'd been caught by a storm, and the ship was pitching something rotten; from seasickness she'd already retired to her cot in her own cabin, which is even smaller, darker, and smellier than ours, tho' the lucky thing don't have to share it.

Tom was bent over his Malay grammars. Often he asks me to test his vocabulary – *ikan*, a fish, *ikan ini*, this fish – but last night we sat in silence, and it seemed to me he was not studying at all: he was taking no notes, muttering no Malay words to himself. His face, in the weak, flickering light that was more shadow than anything else, looked drawn and wan, which was only to be expected with the ship moving about so much, and the tempest battering all around. I was mending one of his shirts that had a rent in the sleeve, and as I put in another stitch, I says, of the storm: sh'd blow itself out by morning, and don't fash yourself,

Tom, it ain't such a monster, I've survived much worse, at sea.

Tom nodded and says: the *Ganges* I must trust is sound, and fear of shipwreck is not now all that troubles me. Then what else is it, my love? I asks. Tom hesitated, but at last he says: I think there are whisperings on this ship of you and Jack and Harriet – or if their names be not known, then at least that before you married Fancourt, you'd taken a lover, and had a child by him.

For the second time in just a few days I thought: O Jack, our secrets told? And again I felt a cold, dark dread. I took a moment to summon my courage, and then I looked direct at Tom and I asks: so you think Mrs. D and Miss W have broke their silence?

Tom did not answer yes or no, but indirect. He told me Ibbetson had earlier cornered him in the cuddy, already the sea was getting up and others must have been keeping safe to their cabins, so 'twas just the two of them, and only one of them with spitefulness in his heart. Ibbetson curled his lip, and sneers: been avoiding me, have you, Raffles? Tom replies, mild and bland: 'tis impossible to avoid anybody on this ship. At this Ibbetson says: aye, and 'tis likewise impossible to keep secrets. Tom refused to give him the satisfaction of asking what he meant, but the rascal told him anyway; he told him he hadn't a hope of surviving this voyage without the truth about me coming out. Again, Tom refused to give Ibbetson satisfaction – the satisfaction of asking: what truth about my wife is this? Instead he turned on his heels and left the cuddy.

From this incident Tom deduced my history is known. But with what I know about the muck Ibbetson is spreading, I thought the so-called truth with which that scoundrel baited Tom was like as not *not* the true truth about Jack and Harriet and me, but his no-truth-at-all nonsense about Tom and me and Mr. Ramsay.

I angled the shirt I was mending closer to the candle, and I says, very cool: There ain't nothing here, Tom, Ibbetson c'd have meant anything. You know I'm a woman to attract lies to me like flies to honey, perhaps they're saying in the cuddy... Here I paused, 'cause the only lies I c'd think they may be telling of me in the cuddy were the lies they actually are telling. So I changed tack, and I says: perhaps they say of me in the cuddy nothing at all? Perhaps Ibbetson was using words as a net to catch you? Aye, I expect he wanted to trick you into saying something ill-judged, and thus give him a nugget of gossip he c'd trade for popularity about the ship. You did very well not to fall into his trap, Tom, very well to refuse to let yourself be wormed.

Tom looked doubtful, but he agreed 'twas possible I was right. He then added whether or not Ibbetson's words had been intended as a trap, he was worried about Mary Ann.

I jolted from surprise and I pricked my finger: a little bead of blood, like red glass, glittered against my skin. I regarded it, admired its glossy scarlet. Mary Ann? I frowns, what worries you about her?

Tom was silent, gathering himself, and then he told me that in truth he'd never felt easy about keeping from his family so many details of my history, tho' for his mother's sake he'd felt he'd had to – it w'd have splintered her heart to think her only son had married a woman who'd had a child out of wedlock. Here I thanked him, as I often do, for his great and uncommon generosity in overlooking all that when he wed me, and he said no, no, how many times must he tell me 'twas selfishness had made him so-called generous; 'twas selfishness, not generosity, that made him want to keep me to him now and in the future, regardless of my past.

At these kind words I put aside my sewing and I went to sit in Tom's lap; there followed some canoodling. 'Twas only after this happy straying we returned to the subject of Mary Ann. Now my poor Tom said I must have realised that ever since Dundas had told him he'd share what he knew of me with Mrs. D, but not to worry, his dear wife was as discrete as a sphinx, he'd been anxious as hell my secrets w'd be no safer with her than they w'd with any coffee house wag or dandy.

I said aye, I was worried too, but for all our worry, there weren't no firm evidence Mrs. D had gossiped about me with anybody but her own sister, which was to be expected, and didn't count.

Perhaps, said Tom, gloomy, but if Mrs. D had indeed kept silent, then her silence up to now was no guarantee of her silence in the future, and whatever his meaning, Ibbetson had spoke the truth: in a small society 'twas almost impossible to keep secrets. It worried him: what if Mary Ann were sometime to pick up hints I'd had a past she c'd not expect of her brother's wife? She was his dearest sister, and how w'd she feel if on this ship or in Penang she learned the truth, which forgive him he must call scandalous, not from him, her brother, and not from me, neither, but from strangers whispering from spite? He continued straightaway she w'd feel excluded, betrayed, and angry. Yes, he said, for many weeks now he'd been thinking we ought to tell Mary Ann that I was not before he wed me a widow chaste as a daisy, and that whatever Ibbetson knew, or didn't know, or thought he knew, but didn't, the man's sneering had this morning confirmed for him that the right course of action was to tarry no longer, but to tell Mary Ann the truth about me *now*, that she may not have any distressing surprises in the future – like taking precautions against poxes, he said. He added his desire to have everything all above board was not just for Mary Ann's sake, but also for his own: if his sister knew the truth, he c'd cease worrying she'd stumble over it; he'd feel happier in himself if he were not withholding from her things he granted 'twere not her right to know. He looked at me, pleading: so w'd I agree to do it? W'd I agree to trust Mary Ann, to confide in his sister, all I'd long-since confided in him?

I c'd not forbear from thinking if Our Mary Ann ever discovered from others we'd kept her in the dark, her distress w'd be slight compared to the pleasure she'd that day take in my scandal. Nevertheless, I agreed to Tom's request, both for his sake, and for my own – I don't never want to give him no grounds to blame me for coming between him and his sister. No. No matter Mary Ann is a rattle young enough to be my daughter, I'll treat her as a friend and entrust to her my secrets. And if she don't keep them? This is another of those things I must worry about later.

Sometime, someplace on the ocean

Mary Ann now knows what loose manner of woman is her sister. Or perhaps I sh'd say what loose manner of woman *was* her sister in one of her former lives, back when she was Olivia Mariamne Devenish?

I will not here try to recount my life story as last night I told it to Mary Ann, with all her interjections, and exclamations, and my hesitancies, and circling, and Tom's kind, firm words guiding here and there, and the ship's timbers creaking, and our damp cabin gently rising, and falling, rising, and falling, for 'twas a calm night with no violent lurching, and the ceiling dripping water, and the quavering beam of the candle's light flickering, and the shadows licking, and the heavy heat pressing, for we are far towards India by now, and damply shiny in our skins, and everything drenched with the mingled smells of hot animals, and hot people, and staleness, and dung.

No, instead I will write the story of my life in a plain style such that anybody may follow, and including even scraps of detail I omitted last night, from the circumstance that Mary Ann already knew them.

I was born in 1771, in Madras. My mother bequeathed to me as my second name, her own name, Mariamne, and also her dark looks that in her youth were said by women to be as obvious as a finger beckoning, and by men to be beguiling. She was Circassian, from that country of Asia which stretches from sea to sea, between the Caspian and the Black, a mountainous country, with the slopes thickly forested, and the peaks clad in perpetual snow, and the air sharp as a knife, and clean as ice. The Circassians are a fierce, wild people, very proud – or so my mother told me. I think she meant their men. Their women, by my mother's testament, they treat as cattle. She told me once: the Circassians are poor, and their daughters are beautiful, and 'tis in them they chiefly trade.

I thought then my mother was perhaps telling me she herself had been of this precious merchandise of daughters? Had she perhaps been sent to Madras a slave? And not one to sweep and clean neither, Circassian girls are acknowledged not made for daytime drudgery. But since I dared not ask I even now remain unsure what took my mother to Madras, nor do I know what she did there before she met my father, this time in her life she rarely discussed, and I w'd not pry; my mother, I thought, had her right to silence, just as I had mine.

My father was George Devenish, of Castledance in the county of Roscommon, a gentle terrain in the west of Ireland. He was in Madras for the textile trade, a dealer in cotton goods, of the white and painted varieties. How he met my mother I do not know, but soon enough he bedded her, tho' they never married. When I was born this good man did not renounce me, nor my mother neither, and for some years she styled herself Mrs. Devenish, tho' few were deceived she was never no church bride. My father must have known his Circassian nearly-wife w'd make a strange, unhappy flower in Castledance, nevertheless he shipped us both to Ireland, when I was but a babe. Alas, he remained in Madras, and he died soon after, of a fever, so I have no memory of him.

My childhood passed in rural Ireland as rural childhoods do. What was I doing at three? At five? At eight? The answer in each case is: nothing of interest, except to a fond mother. At nine I was sent to Cork, as maid to the wife of the Harbour Master there, a childless woman, educated and kind, that taught me to read and write, and treated me almost as her own, except I had to empty her chamber pot. My life as a person of interest to gossips began when I was fifteen, at which age I collided with Captain John Hamilton Dempster, known to me always as Jack.

Jack, like me, was illegitimate, but his father's family was old – tho' what family ain't? – and more than old 'twas moneyed, and well able to wrap the odd bastard in its velvet folds. Then again, he was a man, so for him the stain of his birth was less black than 'twas for me.

Tho' the Dempsters are Scottish, Jack was well connected in London: his half-brother, George, his father's legitimate son, and Laird of Dunnichen, was an MP, and a director of The Company, which is how come Jack was appointed captain of the East Indiaman, the *Rose*.

The summer I was fifteen, this *Rose* was detained several months in Cork, for irregularities of interest to the customs men. My first sight of Jack was along the seafront. He was chatting to a couple of fishermen, who were mending their nets, and I was on my way to fetch a draught for my mistress' nerves, from an old woman who brewed up medicines for all the townspeople. 'Twas a blustery day, grey with massing clouds promising rain, and the sea choppy and dirty with sand churned up from the bottom. An ordinary day – except here was this piratical man, laughing, and relaxed, and he looked at me, or I looked at him – later, neither of us was ever sure – and we met and held each other's gazes, and 'twas like two candle flames at the same instant flaring, or two bells at the same instant pealing, and later Jack told me he looked in my brown eyes, and he at once felt winded, as if another man had thrown a punch into his midriff.

We didn't speak that day – I continued with my errand, and Jack continued chatting to the fishermen. But after that it seemed every time I ventured from my master's house I saw him. I noticed each time he was tall, broad, and shapely – a beautiful man.

'Twas about a week later we spoke for the first time, and I learned Jack's voice was as rich as rum. We said nothing much – the weather grows warmer, miss, indeed it does, sir, or something like – and yet we said everything. We said we knew for sure soon enough we'd be lovers, and soon enough we were. Jack was not the first man I'd lain with, but he was the first I'd loved, and the first that loved me, and the first to bring me joy.

Our bedroom was the fields on sunny days, with hedges for its walls, and the sky for its ceiling. Our sheets were grass, and our bed-hangings branches, and the noises we made flew away into birdsong. All this was very fine, but 'twas not long before I realised I was naught but another lass caught by disaster; I was pregnant.

With a boy from Roscommon, or Cork, my pregnancy w'd have removed from him all choice: the opinion of the townspeople w'd have ensured he wed me, whether he wanted to or not. But at news of my condition, Jack's family called him back to Scotland. That powerful brother George had a goddaughter past her bloom, and a plain old shrew, or so Jack told me. From plainness, shrewness, or some other reason she was not yet wed, and now George insisted Jack marry her, which he did, with a sad and regretful heart.

I had a daughter, Harriet, the sweetest little plum you ever saw, with bonny rolls of fat at her wrists and ankles, and a chuckle to make the stars laugh. Soon after Jack's wife had a son. This boy was adored by Jack's brother George, who was a bachelor, and childless. George in time bought a castle in Scotland, Skibo Castle, and with it half the Highlands; he wanted Jack to settle there, with his family, but Jack was having none of that.

No, Jack was determined not to lose me. He decided to make another voyage to India, with the *Rose*. In secret from George, and also from his wife, he invited me to go with him. Harriet, our little poppet that he'd never seen, was by this time six. Jack arranged for her to be sent to Edinburgh, to be nursed there by the same woman had nursed him as a boy – later he had her educated in that city. I was now free to join him, and that I did, with mostly gladness in my heart, tho' I missed my daughter, and dreaded I may never see her again.

I sailed with Jack for Madras, which tho' 'twas the town of my birth seemed to me as I journeyed to it as strange as the moon. From Madras, Jack intended to sail on to Calcutta. We knew we c'd never now be wed, and during the voyage he suggested that for my own future security I ought to marry in India. He said he'd make sure to find me a suitable husband in Madras, before he left. We first had this unhappy conversation in the bed we shared in his captain's cabin, our limbs naked and entwined, and tangled all about with sheets. I cried, and for that matter so did he, but 'twas true I needed to be married, and I c'd see straightaway the sense in Jack's plan.

Thus I duly married in Madras. The husband Jack found me was Joseph Fancourt, Assistant Surgeon in The Company's service. We told him about Harriet; I wanted to send for her but he said no. It was the first of many blows, tho' that time he did not use his fists. Later, with bruises blooming under my bodice, I decided he must have seen in me not youth and prettiness, but ruin he c'd twist to his advantage to treat me as he liked. Well, to be fair, I saw in him only a roof over my head, and food on the table. No, this was not much of a marriage, and I prefer not to dwell on it. After five years I fled man, marriage, Madras, and returned to London. Fancourt died in 1800, in Ryacotta, a wild region of the Punjab, tho' 'twas not some local bandit killed him, but a fever. News of his death reached me ten months later; it did not discommode me.

Throughout my marriage, Jack and me continued a secret

correspondence. Soon after I returned to London he arranged for me to visit Scotland, to see Harriet – and also to see him. Then his wife died and he came to London, to secure a new command, to be with me, and to discuss Harriet's future, for she was no longer a girl, her schooldays were over, she was near enough the age I'd been when we met and we had to think who'd wed her, given she was merely our natural daughter. Notwithstanding my memories of Fancourt, I had to grant our best chance of finding her a match w'd come if Jack took her with him to India, to cast for one of the many bachelors rattling around out there. So we called Harriet down from Scotland to tell her of our decision. She stayed with me in London, and we saw her father often.

Jack's new command was the *Earl Talbot.* He and Harriet sailed from Plymouth for Bombay on January 7, 1800. I went with them in the stage coach to that city, and as they sailed off I stood on the quayside, waving, weeping, and wishing I c'd go with them, but Jack had said no, our time for recklessness was past, for propriety's sake, and for Harriet's chances, w'd be better if I waited for him in London.

Jack stayed in Bombay only long enough to settle Harriet with his good friend Philip Dundas, a man of substance, Master Attendant of the Marine Board there, who was to act as her guardian 'til she wed. He then set off to China, taking Dundas' wife with him – she intended to return to England via the China route. But a typhoon got up in the South China Sea, caught the *Earl Talbot,* and broke her on the rocks; all aboard were lost. I learned half a year later that Jack was dead. Then I knew what grief was; then I knew what it was to mourn a man properly.

Meanwhile, in Bombay, Dundas married Harriet off to a friend of his, one William Soper. Soon after their marriage Jack's son died – that legitimate son he had with his wife. I never wished ill to this boy I never saw, but I cannot lie I regret his death. When Harriet was growing up in Edinburgh, Old George Dempster paid her now and then a furtive visit, and once his nephew was gone Our Heirless Laird made over his property at Skibo to my daughter, which was a great and unexpected boon for her. She and William returned from India and live at Skibo now; from gratitude for their castle William has added *Dempster* to their name, so their children, if they come, will be called *Soper-Dempster*, and grow up improbably rich and secure, for which I'm very glad.

That is the whole story of my life before I met Tom, and fell in love again after all my reversals. Last night, I told everything to Mary Ann, debarring only that Fancourt beat me, and she greeted my words all agog, with excitement and eager interest writ plain across her face. When Dundas appeared, she exclaimed at the coincidence he now sails with us, and exclaimed again to learn that Mrs. D is his second wife, and asked did that hag know all, and if she did then that explained her horrid treatment of me.

When I spoke of Jack's death Mary Ann throws out her arms and cries: o, 'tis too sad, 'tis too sad. She was perhaps forgetting her brother's presence? Tom is jealous of my past, and by the end of my tale he looked spent from hearing so much about Jack, his ghostly rival – or so I think my husband thinks. Still, he praised me for my courage in speaking. He then told his sister I had done her great honour by entrusting her with my secrets, and enjoined her to keep all to her own dear self. In particular she was not to write to their mother or to their sisters what she knew – this for their mother's sake.

Mary Ann said she'd keep all this from Mother right enough, but may she tell Mr. Thompson – those two grow friendlier by the day. Tom looked aghast; he delivered her a lecture, very stern, more fatherly than brotherly. Aye, 'twas in a most serious paternal voice that he told her she most certainly c'd *not* confide in Mr. Thompson. She was not to go gossiping about this ship. If she let slip any of what she now knew, either by accident, or by design, she'd hurt us both very greatly. Furthermore, she might hurt his prospects in Penang. He said The Company likes its men and their wives upstanding both, and if 'twere widely known I'd sometimes been more horizontal than upstanding then those who didn't like him – and there were many, he said, many – his detractors w'd no doubt use my past to undermine his authority. Yes, he sighed, if this got around backbiting w'd be a heavy drag on his advancement.

Mary Ann blushed and giggled at Tom's mention of upstanding men and horizontal women. Still, when her brother fell silent, she promised she'd breathe not a word to no one, and if she did, then God sh'd at once strike her down dead. She's a good girl at heart, and I believe she intends to keep her promise. Nevertheless I now assume that before too long there'll be yet another aboard knows my secrets: handsome Mr. Thompson.

August 1805, Madras

This heat! I am *melting*. Aye, I am again in my native city, tho' I cannot feel myself its daughter. O Madras! Madras, where I think it possible there is somewhere a house in which my mother once toiled a slave, where I suppose is somewhere else my father's grave, where Jack found for me a husband, and then left me to live with him, where down every shadowed, crumbling alley I risk catching glimpse of the ghost of Fancourt. No, this ain't no place for me to dwell on memories.

So 'tis fortunate, perhaps, that in Madras memory is mostly blotted out by the urgency of sensation, for here everything is everywhere at all moments encountered: the jewel colours of the women's *saris*; the jostling dark-skinned bodies; the babble of native languages, of cries and shouts and noisy chaos; the searing slap of the white hot sun; the golden, juicy taste of fruit quite unknown in England; above all, the smell. O, this smell! This smell of people; of dust, and dryness; of mingled spices; of rotting fish; of jasmine; of strange food cooking; of the smoke of the intoxicating weed called *ganja* curling from communal water pipes called *hubble-bubbles*, 'cause of the gurgling they make; this smell of the cows that wander the streets; of the tame elephants that labour about the town; of the wild monkeys that scamper and dart along roofs and walls; the bitter smell that c'd be human bones burning; the sweet smell of incense wafting from the temples; the smells of warehouses, bazaars, drains, sewers. This, the tremendous, heady smell of India. 'Tis a smell I never forgot, and did not realise how much I longed to smell again, until Tom helped me off the *Ganges* and onto oriental soil, which I never again expected to step on, when last I quit it – and my legs at first all wobbly on land, from being so long at sea.

August 1805, the *Warley*, Bay of Bengal

We have changed ships onto the *Warley*, our course takes us south and east across the Bay of Bengal, and we have as our escort HMS *Blenheim*, which is to be stationed in Penang – she may be a naval vessel but she don't reassure me much she c'd repel privateers, 'tis impossible to look on her and not remark she is all hogged and bowed in the middle.

August 1805, the *Warley*, Bay of Bengal

As we leave the mainland of India far behind, we are starting to see passing by us strange craft indeed – samples of every Eastern boat that swims, says Tom. There are Chinese junks with painted eyes on their prows, so the boats may see where they are going, or so Tom says their crews believe. There are native Malay vessels, some quite large, with wooden stabilisers on each side and woven palm leaf matting rather than cloth for sails, others little tubs so small and crank only an amphibious creature like your Malay w'd trust himself in them – or so says Tom, that has never yet met a Malay. Now we have even seen – far off, thank God – a wicked-looking vessel, fast-moving, low in the water, with a black hull, and a yellow sail. This was a Bugis pirate ship, said Tom, the Bugis being a tribe notorious for their blood lust even amongst the sanguinary people of the Eastward, and if those cut-throats got aboard they'd gut us soon as look at us with their wicked knives called '*krises*', and then take our skulls as floats for their fishing nets.

August 1805, the *Warley*, Bay of Bengal

This Eastern sea we sail upon is a very wonderful one: by day every shade of blue, of grey, of silver, of green, of turquoise, often bruised by great purple or indigo shadows cast by massing clouds; by night gleaming like mercury, if there is a moon. 'Tis a fine thing to stand on deck alone in the late hours, with the splashing splosh of water, and the ghostly billowing sails, and, above, the stars pricking the inky blackness of the heavens, and, below, the unearthly shine of the ocean – and even better to stand at night on deck with Tom, and to hear him say he sees none of this, but only the world that is in my eyes.

September 1805, the *Warley*, Bay of Bengal

It ain't just Tom and me occasionally find moments for spooning in all the squalor and misery of ship-board: Our Mary Ann is another has been standing on deck at night, with only the moon and stars above her, and beneath her the sea, and filling her field of vision another's eyes. This *another* being Mr. Thompson. Aye, he and Mary Ann have reached an understanding, and Tom has given them his blessing, so the work of finding her a husband is speedily dispatched – they will wed the first moment 'tis convenient once we reach Penang.

From there being so few of them, and the Honourable Members of the Court of Directors being so unwilling to meet the expense of sending out more, most of The Company's men in the Eastward take on a plurality of offices, each with its own pecuniary emoluments. Thompson is to serve in Dundas' new government in the posts of Assistant to Superintendent of Marine and Commissary of Provisions and Petty Stores, this latter is especially pleasing to Mary Ann, 'cause 'tis concerned with victualing our naval ships, and Thompson will be able to claim commission on any transactions he makes, which sh'd enable him to put away a tidy profit into his own pocket.

September 1805, the *Warley*, Bay of Bengal

Now our journey is drawing to a close Tom has been trying to explain to me why The Company has chosen to appoint a new, enlarged government in remote Penang. Is not our good East India Company the most extraordinary company that ever existed? Or so asks Tom, not looking for an answer, as he tells me again what everybody knows: The Company has a monopoly on trade between Britain and the East, and in the settlements in India it acts as trading house, government, and army all combined.

Meanwhile, in Europe, the endless wars of our dismal times drag on. The horrid French have long-since overrun the Dutch, and taken Holland. These Dutch until defeated held many possessions in East-Insular India. This much, too, is common knowledge – but now I learn that when the French annihilated the Dutch nation, they seized from the Hollanders their possessions in the Eastward! 'Tis just as if islands and settlements were counters on a gaming table!

Boney, now that he has control of these quondam Dutch bases, aspires to rule the Eastward waves. Our jolly tars – or, in any case, our admirals – have thus been looking for some place in the Eastward where they may establish a naval base, a centre of ship building, and a port from which our frigates c'd sally forth to annoy the tyrant's French ones, and derange his cunning plans.

These matters of strategy overlap with those of commerce. Sailing east from India there is a body of water called the Straits of Malacca, the unavoidable gateway to China, where 'tis agreed in Leadenhall St. there's money to be made. Alas, French warships now lie on the flanks of these Straits. Thus our good East Indiamen, sailing with their cargoes of textiles and muskets from India to China, and back from China to India with their holds full of tea, have no intermediate port of call where they may take refuge from harrying pirates, nor refit after storms, nor take on water, nor re-provision.

These difficult circumstances have prodded the Admiralty and The Company to work together to take remedial measures. By happy chance The Company has had in its possession these past twenty years the island of Penang, towards the northern end of the Straits of Malacca – this outpost it originally took from a local sultan in exchange for military protection against Siamese and Burmese armies then threatening his court.

All this time it's had it, The Company has done nothing much with Penang, and less to defend it; the harbour is poorly fortified and 'tis said one French frigate c'd insult it. But this is soon to change: that Britannia may rule *all* the waves, the Admiralty will now develop Penang as a naval base the equal of any in India; for the sake of the China trade The Company will much expand its presence on the island, and strengthen its government.

Tom says this mingling of interests is why the fellows sailing together to Penang are now appointed to the government there. Tho' I'm grateful for his lectures, I cannot pretend I'm not glad they're over – he does pontificate, sometimes.

September 1805, the *Warley*, sailing along the coast of Penang Island

Penang has hove into view, and as we begin to slip along its coast, I see from the decks an island furred like an animal with a green pelt of densest vegetation – *jangal*, as in India they call this exuberant variety of forest. O, what a green! Splendid. Sparkling. 'Tis a green at all times glistening with wetness, 'cause the air here almost even *laps* – 'tis damper even than in Ireland, tho' damp with a genial warmth, not cold mannered, as in Roscommon.

The terrain of the island is hilly. In some places the hills rise almost from the sea's edge – some cloud-draped they soar so high. Here and there grey outcrops of rock jut from the steep slopes, and in the valleys between sluggish brown rivers snake to the coast, but otherwise the hills are everywhere draped with their vibrant dazzle of jangal.

The shore is an in-and-out affair of sandy bays and rocky promontories. In some places mangroves grow right into the water, and in other places there is a belt of coconut palms fringing empty beaches – these trees I recognise from my time in India. The beaches themselves are broad ribbons of sand, sometimes streaked, or wholly tinted, with muddy brown, or with red in every shade from palest pink to almost crimson – Tom says the soil of this part of the Eastward is everywhere red, as tho' the ground itself were rusted.

September 1805, the *Warley*, at anchor in the roads of George Town

We have survived, Tom and me. We have survived ten thousand miles of storms, seasickness, bad food, bad water, bad smells, horrid living conditions. We have survived boredom, lack of privacy, and the malevolence of our so-called companions. We have survived the risks of disease, pirates, fire. We ain't dead and buried at sea. We have, in short, arrived!

Aye, the *Warley* is now anchored off George Town, the chief settlement of Penang, and we are awaiting the native boats that will convey us ashore. I write now in haste, having retreated to our cabin, whilst all others remain on the decks, so eager am I to record what I have seen.

George Town lies on a spit of land protruding into the water towards the mainland of the Malay Peninsula, which ain't far off. I understood at first sight why they say one French frigate c'd insult it: the fort supposedly protecting it is a long, low-walled building angled to the sea, with a moat, or ditch, surrounding it, but 'tis much tumbled down and crumbled; it has but few canon on the ramparts and Tom says 'tis barracks for but a small contingent of troops. Between the fort and the town – a very little town – is the esplanade that Tom tells me here is called the *padang, w*hich is Malay for *field*.

Not far from the padang a sturdy wooden jetty slices into a blue-green sea so shimmering it c'd be woven from light, and along the beach lie fishing boats and nets set out to dry, black nets and brown, of immense length. By one inlet huddle native shacks built of woven reeds, set on stilts, and thatched with palm. Behind them, some buildings look queer and oriental – Tom says wherever in the Eastward there is trade, there also are Chinamen, and many of them live in George Town, more Chinamen, he says, than Europeans, which number fewer than a hundred, and 'tis Chinamen who occupy the houses with roofs all gaudily tiled and curlicued. Most of the houses fit for Europeans are built of wood, and look much like their counterparts in Madras. Some, built of brick – pukka built, as they say in Madras – have red-tiled roofs and whitewashed walls, and these, from the water, look most pretty. Of the three or four bigger public buildings the grandest, of course, is Government House, where Tom will henceforth work – it faces away from the water, so all I have seen of it yet is its verandah, which is most impressive.

So this little back-of-beyond is where I will dwell from now until I know not when, and content I am to see it after all the endless ocean. Tho' I have no doubt the local fauna must include serpents and spiders of prodigious size, and tho' I ain't got much hope of society here, and tho' I know everything now must be disconcerting, strange, and some of it quite horrid, notwithstanding all that I am as excited as Tom to have arrived at last on this bewitching shore.

I still ain't got no evidence Mrs. D and Miss W have spilled my secrets, so I'm now in high hopes they'll remain forever safe – and happen what may, Tom and me will face it together, two adventurers shoulder to shoulder against the perils of a foreign land.

October 1805, China St., George Town

I have been neglecting my diary this past month, but 'tis difficult to find time to write amidst all the business of arriving in a new world – I c'd say arriving in a new life, except 'tis still this Olivia Raffles living it.

In any case, all has been bustle since last I wrote. First was the happy bustle of a wedding: Mary Ann married her Mr. Thompson not a week after we arrived, and I think there never was a prettier beachside bride.

Once the wedding was done, I faced the conundrum: where to live? At first most of us new arrivals lodged at the Commercial Hotel, and it seemed we might be shifting there some time for the sudden addition of twenty-six new government officials, their wives, and other dependants to the local European population has placed a heavy strain on suitable accommodation here, and rents are shocking high. Still, Tom successfully negotiated for a *bungalow* on China St., and now we are installed.

I sh'd say *bungalow* is the Indian word for *house*, and mine here ain't much different from the one I occupied with Fancourt in Madras – I will not call that place a home, and not say we shared it, neither. This wooden bungalow, like that one, is raised above the ground, against the risks of flood, serpents, and the devouring insects they call white ants. 'Tis so hot there ain't no need for glass in the windows, which are closed by slatted shutters, to provide cool and shade in the heat of the day. The roof is thatched with *atap* – palm leaf – and has wide over-hanging eaves, also for shade.

As in Madras, as everywhere, I suppose, in the torrid zones, we live mostly on the verandah, which is cooled by breezes, tho' even so 'tis scarcely cool. I am on the verandah now, writing at Tom's desk, and I am *dissolving* in the heat – running like butter – not to mention attacked by a regiment of bugs. The mosquitoes are insupportable plaguy! I swear I am nothing but sweat and itch!

The furnishings we had with us in our cabins on the *Ganges* and the *Warley* are now ranged all about the bungalow, and I have tried to make it cheerful by placing big pots of flowers on the verandah and by stitching a few touches from native cloths I buy from traders visiting the *pasar* – that is, the market. These cloths come not only from the *kampongs* – the native villages – of Penang's interior, but also from all the islands of the East Indian Archipelago, for Malays from far and wide come here to trade.

In the space beneath the bungalow are the bath houses. Bathing here is more necessary than at home if we ain't all to stink: 'tis a funny affair; you take a ladle made of bamboo and sluice yourself down from water kept in a *tong*, a huge ceramic jar, filled daily by the water-carrier.

The kitchen is in a separate hut – it contains only a charcoal grill barely even raised off the floor, but Cook manages – he is but one of my seven servants. I much approve that everybody here has multitudes of servants, as in Bloomsbury all I had was one maid, and her little better than a thieving demirep.

October 1805, China St., George Town

Thank God I have this diary, for there is little else in Penang to entertain me. Alas, Mrs. D and Miss W set the tone for all the other European ladies here, hence I am invited nowhere, and through all the damply dragging hours when Tom is flogging himself at his official duties I am alone, unless Mary Ann happens to call, or else I bestir myself to visit her – she has moved with Thompson to Light St., it ain't far, 'cause nowhere is in George Town.

On some days, Dear Diary, I speak to none but you and the servants from when Tom has left the bungalow, to when he returns, bringing with him all the gossip of Government House – he says 'tis as bad as India House for intrigue and backbiting. Already, he finds himself embroiled in disputes: there was a man called Phillips sailed with us on the *Ganges,* to be Secretary to the Government, and thus placed above Tom in the establishment. Alas, his office is perhaps beyond his abilities, for 'tis obvious to all he struggles with his duties.

My generous Tom w'd willingly be as an extra limb to him, but Phillips seems jealous and resentful to have a man abler than himself as his assistant, and he busies himself trying to put Tom in a bad light with Dundas. Happily, he cannot even manage this business of blackguarding, and Tom says the man may as well bark as a dog does at the moon, and with as much effect, for all the attention Dundas pays him.

October 1805, China St., George Town

I wished for a friend and now I have one. Tom found this precious flotsam washed up one raucous night in the Naval Tavern: he found a man newly arrived from Calcutta, very sick, knowing no one here, and with only his three servants to care for him. This man and Tom fell into conversation and my kindly impetuous husband there and then ordered him at once to our bungalow to lodge with us, that I may nurse him back to health.

'Twas somewhat of a surprise when Tom returned through the pitchy Malay night with his arms around another man's shoulders, this other, though taller than him, obviously needing his support, and both of them drunk, lurching, rowdy in their cups, and with three Indian servants trotting along after, one, very old, carrying a lantern, the other two laden down with books, papers, baggage.

'Twas even more of a surprise when Tom's new companion, tho' flushed and swaying, at sight of me at once fell to his knees, flung out his arms and slurred, in a Scottish accent so broad I might not have understood his words, had I not already known them:

> *The wing of time should never brush*
> *Thy dewy lip's luxuriant flush,*
> *To bid its roses withering die;*
> *Nor age itself, though dim and dark,*
> *Should ever quench a single spark*
> *That flashes from my Nona's eye!*

From this I knew at once Tom had told this fellow, whoever he was, that I was the model for dear Trudge's Nona.

This Trudge is the acclaimed poet known to fashionables in London as *Melodious Moore*, 'cause he sings, most beautifully, the settings of his poems to his own piano accompaniment. But to me he is *Trudge*, and to him I am *Wowski*, ever since some years back we attended together at the Pantheon in Oxford Street a masquerade, for which entertainment we dressed ourselves as these two characters, which were taken from a comic opera popular that season.

I cannot deny poor Trudge was more than a little in love with me, and he wrote one year for my birthday a pretty poem, *Ode To Nona*, which, once published, became remarkable famous. As to why Trudge addressed me as *Nona* when my name's *Olivia*, that is a quondam mystery once caused Mother to remark that mine was a ditty w'd do as well for a Fanny as for an Olivia, and then to add that *some* women were ever subject to romantic imaginings. Aye, I replied, and *some* to bitterest jealousy. But since then Tom has told me what Trudge never did: that the Romans believed Nona was the fateful woman who spun a man's thread of life from her distaff onto her spindle, and that even the gods must fear her, let alone poets.

But I stray. I mean to say 'twas from *Ode To Nona* Tom's drunk, sick friend recited, and I saw at once what must have happened: I introduced Tom to Trudge not long before we married, and they got on something famous; Trudge, regretful, but resigned, put aside his jealousy to have lost me to Tom, and Tom, a great lover of poetry, was not jealous at all I had inspired a bard; indeed, he was, and remains, most proud to have won a woman inspired a famous poem. I gathered that from this pride, he had now boasted to his new friend he had at home none other than the lovely Nona of the verses. As to how they came to be discussing poetry, which ain't a likely topic for two drunk men in the Eastward, 'twas no puzzle at all once I learned that the man Tom had brought to lodge with us was, against all the laws of probability, a poet.

Aye, I have now lodging in my bungalow, shivering from the intermittent fever, John Leyden, who has inscribed me already a copy of *Scenes of Infancy: Descriptive of Teviotdale,* a book of verses about his childhood in the border country of Scotland, which won for him considerable fame in Edinburgh and in

London both.

Tho' Leyden is but the son of a shepherd, born in a cottage, he rose to university, and now holds two degrees, one in divinity from Edinburgh, and one in medicine from St. Andrews, so I nurse now a doctor, tho' this one by his own account is plagued by ill-health, and uncommon sickly.

From Leyden's education you'd think him from a great house, and his confidence is supreme even in illness. But his voice is as raw as a flayed rabbit and remains fitter for the cottage, than for the drawing room. Still, he uses it to speak twenty-six languages. Twenty-six! These including Hebrew, Arabic, Persian, Turkish, many varieties of Indian, and, in short, any tongue usually understood by the name of oriental.

As well as mastering their languages, Leyden is interested also in the histories, habits, religions, and cultures of the peoples that speak them. He collects all sorts of manuscript that he may pore over them and thus burrow deep into realms of human thought that until now lay obscured from sight. 'Tis his ambition to publish his various researches. He aims to gain the highest reputation, and to surpass a hundredfold in learning even Sir William Jones, an oriental scholar he claims is very famous, tho' in my opinion *fame* and *oriental scholar* ain't words too often go together.

When not delirious with fever, Leyden is most generous with his knowledge. My Tom, self-educated, ain't never before met such a scholar, and is touching grateful for his willingness to share all he knows even from his sick bed. Indeed, it ain't too much to say Tom has fallen completely under Leyden's spell: he says his new friend's facility for languages must be more like the ancient gift of tongues, than the slow acquisitions of ordinary men; he praises Leyden's wonderful talents and glowing virtues; he remarks often our poet-scholar must command admiration and respect from all who meet him.

November 1805, China St., George Town

There is something about me ensorcells poets. Aye, I cannot help remarking that when poor Leyden looks at me, 'tis with dog-like devotion, and 'tis clear as gin from his yearning eye he has fallen in love with me as completely as did my poor dear Trudge – he bestows upon me ardent glances even when we speak together of our livers and our bowels, which we do often, him being a doctor as well as an invalid, and me being a martyr to interior gouts.

So 'tis fortunate, perhaps, my patient is that rare thing: a poet *not* magnetic. 'Tis true Leyden's eyes are wild and staring enough to count as tortured, but his nose! What a thing! 'Tis so long and pointed it c'd be a poker to stir the fire. And tho' I mostly like what he says, there is that flayed voice – 'tis loud, and grating and it rises to screeching saw-tones when he becomes excited, which is often. No, I esteem the man enormous, but this nose, this voice c'd never tug from me adoration for the man unfortunate enough to possess them, whatever the fame of his verses.

December 1805, China St., George Town

Between rest and the good herbal soups I have been feeding him, Leyden now feels well enough to work. He has come to Penang to absorb Malay, but while it soaks into him, he continues his interest in other languages. In the afternoons I yield Tom's desk to him, and he has begun from our verandah a study of the languages and literature of the Indo-Chinese nations, which is to be an important contribution to scholarship, and will advance understanding of the relationship between Tibeto-Burman and many Chinese dialects – or so says its author.

He don't let up, even in the evenings, when Tom and me now sit listening to him talk and talk and talk of oriental matters. Sometimes my attention wanders – Leyden mixes the vocabulary of learned conversation with native phraseology 'til between his broad Scots accent and his strange words I don't know what he's saying half the time – but Tom drinks everything up, as tho' 'twere good wine, and then he asks for please yet more, which Leyden ever obliges – tho' he is only a little older than Tom he may as well be his kindly professor. Aye, Leyden encourages Tom to set his ambition high, and to pursue in a serious way his studies of Malay, which encouragement is met with enthusiasm so keen 'tis almost shivering.

December 1805, China St., George Town

A party at last! Yesterday, I went to a fine entertainment both gay and grand, hosted by one Syed Hussein, a wily Malay merchant of this town, who wanted to welcome Dundas' new government – and to curry favour with its members, no doubt, for they say he's ever at politicking and intrigue. His party was numerously attended – about sixty guests by my estimation – and 'twas graced by all the youth, beauty, and elegance of this settlement. All of us new arrivals were expected to enrich the evening; it gave me much satisfaction to think that tho' Mrs. D w'd no doubt have preferred me not be there, there was naught she c'd do to stop my invitation.

I wore the dress in which I sat for my portrait by Mr. Plimer: my white muslin with the puffed sleeves, the high waist, and the daycolletay. I was most thankful the fabric was thin, for the night was oppressive hot, with little breeze, and the still air so humid it very near *dripped*.

Leyden, my quondam patient, is now completely well and he has been mixing eagerly in society. He too was invited last night, and we three friends walked together the little distance from our bungalow to Syed Hussein's splendid mansion on Beach St. All along the way the trees were strung with colourful paper lanterns so the light w'd scare off the spirits that wander at night, ready to snatch the souls of the living, or so our houseboy informed me, very frightened and serious, for all the Malays believe in spirits, sorcery, ghosts, divination, astrology, &c, and this tho' they are Mahomedans, which religion Tom tells me w'd say with Exodus *Thou shalt not suffer a witch to live* – no, and nor a sorcerer neither.

Syed Hussein lives most high and keeps many slaves. In the Mahomedan way he has several wives, tho' last night but two of them moved amongst us, one very young, the other old enough to be her grandmother. Both were dressed in the native style that makes a woman look like she's gone out in her chemise – these native women wear a long loose jacket called a *kebaya*, of white calico, like underthings.

The band from HMS *Blenheim* provided cheerful, rousing music during dinner – which dinner was most luxurious, being a soup, a roast fowl, curry and rice, a mutton pie, a forequarter of lamb, rice puddings, tarts, fruit, fine bread, excellent Madeira, for tho' Mahomedans ain't supposed to drink, hereabouts they do.

After dinner we had fireworks over the harbour, and then entertainments from dancers, Indian girls rhythmically swaying their hips to the song – many Indians are kept in Penang as indentured labourers, and these girls were their daughters. Their costumes were wonderful exotic, all flowing, and shimmering, and parrot coloured, and their arms jangled with bangles, and round their ankles were bells. The men that accompanied them, singing and playing those Indian stringed instruments and drums of theirs, were dressed just as rich and glittery.

Once the Indian musicians had packed away their instruments, the band from HMS *Blenheim* struck up again, and we European ladies took our turn at dancing, all brisk and sprightly with our reels. The first was led off by Mrs. D dancing with Phillips, the same bumbling person that is whispering against Tom in

Government House.

Some little time later, I found myself standing alone a few moments by one of the doors onto the verandah, sipping at my glass of Madeira. Tho' the band played on, and there was much bustle and chatter, I heard above the din Leyden's name spoken outside in a snide voice most unhappily familiar: Ibbetson's. I adjusted my position, so I c'd see this villain: he was talking with that other rascal, Phillips; I strained my ears to catch their exchange.

Says Ibbetson: Leyden? I'm not surprised you can't abide him. I've never met a man so *flamboyant*, so *offensive*.

Well! Leyden is for sure flamboyant, but then they say the same of me. I wanted to object: Sir, there is as much difference between *flamboyant*, which can be a gorgeous thing, and *offensive*, as there is between a flame and malodorous smoke. But Phillips was speaking, and I restrained myself, to listen.

Nods Phillips: aye, he is in all ways extravagant, and uncommon boastful too. How many languages is it he claims to speak? He that can barely manage English so an Englishman can understand him. And that voice that he never for one minute stops using.

'Tis true, shudders Ibbetson, 'tis true our yakking scholar suffers a sad inability to refrain from sharing his knowledge, and his opinions.

I've thought the same thing myself, or very like, but I thought it with indulgent affection, not with malice. Then again, the way Ibbetson said *scholar*, 'twas very clear he meant to say Leyden ain't no such thing, but only pretends to scholarship, which charge is both cruel and unfair.

I was already angry and hurt on my friend's behalf, but worse yet was to come. Ibbetson now yawns and says: my dear Mrs. Dundas calls Leyden most presumptuous, she says his manners must revolt the fastidious and alarm the delicate, and 'tis only

Tom and Olivia Raffles w'd have him in their house.

I felt my eyes grow hot and moist, whether for the slights to Leyden, or for those to me and Tom I did not know. But I comforted myself I w'd not for nothing be as stiff and formal and censorious as our good righteous Mrs. D. No, I'd much rather be a woman to pardon peculiarity in favour of originality, than to condemn both as unrefined.

With this defiant thought I returned to the party, determined to show our petty ungenerous society that not only am I willing to overlook Leyden's faults, but more than this I am his ally.

Alas, I now think I was perhaps too successful in proclaiming my loyal alliance. My doubts first began straight after the party, when Tom came into my room. As he climbed into my bed he remarks, out of nothing it seemed, and with both his face and his voice expressionless: there are ever dangers in a poet. Pricked to defensiveness, I demands: what *can* you mean? Says Tom: and beautiful women of refined sensibility are known ever to attract poets. I c'd think of nothing to say to that, so I said nothing at all. Tom now laughs, thank God – not cruelly, not even indulgently, but as at something funny – and then he teases: 'tis a veritable Sarah Siddons I've married, and mine with equal power over her audience as the more famous one at Drury Lane. I still c'd not think what to say so again I stayed silent. Tom began to kiss my face softly, playfully, and betwixt kisses he says: not to worry, it seems to me that what Leyden, dear *shurvaleeay**, wants from you, my darling, is a spiritual, courtly attachment, but *I* want something with more guts than that – and then we began to kiss in earnest.

Then all today Leyden has been acting to me as if I am his sun, the source of all his warmth and light, and I have been prattling about the disarraying effects of too much Madeira, and acting to this man for whom I truly feel a strong and deep affection sisterly, even matronly, and hardly at all *cocketish*, for I w'd not be a tease.

Worst of all, Mary Ann visited this afternoon, and reported, with gay delight, that they are saying about George Town that Tom, Leyden, and me have all fallen madly in love with each other, and ain't this a delicious scandal.

*I consulted Tom, who tells me I sh'd have wrote *chevalier*.

December 1805, China St., George Town

Leyden says he has now mastered Malay, which language he calls childishly easy, tho' I've noticed he relies on *munshis* – native speakers – to aid him in his translations.

Tom, too, is confident he's grasped the tongue. Indeed, my husband is so much enthused by Leyden's support, and by his example, he now announces he will translate for publication, as his modest contribution to oriental scholarship, the *Undang-undang Malaya*, which is the Malay laws, or the maritime codes of the Malays.

Most in the government here care to learn but a few phrases of Malay, and I think Tom and Leyden praiseworthy for their interest in the language, but I must in conscience note it is one thing to *read* Malay, and to translate it from books, and another thing to *speak* it.

There are seen about George Town several women called *nonyas*, the native mistresses of European men, some of them almost wives so long and secure have been their connections with their protectors, and so numerous their children, and so old and stout have they become with no looks left to speak of – and *all* of them with teeth, lips, gums stained red from chewing *sireh*, a concoction of the shavings of a nut called *betel*, and tobacco, and various spices, all wrapped in the betel nut leaves.

Mrs. D & Co. snub these nonyas, so I make sure I don't, and one of them, an ancient creature, the unofficial widow of an

Englishman dead this past decade, becomes almost even my friend – this notwithstanding we both know the gap between us is wider, in many ways, than the sea from here to Plymouth, as it must be between any native and any fair person, even those that share a bed. Or so I suppose. In any case, Martina Rozells is a half-caste who hints she was born a princess of one of our little local courts, tho' 'tis widely known her father was a Portuguese sailor and her mother from Siam.

Here's the rub: I had it from Martina that the Malays love to ornament their speech with jangling rhymes, that their language is rich with riddles, parables, and proverbs; 'tis a language courteously dripping with flatteries and compliments, and one in which 'tis easy to insult when you don't mean to for it boasts myriad ways of saying *you*, *your*, *yours*, &c, depending on the speaker's rank, and the listener's.

Have Tom and Leyden mastered these subtleties? I have to think it more likely they speak Malay no better than w'd chickens, but for the sake of peace between us I do not say so.

Christmas Eve 1805, China St., George Town

Ships sailing where you want to go being so rare in the Eastward and us otherwise as stuck in our settlements as rabbits in traps, we take what we can get. There is today called here a Portuguese ship, *Santo Antonio*. When she quits hence, so too will Leyden, for she sails to Calcutta, and he has booked passage – now he is satisfied he is master of Malay, he feels he must return to that city, there to pursue his oriental studies in busier marts of learning than we have here.

My chevalier's coming departure casts on me an unseasonal pall, and I find myself in a mood of discontent and nostalgia. I remember today with fond indulgence even my mother's carping, and tho' since she was six we only that once spent Christmas together, when she stayed with me in London, I miss too Harriet, and gaze often on her miniature.

New Year's Day 1806, China St., George Town

1805 is gone, and to mark its passing Leyden has addressed to me a poem, *Dirge of the Departed Year*. 'Tis a long piece, and gloomy, full of dark unbodied spirits reminding us weak mortals we will die. For myself I prefer sprightly strains, but Leyden's sad notes commemorate, before he has yet left Penang, the never to be recaptured joys of his time here; his dirge laments, with anticipatory nostalgia, his pain at missing me and Tom – worse it foresees his own early death. When asked pray why so morbid, Leyden replies that Death likes to glut himself on fair people in the East, and between his liver, his bowels, and the intermittent fever he cannot think he'll have the luck to see old age. 'Tis little mitigation of his poem's misery that in one part my dear chevalier imagines his ghost may think itself recalled from the grave by *me* – by what he calls *Olivia's kind bewitching smile*.

Leyden recited his poem, the whole of it, to Tom and me last evening on the verandah, as we waited up to see in this fresh new year that will bring with it what it will. We had not lit the lantern, for dislike of the swarms of little airy flying things its light attracts, so his only illumination was moonlight, and the fitful gleam of fireflies; his accompaniment was all the animal racket of a tropical night, not forgetting the distant throaty grunt that was the roar of a tiger.

Such was the melancholy of the piece that we all wept to hear it. When he'd sufficiently recovered his composure Tom said he liked to hear my smile described as *kind bewitching*, for that it is. I was gratified by my husband's compliment, and gratified too to have been Leyden's muse, as I was dear Trudge's when he wrote my *Ode to Nona*. But when I said so, Leyden replied he was jealous of Trudge and his everlasting Nona, and I sh'd never be be-Nonaed by him, so I pretended to be irked, and scolded him, playfully, and then we all three became a little effusive and allicholy; we drank between us four or five bottles of Madeira, one of port, and a few tots of cherry brandy – did I say before the water here ain't fit to drink, so allichol must do instead, almost even at breakfast?

January 1806, China St., George Town

Leyden sailed this morning for Calcutta. He teased as he wished me adjoo that the moment the *Santo Antonio* got fairly to sea, he expected the Portuguese sailors to address themselves with the greatest fervour to the ship's patron, Saint Anthony, but for himself he would select *me* for his sweet patroness during the voyage.

O, his nonsense! Now Leyden is gone, I find I miss even the irritating whine of his voice, and Tom is very low at the loss of his friend; he goes about muttering we can't expect a letter within two months, and then who knows if Leyden will be able to send good news of his health.

January 1806, China St., George Town

Mary Ann informs me with her usual relish that they are now discussing all about George Town the sagacious question to what degree our recently departed friend Leyden was mad, or merely humoursome? Well! I grant he is unusual strange, but he is for sure his own man, which is more than can be said for most of my insipid, half-alive, half-vegetable acquaintance.

February 1806, China St., George Town

Tom's confidence in his Malay continues to grow. He has pointed out to Dundas that a Malay Translator To Government ain't yet been appointed, and he has suggested that his own name may be borne in mind, since he says he c'd undertake to write in his own hand any letters in the Malay language that may be deemed of a secret nature, rendering it unnecessary for government affairs to be entrusted to the hands of a native.

Meanwhile, his private studies continue apace. In the evenings, he has started in earnest to translate from dusty old manuscripts, often crumbling, the *Undang-undang Malaya*, in hopes the work will not only be very desirable in a literary point-of-view, but will also do everything possible for his reputation at home, and thus for his advancement in the Eastward.

For this work of translation, Tom has begun employing munshis as Leyden does – he has four of them to assist him that he now supports. And since, in time, his translation of the *Undang-undang Malaya* sh'd prove most useful to the government, he has asked Dundas for company funds to pay these munshis. But Dundas says the matter of financial assistance must be referred to the Honourable Members of the Court Of Directors in Leadenhall St. Alas, said Hon. Mems. ain't renowned quick in their decisions – not to mention it c'd take ten months for Dundas' letter to reach them, and another ten months before he receives their reply. No, if we are ever to get our money at all, I fear 'twill not be until long after the *Undang-undang Malaya* is translated into English and Tom is off on some other project – from his endless curiosity he is already investigating such various matters as the chronological cycles used by the Malays, the names they call chess pieces, &c.

March 1806, China St., George Town

That dullard Phillips lately got heartily sick of Penang, and obtained permission to travel to Bombay, to remain there six months on leave, and now he is gone. As Phillips is Secretary to the Government, and Tom is Assistant Secretary, his absence is greatly to my husband's advantage: The Company has so few men here he must now by necessity be given responsibilities beyond his station; indeed he is to be styled for the duration Acting Secretary to the Government.

This title is very fine, but my slight and slender Tom has a delicate constitution and I dread him falling ill from overwork. It don't help he found Phillips' papers in shocking disarray; it seems the man ain't got the skills of his office in record-keeping – which record-keeping Tom says c'd be the poorest in all The Company. Tom, meticulous, and valuing all minutes, reports, letters, narratives, has vowed to Dundas to bring everything to order, for which he has been commended, tho' we don't expect to derive much pecuniary benefit as he can still only be Acting Sec.

June 1806, China St., George Town

On reviewing my last entry, I see 'twas written three months back, and in it I expressed fears for Tom's health. How strange! 'twas not *him* has since become an invalid, but *me*. Aye, I have been neglecting this diary not from sloth, but from indisposition, for I have been ill – almost even mortal ill.

In late March I attended with Tom a ball at the Navy House, with all the beauty and fashion of the island present. I was dancing down the line with Flag Captain Austin Bissell, an officer from HMS *Blenheim*, when I became dizzy, and fell unconscious upon the floor; there was general alarm for my life, which was saved only by the prompt attention of Bissell, who straightaway fetched the surgeon from his ship to attend me.

In consequence of my fall, I ruptured some of the blood vessels in or near my liver, which occasioned a violent haemorrhage. This, in turn, brought on a desperate attack of the liver, which has reduced me to a *mere* skeleton – when I happen to catch sight of my reflection I scarce recognise myself with my eyes dull and sunken, my cheeks lank, my hair lustreless where it ain't fallen out, my skin dry and yellow, and my dresses hanging off my bones like sacks. Still, in spite of my mortified aspect, I live, and I am now convalescing.

July 1806, China St., George Town

Notwithstanding his avowals of devotion, Leyden has been since he left Penang most stingy with his letters. Has he forgot me? Unhappy thought! O fickle man!

Well, if my chevalier has forgot *me*, I ain't forgot *him* – and his forgetfulness, if he be guilty of it, I must confess has been my muse. I know as much about fine writing as I do about Greek, nevertheless, when I was recuperating from my liver, I broke the *ennwee* of illness by writing poetry. Most of my poems displeased me, but one, *Forget Me Not*, I addressed to Leyden, and this I judged not bad, so I submitted it to *The Penang Gazette* – the usual record of ship movements, marriages, births and deaths, which accepts also articles of intelligence, essays, letters, and poetical pieces. To my surprised delight it has now been printed!

I w'd be modest, and I have no wish to make my hand ache, so I will copy out now but the best quatrain of the sixteen I wrote:

> *O thou whom ne'er my constant heart*
> *One moment hath forgot*
> *Tho' fate severe hath bid us part*
> *Yet still forget me not*

These lines please me so much that for all they were addressed by me to Leyden, and not by Tom, to me, I remarked to my husband last night, intending to be playful, that sh'd I predecease him, he must consider them for my epitaph. But Tom took in earnest my banter; he blanched, and he said I must not tease of our inevitable horrid separation, not so soon after I survived my liver, and not in this deadly land where fever can strike at breakfast and kill by tea.

I as well sent my poem in a letter to Leyden; now I dread his reply, fearing our learned pundit will find a thousand and fifty faults in my poor unrefined and incorrect scrawl ... And if he takes from my warm words false encouragement? Good. Let that stand as his punishment for writing me since he quit hence naught but a chit!

August 1806, China St., George Town

It has been known sometime the climate here disagrees with both Mrs. D and with Miss W, and saps from them their vitality; now we learn they are to travel together to Calcutta to recover their health. I think it must be very wrong of me to be pleased by this news, but I cannot persuade myself I am sad.

September 1806, China St., George Town

Our sickly pair Mrs. D and Miss W today sailed for their health's sake to Calcutta. Dr. William Dick, who is on the establishment here as Surgeon, attends them.

My chief tormentor and her sister left aboard HMS *Blenheim*, which is now commanded from here to Africa. That ship remains so hogged she don't look seaworthy – and I that know nothing of ships ain't the only one to think so. Before she sailed, Flag Captain Bissell, who remains my good friend ever since my attack of the liver, told me she is now in such alarming poor condition she requires constant pumping to keep her afloat, but when he protested of this to his commander, he received the taunting rebuke that he may go ashore if he liked. The poor man has left with me a letter composed to his wife, that I am to send her sh'd the ship founder – which sad event heaven forefend, tho' I have often wished Mrs. D to the bottom of the ocean.

January 1807, China St., George Town

My naughty liver has made me ill again these past few months, and I almost thought to put aside for ever this diary as naught but a catalogue of indisposition, but the new year brings with it renewed energy and spirit, and tho' as encouragement from Fate for me to sharpen my goose quill and to dip it in my inkpot, I have good news to report: letters come from London announce Tom has got his money for his munshis that he asked for nearly a year back – still those busy scribes toil at the *Undang-Undang Malaya*. We now learn too Tom is appointed Malay Translator to Government – this in addition to his existing duties as Acting Sec. Alas, his new title brings with it no pecuniary advantage.

February 1807, China St., George Town

Olivia, you are a horrid, shabby woman! Did you welcome Mrs. D's removal to Bengal as deliverance? You cannot deny you did. And now letters come from Dr. Dick informing us that tho' that crook ship HMS *Blenheim* reached Calcutta without incident, a few days later, in early November, first Miss W, and then Mrs. D, succumbed to fever – both lives lost notwithstanding Dr. Dick's best efforts to save them.

Nobody here seems to know the rules governing mourning in the Eastward, and we don't go into black, which is relief to me as I cannot grieve for Mrs. D, nor regret she no longer shades me with her hostility. Still, I find now I pity her as a closed and timid woman, too fearful ever to have turned her face to the dazzling blaze of our Indian sun. And I must in conscience report her death has hit her husband fitting hard; Dundas is more than bereaved, he is bereft. Tom says this is a grief must drag down the whole government, 'cause with the chief desolate and forlorn there must be more than ever opportunity for the different difficult characters in this settlement to make mischief.

March 1807, China St., George Town

Dundas continues low, and almost too ill to work; he more than ever relies on Tom, who, in addition to his new duties as Malay Translator, has now been promoted from Acting Secretary to full Secretary to the Government – this tho' Phillips is returned. Aye, Phillips is back, but he is now shuffled to the posts of Warehouse-keeper and Paymaster and tho' he sits on Dundas' council, Tom says his contributions to discussions are too muddled and feeble to much affect outcomes.

Phillips is aggrieved at what he sees as the lessening of his dignity, and he seems to blame for it my blameless, capable Tom. For his part, Tom says Phillips is an ingrate and the man sh'd be glad to be made Warehouse-Keeper 'cause this is an office will enable him to put away a tidy profit into his own pocket, from those wanting access to the stores.

As for our own accounts, Tom's allowance is now calculated in Spanish dollars – the global currency of trade – each worth we think about five English shillings. He has been on six thousand a year, but this now rises to eight, a most welcome increase 'cause we are ever short of money.

April 1807, China St., George Town

Dundas, our sad chief, today left Penang aboard HMS *Belliqueux*. He takes now a short, restorative sea voyage as treatment both for the low mood brought on by the death of his wife, and also for the physical lowering brought on by our oppressive, humid heat;

the ship's doctor is in attendance.

April 1807, China St., George Town

Dundas that left Penang a man has now come back a corpse. Aye, I am much saddened to report that our quondam chief did not benefit as we had hoped from his short sea voyage, which was not restorative at all: on April 8 he died; the anxiety of losing his wife and bilious complaints brought on by bad air jointly caused his death. HMS *Belliqueux* was then in the Bay of Bengal; her captain immediately turned her around and brought his sad cargo back to George Town.

We buried him two days back with all the ceremony due his station. The whole of the troops at the settlement paraded at half past four o'clock, in front of Government House, and then attended his remains to our Protestant cemetery, where he has been interred, and where soon no doubt we'll raise a most splendid impressive tomb, fitting to his earthly stature.

Forty-five heavy guns, corresponding with the years of Dundas' age, were fired during the funeral procession, and as red Malayan earth was cast upon the coffin more soldiers fired a volley from small guns. Later, as we mourners were filing away I heard a gravedigger complain filling Dundas' grave was awkward work, as the ground there was very narrow.

'Tis now whispered Dundas shook the money tree so well he left his wife (since departed) twenty thousand pounds in three per cents, one thousand pounds in cash, and an annuity of three hundred pounds.

April 1807, China St., George Town

Dundas' funeral has left me unsettled, and has reminded me that, to my bitterest shame, I struggle to feel, as I ought, sure and certain hope of resurrection to eternal life, through our Lord Jesus Christ.

For my troubling doubts I blame my mother. My father's family is Protestant, so that is what I became when I went to Ireland a babe – and so, for show, did my mother. But in earnest she held firm to the ancient Circassian religion – and she still does unless she also now be dead, and the letter not yet reached me. At night, when I was a tiny child, she whispered to me of her beliefs. She held my hand under the blankets and she told me of the spirits she believes dwell in rocks, trees, rivers, and of many gods each with his or her own fiefdom – thunder and lightning, wind, rain. She put her lips close to my ear and breathed that the ghosts of the dead go to the Circassian other world, or underworld, that is just like this one, except chilly, and all in shadows, so that from its drabness the dead may know that they are dead.

This belief in a ghostly other world I put aside before I was ten – 'tis a childish belief, such as no adult not from Circassia c'd believe. But as an infant I believed it, and for believing it then, I have, I confess it, ever since I can remember, asked with some wicked part of me whether Christian beliefs – heaven, hell, a life of bliss or purgatory after this one – be just as childish?

O Olivia, w'd you perish everlastingly, and be flung from the presence of the Lord into the everlasting fire prepared for the devil and his angels, which will consume your body until 'tis ashes, when 'twill be restored, that it may be burned again? No? Then say it with Job: *I know that my Redeemer liveth, and that he shall stand at the latter day upon the earth. And though after my skin worms destroy this body, yet in my flesh shall I see God: whom I shall see for myself, and mine eyes shall behold, and not another.*

April 1807, China St., George Town

There is much bitterness at Government House about who is to be Dundas' successor. Phillips has been appointed Acting Gov. until a permanent appointment can be made. This infuriates Tom; he says Phillips is appointed only by reason of seniority, and the man is barely able to serve even only as Acting Gov.; he worries for the booby's incompetence his own heavy workload is henceforth to become impossible heavy. There is another man, Macalister, he judges more fitted to be made Governor, and he is agitating on his behalf – my husband has drafted for Macalister a letter he will send to Bengal, as if from his own hand, to press his case.

June 1807, China St., George Town

O Fate, cruel Fate! We had yesterday the terrible news that HMS *Blenheim* is lost. After she dropped Mrs. D and her party in Calcutta she sailed for Madras, and soon after quit that port for Africa. During a gale in February she was spotted off the coast of Madagascar flying signals of distress and then she was seen no more. They sent out searches, but no trace of her has been found; there were five hundred and ninety men aboard; five hundred and ninety, and one of them my friend Flag Captain Bissell, he that entrusted to me that letter to his wife 'tis my sad duty now to send. 'Tis very strange to think its recipient probably don't yet know her husband is dead. 'Tis very strange to think the moment *now* in the Eastward is so different from the moment *now* in England, which is to say 'tis very strange Bissell's death, which is in the past for me, is yet in the future for his widow in all likelihood still thinks herself his wife.

August 1807, China St., George Town

From suspecting my own mother was once a slave I have an abhorrence of the treating of people as things that is slavery. Tom shares with me this antipathy, for all his father was a slaver – or perhaps 'cause of it? So we are both in great delight the government at Westminster has accelerated the dissolution of that evil institution: with the customary delay of letters, we have just received authentic reports that in January of this year the British government passed an Act of Parliament abolishing the slave trade both at home and in all Britain's overseas settlements.

Abolition will be like a cleansing wave in the *West* Indies, where those poor enthralled Africans are flogged in the sugar plantations, but it ripples also here in the *East* Indies, where it sometimes seems everybody who *ain't* a slave *keeps* a slave, the natives as well as the fair people.

Aye, all the different Malays of the islands make slaves of each other, if they can, and engage in both slave raiding and slave trading – until now, slaves from all across the Archipelago have been traded in the pasar here. And I'm told that in each little sultanate on the Peninsula a large part of the population is enslaved people, some working the *padi* fields – the rice fields – and otherwise hard labouring, some flogged as domestic servants, and all used like gold or jewels to display their owners' wealth.

Some of the slaves ain't Malays at all, but primordials. The jangals of the Eastward are home to a great variety of primitive aboriginals, pagans all, woolly haired people scattered among them, and these the Malays, Mahomedans, often enslave, for as far as their captors are concerned they are only infidels, and are considered fair booty.

Then again, as often as the Malays enslave them, the primordials just as often enslave each other. The different types of savage are forever at tribal warfare with their blowpipes and their poisoned darts; they hunt each other incessantly, and carry off girls as prizes to their own villages. From the boys they often take their heads, for many of them are headhunters, their horrid shields decorated with the hair of their human victims, and the roofs of their communal houses hung about with skulls. Some of them are even cannibals, from backwardness they do not know that people sh'd not be food – or else these man eaters do not know that people not of their tribe are people at all?

But I stray. I mean to say that with slavery so entrenched hereabouts, and with the Slave Trade Act banning only the *carriage* of slaves on British ships, not the institution itself, Tom knows we will no more be able to do away with slavery overnight in Penang, than they can in any other of Britain's overseas settlements. Nonetheless, he is cock-a-hoop the government here has plans afoot already to introduce as soon as possible measures to stop the importation of slaves into George Town, saying with all his fellow abolitionists: *We have no slaves at home – then why abroad?*

Later, a postscript: it strikes me now 'tis a strange word, this word *abroad*, 'cause where is it, from here? It ain't not England, for all England's half a year's sailing away. Perhaps 'tis China? Aye, I think henceforth I'll make China my own particular abroad.

September 1807, China St., George Town

The implementation of the Slave Trade Act means such an increase in work for Tom, I worry more than ever for his health. He is now spending long hours drafting the orders that will in time he hopes announce the total abolition of slavery in this island – the practice of it, as well as of slave trading in the pasar. He is busy too preparing proposals to the council that they consider compensating slaves for their slavery, tho' he is advised privately by Macalister this be thought unorthodox, as the Slave Trade Act don't call for the emancipation of existing slaves, and the systems of compensation proposed by Westminster are for slave-*owners* in the West Indies who henceforth can't import from Africa new bodies to work their plantations, and not for the sad enslaved wretches in our part of the globe.

October 1807, China St., George Town

We now have word from Calcutta that Macalister is made Lieutenant-Governor of Penang over Phillips, who is much disgruntled, and who is henceforth returned to his quondam posts of Warehouse-keeper and Paymaster.

Tho' Tom is happy and relieved 'tis his friend not his enemy who won the day, he keeps his head down and he has not gloated a bit in Phillips' presence. Notwithstanding my husband's discretion, Phillips, our w'd-be the Hon. the Gov. that's not fit for the role, seems settled into a malignant hatred for him, and acts toward him with inveterate bitterness.

October 1807, China St., George Town

It has been as I predicted: Tom has exhausted himself so much with work he has been desperate ill. He has had an attack of the headache so blinding and dizzying that for some time I entertained little hope of his life. Dr. Dick c'd offer no help but his bedside manner, which, tho' 'tis excellent and soothing, failed to restore Tom to health. When I was quite despairing, Martina Rozells, the ancient nonya of my acquaintance, brewed for Tom, from the root of a common little weed, rather straggly with white flowers that don't look like much, a tonic for his brain. She banished me from Tom's presence when she administered her remedy, as she had to whisper over him magic words most dreadful secret. Lo and behold, three days later Tom was sitting up against his pillows, his vision cleared and his headache much less.

The weed from which Martina brewed her potion is called *Bonglai Kayu*, tho' I don't know its name in English.

November 1807, China St., George Town

Tom, convalescing from his head, applied last week to Dr. Dick for an M.C. – a medical certificate. We now learn he has been authorised to proceed to sea immediately, for a restorative voyage. This is to be followed by sick leave in Malacca, the healthful settlement we have to our southwards that gives its name as well to its famous Straits.

In preparation for our departure we have given up the lease on this bungalow in China St. Tom is now engaged in buying a plot of land on the seaward side of the new carriage road being built along the North Beach. On this plot he plans to build us a bungalow – pukka built, not of wood and atap – but work cannot start until the new year so where we'll live when we return I do not know.

November 1807, the *Scourge*, Straits of Malacca

Once again I find myself writing by candlelight in a hot and airless cabin – one so snug and smelly 'tis more a stall. Aye, Tom and me now sail down the coast of the Malay Peninsula towards Malacca in a small thing, misleadingly named the *Scourge*. Tho' she calls herself a pleasure craft, she is in fact a sieve, offering to her passengers almost total want of decorum. Still, the weather is uncommon placid, so a truce with complaining.

November 1807, the *Scourge,* Straits of Malacca

Tho' the weather continues fine, Tom, who is looking already much pinker for the sea air, tells me we sail into a storm. He says Malacca, originally a Malay fishing village, was captured a few centuries ago by the Portuguese; it became for them an important base for the trading of the spices of the surrounding Eastern Isles.

This was a trade so profitable, in time Malacca attracted the attention of the Dutch. The Hollanders launched a successful war to win Malacca from the Iberians – but once they'd won it, they let the place decline: they built Batavia, on the island of Java, as their main stronghold in the orient; as Batavia rose, Malacca gently fell asleep. And so things went on a hundred years or so. The Company acquired Malacca only recently: after the French conquered their motherland, the Dutch handed it pro tempore into our keeping, to deny use of it to those detested frog-eaters. But now we have it, what are we to do with it? 'Tis these days a poor sort of trading post, and it ain't for the moment suitable as a war port, since the mouth of the river is long since obstructed by mud flats at low tide, and The Company ain't got the money for dredging them. Likewise its defences, scarcely repaired since the Portuguese departed, and in a shocking state, are beyond The Company's resources to rebuild. In consequence of these problems, and bearing in mind too we may have to return Malacca to the Dutch, come the joyful day our dismal wars are, God willing, successfully concluded, the Court of Directors in Leadenhall St. has lately ordered all the fortifications and public buildings be completely destroyed and demolished. The plan is that once Malacca is razed, the building materials and the British officials thus released will be shipped to Penang, to find new use there.

Tom thinks this policy of destruction and demolition is quite insane, and 'tis common knowledge they don't much like it in Malacca, neither. He has heard that not one official from Malacca wants to move to Penang, and he anticipates when we arrive much angry discussion of this matter, tho' he says the destruction is already begun so it ain't clear what use there'll be in jawing.

November 1807, The Stadhuis *, Malacca

I have been in Malacca now a week, and 'tis all around like the destruction of Jerusalem! All I breathe is dust! Tom spoke aright: the place is in the midst of being torn down.

Now Tom witnesses all around him the destruction and demolition he so decries, he is more than ever convinced 'tis madness. He says 'tis certain the ancient fortifications here w'd be less costly to repair than to demolish, and I believe him, for the Fort is built of some strong, reddish stone set in cement. Some of its walls are sixty feet high, and fifteen feet thick! To bring them down requires gunpowder. We are staying with the Resident, Captain William Farquhar. He is an engineer, a soldier trained to design and construct military buildings – and likewise to raze them. Two nights back a large crowd gathered at the Fort to watch him light the fuse w'd set off kegs of gunpowder to bring down a seawards wall. Tom and me joined with all the others, expecting spectacle, and getting instead the fright of our lives. The gunpowder exploded with noise like thunder, and pieces of the Fort as large as elephants – some as large as houses – were thrown into the air and cascaded into the sea. I thought I'd faint from fright and now I'm told the coolies employed on the demolition are afraid of the ghosts and the devils who lived in the stones, and who have now been set free to wander the town, there to steal if they can the souls of the living.

Tho' he lit the fuse, as was his duty, Farquhar is as convinced as Tom 'tis a mistake to destroy Malacca. Most evenings my husband and our host compete in denouncing the Hon. Mems. of the Court of Directors as mad men. They suck on their pipes and agree the H.Ms. are ignorant of the subjects on which they think it necessary to decide. They confirm each to the other that our British presence here is a check to the piracy that ever threatens shipping in The Straits – all the Malay sultans sponsor pirates, 'cause they believe raising money by trade would lower their dignity, whilst piracy is their birth right, and so brings no disgrace. They nod over their wine as one tells the other no French ships can pass Malacca without being spotted from the watchtower on The Hill. They are of one mind the total destruction of the Fort w'd leave an opening for Americans and other neutral flags to move in and build another; they are united 'tis vital a garrison remain here.

Farquhar feels so strongly the H.Ms. have lost their wits he has confided to Tom he intends to spare some of the buildings he is ordered to destroy, which defiance of distant London Tom says shows most admirable character, judicious judgement, and uncommon good sense.

*The Stadhuis is what they call The Residency here. It doubles as the town hall – indeed *stadhuis* is Dutch for *town hall*, for we British inherited both building and name from the Hollanders.

November 1807, The Stadhuis, Malacca

Farquhar is a Scot nearing forty, tall and thin as a candlestick. He has served The Company in the Eastward nigh on twenty years, and he has been the Resident here these past four. He is a good administrator, and an amiable man: his sharp eyes miss nothing, but it ain't his way to criticise; he is patient, tolerant toward everybody he encounters. Indeed, he is most esteemed and popular 'cause of his kindness, his competence, his fluency in Malay, and his interest in the natives.

This interest in the natives extends even to his bed. He lives openly with his nonya, Nonio Clemaine, and they are fonder of each other than many a church married couple. These nonyas are great ones for hinting at grand connections; Nonio Clemaine w'd have me believe her mother was a Malay princess, from the ruling house of a local sultanate, but I know from others her mother was a Portuguese-Malay half-caste. Her father was a French officer. She is about my age, and she must have been pretty once, tho' her teeth and lips must ever have been stained red from chewing that disgusting sireh. She is very fat, partly from overfeeding, and partly from want of exercise. She dresses in the native kebaya that looks so much like a chemise, tho' I grant it must be cool and comfortable.

Nonio Clemaine and Farquhar have together six children. Notwithstanding their skins are tell-tale sallow, this is a lovely, lively set of poppets that frisks about the Stadhuis all day, boisterous, and happy. I play with these pretty ones often, and 'tis my great pleasure to dandle the baby. As I dandle him, I remember dandling Harriet, and I hope that soon I will be dandling another baby of my own, if heaven wills it, which is something that after over two years of marriage I start to doubt.

November 1807, The Stadhuis, Malacca

The Stadhuis stands within the much demolished Fort and is everywhere surrounded by rubble, but Farquhar has today announced 'tis one of the buildings he will save from blowing up. Tho' any man w'd be reluctant to knock down his home, 'tis generally agreed this is a decision he made not from self-interest but from common sense: the Stadhuis is a very necessary building; it houses as well as Farquhar and his family many of his subordinate officials; it has many offices, a prison, a warehouse, &c. Tho' the damp heat of our torrid zones is often the cause for the swift deterioration of paper, it has a records room exceptionally suitable for the preservation of official documents. Tom says this usefulness is on account of the room's thick walls, stone floor, and high ceiling, which together guarantee a cool and dry interior.

For that matter, the whole Stadhuis is delightfully shady and cool, with airy arched corridors leading everywhere to large, dim rooms. It w'd be a most satisfactory building except the exterior walls, painted white, tho' now coated grey with the dust that blows ceaselessly from the general destruction of Malacca, are spattered with red, from where the natives have spat at them quids of sireh. Tom says Farquhar sh'd paint his white walls red all over, to hide this dirtiness.

December 1807, The Stadhuis, Malacca

Tom, who sh'd be resting for his health, instead shadows Farquhar's footsteps and plagues him all day with questions about the running of Malacca – which questions our patient host answers most generously. Tom plagues him too with questions concerning natural history, for Farquhar is scholarly at botanising and zoologising, and is renowned for collecting all kinds of specimen. Then again, he has in his employ a number of Chinese artists commissioned to draw the local plants and animals. I admire his natural history drawings for their beauty; Tom for their contribution to science, which he says is enormous, for all they exist at such a distance from the grand marts of scientific information.

But Farquhar ain't satisfied with pictures, and specimens for his cabinet. No, he has gathered in his garden a *menajery* of living beasts: a porcupine, a great variety of monkeys, and a cassowary, a bird supreme in fierceness, ugliness, and largeness. I am told he had too until it died a leopard, and another creature, unknown before to Tom and me, called a tapir, which Tom says he would have been most interested to see, even only stuffed, except when it died the servants threw its body in the sea.

Tom says he must follow Farquhar's lead and that when we return to Penang he too will collect about him a menajery – he teases me he will not forget to have a cassowary, but I don't like that evil looking thing, and this I swear I will not allow. He says he must as well start collecting in a serious way plants, insects, shells, fishes, birds, reptiles, &c. In preparation for this useful work, he has learned from Farquhar how to preserve the bodies of animals in spirits, and now he keeps in our guest apartment a large barrel full of toddy, in which he puts live animals such as serpents, centipedes, scorpions, and the likes. Two days later he takes them out and places them in bottles where they look just as if they are alive.

I ain't sure I approve this new enthusiasm, for I don't wish to find bottled serpents where I don't expect them.

New Year's Day 1808, The Stadhuis, Malacca

A Malay *proa* – a sailing boat – engaged in the coastal trade has dropped here the mail from Penang, and with it a most welcome packet of letters for us.

One comes from Leyden, and in it there is much to ponder. 'Tis clear his super-eminent abilities ain't not been overlooked in Calcutta, and indeed they have enabled him to enter the circle of his fellow Scot, Lord Minto, since last July The Company's Governor-General of all India, so of East-Insular India also, and of all the settlements in the Eastward – aye, the great personage through whom even our own Lieutenant-Governor Macalister reports to the Court of Directors in London.

This friendship, useful to Leyden, c'd be useful also to Tom. With my husband's preferment in mind, Leyden writes he is anxious Tom sh'd finish his translation of the *Undang-undang Malaya* as fast as possible and send it to him to show to Ld. Minto, for the weight that this w'd give him in The Company.

By happy chance our packet contained also a chit from Tom's munshis to tell him they have at last wrote *finis* at the bottom of their translation, and put down their pens. Is this not timely? Tom, delighted at the circumstance, replies by another proa ordering a copy made, and this he directs his munshis to send to Leyden by the next ship that sails.

On matters domestic, I have had a letter from Mary Ann,

and one that ruffles me: she tells me she is in the family way, and she expects her stranger in the summer. Tho' I try to rejoice as I sh'd for my sister, I cannot lie her news don't make me jealous, for I find myself now more than ever assaulted by longing for another baby of my own. What a cruel twist it gives me to remember how shocked I was, how distressed, how angry, when I realised as an unwed girl of fifteen I'd been caught in pregnancy's dread net. Why is it that since that one time I ain't never been caught again? Not a second time with Jack. Not with Fancourt, which I can scarce regret, and not with Tom, for all he is a most ardent, hungry husband. Is this God's angry judgement on me for conceiving Harriet out of wedlock? But if my Father has punished me for transgression, then why also has he punished Tom? Aye, my husband shares with me my longing for a child. When first we were wed we spoke together often of our hopes, but now, alas, there is on this subject shyness between us, so when I read him Mary Ann's letter – for letters, like newspapers, we think to be shared – he sighed, and he said, wistful, that he looked forward very much to being an uncle. He forbore to add the obvious: 'twould be better to be a father. And I in turn forbore to show my husband's kind forbearance was to me a slap.

I suppose I must remind myself that if other people's happiness is ever hard to bear, then I must bear Mary Ann's as best as I am able.

January 1808, The Stadhuis, Malacca

'Tis now out of fury I take up my quill: Macalister has sent word Tom's leave of absence for his recuperation is cut short. This I think outrageous under the present circumstance of his delicate state of health, but my husband shrugs and says Macalister w'd not have pressed him so hard were the business not urgent – which business is that a vessel shortly leaves Penang for England, and the council's official documents and reports must be on board, 'cause they are required by India House. Well! I say *fie* to India House, but Macalister is clumsy with words, and it seems he cannot make up any dispatches for Court without Tom's assistance. And so Tom is adamant: he must go. Ye gods, this man!

February 1808, Mount Olivia

Tom and me quit Malacca for Penang on that same *Scourge* we took before; now we're back. Work ain't yet started on our new brick bungalow on The North Beach, and, homeless, we stayed the first few days with Mary Ann and Thompson.

I confess I found this time a trial, 'cause I fancied Mary Ann looked at me often through sideways eyes filled with pitying speculation, and she was not above unnecessary waddling, and nor above sighing she has been advised to lift not so much as a *pin*, and her smiles, I thought, were too often simpering. And me trying to pretend, the while, that her gently swelling belly did not taunt my determinedly flat one, and as well that Tom was not as conscious of the taunt as me.

Still, Tom and me are now removed a little way out of George Town, and we are living pro tempore in a wood and atap bungalow on one of the surrounding hills, which hill my loving husband has named Mount Olivia!

Ours is a simple rustic place, isolated, retired, and when, as now, I glance over the verandah rail, I see spreading beyond the compound the glittering green jangal, like a great lady spreading out her skirts, with the birds and the butterflies her gaudy jewels – except in all this overflowing, abounding vegetation there ain't nothing human, no human noise at all, not even the Mahomedans' call to prayer from their mosques, or masjids, which we heard wailing five times a day on China St. Instead there is the ceaseless racket of birds and creatures, and through daylight hours the whine of the cicadas is a constant ringing in my ears, and the song of the frogs is my lullaby.

March 1808, Mount Olivia

After too many excuses from the foreman, a slippery fellow, work is at last begun on our new bungalow, and tho' I will not often be able to visit the site, Tom is henceforth to make it his business to chivvy the builders.

Alas, we now have distressing reason to congratulate ourselves anew we build in brick, for there was a fire in George Town two nights back. It broke out past midnight, when most slumbered unsuspecting of danger. There were no fatalities, thank God, but much of the wooden, atap-roofed housing stock is lost, including Clubley's lodgings – did I say already Clubley is Tom's Assistant Secretary? Aye, this is the one man my harassed husband can rely on to help him, and even with his help I swear Tom's workload c'd defeat ten men.

Poor Clubley suffered much from breathing in smoke as the fire raged, and in consequence he is now confined to bed – he, like many others, is forced to take a room in The Commercial Hotel, we'd have him to lodge with us here, where I c'd nurse him, except he'd rather stay in town.

Clubley's indisposition means all the duties Tom is accustomed to delegate to him, he will for the moment have to undertake himself – in addition to his work as Secretary, and Translator, he is recently appointed also Licenser of The Press. And tho' the press here ain't naught but *The Penang Gazette*, he anticipates from this appointment a load of trouble.

April 1808, Mount Olivia

Clubley was lately granted an M.C., and a few days back he

sailed for his health's sake to Calcutta. My much-flogged husband naturally feels low at the loss of his Secretary, and this lowness has perhaps had general effect, for he told me last evening 'tis becoming clear to him Penang is pointlessly enlarged and a sore drag on Johnny Company's cash. He said tho' the settlement is surrounded by the sea of trees that is the jangal, these are not your Burmese teak, and are indeed quite the *wrong* sort of trees for shipbuilding, and hence, he says, through inefficiency and poor planning, Penang can never become the centre of shipbuilding 'twas intended to be, and as to trade, it here enriches only private merchants, mostly native, plying with their vessels the local, coastal trade in such things as sharks fins, sea slugs, and birds' nests, and not The Company that sends its East Indiamen from one end of the earth to the other, loaded with tea and textiles. He said he is now convinced Penang ain't the place to make him famous, and there ain't no future in this hole for an ambitious man, a man of drive and vision, nor for any poor fellow gets stuck here.

I trust these must be the passing doubts of a man made uncharacteristically pessimistic by overwork, and that if Tom is appointed pro tempore another Assistant Secretary he will be restored at once to his usual optimism and zeal.

June 1808, Mount Olivia

It occurs to me a diary, like the begetting of children, is a hope for immortality? I may never again have no more chicks than Harriet, who is determined to forget me, but perhaps in the far future someone somewhere will read my diary and think: so that was Olivia Mariamne Raffles, once Fancourt, nee, nay, born Devenish?

And what provokes these musings? 'Tis that Mary Ann is safely brought to bed of a beautiful baby girl, Charlotte Raffles

Drury Thompson – *Drury* is for her godfather, Rear-Admiral Drury, Commander-in-Chief on the naval station here, and our good family friend.

Little Charlotte, still so new and crumpled, is lusty and healthful, tho' skinny, and altogether the sweetest babe I ever saw since Harriet was new-born, beautiful even when she's red in the face and bawling. She smells of milk and vanilla: I breathe in her scent, and yearn.

My sister subjected me to a harrowing account of her travail, with no intimate detail sparred. Later, my maid had it from her maid that for Our Mary Ann all went as easy as pulling a plum from a pudding, tho' you'd never know it for her shrieking.

Tom looks on his new niece, the first niece or nephew he ever had, with tender eyes and remarks how glad his mother must be when she at last receives the letter with the news she is a grandmother.

Alas, tho' Tom and me rejoice for our sister, we dare not let our eyes meet over Charlotte's crib, and we are more than ever careful not to speak to each other of our own longing for a child, 'tis become a thing unsayable between us. And us three years married. O, I c'd weep.

July 1808, Mount Olivia

My husband has been noticed in Calcutta, and is held there in most honourable regard! We never knew 'til now whether Leyden received Tom's translation of the *Undang-undang Malaya* but now we have a letter from him, and in it he reports he not only received it, he as well showed it to Ld. Minto, who was greatly pleased by it, and who praised Tom as a gentleman whose intelligence and zeal in the pursuit of knowledge gave the strongest hope of his becoming an ornament to oriental literature, and who said he sh'd be gratified in receiving immediately from its author any communications of a similar nature, for he was clearly a man perfectly versed in the Malay language and manners, and conversant with the interests and affairs of the eastern states.

O, what worthy recognition of my husband's labours! How it delights me to think all the little paltry wretches of George Town will be astonished and nearly maddened to learn Tom has come to Ld. Minto's attention is such advantageous manner!

Leyden also reports he has arranged for Tom's election to the Asiatic Society of Bengal. This most prestigious and scholarly Society examines the laws of the Hindoos and Mahomedans; the modern politics and geography of Hindoostan; the arithmetic, geometry, and sciences of the Asiatics; the poetics and music of the Eastern nations; the trade, manufactures, agriculture, and commerce of India, &c. O kind chevalier! I intend to reply to his by the next ship that sails, in which reply I'll offer him my prayers that all that's good attend him ever.

August 1808, Mount Olivia

The insects scribbling the air are today most moithersome, and I am all together out of sorts with Tom. Why can my husband not profit as other men do through his plurality of offices? For his tactfulness in healing quarrels, his cheerful disposition, and his competence Macalister has now appointed him Court Registrar. O, what a public spirit has my husband! He has taken on this enormous task of Registrar without *fee* or present reward, whilst he continues still in all his other duties – and this at a time when in consequence of Clubley's absence by sickness he is without an assistant, or anyone who can show him the least possible assistance. Indeed, I think Tom has on all sides a vast deal too much on his mind and hands for his health's sake. I only wish he w'd have a little more care for it now than he has hitherto, and I fear the consequence must begin to show itself very soon; I dread another long, lingering fit of illness such as he had last.

September 1808, The Stadhuis, Malacca

I write now not at Penang, but at Malacca, and if, Dear Diary, this seems to you a sudden change of scene, my excuse is I c'd not write until now, for being kept busy by duties in the sickroom. Aye, as I feared w'd happen, Tom fell ill again: intense labour of mind and body brought on a vomiting fever that caused a dangerous jaundice.

I first summoned to Tom's sickbed Dr. Dick, but his bloodletting cure produced no improvement, so in desperation I turned to the nonya Martina, who brewed for Tom a decoction from the root of a common plant that is called in Malay *dakung anak*. She bathed him with this decoction, and then she excluded me from the sick room, and had him drink it, whilst reciting her secret spells.

From dakung anak, magic, or I don't know what Tom's skin and eyes lost their yellow tinge, but he remained ill and quite worn out. I insisted he ask Macalister for an M.C., and permission to take a short sea voyage to renew his vigour, which requests the Hon. the Gov. duly granted.

So it was that Tom and me entrusted ourselves once more to that sieve, the *Scourge*, and after a voyage happily unremarkable we are now a second time occupying the shady guest apartment on the upper floor of the Stadhuis. We find things in Malacca much as we left them: the Stadhuis stands in a field of rubble; the Fort is three quarters demolished; Nonio Clemaine wages war against dust; Farquhar rails against the mad men of the Court of Directors ...

Still, Baby Farquhar now prattles and toddles, and his brothers and sisters likewise grow. Also Farquhar's menajery in the garden is enlarged. The horrid cassowary is now joined by other native birds in cages, there is as well a wild dog, and a tiger. This tiger ain't resigned at all to living in a cage, and he paces up and down all day long, swaying his fearsome head from side to side; if any creature dares to venture close to the bars that imprison him, the furious beast shoots out his paw and swipes it dead.

September 1808, The Stadhuis, Malacca

The sea here is overwhelmed with dugongs, sea creatures Tom says were once confused with mermaids, tho' I think he must be wrong, 'cause they are more like fat little whales, or seals, than sirens. Farquhar has just dissected one and plans to send its skeleton to the Asiatic Society in Calcutta, which Society regularly receives from him specimens of birds and animals, living and stuffed – likewise seeds and plants he sends to that town's Botanic Garden. Tom says now he himself is elected to the Asiatic Society, he must keep up with Farquhar in scientific endeavour, so almost from his sickbed he has employed four natives to help him look for specimens. One he has told to go into the jangal and search for leaves, flowers, fungi, mosses, and so on. Another he has told to find worms, grasshoppers, butterflies, beetles, cicadas, centipedes, scorpions, and the likes. The third he has dispatched to the shore to get coral, shells, fish, and so on. The fourth must go out catching birds and small animals.

So once again I find myself breathing in the fumes emanating from a barrel of toddy and sharing this guest apartment with pickled creatures – Tom preserves in spirits the insects and reptiles his natives bring him. Other animals, birds, and fishes he skins and stuffs. The leaves and flowers he presses between the pages of a large book kept for this purpose. What he cannot preserve he gives to a Chinese draftsman from Macao, very expert at drawing life-like images of living things, and he tells him to copy them in paints.

September 1808, The Stadhuis, Malacca

Tho' I protest he is here to recover, not to work, Tom sits with Farquhar for long hours, thrashing over again and again Johnny Company's mistake of demolishing Malacca, and the excellent reasons for retaining what little remains of its defences. A few years back Farquhar wrote for Leadenhall St. a report arguing in the strongest terms for a retention of the garrison here, as complement to, and not in competition with, the one in Penang. That this report was ignored is evident from the destruction we see all around us. Now Tom says he will write a report of his own, giving new voice to the same general arguments Farquhar employed, and urging the Hon. Mems. of The Court of Directors to reverse their decision to destroy Malacca and abandon the settlement.

Farquhar seems resentful of Tom's enterprise, and he has asked more than once why my husband thinks he will be able to persuade The Court of Directors where he has failed. To which Tom shrugs, and says perhaps he can't do it, but 'tis certain he can't if he don't try.

October 1808, The Stadhuis, Malacca

When Tom ain't at his report, he seems dejected. The doubts he once expressed to me that Penang can't never be nothing but a backwater, that I thought then to be but the passing doubts of a man in a low mood, he now tells me are his settled conviction. Now he is away from it a little while he says he is more than ever persuaded Penang will never offer him the opportunities he hoped he'd find when he was first appointed Assistant Secretary to Dundas. He says 'tis a matter of money: Johnny Company ain't got the money to develop Penang. Worse, he says the settlement gobbles The Company's cash for no return, and an ambitious man w'd be well advised to get out. Hence he has now written to

Leyden, in Calcutta, asking if he knows of any vacancies elsewhere to which he may be appointed.

October 1808, The Stadhuis, Malacca

Farquhar has shot his tiger. A Chinese carpenter was sent to repair some damage to its cage, and the angry beast mauled him. The tiger is to be skinned and stuffed. The carpenter lives, tho' he lost to the beast his left foot.

November 1808, Mount Olivia

Tom is healthy again and we are returned to Penang. I had hoped we might be able to move straight away into our new bungalow, but to my frustration the coolies laying our bricks and roofing tiles slacked off while we were away. Now the foreman, that eel, tells us 'twill be another eight to ten weeks before we can think of shifting from this rustic Mount Olivia to the sociable melyer of North Beach Road.

Tom has submitted to Macalister the report he wrote in Malacca, arguing that the destruction of The Fort there sh'd not continue.

November 1808, Mount Olivia

Macalister has forwarded a copy of Tom's report to London, and another to Ld. Minto in Calcutta. With the copy for London he has sent also a letter commending Tom for his superior talents – and his praise was no less pretty for all that 'twas my husband himself who drafted it!

O, what a boon Macalister is so clumsy with words! Tom has used the letter to London, ostensibly from Macalister's own hand, to point out to The Court of Directors, the unwearied zeal and assiduity with which he has since the formation of the establishment here devoted his talents to the furtherance of The Company's interests, and also to remind said Court that the person holding the situation of Secretary is well able to understand those interests, which understanding, if only a vacancy were to arise, said Secretary – himself, Tom Raffles – c'd apply elsewhere in the Eastward to divers profitable ends.

January 1809, Runnymede, George Town

I have neglected my diary over the Christmas season, not only 'cause I was enjoying the festive gambols, but also 'cause I have been occupied with shifting! Aye, a new year, and we are in our new bungalow at last! Tho' if Tom finds a way out of Penang it may not be too long I have to enjoy it. Still, we exchange the scenery and noises of the jangal for those of town, so 'tis no longer the howling of monkeys swings us from sleep in the mornings, but once again the Mahomedans' call to prayer, that haunting Arabic wail that brings to our green landscape the memory of dusty desert sands: *Aaallaaahuuu aaakbaaar, Aaallaaahuuu aaakbaaar* …

But I stray. I mean to write of our bungalow: 'tis one of a number now constructed on the new carriage road, and has a splendid view of the entrance to the harbour. Our neighbours are Tom's various fellow government officials – including Clubley, who is now returned from Calcutta, quite restored to health.

We have called our house *Runnymede*. 'Tis long and low, and the walls are painted white. We have an open arcade under the house, where are situated the bathhouses. The verandah above is delightfully shady and catches every sea breeze. Here I have placed big pots of scented ginger lily, which is a local flower that much delights me. Our rooms have the customary slatted window shutters, for air and shade, and each bedroom has a balcony with carved railings.

February 1809, Runnymede, George Town

We have now Ld. Minto's response to Tom's report on retaining the defences of Malacca: he agrees with Tom it w'd be highly inexpedient to complete the demolition of the barracks and withdraw the garrison. But we cannot yet know the decision of the Court of Directors, from the circumstance that Tom's report cannot yet have reached them; 'twas sent only last November, and four months sailing ain't enough time to journey from here to London.

June 1809, Runnymede, George Town

I can scarce believe 'tis four months since I last sat down to write the parish news, but I have been indisposed. A blockage of my liver caused in February a swelling of my feet and ankles. In the following weeks the swelling gradually ascended to occupy my whole body, not forgetting my arms and head. This caused my breathing to become difficult, and my thirst great, and led also to certain unmentionables. Fortunately, I never developed a cough, a fatal symptom, as w'd have shown my lungs had been affected. Tom did as the doctors ordered, and had my body tightly bound in strips of cloth, to promote the opening of the pores, and now I am recovered, tho' I remain so weak, and thin, and wan I fancy I am reduced to the likeness of a shadow that departeth.

July 1809, Runnymede, George Town

O, sad news, sad news, and we are all in great affliction, for Thompson is dead. He was taken ill last Thursday, with one of the lethal sudden fevers of the tropics, and by Sunday it had killed him; he was twenty-six. Three days! Three days and he was gone! On Monday we buried him – we c'd wait no longer, for fear of corruption of the body in this heat. He lies now in our peaceful Protestant cemetery where also we buried Dundas, and where so many other Europeans sleep under this hot Malayan sun, and with not yews to shade them, but jangal trees, and if I doubted the words they spoke as they cast red earth on Thompson's body, I prayed I didn't, for I w'd he now has his perfect consummation and bliss in God's eternal and everlasting glory, and when I am delivered from the burden of the flesh, I w'd myself be saved, not damned.

I will not attempt now to write of Mary Ann, 'tis unbearable, impossible, I will say only she is her husband's widow and trust this word *widow* says all I know not how to say.

July 1809, Runnymede, George Town

Mary Ann has given up her bungalow and come to live with us. Tom has written to their mother to tell her of Thompson's death – this son she never met nor never will. He has requested her to allow her other daughters, Leonora and Hannah, to make the voyage out from England and come to live with us too, that they may comfort Mary Ann, their sad sister left behind by her husband, and also to look for husbands of their own – this assumes they remain spinsters, tho' they may be married, and us not know it, from the slowness of the mail.

Our brother, when he died, remained Commissary of Provisions and Petty Stores, or naval agent responsible for victualing our ships. Now Tom, the executor of his will, is authorised by Macalister and by Rear-Admiral Drury – the same that is Little Charlotte's godfather – to occupy this position that he may sign off Thompson's accounts. 'Tis another post that is without fee, but whilst he holds it, Tom will be entitled to take commissions on all transactions, which ought to put rice in our rice bowls, as the natives say.

In her grief, Mary Ann leaves Little Charlotte so much to me 'tis now almost even my naughty fancy the child is my adopted daughter, younger sister for Harriet, this Harriet that she'll never know, and that will never know her. Tom, too, I think sometimes fancies we three are our own little family. O, our pretence! And yet: what to do?

September 1809, Runnymede, George Town

Here's good news, at last: we have authentic accounts from London Tom's report on Malacca is heard. The Court of Directors has revoked its previous order, and the demolition of the Fort is countermanded. For sure, much of Malacca is now rubble, but no more will be destroyed; the wrecking work is finished, and a garrison will henceforth remain in those guardrooms Farquhar has managed to spare.

'Tis evident Tom is in high standing at India House. Macalister has received a letter expressing the Directors' satisfaction at Tom's report, and asking him to tell Tom that they entertain a favourable sense of the talents he has evinced in this matter of Malacca.

Tom is cock-a-hoop, and his hope for a transfer from Penang flares anew, along with the conviction he can win rapid advancement in some other place less dull and more profitable for The Company.

October 1809, Runnymede, George Town

It seems Farquhar is bitter 'tis my husband given credit for saving Malacca. He has written to Tom a most ill-tempered letter, complaining my husband's report that made the difference in London masqueraded as a new view, when in fact it contained naught but arguments he himself had promulgated often.

Tom is much taken aback. He says Farquhar knows he never

pretended to be doing anything but summarising old arguments familiar to anybody with an interest in the future of Malacca, and indeed his report deferred to Farquhar's knowledge of matters pertaining to the engineering of The Fort. He adds Farquhar's letter is less justified rebuke than an expression of his soldierly resentment that in Johnny Company's hierarchy 'tis the civil branch of the service takes precedence over the military, much to the annoyance of our military men.

Christmas Day 1809, Runnymede, George Town

I ain't written much lately, I can't say why. But now 'tis Christmas again, and some variety of wistful dissatisfaction prods me to pick up my quill. Aye, today I find myself remembering winter wreathes of bay and rosemary I used to weave with Mother in Ireland, and regretting Christmas brings not cold to this orient clime, and regretting, too I must use banana leaves for my holly, and for my ivy I must use jangal vines. Meanwhile, Tom says he wishes to God he c'd get a taste of plum pudding.

January 1810, Runnymede, George Town

Here's perfidy! That wretch Phillips has long been watching for a chance to stir up trouble for Tom, and to have a black mark set against his name. Now, jealous and resentful, he has found his shabby pretext.

What Phillips complains of – on behalf of the navy this arrogant hypocrite claims – is that Tom continues in the role of Commissary of Provisions and Petty Stores, or Naval Agent, that he took over from Thompson when our poor brother died, and from which we derive much pecuniary advantage, from the commission Tom claims on transactions on foodstuffs, &c. He uses against Tom the circumstance that he was appointed to Thompson's position for no other reason than to close his accounts. He writes now to the council saying in taking charge of this office Tom acted in violation of Company orders set by the Court of Directors, and he sh'd never have taken a situation so incompatible with that of a confidential Secretary to the Government. He then adds now this violation is remarked upon, he does not for a moment imagine Tom sh'd wish or expect to retain Thompson's situation. In short he is saying Tom sh'd be replaced forthwith.

Tom is furious to be accused so unfairly of grasping for advantage, and it sticks in his craw it sh'd be Phillips to accuse him – he that ever puts his own personal profit before principle – and as to me I think this Phillips is really the most impudent, ignorant, affected, envious old jay I ever heard of.

January 1810, Runnymede, George Town

Tom, as Secretary to the Government, has had to sign on behalf of the Governor and council a reply to Phillips' horrid insinuations. Which reply expresses the council's regret that what it called *the irregularity* of Tom's taking Thompson's situation was tacitly permitted to exist for even a single day, and adding that the indulgence of allowing Tom to take temporary charge of the office in no way sanctioned arrangements unconnected with Thompson's accounts.

Here's loyalty from Macalister for Tom's support! Here's the council's reward for all Tom's public spirit and hard work. What a nest of vipers is this Penang!

February 1810, Runnymede, George Town

Ye gods! No sooner has Tom lost commission on the marketing of victuals to the navy, than his allowance is cut. 'Tis hard to credit, but it seems when he was promoted from Acting Sec. to full S to the G, in '07, the increase in his allowance from six thousand Spanish dollars per annum to eight was never approved by the Court of Directors. Now news comes those skinflint clodpolls have disallowed it, saying the mere pecuniary returns of Tom's office ought to be but a secondary consideration, because of the distinction and status he c'd not have attained in any other way. What stuff! Tom is asked to refund the overpayment, which they claim in English money is one thousand six hundred and twenty-five pounds. One thousand six hundred and twenty-five pounds! Tom says if things continue as they are he that left England a poor man will return home a beggar.

Still, for all he is in a towering rage, Tom thinks this horrid affront has less to do with him, than with the fact Penang, failing as an arsenal, failing as a centre of shipbuilding, is such a drag on Johnny Company's cash, that any excuse the Court of Directors can find for retrenchment, they'll take, and never mind if the retrenchment is made possible only by a quibble of procedure. He is determined to appeal this bad decision, but we don't suppose we'll hear anything for at least a year, and in the meantime we must be shadowed by this alleged debt. O, what unfair, capricious treatment! Tom says he feels marooned in Penang, like a sailor abandoned on a rock for misdemeanour watching his ship slip over the horizon, and he ain't a scamp deserves this punishment.

April 1810, Runnymede, George Town

Tom comes home full of the news our good British military have taken from the French, who had them from the Dutch, The Spice Islands, which lie some way south and east of here, and where gold grows on the trees in the form of nutmeg, cinnamon, cloves, &c. Or perhaps I sh'd say where gold *once* grew on trees? No, the spice trade ain't as enriching as in times past – or even any longer much enriching at all. 'Tis Tom's understanding we took these quondam treasure troves less for the pitiable money they can now bring to Johnny Company, than to deny them to Boney, Britain's most inveterate foe. By all accounts our acquisition was accomplished most welcome speedy, there being no resistance to a raiding party we put ashore.

May 1810, Runnymede, George Town

The slowness of communication between London and India has produced a blundering, bewildered muddle: news now comes from Bengal we took last month The Spice Islands without authorisation from India House to do any such thing. This circumstance has put Ld. Minto in a quandary about how now to act.

O, what a happy quandary! What happy confusion! God willing, this little tumult c'd be Tom's passage out of Penang!

It ain't an obvious path from *here*, to *there*, but our friend Rear-Admiral Drury has written to Ld. Minto with the idea Tom sh'd proceed at once to Amboyna, Chief of the Spice Islands, and be put in charge pro tempore of their governance, until instructions arrive from London about what next to do.

Drury is so keen for this plan, he has suggested Tom sh'd take leave from his duties here, and sail for Calcutta, to press his case to be appointed to Amboyna direct to Ld. Minto.

Tom is determined not to let this chance of Amboyna slip. He has today obtained from Macalister permission to go at once to Calcutta, and to remain there two months to petition his lordship.

Even as I write this, Tom is writing to Leyden, telling him to expect us shortly, and asking if we can lodge with him in Calcutta – aye, I will travel with my husband to see for myself our famous capital in India. Tom's request is for form's sake only; Leyden w'd be most offended were we not to lodge with him, in any case we may see him before he gets the letter.

Tom now exists in a frenzy of preparation for his leave: he writes many, many notes and memoranda for Ld. Minto on the subject of Amboyna, and also exerts his mind to intensive study of Java, a big island south of here.

Until the upheavals in Europe, Java was another of those places held by the Dutch, who made their headquarters in the Eastward at Batavia, the chief port for the island – the port which, rising, caused Malacca to sink. But now Boney has Batavia and Java both. This is a circumstance that much annoys Tom, who grows quite obsessed with Java. Indeed, he has taken to quizzing the poor Malays about Javanese politics, geography, trading, &c, until they are dizzy with his questions. He learns the little local sultans on the island, ever engaged in their own plots and intrigues, wars and battles, think well neither of their old masters, the Dutch, nor of their new ones, the French, and c'd be persuaded to Britain's cause. He learns the Dutch marooned there are demoralised, a people cut adrift without even a motherland to anchor them, now theirs has been overrun, and with even more reason than most to detest the French. Meanwhile, he is assured the French garrison has neither so many men nor so many cannon as to render it invincible. He concludes from his inquiries The Company c'd seize Batavia with relative ease, and make all Java its territory. More, 'tis his opinion this is something The Company *sh'd* do. Aye, he is quite persuaded Java is of some considerable importance, both trading and strategic, and Johnny Company ought to have it.

His reasoning is in part geographic: Java lies on the flank of the Calcutta-Canton trade route, well placed, he says, to enable the power which possesses it to control all the Eastern Seas, and hence to control as well access to the treasure chest that's China. Moreover, he thinks Java is in itself its own little treasure chest.

Aye, he learns from his Malay informants, that as well as rice Java grows also coffee, pepper, tobacco, and indigo, which products 'tis his opinion c'd be sold so well as to undercut every other settlement in the Eastward, making it a most attractive prize.

Hence, as a second string to his bow, sh'd Amboyna come to naught, Tom is writing for Ld. Minto a long memorandum on Java. 'Tis his argument the conquest of that island w'd provide both unparalleled opportunity to enable our navy to gain supremacy in all the seas of East-Insular India and also unparalleled opportunity for The Company to add to its treasury – he confides privately to me that Java, if we had it, w'd likewise offer unparalleled opportunity for Tom Raffles, if he ain't needed at Amboyna.

June 1810, an Arab dhow, Bay of Bengal

O, the misery of ship-board! Tom and me have commenced our voyage to Calcutta and we sail, the only Europeans, on a weather-beaten dhow, dangerously light, carrying Chinese crockery-ware to India. Alas, no other ship was available but this frail thing, and such is Tom's eagerness to seize his chance of Amboyna he w'd not wait for something safer, notwithstanding his dread of drowning.

Tho' our dhow is mastered by an Arab, 'tis crewed by Maldivians prodigiously addicted to sorcery. Their magic is planned to keep far from the dhow the *jinn* – malevolent spirits – they believe dwell in both sea and sky. The Maldivians conjure the jinn away through incantation, and through burning sweet leaves, so the hungry spirits become distracted from wickedness, and long to feast not on human souls but on the aromatic smoke. Perhaps this sorcery has its own kind of success, for today the weather is placid.

July 1810, Leyden's lodgings, Calcutta

To my relief, the jinn left off causing our dhow mischief all across the Bay of Bengal, and now I am in Calcutta, jewel of the East, and I breathe once again the heady smell of India that contains within it every other smell, delicious or disgusting, that ever wafted o'er the world.

Unlike Madras, this Calcutta holds for me no ghosts. 'Tis a lively, vital city, seething with people, irreverence, ideas, lies, scams, stories, languages, possibility. There are sometimes appearing in the streets jesters or musicians or puppeteers, but they provide but a fraction of the entertainment for there are also: hawkers; fishwives; fishmongers; flower-sellers; servants; the tax collectors called here *scavengers*; wealthy, educated Indian gentlemen called *babus*; Jews; Armenians; scrawny palki-bearers staggering under their palanquins, and in those palanquins Persian lawyers, or Christian missionaries, or The Company's merchants; the Hindoo priests called *brahmins* singing, and carrying images of their many-armed, many-headed gods and goddesses; mendicants crying for alms; opium addicts; old men banged up to the eyes by the ganja smoking in their hubble-bubbles; vegetable sellers drunk from visits to the grog shops, &c. Tom says there are also cremators, but such grim tradesmen I choose not to see – tho' I've seen where the natives burn their dead, at the *ghats*, by the river – and nor do I remark the eunuchs, and nor the saucy dancing girls that dance only at night, in shady parts of the city, and that ain't given their tips until they give their patrons kisses.

'Tis Leyden who has shown me and Tom about. O, what a joyful, tearful reunion we three have had! Our friend, and host, has taken a house, much decayed, in a mostly native part of town – the dark alleys litter-strewn and higgledy, the buildings jumbled close together. His living quarters are on the upper floors – large rooms, but the plaster peeling from the walls and very untidy, with everywhere books and papers in great profusion. On the ground floor he accommodates his munshis, and above he has access also to the house's flat rooftop, a cool and breezy spot in the hours when the sun ain't blazing, with a low wall all around. Here we sit at night on oriental cushions, and look upon a patchwork view of other rooftops where natives likewise loll, and 'tis our pleasure to pass between us the bottle, so we become quite allicholy, and happy we are in our jawing.

To my content Leyden, faithful knight, seems as smitten with me now as he did when first we met. At every chance presents itself he directs to me sighs and yearning looks and teases. I confess I cannot prevent myself becoming a little playful in return, for I welcome his admiration, notwithstanding I cannot return it – as for Tom, he sees my flirting, but he don't mind it.

July 1810, Leyden's lodgings, Calcutta

Tom's campaign to win for himself Amboyna is launched: we have met Ld. Minto, who held last night at Government House an elegant dinner that we attended with Leyden – I wore my new blue with the bows I brought with me for just such occasion, and all remarked how well it became me.

We were most kindly received by his lordship. He ain't a swaggering man: tallish, he is in late middle age, slightly stooped and balding, with a build as fragile as Tom's. His face is gentle and mild. He has not the air of his office, and don't seem to take the deference of his subordinates as something properly due a superior person. Indeed, he appears most uneasy with the pomp that is his lot – even in his private rooms at Government House his servants give him regular military salutes, and he has besides four or five of them running before him with maces.

Still, modesty is one thing, and rank another. No, notwithstanding his unassuming nature, none can deny Ld. M is the Governor-General, so when, as a visiting lady, I was seated next to him at dinner, I did my best to charm him. It seems I was successful, for Leyden now reports his L was much struck by my height and by the originality of my dress. He says he found my countenance lively and *spirituelle*, and that he thinks my conversation deserves the same epithets. He says too his L found me quite the great lady, accomplished and clever, and that he much admired my dark eyes, which reminded him of his wife – she remains in Scotland whilst he is in India, so they must be uncommon devoted, to withstand the separation, or else indifferent to each other. He assures me The Governor-General is on fire for our closer acquaintance, 'cause he has told him I am one of the beauties to whom Melodious Moore addressed his amatory elegies.

I am pleased to be described *lively and spirituelle*, tho' I ain't happy to be disdained *quite the great lady* – still, if I must be condescended to, then let it be by the Governor-General for notice by him spells fortune.

July 1810, Leyden's lodgings, Calcutta

Bad news: I ain't not to be the Lady of Amboyna. Alas, Tom ain't appointed pro tempore to the governance of that island; we now learn the post has already been disposed of. I w'd fear the disappointment must undermine Tom's health, except Leyden says he will not suffer or permit him to be unwell here, and in any case we learn too Ld. Minto has Java often in consideration, and has lately been thinking how to clear the French out of that island. Indeed, he wrote to India House in March, proposing to the Court of Directors that he sh'd be allowed to reduce Batavia – to destroy it, so use of it be denied to the French – and then, once the plunder was complete, to quit the scene and give up the island to the natives.

Tom says 'tis a most favourable situation he has with him his memorandum on Java, and he is hopeful our arrival here was well-timed, notwithstanding another man has got Amboyna.

July 1810, Leyden's lodgings, Calcutta

Here's surprise! I have had a most happy, startling letter from Mary Ann: it seems my sisters Leonora and Hannah, that Tom last year invited to come live with us, have arrived in Penang! They came on an East Indiaman that reached the island a fortnight after we quit it. Apparently a letter was sent from London, and another from Madras, both letters announcing they'd be coming, but I never received neither letter, and when a runner came from the harbour, with the news they were arrived, Mary Ann was most astonished – as now am I, and so also is Tom.

Mary Ann writes she commences at once the work of finding husbands for her sisters. Alas, neither of these two single ladies is remarkable pretty but since a woman's looks don't matter over much in the Eastward, I am optimistic she'll find them matches – I shall reply by the next ship that sails, asking that she keep me abreast of what's doing.

August 1810, Leyden's lodgings, Calcutta

Tom is cock-a-hoop for he now anticipates having a much finer game to play than he has hitherto had, and one in which Amboyna ain't in the least to be compared. To wit: Java.

Aye, Tom has presented Ld. Minto with his memorandum, and his L has bestowed upon him as its author the most cordial attention. Indeed, Tom says when Java was first mentioned between them his L cast upon him a look of such scrutiny, anticipation, and kindness as he shall never forget. Yes, says his L, Java is an interesting island. I shall be happy to receive any information you can give me concerning it.

But Tom don't stop at conveying information. No, he now devotes all his energy, bends all his views, all his plans, and all his mind to creating for Ld. Minto such an interest regarding Java as sh'd lead him to embark on nothing less than the annexation of the island to The Company's territory in the Eastward.

Tom understands annexation is a more ambitious thing than Ld. Minto's idea of reducing Batavia, clearing out the French, and then quitting the scene. He understands too his own notion of capturing and keeping all of Java may not please them at India House, 'cause Johnny Company don't never much want new territory – not beyond what it needs to protect its narrowest trading interests – 'cause administering territory costs money. However, he is hopeful he can persuade Ld. Minto 'tis his patriotic duty to annex Java, to give Britannia the splendid prospect of expelling utterly her European rivals from the Eastern Seas, and keeping to her own dear self the China trade. Moreover, Tom has provided his L with details of the profits to be had from Java, from the trade in indigo, coffee, pepper, &c, and has explained that if we had Java the pecuniary returns from the produce of the island alone w'd soon be much more than the expenditure. Time permitting exploration of his novel argument, he thinks it ought to sway them at India House where 'tis an acknowledged fact every colony does, or ought to, exist for the benefit of the motherland.

August 1810, Leyden's lodgings, Calcutta

Leyden has a liking for the native ganja, and now Tom and me partake of it too, for 'tis a weed that blurs the world pleasantly, and the bubble-bubble of the hubble-bubble is heard most evenings on our rooftop. Sitting with the pipe and wine, Tom and Leyden become quite carried away with the idea of making Java ours.

More, they wave their arms and say if only we had Java we c'd from this fulcrum conjure an entire empire east of here – nothing less than a British empire in the Eastern Seas. This, they say, not only that Britannia may profit from it, but as well to further the cause of philanthropy, by diffusing the light of civilisation even unto the remotest, darkest island jangal. Aye, they assure each other 'tis our charitable duty to rescue the Malays, in their various scattered nations, from the vassalage and oppression of their feudal systems, and the barbarity of their tribal ones. They say that, like children, the Malays are easily led, and though little can be expected of them at the current moment, if only they c'd be brought on by simple ideas, simply expressed, and governed under the justice, humanity, kindness, and moderation of Britannia's principled government, we c'd do great things with them, and in time they must become less indolent, and feeble than now we find them.

Does this not sound grandiose? For myself, I am tempted to disparage Tom's and Leyden's talk of an Eastern empire as the ravings of two dreamy drunken fellows, two fellows banged up on ganja, encouraging each other to ever more outlandish fancies. Still, I hold my tongue, and I suppose I cannot disagree the European is so superior to every other race he has the right to insist his ways prevail.

September 1810, Leyden's lodgings, Calcutta

My husband has been so persuasive Java is an attractive prize that, to his great satisfaction, Ld. Minto now announces he is firmly set on invasion. The attack will take meticulous planning, and his L has asked Tom to return to Penang forthwith, to commence investigating practicalities – 'tis from Penang the war fleet will depart.

Alas, once the invasion is achieved, if 'tis successful, Ld.

Minto plans only to reduce Batavia. My bold Tom thinks this reluctance to annex Java is most unfortunate timidity. Still, he is sanguine he can sway his L to more fitting ambition, and he sees no need yet to abandon his dreams of an eastern empire.

'Tis probable them at India House as yet know nothing even of Ld. Minto's cautious plan. No matter: his L has no scruples about awaiting official approval when he is set upon a course of action he believes to be correct. Tom much commends his most necessary decisiveness, saying wavering won't do when dealing with the French.

In consideration of mysterious maritime things – monsoon winds and the rains they bring, and the sea currents and the tides – the date for the invasion of Java is fixed for next June.

October 1810, Leyden's lodgings, Calcutta

O my in every way worthy husband! In recognition of Tom's talents Ld. Minto appoints him now Agent to the Governor-General with the Malay States.

Agent to the Governor-General with the Malay States! What a most resounding, ringing title! How it must annoy Ibbetson, Phillips, & Co. when they come to learn of it!

In his new role Tom's orders are various: he must carry out any arrangements, any investigations, any tasks Ld. Minto may have in mind regarding the invasion of Java. The moment we reach Penang he must establish an intelligence network of native spies to discover the likely movements of the French, and the state and nature of the fortifications at Batavia. He must commence communication by letter not only with all the native rulers in Java, but also with those throughout the rest of the scattered Malayan nation. Many of these rulers he hopes will give us support, and some of them he c'd well recommend we arm. All he must do, he must do in utmost secrecy, lest the French get wind of it.

That Tom may better fulfil his intelligence gathering, and other preparations for the invasion of Java, Ld. Minto has given him a secret letter, strictly confidential, to deliver in Penang to Governor Macalister informing him of the Great Plan, and requiring him to allow Tom to indent for any supplies he needs.

October 1810, Leyden's lodgings, Calcutta

When Tom and me quit hence, we will take with us the Malay munshi, Ibrahim the son of Candu. This Ibrahim has lately been helping Leyden translate the *Sejarah Melayu*, or *The Malay Annals*, a literary work of mystical history chronicling the doings of Malay kings of former times. But the work of translating is now done, so Leyden can spare him.

October 1810, Leyden's lodgings, Calcutta

I write in defiance of a thumping head, 'cause in another hour Tom and me must go to the wharf to quit Calcutta. Last night we repaired one last time to Leyden's rooftop, and there sat up with him, and invited as well our good friends allichol and ganja. Even sober Tom remains hopeful he can sway Ld. Minto to the annexation of Java, notwithstanding his arguments he must henceforth promulgate by letter. Last night, woozy, he slurred Java is his land of promise, and confided he has the vanity to hope that if 'tis annexed, its administration sh'd be entrusted to his individual charge. He and Leyden then fixed it between them that the instant Tom is Lieutenant-Governor, Leyden is to be his secretary.

Alas, when we stopped talking of such magnificent things, our mood was most melancholy, and we became like to cry. Leyden compared me to the waxing moon hanging silver above us, filling the night with her mysterious beauty, and he said he was indeed envious of Tom, his friend, for having the luck 'twas him who got to offer me his protecting care. I said in reply I was *enchantay* at this celestial comparison, and Tom said if it came to that he was enchantay to be remembered as a protecting friend.

After, in bed, Tom asked was I not pleased he took Leyden's flirting with me, and mine with him, in such good part? How sh'd any wife reply to a question such as *that*? For want of ideas what to say, I kept silent. Tom laughed he'd hazard Leyden needed to love me as inspiration for his poetry, but were I ever to open my arms to him, no doubt our dear poetical chevalier w'd be too frit to respond. I still said nothing, tho' in my heart I c'd not disagree. Tom then added he'd likewise hazard I'd be frit as a mouse faced with a cat if ever Leyden made advance to hold me in his arms, notwithstanding I so plainly relish his admiration. Ye gods! Was this cool confidence not impudent, for all Tom is my husband? I was momentarily minded to take umbrage, but then I thought: well, Olivia, 'tis true you like the power to flirt, and tease ... So I did not show my husband my back, but instead from all his talk of opening arms, I did that very thing.

Later in haste, the *Ariel*, riding in the roads of Calcutta: Tom and me have boarded The Company's brig the *Ariel*, and we are ready to be underway, awaiting only the tide. Our cabin is a goodish one, including even a window, so I am in hopes this voyage won't be too horrid – in any case for us, tho' Ibrahim has only a corner of the hold.

November 1810, Runnymede, George Town

Tom's two months leave turned into five away, but a truce with complaining, for we are now safely returned to George Town, and to happy chaos! What a joyous reunion we had with Leonora and Hannah, and with Mary Ann too, and how pleased I was to coo again over Little Charlotte – much grown since last I saw her.

Now we are returned Leonora is to wed John Loftie, our widowed Acting Surgeon here. He ain't a man to set a girl's heart thumping, but also he ain't so old or so stout or so pompous Leonora, a practical girl, c'd much object to him. Aye, tho' Mary Ann never wrote me of it, those two have hit it off, and have come to an understanding. Tom, all too glad to have got rid of one of his sisters so speedily – and who claims, bye-the-bye, without any reason for it the credit for this getting rid of – has given his blessing: they are to be wed next week; Mary Ann is arranging the ceremonials. This widowed sister has confided in me she now starts to look around the world for a second husband of her own, and since she ain't lost her looks I trust she'll soon find one, tho' her bloom is gone.

Runnymede is now so crowded, that for want of other space Ibrahim sleeps on the verandah. His first evening here he was most concerned I sh'd not serve him food in dishes had touched pork, but I reassured him that since my servants like him are all Mahomedans they won't countenance pig meat in the kitchen, so now he is happy and ain't no trouble, except he cuts an odd figure at our table, 'cause like all these Malay munshis he dresses in the native style, of *turban*, *baju*, and *sarong* – the baju is a loose, long jacket or shirt, and the sarong a length of cloth worn around the waist that w'd be called a skirt in England, for all 'tis worn here by men as well as by women. A turban, meanwhile, is a hat of wound cloth shaped something like a tulip.

November 1810, Runnymede, George Town

Leonora is wed, but I ain't got time to write of that – I am too full of confusion and trouble to write but a few lines, 'cause Tom has decided on Malacca, not Penang, as the headquarters for his communications and investigations in preparation for the invasion of Java, and as the mustering point for the troops. This 'cause 'tis two hundred and fifty miles closer to Java than Penang, and also 'cause he thinks it will be nigh on impossible to pursue his secret mission under the jealous eyes of his enemies here, who are bitter to a man he has been noticed by Ld. Minto, and galled they ain't considered worthy to know the nature of his shadowy work, and who have all of them mouths filled with scurrility against my husband and who spread it about he's let himself run away with the temporary elevation of being Ld. Minto's Agent. These jays! They none of them think of strategy and glory, but only of themselves.

So at a snap our household is to move to Malacca – this to include Leonora, for all she is got rid of, and with her Loftie, too. Whatever the outcome of the invasion, Tom don't wish to return to Penang after, so he has put Runnymede up for auction. It has been advertised in *The Penang Gazette* as a valuable and very eligible estate. I expect much interest, and am in hopes of some little pecuniary advantage to us. Tho' I am sad to imagine some other woman enjoying my pretty balconies with the carved railings, I remind myself 'tis only a house.

December 1810, the *Ariel*, Straits of Malacca

Tom retained the *Ariel* to bring us all to Malacca, so once more I am at sea, and glad to be so too, notwithstanding the usual privations of a ship, for the weather is fine and calm, and I hope this short voyage will restore my health, which begins to fail from all the recent turmoil – the nonya Martina gave me as a parting gift a tonic she'd brewed for nervous exhaustion, and I drank down the whole bitter dose and I lied I felt better.

December 1810, the Chinese Kapitan's house, Malacca

Behold me once more in Malacca, Dear Diary, and I sh'd report at once that when Tom made his first visit to Farquhar, the Resident presented to him a most bitter face, still sour 'twas my husband, not him, made the difference in getting the order to destroy Malacca countermanded. Farquhar did not trouble with the customary greetings, but at sight of Tom at once commenced protesting that in his famous report that won the day he restricted acknowledgement of his, Farquhar's, contribution to nothing more than matters engineering. Tom, replied, with his usual sweet suavity, that 'twas not his intention to dishonour, and he respected enormous Farquhar's opinions on matters political and strategic. Now they are almost friends again, which is relief to me, and also to Nonio Clemaine, as we did not want to see estrangement between our husbands.

Alas, my health falters, which makes harder all the thousand-and-one things at any time need doing when a household is uprooted and replanted. Tom has taken for us a house on The Hill, just outside the only one of the old Portuguese gates to the Fort that remains standing – Farquhar spared it in the first instance 'cause it has guardrooms attached, useful to our military. 'Tis sad to see the remains of most of the rest of the Fort lying around the foot of The Hill, little better than a heap of rubbish. Tom looks on the destruction and calls it a most useless piece of gratuitous mischief.

Our house is adequate but unremarkable – except that 'tis owned by the Chinese Kapitan of Malacca, the representative to Farquhar of all the Chinamen in the population here.

As well as our pretty numerous family, our house must also find room for Tom's secretariat, which is now only the munshi Ibrahim, but which he hopes to expand quickly, by the engagement of native copyists, to draft appeals to all the rulers of the Malayan nation, and especially the sultans of Java, to abandon their alliances with the Dutch, or French, and to assist our British forces in the forthcoming invasion – he has written to

Leyden asking him to send a dozen pairs of good spectacles for these scribes he is yet to employ.

Tom himself exists now in a perfect combustion of planning for the Great Project – he is working from before dawn breaks until after dusk falls. Tiredness is I think making him uncharacteristically choleric; this morning he went banging about the house in a towering rage with the government in Penang, which is charged to expedite the sending of military stores, but which ain't done so. Tom says from that settlement he can get nothing, and the narrow-minded jealousy and envy of the officials there disgust him. He holds accountable for the lack of his supplies not only the Hon. the Gov. Macalister, who knows full well the nature of his mission, but also that rascal Phillips, second man on the council, who remains ignorant of it for secrecy's sake, and who harbours for Tom a most rancorous hatred, on many accounts.

December 1810, the Chinese Kapitan's house, Malacca

My health has been bad again, on account of my old problem, an attack of the liver, which for a few days made my eyes yellow as egg yolks, and brought with it a fever sapped near all my vitality.

January 1811, the Chinese Kapitan's house, Malacca

Alas, this new year starts with sadness, for we have today a letter from Clubley in Penang announcing Macalister is dead of a fever. Tom is remorseful now he berated the departed for not acting speedy in sending military stores, and he is most bitter regretful at Clubley's other news: 'tis Phillips who replaces Macalister, tho' only pro tempore, as Acting Gov. Tom must now tell his old enemy the nature of his secret mission, and he expects he'll act petulant, for not having known before.

January 1811, the Chinese Kapitan's house, Malacca

My health again confines me much to my bed – I am thin as a skeleton and almost as rattling. Tom can't disguise he is alarmed by the precariousness of my constitution – and my poor husband, anxious about me, is now also much anxious about his prospects. 'Tis a fine and indispensable thing to be Ld. Minto's Agent, preparing the way for the invasion of Java, but after 'tis achieved, if all goes well, what then? He is in hopes still that in that case we will do more than reduce Batavia and then leave it for the natives, but we will instead annex Java for The Company, and if that is the course decided, then he believes Ld. Minto w'd have it in mind to make him Lieutenant-Governor – but what if he don't?

This uncertainty is agitating, and Tom has written to Leyden asking him to try to ascertain from Ld. Minto what part of the play he is to act hereafter, which is to say Ld. Minto's most recent opinions on what to do with Java, sh'd we take it, and who sh'd govern it, in that instance, and if there are yet any instructions from London, which he doubts. But Leyden ain't yet replied even to his request for spectacles for his munshis, so we don't hold out too many hopes of a swift response.

February 1811, the Chinese Kapitan's house, Malacca

Tho' I remain weak, I have recommenced almost all my household duties – and 'tis a growing household, since Tom has by now hired a full complement of munshis.

Toward one of these, Abdullah, a boy of fourteen, I grow fond. Notwithstanding his tender years he has already Arabic, Tamil, and Hindoostani as well as English and Malay. For his gentleness and his skills in language I have adopted him almost as my private tutor and ask him often how the Malays say this or that – 'tis useful to me to grow my vocabulary, if only to understand what my servants are saying about me, when they think I can't follow.

Tom uses Abdullah not only as interpreter to communicate with the native rulers in their language, but also as scribe and copyist for preserving Malay literature and manuscripts. 'Cause my husband's interest in these things is known, people bring all day to our house books and manuscripts to sell, to the number of many hundreds, the whole of Malay literature, it sometimes seems. The books ain't printed, but written in longhand, sometimes not even on paper, but on bark, and Abdullah has confided in me he worries sh'd our house burn down, for then 'tis his belief he'd have not a single book to read in his own language. More he complained to me 'twas wrong of his people to sell his inheritance, and theirs, for money. I said I didn't think them wrong, I thought them worried how they'd fill their rice bowls and he said he was grateful 'twas us put rice in his.

March 1811, the Chinese Kapitan's house, Malacca

Astonishing news! Tom has had his package of spectacles from Leyden, and with it an almost incredible letter: it announces Ld. Minto himself is to come to Malacca! Aye, the Governor-General of all India is to accompany our good British fleet on the invasion of Java! We are all so honoured and surprised I don't know how to write it!

Leyden adds he is himself appointed to Ld. Minto's staff on account of his expertise in Malay, and so my dear chevalier will travel with the government party here to Malacca.

Alas, on the heels of these happy announcements, Leyden reports less welcome news: Ld. Minto is still fluctuating between the two old plans of reducing Batavia, and then quitting the scene, or annexing Java to The Company's territory. And if the choice falls to annexation, then he is unable to say whether in that case

Ld. Minto intends Tom as Governor. As consolation, perhaps, he then reports Ld. Minto talks of Tom always with kindness, and is exceedingly well-disposed towards him, and desirous of giving him every opportunity of distinguishing himself, and rewarding him as highly as the imperious nature of circumstances will permit.

Tom ain't at all content he has no better assurance his ambition to be Lieutenant-Governor of Java is ever to be achieved.

March 1811, the Chinese Kapitan's house, Malacca

I have just come from the room in our house where the munshis work, where I paused, after a trifling domestic consultation with my husband, to greet Abdullah.

The boy was curved over his desk, working at a letter to be sent in Tom's name to the Sultan of Palembang. This Palembang, on Sumatra, is a dependency of Java so 'twas formerly a Dutch possession, and is now ruled by Boney's administration from Batavia. Tom was writing to tell the Sultan of the feeling regard for the interests of humanity which always distinguishes the British character, and to ask him to ally himself to us, and to throw out the Dutch remaining at Palembang, the cruel Dutch that were ever desirous of enriching themselves from the property of every Prince of the East, so that we may more easily drive from these parts both them and the treacherous French, and bring peace, stability, and prosperity to all the Malays.

I read this letter in English, in the draft Tom wrote for Abdullah to translate. I c'd not read the words Abdullah wrote, or even recognise the letters, 'cause he was writing in the local Jawi script – 'tis like Arabic, but adapted to the words of Malay. Still, I c'd see for myself what everybody says: he is a most skilled calligrapher. The swoops and dots and lines issuing from his quill made on the page an intricate, graceful pattern as tutored in the ways of art as even Tom's clear, flowing hand.

The paper Abdullah wrote on was notable beautiful, too. There is in this part of the Eastward much concern with *tiu lien*, which is a Chinese term used also by the Malays. *Tiu* is Chinese for *lose*, and *lien* is Chinese for *face*, and by this *lose face* the locals express their dread of lessening their dignity and seeing their standing fall in the eyes of others, which to them is serious mortification and absolute misfortune. Aye, 'tis very important Tom don't cause the local sultans to tiu lien, which they w'd do if 'twere thought they were not dealing with a man of their own rank; no, he must not appear in the eyes of the native kings as a mere cat's paw, or they'd be insulted to deal with him.

For this reason he makes his letters most regally splendid: he has them written on gold-speckled coloured papers stamped with gilded borders of floral motifs, and he sends them wrapped in yellow cloths – yellow being a colour much associated with royalty hereabouts. The rulers with whom he corresponds reply with similar sumptuousness – their letters now come in daily, from all over the Archipelago – and never mind what's said I think there cannot exist anywhere exchanges of letters more flattering than those betwixt Tom and the various sultans.

March 1811, the Chinese Kapitan's house, Malacca

Tom is now forever writing, writing, writing, breaking quill after quill. Even at night he writes; he has taken to retiring each evening about six to his study, where two candles light his desk that he may work in spite of the darkness. His desk is large, and when I peek in on him, I sometimes see him lying flat on his back upon it, with his eyes closed, as tho' he is sleeping – but then he'll jump up and start his scribbling again. He continues this way every night, up to eleven or twelve o'clock, when he goes to bed – and never now comes to my room to say goodnight.

When I protested to Tom it vexed me to be ignored, and he

w'd make himself ill again with all this working, he replied he did not like to disregard me, and nor his health neither, but, God knows, he has no choice, 'cause as well as writing to the many sultans of the Malayan nation, to understand their squabbles and alliances, and to seek their help in the Great Project, he must also compose secret missives to the Dutch remaining on Java, to be distributed in their language by his agents there, urging them to reject the brutal French and welcome the blessings of British government, or else face the consequences when we prevail, and what's more he must also compose many, many memoranda to Ld. Minto, with reports on the military and naval strength of the French, and all other information relevant to the invasion.

March 1811, the Chinese Kapitan's house, Malacca

Farquhar is cross with Tom again. Some of the memoranda Tom sends to Ld. Minto are on the state of the island of Java: its roads, waterways, ports, &c. Since Farquhar is one of our cleverest engineers, Tom naturally asks him about these things. But now Farquhar, who ain't to be part of the invasion force, but is to remain here to govern Malacca, grows resentful and complains Tom obtains from him information and maps, which he then transmits to Ld. Minto without acknowledgement. Tom, as ever speaking in smiles, replies 'tis not his way to claim others' intelligence as his own, and that when he quotes from Farquhar's memoranda to him, in his own memoranda to Ld. Minto, he mentions him by name.

Alas, Farquhar don't seem satisfied by this, and goes about looking very sore – and in turn Nonio Clemaine is sore with me, which I regret, and, probably, so does she.

Out of time, a wasteland

O my daughter! Seven months cold dead! Seven months!

Out of time, a wasteland

But she denied you. Aye, she did, but no matter; denial c'd not rent the sticky cobweb threads that ~~bind~~ bound us. But she was in Scotland. Aye, she was, but 'tis no use claiming distance made her whilst yet she lived as good as dead to me, for there is as much difference between *as good as dead*, and *dead*, as there is between *dead* and *living*. Aye, my daughter once *was*, and now *is not*. What else of anything is left to say?

Out of time, a wasteland

My daughter is dead, gone, delivered out of the miseries of this sinful world into joy and felicity, to be raised incorruptible at the last trump, when her mortal body will put on immortality … Or else to be carried a ghost on the wings of hornbills to the peak of a sacred mountain as I'm told some of the jangal primordials believe is the fate of the dead.

Out of time, a wasteland

I doubt my Harriet was barren, and yet I wish I knew for sure she weren't. I wish I c'd be certain her face – my face – is passed down. My only child is dead, and I am resigned, now, I'll never have another, but I wish I knew if I am a grandmother, notwithstanding my grandchildren, if existing, must ever be strangers to me, and more distant even than was Harriet from Mother … O, God, how can I write to Mr. Etherington, that he may break the news to Mother her granddaughter is gone?

May 1811, the Chinese Kapitan's house, Malacca

'Tis a month now since I received from William a line to tell me Harriet is dead of a furious fast consumption – aye, that prig bothered to write, tho' I won't feel grateful to him for it.

In my dragging month of sadness I have scarce taken my eyes off my Harriet's miniature that Mr. Plimer painted. I have kissed my daughter's likeness, wept over it, and wished to embrace it, tho' not as much as I have wished to embrace once more my living daughter.

But my lost month was not lost to others. At the end of April there arrived here from Calcutta the first part of the British force that is to invade Java – what a multitude of lively men, dashing in their tight-fitting scarlet coats, and their shiny black boots – and our widowed beauty Mary Ann quickly made her choice. Now, two weeks later, she is wed.

The ceremony was yesterday, here at our house, and I will chiefly remember it for Abdullah remarking to me after 'twas done that he c'd see Tom and me were happy married. He said 'twas clear Allah had joined us together, making us of one mind, like a ruler and his minister, like a ring and the jewel set in it, like sugar in milk.

I ain't so sure Mary Ann and her new husband, Captain William Flint, a commander in the navy, will be as sugar in milk. I grant he is well connected – his brother is Secretary to Wellington – and Tom, delighted to have got rid of another sister, claims to find him amiable, but his manner grates me. I find him argumentative, self-satisfied, self-aggrandising, unseemly. In any case he is so fat about the face his little eyes look like currants sinking into dough.

May 1811, the Chinese Kapitan's house, Malacca

Poor Hannah is low to be the only single lady remaining of our household, and fears never finding a husband. Alas, tho' looks don't much matter in the Eastward, hers are so honest-like 'tis possible she'll remain forever a spinster, for she is already twenty-five.

May 1811, the Chinese Kapitan's house, Malacca

Toward the end of April, when I was still absorbed by grief, Tom received a mark of attention from the Sultan of Acheen – a court on Sumatra that guards the northern entrance to the Straits of Malacca. This Sultan is friendly to the English against the French, and in consequence of some help Tom gave him, he wrote honouring him with membership of the Order of the Golden Sword, and conferring upon him the title His Excellency the Nobleman with the Golden Sword.

I ain't much impressed by orders and titles for thinking too often 'tis featherbrains that have them. Tom, tho', w'd fawn upon even the Duke of Puddle Dock. More, he likes to pretend a few drops of blue blood flow through his veins, thanks to some distant ancestor as aristocratic as fictional, and he dreams of winning for himself in the Eastward at least a baronetcy, if not a dukedom. But until the glorious day Sir Tom Raffles, Bart, can strut his hour, he acts off-hand about his Order of the Golden Sword. Alas, if he fools himself, then he don't fool none other, and 'tis obvious he is in his heart delighted. I find his ill-concealed pride in his honour touching, but I hear whispers others don't, and mock him for it, and call his honour ludicrous, which cruelty I hope don't get back to him.

May 1811, the Chinese Kapitan's house, Malacca

As the invasion of Java grows closer, transports from Bengal now daily, hourly, deliver troops to Malacca, which is transformed all along the shore by encampments of soldiers, their tents pitched in long, orderly rows of white canvas. The troops include even also *sepoys* – Indians serving in our army. Notwithstanding their redcoats, some of these look remarkable strange: be-turbaned, moustachioed, or their faces smeared with ashes or earth to make their Hindoo caste marks. The Malays seem notable nervous of them and skirt about them with averted eyes.

It ain't just transports riding in the roads: more ships arrive every moment to add to the war fleet gathering out at sea; it consists already of battleships, frigates, gunboats, and I don't know what. Between transports and men-of-war I never saw so many ships in all my life as are gathered in the roads of Malacca now – Abdullah says they are so full that the masts of the vessels look like poles of a fence.

May 1811, the Chinese Kapitan's house, Malacca

Such cheering and bunting and excitement! Malacca is pro tempore the seat of the Supreme Government of all India! Yes, the Governor-General is here; Ld. Minto has arrived – and with him my chevalier, Leyden.

Their ship, the *Modeste*, appeared in the bay this morning. Once she'd dropped anchor, Tom and Farquhar went out in a pinnace to escort his L ashore, whilst the myriad ships in the roads all fired their guns.

Ld. Minto was welcomed by crowds of cheering natives – who for all their loyal noise were perhaps unimpressed? He was dressed in a black coat and black trousers and the dignified sobriety of this British costume disappointed Abdullah, who told me later he assumed the great Sultan w'd be gorgeously dressed in yellow silks and adorned everywhere with gold and jewels.

There was a parade of soldiers and cavalry, with each part of the troops presenting arms, and all the flags of Malacca flying.

After the canon had stopped roaring and the ceremonials were done Ld. Minto went with his *ontoorage* to the Stadhuis, where Tom was consulting with him most of the day.

Now at last my husband is home, and he brings with him both Leyden, to lodge with us, and news just as welcome: he is henceforth to be styled Secretary to the Governor-General!

May 1811, the Chinese Kapitan's house, Malacca

Tom and Leyden are thwarted, bitter, and complain much that in India House profit trumps all other considerations of patriotic duty, of glory, and of philanthropy. This 'cause dispatches come from Calcutta relaying that the Court of Directors in London has at last instructed Ld. Minto how to proceed in Java – and that body of Wapping Peddlers tells him only to destroy the fortifications at Batavia, to distribute the ordnance, arms, and military stores amongst the native chiefs and inhabitants, and then to retire from the country for, say the dispatches, Batavia without the French ain't no threat to our trade. They contain too the rebuke that for the sake of the shareholders The Company can't risk the money required to administer Java as a settlement.

May 1811, the Chinese Kapitan's house, Malacca

O happy reversal on reversal! Tom's and Leyden's dreams of an Eastern empire flare again as bright as sparks. This 'cause Ld. Minto has decided to disregard instructions from London, saying they do not begin to understand in Leadenhall St. the conditions and circumstances of the East; they do not begin to understand the strategic importance of Java, or the riches it can bring to The Company and hence to Britain. Aye, for the sake of our naval supremacy, and of our trade, his L has decided the aim of invading Java will be not merely to reduce Batavia but to annex the island to The Company's territory, and to establish there an administration.

If we are successful, as we must be, then when in due course they learn Java is ours, what will the Court of Directors say to that? Tom shrugs and says from them at India House 'tis always better to seek forgiveness than permission and if the Hon. Mems. disapprove of Ld. Minto's admirable boldness, by the time they can protest the rice will already be porridge.

May 1811, the Chinese Kapitan's house, Malacca

In the case Java is taken, who is to be its Lieutenant-Governor? Tom? Alas, on this Ld. Minto remains distressing coy. On the one hand he warns 'tis from circumstances impossible for him to pledge himself to the fulfilment of his own wishes, interests, and intentions. On the other he says Tom must not doubt the prospective interest he has always taken, and does not cease to take, in his views and welfare, and that he has a very strong desire that the utmost will be done to secure for him the best situation worthy of his services, and the high esteem in which he holds his person.

With these hints my poor Tom must try to be content.

May 1811, the Chinese Kapitan's house, Malacca

I was yesterday sitting sewing with my sisters, when Leyden came to distract our company of busy women with his nonsense calling me his *dear amiable Olivia* and other such pretty things. Then he says – in front of my sisters, mind – he says he must tell me again how much he loves me. Don't start now at the term, he says, for I repeat it. I love you with a true brotherly affection, and never think of you without the kindest emotions.

I confess I *did* start, notwithstanding Leyden called his

affection for me brotherly, and my sisters looked as shocked as three Dame Grundys. But this was such gaudy exuberance, such public enthusiasm, such spaniel devotion, that within ten minutes I'd quite put it from my mind, as a trifling jest – or if not a jest, then in any case not as something earnest.

I thought no more of it until Tom came into my room last night. But as he climbed into bed he told me Mary Ann had earlier cornered him, and said from sisterly duty she felt she must warn him Leyden was making love to me! Well! Tom said he did not like this meddling, but he did not rebuke his sister, instead he coolly remarked he was complimented his brilliant scholar friend admired his wife. He then meets my eye, pinions my gaze with his, and adds: my *loyal* friend, my *constant* wife. He then set to reminding me why 'tis I'm so constant.

That Mary Ann! And her twice married! She sh'd know better than to interfere between a husband and a wife.

May 1811, the Chinese Kapitan's house, Malacca

Tom and me dined last night at the Stadhuis with Ld. Minto and some of the officers soon to be departing for Java, including General Sir Samuel Auchmuty, a loyalist American, who is Commander-in-Chief of our troops, and who will lead the invasion.

The dinner was very fine, including a roast of buffalo meat, which is the beef of the Eastward, but the evening was suffocating hot, and the mosquitoes terrible moithering, and I sat between two men who both discomfited me.

To my left was Ld. Minto's son, George Elliot, who is captain of the *Modeste*. I do not like him. He was I grant most gracious towards me – but in a sneering way made me feel his graciousness was a favour for which I sh'd thank him.

On my other side sat Colonel Rollo Gillespie, Second-in-Command under Auchmuty. Gillespie is Irish and he knows the terrain of Roscommon, so we talked of that and if he noted he is from the landed gentry, and I ain't, he did not let me note he noted it.

Terrain ain't the most interesting subject, but 'twas at least safe enough ground from which to confront a man I must think is most unsafe. Gillespie has a soldier's glamour – indeed he is a famously tenacious warrior, of such derring-do and reckless bravery they call him *Rollicking Rollo*. They say he inspires in his men admiration verging on adulation – and in women the same. I w'd never stoop to adore a man – let *them* do the adoring, say I – and yet 'tis true Gillespie has about him something powerful compelling. He is tall – taller than me, and older, his hair speckled a canine grey – and his uniform fits him most becoming. Then again, he looked at me, through glowing eyes, in a way unmistakable: not irritating eager, but nonetheless admiring, savouring, so I felt myself growing more expansive under his gaze. His animal closeness set my skin to pricking as if there were needles everywhere sticking into it, and I thought: Olivia, there are dangers here. And with that thought I decided once we'd done with Roscommon I'd better not speak to him no more, so 'twas all in all a most difficult evening.

May 1811, the Chinese Kapitan's house, Malacca

Ld. Minto has had presented to him most extraordinary gifts sent here by native nobles. There is in these parts a kind of monkey the Malays think almost human, calling it *orang utan*, which means in English *man of the forest*. Ld. Minto has had from the Sultan of Pontianak, a court on Borneo, a pair of young orang utans, a male and a female, very fond of each other, that we have named Baba and Nonya – that is Husband and Wife – and Abdullah remarked to me that if orang utans can love one another as man and wife, how much more sh'd we human beings do likewise.

141

Meanwhile, from a rajah of Bali, Ld. Minto has had five slave boys and two slave girls, none more than seven years old. These unfortunate children his L emancipated from slavery immediately, but now they are free what are we to do with them? Captain Elliot took one, to serve him on board the *Modeste*, and the rest are now staying with me. They will probably grow into very good servants, and Tom has agreed to pay the upkeep of one or two until we can use them, but the others Ld. Minto must support – he remarked to me the girls w'd be a puzzle, and he teased he had some thought of baking them in a pie.

I now have in my house all the family, Leyden, all Tom's Malay secretariat, the servants, and now these orang utans, and these children. We are packed close as dates in a tub and feeding this host has Cook in a frenzy – tho' the orang utans, at least, eat naught but fruit.

May 1811, the Chinese Kapitan's house, Malacca

Tom grows very fond of Baba and Nonya. Baba he dresses in trousers and a coat and hat. Both these monkeys he allows to range free about the house – and various other birds and animals he keeps in pens and cages in the garden, for when he can find time he is still often at his natural history. He has now even a cassowary, and I still don't like that big bird, tho' he tells me some primordials believe the world was created from its feathers.

May 1811, the Chinese Kapitan's house, Malacca

I am coming to loathe Ld. Minto's peevish, horse-faced son, Captain Elliot. It seems to me he is jealous of his father's cordiality for Tom, and of the way he promotes his interests. If jealousy were his private torment, I w'd pity him, but it seems to me he looks at Tom with an eye blatantly disparaging. Tom don't say nothing, but I think he notices Elliot's disdain, for he is nervous in his company – he lacks the social confidence to belittle them that belittle him.

Meanwhile, I have it from Mary Ann, as aggrieved as me, that Elliot mocks Tom behind his back for his membership of the Order of The Golden Sword. She says Flint says Elliot spreads it about that the Order of the Golden Sword is neither old, nor noble, and naught but a native bauble bestowed by a petty king on coxcombs. She says 'tis said he sneers Our Sir Knight, or Our Sir Golden Sword, is self-opinionated, pert, forward, assuming, and says: *here's* one neither born nor bred a gentleman.

Well! I sh'd like to corner Elliot and say my mind freely, but since the laws of society forbid it I instead told Tom last night I'm proud of him for what he's achieved, notwithstanding his unhelpful beginning.

June 1811, the Chinese Kapitan's house, Malacca

We celebrated yesterday the King's birthday, for all rumour reaches us even here the king has at last gone completely mad – irretrievably lost, suffering violent paroxysms. No matter: at dawn, salutes were fired by the men-of-war anchored in the roads, and by the batteries on-shore, and then at noon we had in the square outside the Stadhuis a further seventy-three gun salute, marking the age of the sovereign (now insane).

But mere booming was not the end of it. Hereabouts, it ain't just natives keep slaves: every private Dutchman in the Eastward has poor enthralled wretches to do his work, and in its day the Dutch government, too, kept many poor creatures as its chattels. Our own Honourable East India Company inherited some twenty of these Dutch government slaves when the Hollanders entrusted to us Malacca. Twenty born into slavery! Twenty who thought their children w'd be slaves after them! It ain't not to be tolerated

– and this morning, Ld. Minto held at the Stadhuis a ceremony emancipating these unfortunates to each of whom he presented four Spanish dollars, and a certificate of freedom.

Later, his L went to the gaol and released all those imprisoned for debt. When the gates were flung open, the prisoners ran free, screaming praises to Allah – and also to Ld. Minto.

There was in the gaol a most notorious dungeon, called in Malay *terongko galep*, the dark dungeon. Ld. Minto visited it, and ordered it destroyed. Within were found various instruments of torture; his L at once proclaimed such things sh'd never again be used in Malacca. Those of wood – racks, wheels, gallows – he had burned at the foot of The Hill. Those of iron – various articles for screwing thumbs, wrists, ankles, and other contrivances of the diabolical sort – were put in a boat, carried beyond the roads, and sunk in deep water, never to rise to screw poor people's bones and joints again.

Tho' I protested the visions we had in our heads were all the cautionary mementoes we needed, Tom took a few of these iron torture instruments to keep as a dark reminder we must never again permit the use of such abhorred devices.

After this good work of freeing slaves and debtors, and destroying racks and screws, Ld. Minto gave a dinner at the Stadhuis, 'twas for men only, but there followed a ball, which I attended with Mary Ann, Leonora, and Hannah. The company numbered some one hundred and fifty army and naval officers, but there were only twenty ladies present, so those of us of the female chapter were kept busy all night dancing.

I had the honour of leading off the first dance with Ld. Minto. His L was gracious to me, saying Tom is a very amiable, able, active, and judicious man, and adding he was glad to see him so happy in his interior, and 'twas pleasing to find a man such a true admirer of his lot. He told me also that tho' 'tis his duty to friskify off to Java, he never engaged in any affair with greater interest, or with more pleasure.

For my part, I itched to ask what he intends for Tom, sh'd we take Java, but since the rules of society forbade it, I spoke instead of the fiddlers, which musicians played uncommon loud.

When I went down the line with that dashing man Gillespie, he cast upon me his wolfish glances that I pretended not to notice.

June 1811, the Chinese Kapitan's house, Malacca

The invasion of Java is launched. Our fleet, above a hundred vessels under sail, is too big to pass as one body through the narrow waters between the many islands of the Archipelago. On account of its unwieldy enormity, passage for the fleet is to be effected by its sailing in small divisions of transports, protected by frigates or other men-of-war; the divisions will all depart in the space of the next month, or six weeks farthest; today the first of them is gone, looking deceptive peaceable, like a drift of blossom caught by the wind, as it blew them away from the harbour.

Our ships in bloom make initially for the Straits of Singapore – this Singapore being a small island off the southern tip of the Malay Peninsula. Leyden unrolled his map to show me where it may be found – 'tis so tiny it appears on the chart as naught but a dot. Still, Leyden says there was on it in the distant past a thriving city, mentioned often in *The Malay Annals* – the same that Ibrahim and him translated. Alas, he sighs, alas the island is today naught but a haunt of pirates that has on it only jangal and a fishing village, and it ain't now of no interest to nobody much. No matter: 'tis in its waters our scattered fleet will reassemble, before sailing the next stretch of sea leading to Java, Tom's land of promise.

June 1811, the Chinese Kapitan's house, Malacca

I have had to take my leave of Abdullah. Tom wanted to take him to Java, but his fond mother w'd not allow it. So now he is leaving us, to return to his home with a letter of recommendation and forty Spanish dollars – ten of them a gift from me. When we parted I gave him also a piece of leaf-patterned muslin, to make a jacket, and he gave me a verse he had written comparing Tom and me to a pair of goldfish swimming together in a bowl, sharing every thought and move – or so he told me, I c'd not read it for myself, 'cause 'twas written in Jawi. We were both very sad. Abdullah said Tom and me had been as a mother and father to him, and I w'd have said he'd been as a son to us, except I was crying.

June 1811, the Chinese Kapitan's house, Malacca

O, what a patron! Ld. Minto, dear, kind man, has communicated to Tom the news we have longed for: after the invasion of Java, in case of success, Tom will be appointed Lieutenant-Governor!

For now my discrete husband has confided his elevation, assuming our conquest, only to me and to Leyden, but we three exalt enough for multitudes. Last night we drank much, and the two men spun again their golden dreams of establishing for Britannia a civilising empire in the Eastern Seas, and they reconfirmed that when Tom is running it, he must be aided by his able Secretary, Leyden.

June 1811, the *Preston*, Straits of Malacca

Did I say already I w'd accompany my husband to Java? No matter: I say it now. Indeed I this morning embarked in one of the transports, the *Preston*. I sail with Mary Ann and Flint, Leonora and Loftie, and Hannah, our single lady. Charlotte is left pro tempore in the care of Nonio Clemaine at the Stadhuis.

The *Preston* carries about two hundred troops, mixed English and Indian. Tho' I have my own cabin, ship-board must be the usual horrid. Still, the weather is fine, so a truce with complaining.

Tom is to quit Malacca at the very last; he will not sail for a day or two yet. He is to sail on the *Modeste* with Ld. Minto, and that contemptible Captain Elliot. Still, Leyden will also be aboard, as his ally, 'cause 'tis his job to supervise the munshis of the secretariat that necessarily sail with Ld. Minto to run the government.

July 1811, the *Preston,* Straits of Singapore

Our battleships, frigates, sloops, cruisers, transports, gunboats, schooners, &c, have reassembled as planned off Singapore, and the little ink dot I beheld once on Leyden's map now appears before my eyes, as a little dot of land poking up from the ocean, one rimmed by beaches so white they look like sheets of cotton – or else like shrouds? Aye, the sands of Singapore are littered, I'm told, with the skulls of men robbed at sea, 'cause whenever a boat or ship is plundered 'tis brought to this place for division of the spoils.

The weather has been foul, with the wind thrashing the sea to a fury, and lightening cracking all about, and the rain hurling down. Still, 'tis calmer now, and we soon get underway again, and commence to navigate the narrow Straits between Singapore and the mainland of the Peninsula – if any natives stand on either shore they must watch the passing of our enormous fleet with awe and astonishment.

August 1811, the *Preston,* Bay of Batavia

I am so close to Java the breeze brings with it the scent of the place: rain, rotting jangal vegetation, a fishy whiff, an animal musk, and spice. Aye, our fleet has reached its destination – and it has done so without loss of a single spar to any ship, or slightest accident, which is a great relief to all, but especially, I sh'd think, to Tom.

The fleet is anchored in the Bay of Batavia, a little way east of the town that gives the bay its name. From the decks 'tis possible to see a native village, a collection of huts, apparently deserted, set back in a clearing in the jangal at the mouth of a sluggish river, one side of the huts projecting over the surface of the water, supported on stilts, giving them a rather amphibious appearance: tomorrow this village is where the invasion commences.

Tonight, my thoughts are all with my husband, so close by on the *Modeste*, and for all that so distant he may as well be on the moon. How must he feel to see all the divisions of the fleet reunited, in sight of his land of promise, where soon he is to be Governor, if heaven wills it, and bring to the languishing people there all the improving benefits of British government? He must think today a fine day; tonight he must be as happy as 'tis possible for a man to be ... Unless he ain't? Perhaps he is sombre? Perhaps he reflects, as he looks at Java, that tomorrow his hopes, his ambitions, may be hideously snapped, like a chicken's neck, as the housewife kills it for cooking? Aye, he must surely reflect that tomorrow cool reality takes over from all his dreaming.

In any case, whatever else Tom thinks tonight, he surely thinks this: conquer we must.

August 1811, Molenvliet

Java is ours!

'Tis almost a month since last I wrote 'cause all has been too anxious, confusing, and exciting mixed, to allow me to settle to my diary, and too noisy for concentration, and with much going about from here to there. But now I have at last peace, a slope, a desk to set it on, a quill – and with them this great news to report, that I wrote already: Java is ours.

'Tis now my happy task to write the gist of how we won it. On August 4 our troops landed unopposed at Cilincing – the deserted village of stilt-huts I c'd see from the deck of the *Preston*, that night our war fleet first anchored in the Bay of Batavia.

Tho' he is a civil servant, not a soldier, Leyden, dear, flamboyant man, was the first to splash through the shallows to land – and for his love of theatre he did so dressed as a pirate, in a red tasselled cap, with a patch over one eye, and armed with a cutlass and a pistol in his belt. Now our Calico Jack boasts he bore the brunt of the enemy's counterattack. But since the E had already fled Cilincing, he admits, cheerful, this brunt of the attack came from a flock of barn-door fowls headed by an aggressive rooster.

Four days after we took Cilincing, an advance column under Colonel Gillespie captured also Batavia, still without meeting much resistance, for the French had withdrawn, after first opening up the storehouses so the natives c'd loot them, and thus deny to us their contents – Leyden told me the streets were covered with coffee and pepper as with gravel, and in other places with quantities of sugar, these commodities the natives either having flung about, or dropped as they made off with more valuable booty.

Next to fall was the military station of Weltevreden, which is an odd sounding name, like all these Dutch ones. Here, at last, the E put up a fight, but Gillespie was himself, as Tom put it, and attacked with spirit and judgement. After two hours of the hand-to-hand fighting the military men call *hard service*, we prevailed with on our side trifling loss of life, and the E all fled.

At Weltevreden the E abandoned a fine country house, elegant and airy, with a lake in the grounds, and beautiful flat lawns, for riding. This house Ld. Minto at once took as his headquarters and billet, installing along with himself, a portion of his officials, tho' Tom and Leyden were billeted in another house close by, on the canal at Molenvliet.

'Tis at Molenvliet that I now write my diary, for 'twas judged safe for me to join my husband, and I made haste to do so – Mary Ann, Hannah, and Leonora remain still in their births on the *Preston*. I see Tom every day, but Leyden moves between Molenvliet and Batavia, where there is a library of Malay manuscripts and Dutch archives Ld. Minto has committed to his charge, for him to study and to catalogue.

Two or three days after I arrived here, the battle moved southwards, to a new-built Dutch stronghold called Meester Cornelis, and 'cause it ain't very distant, we started to hear the booming of heavy artillery coming from there. 'Twas a nervous time; we knew the E much outnumbered our good British redcoats, led again by Gillespie, who, 'tis reported, was everywhere – he was so energetic in his harrying of the E, that at the height of the battle he collapsed with fatigue, but carried on fighting after a swig of grog, and all now call him *gallant hero*, for we prevailed. Aye, with great rapidity the E was vanquished utterly. What a rout! Boney's poor fodder for our bayonets all running everywhere in panicked confusion, and their leaders fled pell-mell through the jangal, chased away by our grape and musketry – it can be but a matter of time until we catch them.

All this we achieved with a loss of fewer of our own than one thousand killed and wounded, which low number can be no consolation to the dead, but 'tis a relief to those of us still living. As for the E? The whole of their army was killed, captured, or dispersed. We have five thousand prisoners – men who must give thanks they survived. Their less lucky comrades were scythed especially in the retreat; the rivers are chocked with the dead, their corpses bloated and stinking, and the huts are filled with wounded men, some of them soon to expire – the shocking variety of deaths had better not be imagined, so, to forestall imagining, I now put down my pen.

August 1811, Molenvliet

All around us happy drunken men are celebrating victory, but Tom and me are plunged into deepest anxiety: Leyden has been these past few days in Batavia, which is notorious in the Eastward for an unhealthful place, a stew of fevers, 'cause of bad airs and smells emanating off the swampy mudflats that surround it, and off the canals the Dutch built – the arrogant Hollanders wanted to make Batavia the Amsterdam of the East, but their canals quickly silted up with stagnant slime, so these days they ain't naught but breeding grounds for mosquitoes and vermin, and they exhale an intolerable stench and the water in them is yellow as pus.

Leyden was in this wen examining the library he is charged to catalogue, but now he is returned in a bad way with his old trouble, the intermittent fever. It came on very sudden this morning, when, unwise, he went, heated, into a closed room within the library. The stale air was full of dusty moulds, and 'cause 'twas cool and damp it reacted badly with his heaty blood. Such mixing of cool and hot is ever dangerous, even in healthful places, and Leyden fell at once to shivering, and to sweating.

He was too ill to ride back to Molenvliet, so his servants loaded him into a bullock cart, and brought him here, for me to nurse. Bullocks ain't hasty creatures, and the journey that by a horse even only walking w'd be but an hour and a half instead took nearly three.

We got Leyden to bed, and I have brewed him a cooling infusion of bitter gourd, but 'tis a struggle to get him to drink, and he has taken but sips, and whispers that for inhaling pestiential air he is on the brink of the grave.

August 1811, Molenvliet

Leyden is worse. His sheets are soaking the minute they are

changed; he shakes and raves at shadows; he don't know me, and nor Tom neither, and when Tom, distraught, tries to boost him by reminding him of our victory, and saying this is the instant of his triumph, for he witnesses the beginning of that Eastern empire the two of them long since dreamed of, he is too ill to take it in.

August 1811, Molenvliet

O, this deadly Malayan shore! With what cruel timing it has robbed us! Aye, Leyden is dead. Tom attended him from the first to the last of his dying which after three days of struggle finished in my husband's arms. We bury him before sunset. I cannot for my tears write more than this.

August 1811, Molenvliet

This page in my diary sh'd be bordered in black, bordered in sorrow, for yesterday we committed Leyden's dear body to the ground in the Dutch cemetery of Batavia, under a stinking sun that for all its blazing c'd not warm his cold remains. Ld. Minto spoke the eulogy, saying no man but Leyden ever possessed a mind so entirely exempt from sordid passion, so negligent of fortune and all its grovelling pursuits. The open grave was as horrifying as open graves always are, and what else of a funeral is there to say?

August 1811, Molenvliet

Was Leyden as confident as he ought to be – as *I* ought to be – that truth grasped by the European mind trumps all other truth? I ask from pondering that for all my dear chevalier was a doctor of divinity, I never once saw him reading a book of Christian theology, indeed I saw him reading books on everything *except* this subject. And I never heard him talk any more than Tom of spreading the light of Christian Revelation through the Eastward – such talk my husband leaves to the missionaries, saying he is too interested in the here and now to worry over much about the hereafter. What I am coming to say is: Leyden was an orientalist. He studied the Hindoos, who believe, like my mother, in many gods, and who believe not in the resurrection of the body, but in the reincarnation of the soul. Yet Hindoos, like Christians, claim their beliefs are *true*. But it cannot be the fate of the dead to be both reincarnated, and resurrected incorruptible. So what did Leyden think w'd happen to him after he breathed his last? And ain't this close to asking: how to decide between them when the teachings of faiths conflict?

O, what sinful audacity! Shut your mind, Olivia! Can you not feel the hell fires lapping? Do you wish to suffer the bitter pains of eternal death? Then cling fast to the pieties.

September 1811, Molenvliet

I am tonight to be called the Lady Governess of Java. Ld. Minto this morning proceeded in state to the council rooms at Batavia where our British conquest of Java was formally proclaimed to a salute from the Bengal Horse Artillery, and where Tom, looking haggard from lack of sleep and weeping – loss of Leyden, he says, is loss of a host of men – where Tom, my grieving husband, was officially appointed Lieutenant-Governor.

Several tedious proclamations were read, and my mind wandered often to Leyden. My dear, departed chevalier! Did he not once imagine my bewitching smile c'd summon him from the grave? W'd that my smile had really that power! W'd I c'd hear again his screeching voice, clacking, clacking!

September 1811, Molenvliet

Tom sorely misses Leyden as advisor, and as inspiration, and goes about reminding everybody he w'd have been his private secretary, had he lived, and demanding what w'd he not have done with the latitude he sh'd have given him? He knows there are some, a very few, who have no delicacy, and who say Leyden w'd have made a poor fist of the job, and these he denounces as villains whose tongues out venom all the worms of Nile.

September 1811, Molenvliet

It seems wrong Tom and me sh'd smile together with Leyden scarce cold, and yet now and then we cannot help but smile. For all that I'm no lady, merely, from my husband's position, the Lady Governess, Tom teases me Your Ladyship. And here's a strange thing about elevation: tho' I laughed at it before, now I find I approve it. I have written to all my correspondents in England to tell them I am Lady Governess, the packet including as well a letter to Mother, to be read to her by Mr. Etherington.

September 1811, Molenvliet

Ld. Minto has written to the Court of Directors to inform the Hon. Mems. he has ignored their instructions, and done what is right and best for British interests; that is he has taken Java and now intends it sh'd be made an English colony as soon as we can, by the introduction of English colonists, and English capital, and also that Tom is to be the Lieutenant-Governor of this new colony.

In case these unlooked for developments alarm the Court, he has offered reassurance Java is a much greater country than is generally conceived in Leadenhall St., and 'tis more yet than simply another island in East-Insular India, but is in fact the *other* India, and that the opportunity of obtaining it was rightly not cast by, 'cause the monies flowing to London from this golden isle will very soon enrich the Hon. Mems., and line the pockets of the shareholders, which enrichment and lining is Johnny Company's only purpose, tho' I don't suppose Ld. Minto wrote it that way.

September 1811, Molenvliet

Needs must we think of future European statecraft. Once the world is rid of Boney's tyranny – as it must be – England will want Holland, her neighbour across the North Sea, as an ally against Prussia, Russia, Austria, &c, for if a fair balance of power ain't maintained, the world risks another war.

Hence my naughty Tom claims to think it a threat what most men think a hope: general peace in Europe. This 'cause in that event, as part of the settlement, to conciliate the Dutch, our government will most likely return Java to them to rule. And what then for Britain in the Eastward, and for him, and for all his dreams?

Still, Tom don't think this threat of losing what we now have sh'd prevent us from improving the condition of the Javanese, the mild and simple people that has become tributary pro tempore to our British authority, and tributary too to our prosperity. No, 'tis his charitable belief that whilst we are here we sh'd do as much good as we can for the natives – tho' without spending too much of Johnny Company's cash – and release them from the state of bondage and arbitrary oppression in which most of them now live, for the life of a village cultivator is wretched; the sultans don't notice their little people at all, except as beasts of burden, and the Dutch ain't no better, but treat even free natives almost as their slaves, and load upon them many cruel dictates that undermine their sovereignty and self-determination. Aye, 'tis Dutch practice throughout the Eastward to insist cultivators grow the crops they specify, not the crops they want to feed their families, and then the poor things must sell to their greedy Dutch overlords their coffee and pepper, &c, at ridiculous low prices, so that when they ship these goods to Amsterdam the merchants are assured of a great profit on the markets there.

Tom will stop the tyrannical and rapacious Dutch practice, adopted here also by the French, of forced cultivation. Indeed, he says he can't run Java for bare mercantile profit, but must consider the common good, and connect the wellbeing of the Javanese with the general prosperity of the colony. To this end he will put the cultivators, their needs and interests, at the centre of his agricultural policy, and he will ensure for them the right of property in the land – this important right being alien to them, at the current moment.

My husband don't intend his philanthropic improvements sh'd stop with agriculture, neither. No, in accordance with British law and our enlightened principles, he intends here, as in Penang and Malacca, the banning henceforth of all purchase of slaves, and of the torture and mutilation of criminals. He will suppress too gaming and cock-fighting – 'twas through gaming that his father plunged his family into almost direst poverty, and in consequence of this Tom has a particular horror of that vice. Alas, the Malays are mad for cock-fighting, and men may gamble their children, their wives, and lastly themselves into slavery in satisfaction of bets placed on fighting cocks.

October 1811, Molenvliet

We have had at Government House a victory ball and supper given by the officers of the army for Ld. Minto and Auchmuty, who entered hand-in-hand like two dandies smelling at one nosegay.

The French had done for us some of the work of preparing for this ball; they had left Government House near enough decorated. This was 'cause as our fleet assembled in the Bay of Batavia, they were preparing to celebrate Boney's birthday, which celebration we disturbed by landing and getting possession of Government House, decorations and all, a few days before the grand occasion.

For all we want to make Java an English colony, Ld. Minto and Tom are agreed: the Dutch, resident over generations, they will allow to stay. 'Tis already announced some Dutch gentlemen, employed also by Boney in his civil service, are to continue in their posts – this from necessity, since there ain't the money to ship replacements out from London. These Dutch are already grateful to us for rescuing Java from Boney's tyrant grasp; to encourage them to further embrace their duties of allegiance and attachment many Dutch officials and their wives were invited last night.

Some of the Dutchmen, I think, had been born in Java and had perhaps not ever visited Holland? For sure they have been long cut-off from Europe, 'cause of Boney's wars, and in outward appearance they were a peculiar group: they were dressed very fine, but in antique style, with embroidered velvet coats down to their heels, notwithstanding the climate.

Meanwhile, their women were barely European. The Dutch, it seems, are reluctant to allow their women to come to the Eastward, so the men have for many generations lived with native women, whose daughters, gradually borrowing something from the father's side, and becoming a mixed breed, are now the wives and ladies of rank and fashion in Java.

As I am Lady Governess, I must now improve by example these mixed breed Dutch quizzes in etiquette, and this I think will be a demanding task, for they seem to possess no idea of social intercourse – indeed, no idea of anything at all. They ain't educated, for instead of taking lessons from their mothers they are attended from their cradles by slaves, by whom they are trained in helplessness and laziness, and from whom they acquire nothing in the way of opinions, or accomplishments or refinement in manners, or any language other than Malay.

They are all of immense size through greediness and inactivity and they seem not to care how they dress: they wear native kebayas, and these loose, white-cotton jackets they fasten with a negligence of pins w'd disgrace a village girl in Roscommon. Their white skirts look like petticoats, their coarse stockings and wide, thick-soled shoes are ugly. 'Tis only the back of their heads look properly dressed: their hair they wear in buns stuck about thickly with gold pins ornamented with rubies, diamonds, sapphires, and by these crowns of pins you know their rank.

For myself, I wore one of the white muslin dresses, daycolletay, with a high waist and puffed sleeves, that I like so much, and Tom cast on me a most approving eye and said ye gods, he looked around at all the Dutchwomen without once regretting that he was married.

Auchmuty proposed a toast to Ld. Minto, which he said c'd never have been given before we won this part of India in the Eastward: Ld. Minto, Governor-General of *all* India. Other toasts were proposed, each accompanied by its music, and various speeches were made, and all the men got loyally tipsy.

Dancing followed. The music was lively, but the Dutch were lame in English dances, of which they knew neither the steps nor the figures, and we did not know how to dance their waltzes, so between ignorance and the drunkenness of the men, the dancing was all abroad, and as awkward and crippled as anything.

One reel I went down the line with Gillespie. O, this Gillespie! He teased he wished our reel were a waltz, but 'twas relief to me 'twas not, for during their Dutch waltzes they revolve not allemande, but the man takes his partner fairly in his arms to hug her, and what w'd Dame Grundy say to *that*?

October 1811, Rijswijk

Tom and me have taken possession of what is henceforth to be our official residence in Batavia. 'Tis a house called *Rijswijk*, which ain't a name as pleasing to me as *Runnymede*, and tho' the house is very fine and large, 'tis swarmed with mosquitoes so many and so thick they float like scarves of gauzy grey through every room.

The house has two stories, built in the European style, and its gardens run down to the Ciliwung River, that flows through Batavia – *ciliwung* means *turbid water* and the river is well-named for 'tis the muddiest thing I ever saw.

Mary Ann and Flint, Leonora and Loftie, and Hannah have joined us. Now we are settled, Mary Ann w'd send for Charlotte to come here from Malacca, except Flint has no patience for her daughter, and so she has delayed. When she told me this, I c'd not help wincing to remember Fancourt telling me I may not bring Harriet to Madras. Well, I must hope my sister's second husband is not such a bully as my first.

October 1811, Rijswijk

We have taken our turn to celebrate the great victory which has enabled Tom to be elevated to the Lieutenant-Governorship of Java, and this we have done in style, by giving here at Rijswijk a grand dinner and entertainment in honour of Ld. Minto, before he returns with his ontoorage, and most of the troops, to Calcutta.

In the garden where the guests came in, we created an avenue, illuminated by strings of Chinese lanterns, leading to a temple, built of bamboo, in the classical style, not the native. On the pediment of this temple we arranged to be picked out in candles the name *Minto*. To each side of the temple we erected bamboo stages, on which richly costumed Chinamen performed their screeching sort of opera. Our temple and our Chinese tableaux were both much exclaimed upon, with admiration and envy.

I had as my guests here both Dutch and British government officials, and civilians, and their wives, and army and navy officers. Indeed, we invited all <u>the beauty and fashion</u> of Batavia – I mean to say by my underlining 'twas a strange sort of beauty and fashion, for once again, the ugliness and the queerness of the Dutchwomen was remarkable.. These Dutch women! 'Tis impossible to give anything like an adequate notion of the total absence of beauty amongst them. Tom said later there never was a dozen of women assembled in Europe without a few attractions, but here there was no difference, except in varieties of ugliness and ordinariness of dress and manners.

Ld. Minto took the opportunity of paying some very handsome compliments to the army, to whom he certainly feels very grateful for his conquest, and a great many bumper toasts were given – when it came to the toast *The Company* we drank it to the tune *Money in Both Pockets*. A good many of both nations, Dutch and British, got a little tipsy, but the harmony of the party was not disturbed.

I led off the dancing with Ld. Minto, to my old favourite, *Off She Goes*. We had only reels, not these Dutch waltzes, so of the English cavaliers and damsels all were most graceful.

When I danced with Gillespie <u>I did not regret at all</u> we progressed allemande, and he had not his arm around my waist.

October 1811, Rijswijk

I had supposed – hoped, feared – I'd soon be rid of Gillespie's needling presence, trusting he must shortly return to Calcutta with Ld. Minto. But now his L has announced that when he and his party quit hence, 'tis Gillespie will stay to be in command of the troops left behind – some seven thousand men – as he has been the great hero, and the chief means of our success.

Perhaps Ld. Minto too sees trouble in Gillespie's continued presence in Batavia? Certainly, he has seen fit to remind Our Rollicking Colonel that where The Company governs foreign settlements, 'tis the civil power has recognised seniority over the military – that is to say, Tom will soon be set over him on the establishment. I suppose he thought this reminder necessary not only 'cause Gillespie is older than Tom, but, more, he is a distinguished fighting man, trained to attack the world with a belligerent swagger, and such must ever chafe to be subordinate to civilians.

In any case, Java's two new chiefs are both men of talent, self-belief, ambition, and strong-will. 'Tis hard to see them co-existing peacefully – especially if Tom ever comes to suspect I succumb to little reveries, now and then, of dancing waltzes with Gillespie.

October 1811, Rijswijk

O sad day! Ld. Minto, Auchmuty, their ontoorage, and a great part of the troops have all set sail for Calcutta, and when shall I ever see him again, this dear patron who is the cause of Tom's elevation, and the sweet happiness it brings?

I said my farewells here at Rijswijk, but Tom accompanied his L to the wharf in an old carriage-and-four left behind by the fleeing French. While crossing the bridge over the Ciliwung a wheel gave way, and the carriage overturned. The horses broke free and bolted; in the confusion Ld. Minto and Tom were tipped to the ground. Tho' alarmed, they were, thank God, unhurt. After they had collected themselves, and dusted the dirt from their clothes, they continued to the wharf in another carriage. There they parted; Ld. Minto was conveyed in a barge to the *Modeste*, which waited at anchor in the roads, Tom watching the while from the shore.

Henceforth, in this remotest of remote regions, my husband must exercise in his own name and person all the powers of government. He is here alone without any advice, in a new possession as large as England with a native population of six or seven million people, a small civilian European population including as well demoralised Dutch and a few resentful French, and a standing army of not less than seven thousand men. Is he daunted? I think he must be, tho' he don't show it, and I hesitate to ask. But perhaps he ain't? Perhaps my Tom has so much trust in his own abilities there ain't no room in his head for self-doubt?

October 1811, Rijswijk

Tom is hard at it, governing, and I too have my work. Aye, I have started on bringing the elegance of English ways to the local Dutch women and to the natives both. I have banned already sireh from Rijswijk; I will not offer it to visitors, nor tolerate that nasty spitting of the quids; our walls will not be stained red as are those of the Stadhuis in Malacca. I will henceforth insist that shoes be worn on official occasions, for the Javanese, who go everywhere shoeless, must be taught that bare feet are unacceptable in civilised society. I will likewise require ladies of all races to sit on chairs, not on the floor, and to eat with a knife and fork, not with their hands. These orders, I hope, will be the dawn of still greater and more important amelioration of public behaviour in Batavia.

October 1811, Rijswijk

Java cannot yet pay for itself, and must for now be funded from Bengal. But Tom dare not keep drawing on the government there indefinitely, 'cause of all the assurances he gave Ld. Minto of the capability of the island not only to maintain itself, but also to bring increase to Johnny Company's cash. He has now lit upon the idea he can help the treasury in Leadenhall St. by creating here a market for cheap printed cottons imported from the mills of England, and he is most sanguine in his expectations of success provided strict attention is paid to patterns and sizes. Accordingly he has written to The Court of Directors, asking the Hon. Mems. to send out a consignment of cottons forthwith.

November 1811, Rijswijk

The rains have begun – not the rain, but the rain*s* – and all day said rains lashing down, lashing, lashing, as if water is in a frenzy to thrash its rival, earth. The sky is at all times like a dirty dishcloth, and the puddles around the house swarm with mosquitoes; I am bitten half to death, and maddened by itching. The wringing air that always smells bad now stinks of putrefaction, so every breath is suffocation and gagging; the exterior walls of my house are all dripping and coated with green slime, and in places the interior ones also. Our sheets and clothes are never now dry, so my skirts seem to bloom with mildew even as I don them, and my shoes rot. Meanwhile, the drumming of the deluge on the roof all day is an incessant rhythm in my ears, so I don't know how a woman's to stand it, in truth I don't.

November 1811, Rijswijk

What a place is this Batavia! What reeking heat, reeking muds, reeking canals, bad waters, and unsafe airs. I remark often to Tom no people in their senses w'd, without absolute necessity, venture to encounter its pestilential atmosphere. More, I remind him his constitution is delicate, and I say I do not want this deadly shore to see him off as it saw off poor Leyden, and so many others that stuff the European cemetery. Indeed, I have told him I will not live in Batavia, and that we must move, and this he has agreed we will do.

November 1811, Rijswijk

'Tis all decided: in the new year, Tom and me will leave this swamp, Batavia, and move about forty miles southwards, to Buitenzorg, where is to be found the former Dutch Governor-General's palace. We cannot shift sooner as the palace is in poor repair, and needs work to make it habitable. Moreover, Tom is planning to undertake soon a journey of diplomacy to two of Java's native courts, east of here, in the central part of the island, and we cannot shift until his return.

These eastern courts, Surakarta and Yogyakarta, have long been the bane of European authority in Java, and they are minded now to resist our British right to insist on their obedience. Tom says the reason the sultans won't accept they must submit to us, is 'cause in former times the Dutch confined themselves to the coasts, and sent their residents to Surakarta and Yogyakarta more as ambassadors than as rulers. But Tom thinks you can't run an empire from coastal strips, you need firm control of *all* a territory's territory to govern effectively. Hence it is now his plan to inform the sultans the ways and extent to which the treaties they made with the Dutch may or may not henceforth be respected, and to tell them that tho' they never submitted as they ought to Dutch power, and nor to French, they will indeed submit properly to British.

Christmas Day 1811, Rijswijk

Here's a miserable Christmas. Tom is away at the eastern courts, and today, when all sh'd be merry gambols, I worry for him – when I consider his very delicate state of health, all that he has done, all that he is doing, the fatigue of his journey, I am indeed astonished he don't collapse. Then again, I grow resentful of his absence, and feel I am a loser by it for I am deprived of the happiness of his company, and I am neglected, and I do not think touring about Java without me is a nice way for a husband to treat his wife.

New Year's Day 1812, Rijswijk

Tom has returned healthy this first day of 1812, which I think a good omen for the new year. He is full of tales of his journey, and hopeful he has stamped his authority on the eastern courts.

He went first to Surakarta, where I now learn the sultan is called the *Susuhunan – object of adoration –* and where said Susuhunan farms rocks for birds' nests. These he sells to China to be made into birds' nest soup, believed by the people there to strengthen the lungs. In exchange for an annuity, he agreed to give up to The Company the profits from this lucrative trading, as indeed he ought now we have Java for all resources such as pearl reefs, salt-pans, bird's nest rocks, &c, sh'd remain government property, and likewise he has agreed to give up his teak forests, so all is satisfactorily settled.

Before he left Surakarta, Tom came across one Dr. Thomas Horsfield, a physician and naturalist from Pennsylvania who has been living in Java almost a dozen years, studying the useful and medicinal plants of this island, and every branch of its natural history.

Tom continues to accumulate specimens of plants, insects, shells, fishes, birds, reptiles, &c. From enthusiasm, he called on Dr. Horsfield at his house, where he devoted several hours to the patient examination of his cabinet.

As well as productions of the animal, vegetable, and mineral kingdoms, Dr. Horsfield has in his possession a great variety of ancient carved stones, fragments of Hindoo statuary, cracked and chipped panels showing pieces of deities, &c. Tom says he was much amazed by these things, and gratified to see them, adding that in the long distant past the people in *all* of India, including also East-Insular India, followed the interesting and estimable faith of Hindooism, since supplanted in these parts by Mahomedanism. He says 'tis evident Horsfield's statues are relics of the time before the Mahomedans arrived, at which date he supposes the Malays ceased flourishing, and, indeed, commenced their slow decline 'til they were reduced to the miserable state of slackness in which we now find them.

Tom noticed in particular several antique heads of the one called the Buddha, decapitated from their bodies. These, Dr. Horsfield told him, were found at a place called Borobudur, a most wondrous, isolated temple now slowly, sullenly being eaten by the jangal. On hearing this, Tom immediately determined to send a surveyor to see this Borobudur before the jangal obliterates entirely the works of man – just today he selects for the task Lieutenant-Colonel Mackenzie, one of our more mature and distinguished military engineers.

On being asked why, pray, there sh'd be heads of the Buddha on an island he says was Hindoo before it was Mahomedan, Tom dismisses airily they must have been carved at a period when the worship was not separated.

Once he was done in Surakarta, my busy husband journeyed on to Yogyakarta. The Sultan met him outside his *kraton* – his palace – which Tom says is more like a small town or large village than a palace alone, being some three miles in circumference, and housing as well as the Sultan, his wives, their children, and all their extended families also courtiers, guards, cavalry, infantry, slaves, servants, retainers, clients, pensioners, &c.

There was some difficulty about whether Tom's coach or the Sultan's sh'd ride into the kraton first, for the native sultans are touchier about precedence than any English duchess. 'Twas all a matter of tiu lien: Tom knew he must not be the one to lose face, and this not on his own account – his own honour he easily puts aside – but for fear of lowering Britain's dignity and rightful prestige, so his coach went first, and 'twas the Sultan snubbed, not Britain's representative.

Once they were inside the kraton, there was more difficulty over chairs. The Sultan led Tom and his ontoorage to an open pavilion, its roof rising in tiers above heavily carved columns painted yellow and white. Here the Sultan had placed upon a dais two carved and gilded teak chairs, one slightly behind the other. To test the quality of the man he had to deal with, the Sultan indicated Tom sh'd take the chair in the inferior position, as if he were a mere petitioner for his favour. Infuriated by this insolence, Tom demanded the chairs be placed side-by-side. The Sultan refused; his courtiers and guards – of which he had scores, hundreds, hordes – his courtiers and guards in unison drew their krises with a menacingly sibilant swish.

Much to his own astonishment, and to my very great alarm when I learned of it, my meek Tom, who is by nature as milky as a kitten, found himself drawing his own sword in response. This risked touching off a bloody massacre of the British, for he had few troops of his own with him, and the Malays are notorious for being easily roused to fanatical frenzy. A moment later, realising he did not wish to die, he came to his senses and he sheathed his sword again. He said he didn't quite know what he intended by drawing his sword, but by sheathing it he intended conciliation – tho' not submission. But whatever he intended his act was received as one of authority; 'twas received as the cool, confident action of a man who assumes he's made his point.

The Sultan took the inferior chair, his guards and courtiers sheathed their krises, and Tom too sat down. A treaty was signed, regulating dealings between Britain and Yogyakarta, but Tom is convinced the Sultan has little intention of honouring it, and he says he expects further trouble from that quarter. He decided not to pay the kraton a second visit before quitting Yogyakarta, a calculated breach of etiquette intended to make the arrogant Sultan aware who it is yields power now.

January 1812, Buitenzorg

Tom and me have moved from the poisonous swamps of Batavia to the sweet, clean air of Buitenzorg. 'Tis situated in a delightful, healthful spot on high ground. Torrents tumble past it and two burning mountains stand behind it. The mosquitoes here are fewer, less moithersome, than in other parts of the Eastward, and the climate is good, the heat less like a panting creature crouching to pounce – today 'tis almost as cool as summer in England. Still, the palace we now inhabit ain't very comfortable, and w'd not be called *palace* at home, so 'tis perhaps fitting we rename it Government House – Tom teases he is *at present* satisfied with this less grandiose title for his residence. Notwithstanding the repairs made over the last few weeks the roof leaks. What's more the floors and ceilings are in places more gap than good wooden plank; newly replaced doors warp in their frames; the servants wage constant battle against white ants, and Cook yesterday chased from the kitchen a badger called a *teledu* that is a notorious stinkard.

For all that, the building is a handsome one, something in the nature of an old English mansion. The main part of the house is a circular-fronted building, with to each side a wing connected to it by a covered walkway. Behind, there are the servants' quarters, and the kitchen, and various outbuildings and offices.

Tom and me occupy the central building, which has the largest, lightest, airiest rooms. This portion of the house also holds the principal offices of government, and here too are billeted Tom's ~~aides-de-camp~~ ~~aid-des~~ aide-de-camps who are mostly young and boisterous – one of these, Travers, is super-eminent in his loyalty to Tom, and tho' I must call his manner of speech dull and pompous, and tho' too his eyes bulge most unnervingly, like boiled eggs, none c'd fault his steadfast desire to serve my husband's best interests. The secretariat is accommodated mostly in the wings, but with some munshis in the outbuildings.

Tom will make often the forty-mile journey to Batavia for council meetings, and other official engagements; he will spend each week two days or so in town. I will go now and then to hold Drawing Rooms for the ladies there, or to act as hostess at official receptions. The journey is at its quickest about four hours, and our stud is necessarily large, as no one can travel with fewer than four horses, and often Tom takes six. We have at present more than sixty horses in the stable – native ponies that we love and think the most beautiful creatures in this world.

We have also fat oxen in the stall, and extensive farms and gardens; here we will grow our potatoes, and almost every description of English vegetable, not forgetting water-cresses, and sweet grasses as provender for the animals.

Leonora and Loftie and Mary Ann and Flint remain in Batavia, so 'tis only my spinster sister Hannah has moved with us and I shall lead henceforth a retired life, unruffled by the squalls of town.

January 1812, Buitenzorg

There is in these parts a primitive orchestra called a *gamelan* – an ensemble of xylophones, drums, and gongs, the instruments gorgeously carved, sometimes to resemble mythical animals, and painted red and black, and with their various curlicues all gilded. Tom has now bought a gamelan – for the sum of one a thousand Spanish dollars! – and he has hired musicians to play it, so we have all day its music spilling through the house. Some say the gamelan sounds like bells, but to me it sounds more like cold, clear water, dripping, dripping.

Tom bought his gamelan 'cause he thinks this orchestra's

presence in the Eastward predates the coming of Mahomedanism, and he is minded to make a comprehensive collection of such relict things. Accordingly, he buys also other objects he thinks have an antique link with past richness: krises, and curiosities, and leather puppets from the *wayang kulit* – a strange type of wordless entertainment in which puppets, thin as shadows themselves, throw their jerking shadows on a screen, as if they were cut-paper silhouettes that started moving. Wayang kulit tells of the epic adventures of Indian gods and heroes, and c'd there be better evidence, asks Tom, that the Hindoo faith once held sway in all East-Insular India?

Tom intends one day to ship his curiosities to England, for he thinks if only he c'd show in Leadenhall St. the past achievements of Javanese artisans, and thus prove to the Court of Directors that in spite of the crude impoverishment of its present, Java was once home to a society far advanced towards civilisation, then the Hon. Mems. w'd take greater interest in our land of promise than they are now wont to do.

Alas, it ain't just his gamelan, all Tom's collections gobble dollars. The servants cannot understand his expenditure has a purpose beyond mere heedless acquisition, and I know they complain in the kitchen he cares arrogantly little for money, and if there is anything he wishes to buy he pays for it, and 'tis shocking the money paid out daily from his safe.

I do not begrudge my husband his enthusiasms, but I must in conscience confess 'tis no wonder we seem always to be in debt.

January 1812, Buitenzorg

Tom is so busy and so much in Batavia I never see him now oftener than once in eight or ten days – ain't this sad, miserable? – but I will not again whine as I did when he was away at the eastern courts, instead I will look upon the world and be content. This beautiful Java! This fertile soil! Tom says all he must do to have a plant is to spit out a seed, and where it falls vegetation grows up and shoots out great branches.

Everything here is enchanting – tho' this can be a violent land. From where I write now, on the verandah, I can see rising in the distance our two mist-veiled burning mountains called Salak and Gidi, neither presently spewing fire and cinders, tho' each evening the sun as it sets seems to send tongues of flame licking from their summits. As warning one will blow, we are told, we will see lightening round its peak, and all the animals living on its slopes will flee. Sh'd these warning signs be seen, on either mountain, a witch doctor will circumambulate its slopes quoting verses from the Mahomedan holy book, to soothe the mountain's angry guardian spirit.

For doubt of the protective efficacy of charms and prayers I now think it possible I may die an ashy death not often met by Englishwomen.

March 1812, Buitenzorg

Nothing of importance has happened in this parish these past two months, but now there is much commotion, and I have been given most distressing cause to remember that letter I once read from Tom to the Sultan of Palembang, when I interrupted the work of the munshi Abdullah, who was in the midst of translating it from English into Malay, for reports now reach us of despicable horror and insurrection at that depraved Sumatran court.

Aye, the Sultan there turns out to be a murderous, wayward, wicked man who some months back massacred the local Dutchmen and allowed his troops to rape the Dutchwomen, and now his crimes have come to light that villain tries to justify his villainy by claiming Tom *ordered* the massacre, when he wrote comparing the cruelty and greed of the Hollanders, to the beneficence of the British, saying Tom told him to strike out and finish utterly the Dutch, and he now refuses to submit to Britain, or to swear fealty to King George, for all that Palembang is a dependency of Batavia, and so now 'tis us that has it.

Tom, outraged in all directions, has decided this infinite and endless liar must feel the force of our troops to teach him how to be good, so he has ordered Gillespie to Palembang, to mete out justice, and to place on the throne a sultan less treacherous, more tractable than the one now occupies it.

Tom takes this initiative without first receiving authority to do so from Ld. Minto. In acting thus, he is aware he takes too much responsibility on himself, but the expedition must be dispatched at once, or wait another whole year 'cause of the winds. Still, he don't think he deviates too materially from instructions, and he is confident he and the Governor-General are of one mind with regard to Banca and the tin.

Aye, here's the rub: from Palembang is controlled an island, Banca, which is so rich in tin Tom says it may be considered an immense mine. The tin is traded with China, where 'tis made into cooking pots, for enormous profit, and Tom and Ld. Minto have long thought Banca ought to be occupied as they want that profit for The Company. Hence Tom has now told Gillespie possession of Banca is to be the indispensable condition of his conquest of Palembang.

I sh'd not confess it, but 'tis good to have excuse to write Gillespie's name, I ain't seen the man now for months. But if here is reason to regret the retired seclusion of my country life, then I confide it in none but this my diary of my most secret self, which being dumb can't tell it.

April 1812, Buitenzorg

I am exhausted by the activities of the past fortnight. We have had staying here the sultans of Cirebon, a region on the north coast, hitherto independent and lawless, now newly brought under our control. The sultans arrived with their numerous retainers on March 25, to render their fealty to the British government. We had also visiting at the same time a noble from the court of Surakarta bearing a name so impossibly long and difficult to pronounce we called him simply *Pangeran*, that is, *Prince*. Pangeran had with him three of his sons, and some of his troops, so for a while 'twas a full house I had.

Tom received the sultans ceremoniously with due display of guns and cavalry. After they'd rested a few nights, we removed all the party to Rijswijk, where over the succeeding days we gave many elegant receptions and entertainments, introducing our guests to all the civil and military officers of Java, and inviting also prominent Dutchmen.

Most memorable of all our *fetes* was a fishing party we organised on a pretty stretch of the Ciliwung River three miles or so outside Batavia, where the banks had been cleared to make pro tempore a park.

The weather smiled on us, and the townwards bank was lined, that morning, by so many carriages bringing guests from Batavia it c'd have been a fashionable drive in London.

The sultans of Cirebon wore native dress, of baju and sarong, but Pangeran looked very splendid in British military uniform, with medals on his chest, and most impressive epaulettes of gold braid. Alas, none of our military men c'd identify his intended rank, or what regiment he meant to compliment by donning this uniform, and none dared to ask him.

We had set up seating and a stage on our rough newly-created lawn, which was soft and slippery, so my skirts became muddied. The sultans, their retinues, and our many guests, were first entertained by Javanese dancers, accompanied by the gamelan. Alas, this entertainment I c'd not count a success – indeed, quite the opposite, for I must call it bawdy. The English spectators were most surprised by the dancers' uncouth attitudes and gestures, tho' the rude Dutch relished them, and they evidently delighted too the Javanese nobility – and tho' I c'd not show it, for being Lady Governess, they in secret delighted *me*! O, what a struggle to keep my features in order! To look at the shocked faces of the English ladies, you'd think Dame Grundy had left her home in England and moved to Batavia.

But tho' I laughed behind my hand, I was most confused. I had seen before only courtly Javanese dances, and those were never dances such as these. Later, I discovered from quizzing the natives, we had through absolute misfortune laid on a type of dance called *tari kawulo*, that, 'cause of its gestures and nuances, is called *the dance of the prostitutes*. I am told tari kawulo is popular in peasant villages far from the Javanese courts, tho' it ain't not seen often in the kratons.

After these unseemly dancers had retired, breakfast was served in an atap bungalow erected especially for the purpose, and all ate *kitchri*, a native mess of rice and onions, and fruit, and bread, and drank much coffee with sugar, and everything laid out with taste. Tom's band – The Governor's band – played during the repast several popular tunes and pieces of music.

Once we were done with *dejoonay*, we moved by means of a bamboo bridge, somewhat precarious, to a second temporary bungalow, set up to be floating in the centre of the river – the ingenious floor of which bungalow was able to trap fish! Other fish we caught by tipping into the river a secret jangal poison known only to the Malays, brewed from some intoxicating vegetable, by which the fish became immediately inebriated, so 'twas easy to scoop them from the water.

After the fishing party our guests stayed on a few days at Rijswijk, until the sultans of Cirebon caught an Arab dhow bound for their home. Tom and me then brought Pangeran, his sons, and their retinue back here to Buitenzorg; now they have left overland for Surakarta and thank God all is quiet again.

April 1812, Buitenzorg

From returning after being absent a few days, and from the blessed relief all my guests are gone, I now come to a happy realisation: my house ain't the best appointed, but this beautiful Buitenzorg is my *home*. And from this realisation comes another: I hitherto never truly thought of any place as home. Still, from not belonging nowhere I was at least mostly spared the misery of homesickness, a useful sort of sparing for this rambling life of mine.

April 1812, Buitenzorg

So much for flattering Pangeran with lively dancers and inebriated fish. It seems quondam Dutch laxity encourages the Susuhunan of Surakarta, and likewise the Sultan of Yogyakarta, to dream still of maintaining a state of absolute independence from Britain, which Tom cannot tolerate. Aye, our informants have told my husband of a secret correspondence between those two troublesome courts, which are together plotting rebellion, and have treacherous design in agitation.

Tom is much alarmed by the uppity sultans' disloyalty, tho' he knew all along to expect it, such are the devious intrigues of the natives. The conduct and disposition of the Sultan of Yogyakarta in particular are so unfavourable and unsafe that his removal becomes necessary. Tom hopes to be able to effect the change quickly, and without bloodshed, but for all that he is peaceable he has ordered troops to Yogyakarta, and prepares to journey there himself, to deal with the dissension from that court – his spies report the sultan is strengthening the walls around his kraton, against our canon.

April 1812, Rijswijk

Since I grew so lonely and felt so neglected last time Tom went touring the eastern courts, I now insist on accompanying him to Yogyakarta. Hence we are both in Batavia, preparatory to our departure, and here our good military officers last night gave a ball in my honour.

I wore a new dress, white, with puff sleeves, as is my style, and to my delight the younger Dutch women are beginning to copy from me this elegant European fashion. Indeed, 'twas remarked on all sides how great an improvement has been introduced in respect to the attire of the Dutch ladies since I became Lady Governess, and the kebaya is already almost disused, except amongst the older chapter, and all I regret is I have no power to improve the Dutch women's faces, which remain a queer set of phizes.

Everything at the ball was in the first style, and my military hosts were kindly unremitting in their attentions to me – Gillespie not amongst them, as he is still away to Palembang, tho' I did not much note his absence. But, alas, I c'd not join in the dance to which I am usually so partial, and partake of with much spirit, and, let me say it, success, for I was feeling poorly, and still do, and our family doctor, Sir Thomas Sevestre, who lives with us at Buitenzorg, has directed me to drink daily from a draft of mercury salts, and this I will do tho' mercury tastes bitter vile, and causes in me interior gouts, not forgetting the cure ain't working if it don't set a mouth to drooling and slobbering like a hungry dog.

Later: Well! She daren't quite say I'm naught but winter fodder, but Our Mary Ann ain't never averse to reminding me by little nudges that I am turned of forty. Now my sister has called for the sole purpose, I think, of conveying 'tis the opinion of the *young* wives of our good British army officers arrived fresh from Calcutta, that the European fashions here are so backwards as to be almost fantastical, and 'tis *them* must henceforth set the tastes in Java! Ye gods! And them with not an inhabited head between them!

May 1812, The Residency, Semarang

Tho' my health remains delicate, I was able, as planned, to take my place in the buggy, to accompany Tom and his ontoorage here to Semarang, a congenial and pretty port east of Batavia, from its position well-placed for marching on Yogyakarta, due south over the mountains.

The Residency here, where we now stay, is remarkable for its garden, for scattered across the lawn are to be found fragments of strange stone carvings: women's limbless torsos, almost naked and shocking lifelike; half of a man holding a kris; many pieces of the Buddha. Tom says these relics come from the ruins at Borobudur, which ain't far off, and he has written to Mackenzie to ask: how goes along the survey?

May 1812, The Residency, Semarang

The European and half-caste inhabitants here number together about five hundred, and last night the local fashion and beauty, including the principal Dutch fashionables, held for us a ball and supper – one much enlivened by the bewitching power of Bacchus. Indeed, Travers, who travels with us, and some of Tom's other young aide-de-camps became so noisy, boisterous, and convivial, and their joshing became so rich and ripe 'tis as well for them I am no sister to Dame Grundy.

June 1812, The Residency, Semarang

I don't say I note it in particular, but Gillespie has arrived at

Semarang to lead our troops in the forthcoming action against Yogyakarta.

Our Rollicking Colonel rushed his men here direct from Palembang – where he was most disappointed to have been deprived a fight. Aye, when he and his troops arrived at the battlements of that benighted court, they found military action was unnecessary: the inhabitants had risen up against their wicked sultan, and gone on the rampage, and fired and ransacked the palace, and forced their oppressor to flee, so 'twas without hard service, or even any fighting at all, that Gillespie hoisted the Union Jack, and placed on the throne a Sultan friendly to us.

This Sultan has agreed we can henceforth take control of all the income from the tin trade at Banca – which income is more than ever necessary 'cause to Tom's surprise and distress, The Company's expenditure in Java continues much more than its returns.

June 1812, The Residency, Semarang

It cannot be good the Lieutenant-Governor's wife cannot look her husband's Commander of the Forces in the eye, yet when me and Gillespie must meet – which is often – I am unnatural polite to him, and he to me, and when our gazes do by accident collide, it seems to me he sees my innards, and I seem to see the flesh beneath his uniform – and, ye gods, how I hope Tom don't find this diary.

June 1812, The Residency, Semarang

I am all restless and in worried agitation: Gillespie is soon again to be in the thick of it, and Tom must now face dangers to his civil authority, and to his reputation; the two men rode for the kraton of Yogyakarta yesterday, to put a stop to the wily sultan's treachery with troops about a thousand strong. The certainty of a fight causes my husband, no warrior, and gentle, deep anxiety, just as it does me, but 'tis to Gillespie's great satisfaction.

June 1812, The Residency, Semarang

O what relief! A rider came today, to report that after brief hard service both within and outside the walls, Gillespie and his brave troops quickly captured the kraton at Yogyakarta, with scarcely any loss of life on our side and with on theirs much tumult, disturbance, clamour, and fuss, so they were utterly broke and defeated, and we have removed the unsafe sultan and placed on the throne his son, the quondam Crown Prince, who is said to be malleable, and minded to promote our interests.

Now that Yogyakarta has felt the full weight of British might, and, indeed, suffered moral collapse in the face of the discipline and bravery of our redcoats, 'tis expected traitorous opposition to our rule at Surakarta will float away like smoke.

For all the gladness of this news, I feel most unwell, and this morning my skin takes on a yellowish tinge.

September 1812, Buitenzorg

Do not charge me, Dear Diary, with neglecting you, there is a reason I ain't once picked up my quill since June: in that month a recurrence of my liver left me labouring under a very severe illness. Aye, as soon as news came we had prevailed at Yogyakarta, where Tom remained so c'd not help me by his presence, an abscess burst in the right lobe of my liver. The quantity of mercury which my doctor at Semarang decided 'twas immediately necessary to throw into this dangerous organ, to save my life, so effectually reduced my strength and shook my constitution that there was serious alarm I'd die.

Tom, when he returned found me all over yellow, and raving so sickly he told me later his nerves came all unstrung and his ideas were so confused he hardly knew what to say.

The crisis came, and I survived it. After, Tom stayed with me in Semarang for my convalescence. Travelling was for many weeks impossible, and 'twas not until the beginning of this month that my health was sufficiently re-established to admit the possibility. Then, as soon as was practicable, Tom brought me by easy stages back here to Buitenzorg.

I suppose I was as little ravaged by this journey as c'd have been expected, but I am still extremely weak and indisposed, tho' I hope the delightful climate of Buitenzorg will soon enable me to resume my habitual duties and activities. 'Tis such a relief to be back here, and to feast my eyes on the view I may not have lived to see again. How it moves me by its beauty, even more now than before, 'cause of my liver's reminder: you will die, Olivia. And how the view and my liver together conspire to make me ponder eternal things. Now, when I look upon our two burning mountains, I ask myself: what god c'd create both beauty such as I see with my own eyes, and also the horror that we are told is hell? What god c'd create both the stars sprinkled like salt across the heavens, and also have me believe that when I am dead my body will be consumed by fire, and, once consumed, reassembled to be burned again, and all for asking: is it true, God, you made the heavens? No, beauty, for existing, seems to me to deny 'twas made by a god w'd from jealousy damn his creatures 'cause they doubted him – is it not likelier the world was made from the feathers of hornbills and cassowaries, such as our native primordial believe?

October 1812, Buitenzorg

Death that pro tempore spared me, has scythed another: news

reaches us from Mrs. Raffles in Walworth that her husband, Tom's unsatisfactory father that I never met, died some months back in the almshouse for derelict Old Salts where he lived these past few years.

Tom reacts to this news with an indifference which don't seem studied. His disregard much saddens me; a son, I think, *sh'd* weep at his father's death, however inadequate was that father. But I cannot say so; I hold my tongue, and regret in silence all that Tom has lost, which ain't as much as his father has lost, but still he has lost all possibility of communion with the man that sired him, and here's sorrow.

October 1812, Rijswijk

Tom is to have a ship named for him – and 'tis me will name her! Aye, I am at last well enough to be driven into town in a carriage, and so I find myself once again at Batavia, whither I have travelled to break the bottle of wine over the bow.

Mary Ann and Leonora, of whom I have seen sadly little since before I went to Semarang, have both called on me today. They are both well – and so to my delight is Charlotte who is at long last reunited with her mother; the girl grows up beautifully, tho' Mary Ann don't seem to notice it.

October 1812, Rijswijk

I have completed to general satisfaction my ship naming duties! the *Governor Raffles* is a fine sloop, and, to hearty cheers, I broke the bottle at the first attempt, which sh'd bring her luck. She belongs to a Dutch magistrate here, and after the jolly work of naming was done he threw a ball at his mansion. Alas, I c'd not from continuing weakness partake of the delights of the sprightly dance. Instead, I sat on a sofa and drank wine, and many of my acquaintance came to tell me how regretful they were indisposition had so long deprived them of my presence at Batavia, and to flatter me this splendid party was so much more splendid for my presence.

Gillespie sat by me longest of all, and lied my looks had not suffered from my illness, and dared to take my hand a moment – such effrontery, tho' I can't in conscience pretend I was affronted – as he told me these past few months he'd often asked himself how long 'twould be before he c'd promise himself the happiness of my fascinating society.

We bantered until Tom came to fetch me to the pleasures of the festive board, whereupon Gillespie stood, and left us – I will not say he looked guilty, tho' Dame Grundy may. Once he'd gone, Tom's eyes go hard as peach stones, and he says: I grant he is courageous but I never thought you'd be a woman to value brawn over brains. Well! Notwithstanding I'd have flounced away in umbraged dudgeon if I'd had anywhere to flounce to, my traitorous cheeks set to blushing, and since I c'd think of nothing to say, I said nothing at all.

November 1812, Buitenzorg

Tom says, rueful, his talent ain't not for making immediate profit, and this 'cause the cottons he ordered last year to wring for The Company a market out of Java arrived about a fortnight back, and began to be sold in the pasar. These cottons are such remarkable well-travelled cloths their patterns c'd be woven from latitude and longitude, so to speak – as c'd the patterns of my life, now I come to think of it. I mean the cotton for them was grown in the West Indies, imported by The Company into Liverpool, spun and dyed in Lancashire … And now here they are in Java. But, alas, the dyes ain't fast, and the colours run at the first wash, and now this is known, nobody will buy them.

In consequence, Tom is more than ever anxious they will in Leadenhall St. see Java as a drain, for instead of the surplus revenue which for giving importance to the conquest, he asserted to be forthcoming from this island, he now finds it cannot be maintained without the treasure, as well as the troops, of Bengal. For fear of the harm done to the colony if he permits a continued expenditure beyond its means, he attempts now the renovation of the whole economy.

To bring more funds *into* the treasury he is raising new taxes: on horses and carriages; on the native allichol called *arak*; on candle-manufacture, &c. He is levying tolls on the roads, bridges, and ferries. He has introduced a poll tax on the Chinese. He also taxes opium, but less for profit than 'cause he thinks that wicked trade in lives and hazy stupefaction sh'd be eradicated, which don't go down well in Calcutta – Johnny Company regards opium as a source of revenue, no different from tea.

To prevent too much flow of funds *out of* the treasury he is determined to make economies in government expenditure. Since the internal resources of The Company are so horribly confined by the actual state of exterior commerce at the present moment he is removing from official employment a number of civil servants. Those that remain have more than ever a plurality of offices from which to line their pockets so Tom don't feel too guilty if he now introduces a system to control their expenses.

The most severe charges on the treasury come not from the civil service, but from the army. Tom knows there ain't no security for colonists without a judicious disposition of military force, nevertheless he thinks there are too many troops on Java, and wishes to drive their number down, and also to reduce expenditure on supplies. This has caused a severe rift with Gillespie; they squabble incessantly over the rations and living conditions of the troops; over army pay and allowances; over the sale of cavalry horses, which one thinks necessary, the other foolish; over the construction of a new arsenal, which one wants continued, the other stopped; over the great expense of maintaining the heavy artillery, which one thinks perfectly useless since those guns can't go nowhere in the jangal, and the other thinks essential. Every day brings some new point of contention.

Travers tells me Gillespie says by Tom he feels thwarted and misrepresented, where 'tis reasonable to expect cordial support and liberal confidence. Tom says that from Gillespie he encounters naught but provoking slights and petulant opposition. 'Tis clear as gin to all abroad there ain't no congeniality of sentiment between them, and Travers says 'tis common gossip at Government House the estrangement between the two chiefs must be attended by serious consequences to one or the other.

I refuse to wonder does my husband's antipathy to Gillespie, and Gillespie's to my husband, have anything to do with *me*?

November 1812, Buitenzorg

It has occurred to Tom that to bring increase to the treasury, he c'd transfer public territory to the management of private individuals – which is to say that public land may profitably be sold off to Europeans. He has accordingly had announced in *The Java Government Gazette* the outright sale by auction of such lands, for the benefit of the government. When he proposed this plan to his council, Gillespie was obstructive and said Tom ought to seek sanction from Calcutta, but Tom ruled there was neither need nor time for that, and the auction is now set for January.

January 1813, Buitenzorg

I see it is two months since last I wrote, during which time nothing very important has happened in this parish – except I have been in better health than of late. Aye, my liver has held up, and I engaged in the gambols of the Christmas season with spirit, and Tom said I partook of them beyond what his most sanguine expectations c'd have hoped last summer.

Now I pick up my pen to report the public lands Tom ordered sold to private investors have been auctioned off. Alas, the sale has provoked much querulous gossip and envy from those disappointed and bitter to lose the bidding. Some hint darkly *certain* investors seemed to have been given preferential treatment, or that plots were too large in acreage to give much chance to small investors, or that plots were valued too low so investors got them for too little money, which, these jealous carpers moan, was wicked cheating of the treasury – tho' they'd have sung a different tune if they'd won in the auction.

To give confidence to investors the lands will not be snatched back into the public domain by capricious fiat, neither of Calcutta, nor of some future Dutch administration, Tom himself has bought four lots of coffee plantations, he paid just under thirty thousand Spanish dollars, all of which he had to borrow, so we are now once more greatly in debt, and I must hope this investment is a wise shake of the money tree.

For all the trouble and backbiting about these land sales, the profit from them has brought considerable increase to the treasury.

January 1813, Rijswijk

Wellington has smote the French at Salamanca, which smiting occurred last July, tho' news of it reaches us only now. In consequence, Tom last night hosted a triumphal ball here at Rijswijk, a very grand and superb fete, fully attended and brilliant in both beauty and jewels. Notwithstanding our load of debt we bore all the expenses of the evening, which irks me, but Tom says he is the *Governor*, and we cannot appear as *paupers*.

The Commander of the Forces and the Lady Governess –

Gillespie and me – c'd not avoid leading off. O, what pleasurable torment to go down the line, my hand in his, and for the pleasure of that torment I completed our dance with my usual spirit, and, let me say it, my usual grace. Indeed, my health allowed me to keep up the sprightly dance with uncommon animation till half past twelve, when the party was summoned to the supper tables, which were decorated with the utmost taste, and covered with every delicacy and luxury Batavia can afford, not forgetting chocolate puffs and candied pineapples, and the whole conducted in a superior style of costly elegance.

Many appropriate and patriotic toasts were proposed to the King, Prinny, Wellington, and the army in Spain, &c, each one accompanied by bumpers and its music. Gillespie, very feeling, proposed *Mrs. Raffles and the ladies of Java*; its accompanying tune was *I would make you be willing to follow me*.

I went to my bed happy, but Tom had barely left this morning before Mary Ann was calling on me for no other reason than to purse her lips and to tut that last night Gillespie and me danced in such a high style she considered such a pair as us were not in the room. Tho' her words made little sense, I caught her meaning well enough.

Worse, I now learn from one of my maid servants, who had it from the water-carrier, that about the time Mary Ann was calling on me, Tom was calling on Gillespie at the barracks. My maid said she c'd not tell me why, and when I tried to discover from Travers what's doing, he looks shifty, and he mumbles: everything is settled to keep up appearances better in the future.

And I never did naught but *smile* at Gillespie, and blush in his presence, which is the honest amount of my confessions.

January 1813, Rijswijk

O, disarray! O, disorder! O, tumult, and confusion!

Gillespie and Tom have had a most furious intemperate disagreement ostensibly about the land sales – on which pretext I will not comment. This in Tom's office at Government House, and all the secretariat c'd hear them at it, and the servants all stopped their work and went to stare.

In the heat of passion Gillespie accuses Tom: sir, behind a show of public service you have been feathering your own nest, and besides being corrupt in the land sales you are quite impractical, your measures towards the army are ill-conceived and dangerous.

Tom don't in so many words call Gillespie a dullard, but he flashes back: sir, a man of action cannot be expected to understand the workings of the economy, and 'tis no dishonour to a soldier if he cannot grasp the business of government.

Gillespie, touchy, rash, and proud, at once resigns as the Commander of the Forces, which resignation Tom, over-sensitive, angry, and immoderate, at once accepts.

Before Gillespie had even stormed out of his office, Tom was at his desk, writing to Ld. Minto, to inform him what had happened. This I know 'cause my husband, flushed and fierce, later made particular point of telling me he'd *wasted no time* seeking advice from Calcutta who it is will relieve Gillespie. No, he says, No, Olivia, I won't give this whelp of a hag time for second thoughts.

I feel all unstrung, and must retire to bed with a bottle of cherry brandy.

February 1813, Buitenzorg

Home. But my health which I had thought recovered has taken a turn for the worse. I am severely afflicted with the gout in my head and stomach. Tom too is in poor health, and feels the effects of the climate very sensibly. Or else we both suffer the effects of his quarrel with Gillespie? In any case, I am much cast down, and

I find it difficult to retain my wonted spirit and animation, tho' I try to act in front of Tom invariably cheerful, for not wanting to alarm him, from one cause or another.

It don't help that until his replacement arrives Gillespie must remain in place, however much it galls him, and aggravates Tom, and discomforts me. Of course, there is as yet no word from Calcutta who is to relieve Our Rollicking Colonel, who is like to be here months yet.

February 1813, Buitenzorg

Authentic reports arrive we have been since last June at war with America – this over our British practice of pressing American seamen into our navy, an insult, they claim, to their national pride. Tom now goes about saying Americans ain't naught but opportunists who require our most watchful attention, and he never did trust them. As his contribution to our war effort, he has ordered that throughout Java there sh'd be imposed immediately a blockade on American ships.

It occurs to me the Americans purchase more Javanese coffee than any other nation, so Tom's blockade will hurt Java considerably more than America, but this opinion out of wifely discretion I keep to myself.

March 1813, Buitenzorg

The war with America has halted the coffee trade, and coffee is rotting in the stores. Alas, there seems a total want of demand for the other produce of this colony, excepting perhaps pepper, and even pepper prices are falling, and the profits from the Banca tin illusory, which fact weighs heavily on Tom, who is much harassed by the lamentably deficient state of the economy.

April 1813, Buitenzorg

Tom has lit upon a new idea for making Java profitable: he will establish from here trade links with Japan, which he calls the Great Land of the Rising Sun, and establish there a market for our goods. And this tho' Japan is a country that values her seclusion so high that, debarring one port she keeps open in Nangasaky as her chink onto the wider world, she has excluded all other nations from her shores, and confined herself within her own limits, at least these past two hundred years.

Notwithstanding this jealously guarded isolation, Tom is sanguine of success, for from studying the map, and noting Japan's latitude, he concludes the country must possess a climate where European manufactures are almost a necessary comfort, and where, if The Company acts judicious, the consumption of woollens and hardware may be rendered almost unlimited. He has written to warn the Court of Directors that if the attempt be not made to sell our stuffs to Japan whilst we have possession of Java the opportunity lost may never be regained.

Tom's ideas about his Great Land of the Rising Sun I think quite fantastical – altogether chimerical and impracticable – but I hold my tongue.

May 1813, Rijswijk

Behold me again, in Batavia, Dear Diary, and I sh'd confide straight off I ain't seen Gillespie not once while I've been in town, and nor w'd want to, neither.

But enough of that. I travelled here to feed bananas to a white elephant. Aye, in furtherance of his aim of establishing in Japan a market for our stuffs, Tom is soon to dispatch to Nangasaky a messenger with presents for the Emperor: plants, sheep, birds, wine, and decanters, a ground up Egyptian mummy, for its magical powers of healing, a clock – and this white elephant just arrived in Batavia from Siam.

Tom tells me that in Siam they believe white elephants to be sacred, and that for a king to be able to keep at his court one of these rare, magnificent holy beasts shows he reigns with justice, and that while the elephant lives the kingdom will be blessed with prosperity. Ergo, Tom trusts the Emperor of Japan will understand by his gift of a white elephant he intends to say he is a wise, just ruler, kind to his people, and able to furnish them with rice in abundance.

I worry Japan is very, very far from Siam and that my husband has lost his wits, for all Madame Elephant is very pretty and tame.

July 1813, Buitenzorg

Nothing worth telling has happened in this parish since I was last at my diary, in May. But we now hear from Calcutta Gillespie will be relieved by one General Sir Miles Nightingall. Ld. Minto writes he is an able and experienced commander, who has his backing as a man of honour and a gentleman in the highest degree. He sh'd arrive sometime in October, when Gillespie will quit hence.

I hear conflicting reports how Gillespie goes along. Some say he swaggers about town boasting he is pleased to be leaving, and wishes good riddance to Batavia; others say he was shocked Tom accepted his hasty resignation, and w'd have tried to withdraw it, except he has his pride.

I know what it is to be in two minds: o, when I think of Gillespie off to discompose some other settlement ...

August 1813, Buitenzorg

Reports come from Japan saying the people there have rebuffed our offer to sell them woollens and hardware. Still, Tom ain't too cast down, 'cause the Emperor accepted all his presents, debarring only the clock and the white elephant, and this acceptance Tom regards as an unusual favour.

The Emperor did not accept the clock 'cause, as we now learn, to our distress at the blunder, the Japanese have a horror of them as gifts, believing they indicate the giver wishes the receiver's time slipped away.

Meanwhile, Madame Elephant c'd not be persuaded into the sling intended to lower her onto a barge to ferry her from ship to shore, and even if she c'd have been, it was decided she w'd have sunk any barge available in Nangasaky. The Japanese came out to gawk at her, and to sketch her, but she never disembarked, and I think our Madame Elephant will be remembered as a most troublesome, burdensome gift, for all she is so beautifully white, and now she is to be returned to Siam, to be indulged and petted there.

Notwithstanding Nangasaky was cool to our overtures, Tom is convinced his messenger has paved the way to further and more decisive attempts to establish trade links between Java and Japan, with every prospect of success, and he is most delighted with accounts of the Japanese. These, he declares, are a people whose bodily and mental powers must assimilate much nearer to those of fair-skinned people, than do Asiatics in general, and they are indeed remarkable for their frankness of manner and disposition, for intelligent inquiry, and for freedom from prejudice – all this, he says, 'cause the Japanese exist at a similar latitude to Europeans.

September 1813, Rijswijk

Nightingall, our new Commander of the Forces, is expected in the next few days, and so Gillespie must now be away to Calcutta.

Our Rollicking Colonel let it be known he wanted to go off quietly, but for all the difficulties between them, this Tom w'd not allow, as 'twould have reflected badly on the dignity of his person, and on his government, if he had let his Commander of the Forces slink away like a disgraced dog.

Thus we held for Gillespie last night a magnificent ball and supper. All the *bo mond* of Batavia attended, and the beauty of the grounds here was heightened by the brilliancy of the illuminations, which were tastefully arranged. The hours of the evening flew rapidly along in the amusements of dancing, music, and cards, till we retired to the festive board, which was covered with all that luxury c'd wish for, and decorated with more than usual elegance.

A great deal of wine was drunk – so much I fancy few of the number present witnessed before so drunken a scene. Tom I think drank to blot out a secret shame he'd acted childish towards Gillespie, mixed with relief the man is going. As to Gillespie, I doubt not he was trying to blot out many things, on divers counts.

In any case, Tom and Gillespie were both in their cups, and to a person unacquainted with preceding events they must have appeared the best of friends, for they partook of a most unreserved conversation, with reiterated professions of goodwill, tho' I think it doubtful either knew at the time what he was saying, or can remember now what was said, and then first one man, and then the other was chaired around the room.

Later, I retired to the verandah, to breathe air slightly cooler than that in the ballroom, and from there I went into the garden, and took a secluded path, and walked and cooled my face. I did not mean to catch Gillespie's eye as I slipped outside, nor as I slipped into the garden neither, but still he saw me go, and followed me. I halted beneath a palm tree, its leaves fanned flat against a sky all embedded with its stars. Gillespie swayed to join me, and he took me by both my hands, and he slurred he'd depart Java with but *one* regret, and, tho' drunken, by tone of voice, looks, gesture made clear as gin the nature of that one regret, he then took me in his arms, and pressed his mouth to mine, and kissed me.

O, the dizzy, giddy swirl of a kiss! But I did not feel it then. No, Gillespie's kiss turned to ashes in my mouth, and for a shocked moment my vision filled with the palm fronds fanned above me, like a peacock's tail, and each feathery leaf with its eye – Tom's eye, hurt, betrayed, angry, judging – until I felt myself watched a hundred times by my husband. So I roused myself, and I pushed Gillespie away.

Gillespie's eyes widened – went very wide. He blasphemes and then he slurs: what, you? Just another prissy tease?

Ye gods! A tease? Says I: Sir, I am a married woman and never teased nobody and am no more prissy than a piss-pot. All the reply I got was a grunt, and with this grunt Gillespie turned and lurched away, and so ended all my pretty dreamy notions of him, and all that's left of them now is regret at what I did not do, and exasperation with myself, and with Tom, that if my husband knew of this scene, he'd no doubt smile he'd known all along I'd be too frit to be bolder.

October 1813, Rijswijk

Here's consternation! Gillespie has quit hence, and to make sure he'd gone, Tom sent as his representative Travers, to say farewell, and also to warn him, by hints and covert, indirect suggestion, that when he reaches Calcutta he sh'd not from malice or envy blackguard my husband's good name.

Travers, super-eminent in conscientiousness, saw Gillespie off not only as far as the beach, but followed even him on board the ship – and then: calamity. I can hardly write it for dismay, but I have it from Mary Ann, who had it from Flint, who had it direct from Travers himself, that Gillespie had barely got aboard before he was telling all who cared to listen 'twould be his duty, when he got to Calcutta, to expose Tom's dishonesty, speculation, peculation, and deceit in the matter of the land sales, and likewise his high-handed incompetence in matters military. He bragged this w'd be his revenge 'cause Tom went behind his back when he wrote to Ld. Minto that he, Gillespie, was not fit for the Java command.

'Tis evident to me, as it must be to all Batavia, that Gillespie is affronted he is bettered, and sore 'tis him quitting Java, not Tom. But will what is evident here be likewise evident in Calcutta? Gillespie is a man of good family, an officer, a dashing soldier; Mary Ann says Flint and Travers are united in the opinion he must be believed by society in Calcutta, whatever false charge he concocts.

My nerves! I again feel all unstrung and it must be at least two months – more likely three or four – until we can know how Gillespie gets along.

October 1813, Rijswijk

I am low in spirits and far from well, with continuing severe fits of the gout in my head and stomach. I tell myself these gouts are the effects of the hot climate, and in any case 'tis true I will not be able to remain in the Eastward many years longer, for the way the heat withers me.

October 1813, Rijswijk

Nightingall has arrived aboard the *Nearchus*. He seems a most upstanding fellow, with a fine flow of spirits, entirely free from arrogance. His wife accompanies him, and her too I liked at once. Florentia is a warm and open creature, affectionate, and affable. Indeed, even only at our introduction, she confided, in an altogether unsolicited manner, that 'tis her husband's fixed intention to keep clear of any difficulties and differences which have taken place here previous to his arrival. Aye, these two seem set to become most happy ornaments to our little society, and I think it certain that henceforth relations between the civil and the military arms of government will be less jealous and peppery than of late.

October 1813, Rijswijk

Now Tom can leave Batavia to the charge of good Nightingall, he announces 'tis both his pleasure and his necessary duty to make another journey to the eastern parts of Java. 'Tis his *pleasure* 'cause he is eager to visit the ruins Mackenzie is surveying at Borobudur. 'Tis his *duty* 'cause he must show himself at those annoying courts of Surakarta and Yogyakarta, to remind both their sultans and their people who is ruled, and who is ruler. Notwithstanding my health, I am determined to accompany Tom on this journey, for if I now return without him to Buitenzorg my lot there must be loneliness and misery.

November 1813, the *Malabar*, off the coast of Java

Behold me again at sea, Dear Diary. This morning Tom and me boarded the *Malabar*, and now we sail for Semarang, on our way to the eastern courts.

They gave us a good send off at Batavia; we were accompanied from Government House by a great crowd of military men and civilian officials, and an escort of hussars. At the wharf we were received by a detachment of soldiers, and as we were ferried from the shore to the *Malabar* salutes were fired, both from batteries on land and from ships in the roads. More salutes were fired when we boarded, and then we got underway in the company of the East Indiaman the *Aurora*. I hope this short sea voyage will do much to restore my health to full robustness.

December 1813, The Residency, Semarang

I have been in Semarang about ten days, but I ain't until now found time to write for the whirl of dinners, balls, breakfasts, &c, held to welcome us, and for taking an excursion of three days, to visit the ruins at Borobudur.

Mackenzie was our guide, and with him his assistant, a young Dutch engineer he rates most high. The last part of our journey was on foot, along a barely passable jangal track, all mud, roots, vines, leaves, and whining skeins of mosquitoes. We c'd not have made progress without our porters' *parangs* – heavy native knives made to slash through the densest undergrowth – and we were not ten yards into the forest before I was slithery with exertion, my skin running beneath my skirts with veritable *rivulets* in a variety of unmentionable places.

At last we came to a hill of stone, carved by man, but now much under attack from the vegetable kingdom – mosses obscured friezes, roots pushed through cracked slabs, and vines everywhere dripped down tumbled walls like candle wax.

For all its decay, and the encroaching jangal, and for being half-buried in ash spewed from the burning mountain that stands not far off, the beauty of the ruins spoke of the building. The hill was magnificent: a stepped pyramid formed by terraces carved all about with mysterious reliefs, a thousand years old, Tom said. A crumbled structure occupied the whole top of the hill – 'twas once a dome, tho' now its roof is fallen in from being shaken about by the occasional earthquakes of this violent land.

The Buddha was everywhere, his statue here standing palms raised in benediction, here kneeling cross-legged, one hand on the earth, here likewise kneeling, but with his hands to his navel. His face in every statue looked so serene 'twas almost blank.

On seeing all the tumbled stones, and the smashed carvings my husband became almost overwrought. O, he says, o, what noble monuments to the ancient splendour of religion and the arts now submitting to the destructive hand of time and nature, and how melancholy that the art which raised them has perished before them, and more melancholy still that the faith which they were to honour now has no other honour in the land.

I reminded him we had with us a picnic. An immense slab of granite served us for a table, and limbs of mutilated gods and goddesses were our chairs.

Before we retraced the track that had led us to this wondrous site of Borobudur, Tom ordered many detached pieces of sculpture be taken away for his collection – Buddha heads, a voluptuous dancing woman, as w'd have shocked Dame Grundy, a carving of the long-stemmed flower called *lotus* – all bearing silent witness to the pre-Mahomedan grandeur and magnificence of Javanese culture.

But enough with Java's past glories; Tom must contend with the present: tomorrow we quit hence, for Surakarta; we will be accompanied by a military detachment, as well as civilian officials, and the journey will take two days; we will break it overnight at a fort conveniently situated on the route.

December 1813, The Residency, Surakarta

Tom and me have arrived in Surakarta with all our ontoorage. We stay with the British Resident, Major Jerimiah Johnson, whom I must describe as nondescript. Tonight he is to host for us an elegant dinner, which he promises will pass with much conviviality and many favourite toasts, and where he will introduce us to various officials, both military and civilian, both British and Dutch, and their wives. Tomorrow, we pay our respects at the kraton.

December 1813, The Residency, Surakarta

What a day of pomp and processions: soldiers, both redcoats and

Javanese; booming salutes of artillery; sharp, clattery volleys of musketry; drums beating; trumpets sounding; colour; opulence; excitement; exhaustion.

But I rush ahead of myself. As Tom and me this morning approached the kraton, our carriage accompanied by our cavalry, we found the road lined by hundreds – thousands – of bare-chested, barefoot Javanese spearmen, dressed in sarongs richly woven with gold thread, with their krises tucked into their belts and their black hair hanging loose and long about their proud faces – they w'd have looked most warlike and fearsome except to be peaceable the points of their spears were covered with native cloths.

We entered the kraton, and halted at an outer court. On alighting from our carriage we were greeted by the Susuhunan, a plump man in middle age, and his official consort, much younger, together with the Crown Prince, our old friend Pangeran, and various milling others, including ladies I supposed must be the Susuhunan's other wives, and all of them, both men and women, diminutive.

The Susuhunan's official consort is called *Ratu Kencana*, or *Golden Queen*, a fitting title, 'cause she was so covered in gold she c'd have been gilded. She was dressed in a kebaya woven with much gold, and she was everywhere hung about with yet more gold – bracelets, necklaces, nose rings, earrings, hair pins – and as if gold were not enough she glittered as she moved with precious stones of all colours that were stitched and tucked about her person, not forgetting pearls. The Susuhunan, who was shaded everywhere he went by a yellow umbrella held by a slave, was likewise glittery and swathed in such a quantity of golden sarong I think a man-of-war c'd have had a mainsail from it.

I c'd not speak to our golden king and queen, nor they to me, since they know no English, and I know too little Malay – and Tom says they anyway do not deign to speak Malay, which they regard as the gross tongue of the common folk, but must speak in High Javanese.

Ratu Kencana, speechless, but jangling with her jewellery and smiling, escorted me through a guard of yet more bare-chested Javanese spearmen to the audience hall. Tom, Major Johnson, the Susuhunan, The Crown Prince, other members of the Royal Family, various officials both Javanese and British, and troops of both nations all followed us.

The audience hall, or pavilion, had a tiered roof, much carved, gilded and painted, but no walls – the best sort of room in the heat of the tropics. The ceiling and the columns supporting it were as ornate as the roof. The floor was of worn stone, smooth and cool like the surface of a still pool. Those of us of the British chapter walked upon it shod, our heels clicking, the Javanese all went shoeless, their footfalls silent.

Gilded chairs of state were waiting on a dais – heavy chairs, all carved about with flowers, leaves, monsters. Tom took the one to the Susuhunan's right, I sat on his left. The Crown Prince and the court officials sat on the floor in a double row; our officials stood.

Volleys of musketry were fired, both within the kraton's walls and outside them. The Resident's band played *God Save The King*, and then gamelan music rippled everywhere, the instruments played by the court musicians.

Tea, coffee, and wine were served by female slaves I was told came from Bali. Several toast were proposed – those from the Malay chapter to our British one elaborately flowery, if our translators had them right.

Speeches followed, very windy.

I trust I bore the due ceremonies with spirit and dignity, and now I am weak and wan and languid from tiredness, and I must put down my quill that I may sleep.

December 1813, The Residency, Surakarta

Tom took me today to visit Dr. Horsfield, the natural historian who told him of Borobudur, the same he met the first time he was in Surakarta. The good doctor lives in a splendid, spacious mansion, and, just as Tom had promised, this serves both as his dwelling, and as a giant cabinet of curiosities. We wandered his garden a while, to see the statuary strewn there, and then Dr. Horsfield took us inside to see his many botanical, zoological, and geological specimens.

He also demonstrated to us the thrillingly deadly effects of the sap of the Upas Tree – *upas* is a local word for *poison*. The primordial people of the jangal, those that creep about with their darts and blow pipes, make deadly use of this notorious tree, which is said to be so dangerous it can kill a man standing downwind of it, who breathes in its mortal miasma. Be that as it may, the primordials dip their darts in its sap, and with these deadly darts they slay their monkeys they feed off, and their other prey.

The sap is a milky gum, and this venom Dr. Horsfield injected into a poor unfortunate fowl and a dog, which both twitched and writhed to death within minutes, the dog howling the while. I was not happy at this display, and nor was Tom, but the killing work was done for the sake of scientific understanding: Dr. Horsfield is trying to uncover how it is the upas poison works, for he thinks it c'd have medicinal uses, and if animals must suffer that humans may not, so be it.

December 1813, The Residency, Surakarta

I held last evening a Drawing Room for the British and Dutch ladies of Surakarta, which was followed by a Javanese play. This I trust was greatly enjoyed by those with the language to understand the plot and dialogue.

Once the play was finished, I welcomed to my Drawing Room the male chapter of the Europeans residents here, and from the kraton the Susuhunan, Ratu Kencana, the Crown Prince, and their various attendants.

We had a most splendid exhibition of fireworks in the garden, and then two sets of dancing girls belonging to the Susuhunan gratified the company with a very excellent specimen of Javanese dancing.

At half past midnight the party adjourned to the supper tables, where we ate great quantities of duck, and greater ones still of rice and relishes. Tom proposed a toast to the Susuhunan, who in turn proposed a most effusive gracious toast to me, or so I was assured.

Later, in the ballroom, the Susuhunan and me led off – I was so much taller than him I felt like a giantess. We danced very badly, the steps being unfamiliar to him, and me being unable to explain them to him for my lack of Malay, let alone of High Javanese, and his of English. Meanwhile, Tom danced with Ratu Kencana.

Tom has since told me he thinks this may be the first ever time the Susuhunan danced with a European lady, and 'twas certainly the first time Ratu Kencana ever danced with a European man. I replied 'twas likewise the first time he'd danced with any Ratu Kencana, or me with any Susuhunan.

December 1813, The Residency, Surakarta

Today I must describe as difficult, 'cause I witnessed four tigers slain, and I do not care for blood sports, even when all that dies is a fox. The first death was in a fight between our unfortunate cat, and a buffalo. This horrid duel was at the kraton, where buffalo-tiger fights are apparently a standard royal entertainment.

Aye, hospitality swung back to the kraton today, and on our arrival this morning the Susuhunan conducted us to seats giving view of an *alun-alun* – a grassy square – guarded by a pair of shaggily sacred banyan trees, and now hemmed about by wooden palings, into which enclosure the buffalo and the tiger were forthwith admitted, and once admitted were goaded and roused into anger at each other by the watching crowds who poked at them with long poles thrust through the palings, some tipped with smouldering rags.

I had thought the tiger w'd at once dispatch the buffalo, but the poor, noble cat was gouged to death on the buffalo's horns, amidst much blood and feline screaming. A second tiger only narrowly escaped the same fate by creeping along the paling fence, crouching out of the cruel horns' jabbing reach.

Apparently, 'tis always this way: the buffalo bests the tiger. This reliable result is even more greatly pleasing to the Javanese than the anguish and the blood of the fight, for they are accustomed to compare the buffalo to themselves, and the tiger to the European, so it may readily be imagined with what eagerness they look forward to the success of the buffalo.

After the tiger-buffalo fight was done, we moved from the alun-alun to a pavilion where a square stage was lined by Javanese spearmen along its boundaries. Here we witnessed another horror: a *rampong macan*, or tiger-sticking. Into the square were introduced three tigers and a leopard; all four cats were promptly speared.

December 1813, The Residency, Yogyakarta

We have driven in our carriage with a military detachment and all our ontoorage from Surakarta to Yogyakarta. Our host, the Resident here, one John Crawfurd, is a most inhospitable man: a granite-eyed Scot of grim manner and beaky appearance, who keeps a stingy table. Tom says notwithstanding he is touchy, tight-fisted, and not very popular, he is a sound appointment, shrewd, and practical, fluent in both Malay and Javanese, and most effective in his dealings with the natives – in short a clever fellow he doubts not will have his day. But then Tom must defend Crawfurd, for 'twas my husband who appointed him.

December 1813, The Residency, Yogyakarta

We this morning paid our respects at the kraton, where we were met by the Sultan, and by his Ratu Kencana. The Sultan – the Crown Prince until last year's insurrection here led to our placing him on the throne – is most grateful to Tom for his elevation, and he showed a most unaffected pleasure at their meeting.

Today was another to demand of a woman much patient politeness in the face of all due honours: spearmen; slaves; refreshments; toasts, volleys of musketry; gamelan music; speeches, more speeches, &c. Alas, there was another buffalo-tiger fight to endure, and – ye gods! – another tiger-sticking.

The sky today was like a blue benediction, but beneath it was no compassion: the grisly duel between the tiger and the buffalo lasted a merciless hour. Then, to the gasps of the Javanese, the tiger unexpectedly emerged victorious. O, what consternation! In order, I suppose, that the natives may not think the spirits were set against them, the Sultan at once ordered a fresh buffalo into the alun-alun; it promptly did its duty and gored to death the exhausted tiger.

During the tiger-sticking that followed two more cats became carcasses.

December 1813, The Residency, Yogyakarta

These past few days have been as hospitably busy as those at

Surakarta, I have been at one moment a host, the next a guest, but tomorrow we depart Yogyakarta, so we have made our farewells at the kraton. The Sultan received us with ceremonies and compliments, and then he led us on a tour of the kraton, an enormous complex, home to thousands, that consists of many open-sided, tiered-roofed pavilions, a mosque, dwellings, barracks, rice granaries, &c.

When we put down the quondam sultan's insurrection, there was by all accounts much conflagration and general destruction within this kraton, not forgetting the looting that was our troops' due reward for their bravery, tenacity, and skill – our civilian officials got their portion too, but apart from some rough diamonds, Tom's share of the prize was only books and manuscripts, and various curiosities of interest to him tho' of no pecuniary advantage to us. But I stray. I mean to write the damage done by us to the kraton here has by now been everywhere repaired, and 'tis as gilded, carved, painted, and splendid as its cousin at Surakarta.

One part of the kraton was most interesting and pretty, the *taman sari*, a walled water garden, very old, that is a series of canals, fountains, water tanks, and pavilions surrounded by artificial lakes, the level of water within controlled by gates, and in all worthy to be called *taman sari*, which means *beautiful park*, and beneath it a network of tunnels, cool and damp that the Sultan showed us; they lead to a sacred pavilion, that can be accessed no other way, for it sits on an island in the centre of an expansive lake.

After we'd finished wandering the taman sari, our party proceeded to the audience hall where refreshments were served by slaves – woolly-haired primordials from Borneo. After, Tom and me were conducted by the Sultan and his Ratu Kencana to the palace's private apartments, where we were introduced to the Sultan's other wives, his mother, and various princesses of the court. One tiny, wizened old lady – perhaps the Sultan's grandmother? – made it obvious by her gestures she intended to be most loving toward me, and I felt in return most tender to her, tho' we c'd not exchange a single word.

This visit was another great and unprecedented honour for Tom, 'cause no other European man has ever been admitted into the Sultan's harem before.

Later, a postscript. Tom has just now told me the purpose of the pavilion in the centre of the artificial lake in the taman sari: 'tis where the Sultan is sometimes privileged to entertain at night Loro Kidul. This Loro Kidul, beautiful and terrible, cruel and carnal, is both the temptress and the goddess of the southern sea, beneath which she has her palace. She is the protectoress of Yogyakarta, and 'tis through her demon grace the Sultan rules – or so Tom says the natives believe, for all they are Mahomedans. What the Sultan's wives make of his alleged consorting with a goddess I can't imagine – which is to say I can imagine it all too well.

February 1814, Buitenzorg

I have written nothing in my diary these past two months, from the unhappy circumstance of having lost it on the journey back from Yogyakarta – or so I thought. But now I have found it again, wrapped with some of the gifts we collected on our journey to the eastern courts, and which I only now find time to unpack.

February 1814, Buitenzorg

Today I turn forty-three, and from a fleeting melancholy I feel for the moment that birthdays sh'd not be celebrated, but mourned as the passing of another year – another pearl let slip into the ocean. But I cannot say so to Tom, who will tonight throw me a party.

February 1814, Buitenzorg

I have had my party here at Buitenzorg, which was decorated for the evening with streamers and swags of coloured linen and massed jangal flowers. Dancing commenced about eight o'clock, and its mazy evolutions were performed with great spirit until near twelve o'clock, by a numerous band of the beautiful and the gay. Supper combined all that fancy c'd invent, with all that luxury c'd wish for. I was toasted in Champagne, and afterwards dancing continued until the early hours of the morning, and throughout it all I felt myself old, ugly, invisible.

February 1814, Buitenzorg

These past few months it has been every moment a shadow at the back of my mind what Gillespie intended in Calcutta. Now it has happened as I feared, and Tom too: Gillespie has had his base revenge 'twas my husband got the better of him, and sent him away from Java.

Never shall I forget this morning, when Travers came to find me here in my private sitting room, to tell me that from bitterest resentment Gillespie now engages in Calcutta in hostile machinations, and lays against Tom charges most serious concerning those dratted land sales, God rot them!

Worse, rather than dismiss Gillespie's allegations as the product of a rancorous, addled mind, from the circumstance of his being a gentleman the misguided government in Bengal now prosecutes his trumpery charges, so Tom must provide an explanation for them.

Tho' Tom and me now never speak of Gillespie, at this bad news I hastened to my husband to discuss what's doing. I found Tom at his desk, white from shock, and the hand that held the dispatch from Calcutta shook as he showed it to me. Still, armed strong in innocence, and the consciousness of his own honesty and uprightness, he held himself in order, and to his great credit he coolly and dispassionately detailed to me the particulars of every false charge.

In gist these are that an extensive alienation of the public domains in any overseas territory, and transferal of the same to private gentlemen was too important a measure to be taken without the sanction of the Court of Directors in London, and that this was doubly the case here, whilst there remains such uncertainty over the restoration of Java to the Dutch that ours may indeed be considered a provisional government, the duration of which is more than precarious; that Java has neither capital nor capitalists enough – that it ain't got the necessary markets – to establish a fair valuation of the land; that if capital had to be raised, this sh'd have been effected by small and partial sales of land on short leases, not in perpetuity; that Tom sh'd not have sold off public lands as Lieutenant-Governor, and then bought them back at below fair value as a private gentleman.

In short, Gillespie alleges Tom allowed his behaviour to be contaminated by errors of judgement so severe an impartial judge must call him rotten.

O, how I wish today I'd never met that vindictive, vengeful, venomous Gillespie, nor let him make eyes at me neither, and 'cause of his spite I no longer regret I did not swoon into his manly arms when he kissed me. This Judas! No, today I can no longer regret I am in my heart a good wife, neither shameless nor indecent. Indeed, if I were naughty in my thoughts I console myself in any marriage no longer new there must now and then be temptation, and from the outrage I feel now on Tom's behalf I know better than ever my love for him is true – it drenches me, like our drenching rains.

February 1814, Buitenzorg

When I wrote last my calm was so scattered I forgot to say the horrid dispatches from Calcutta brought yet more unwelcome news: Ld. Minto is recalled home. Our dear patron himself wrote this in a private letter to Tom, dated November and saying he will soon be leaving India, so we assume he has by now left. His successor as Governor-General is one Ld. Hastings, who is apparently already in place.

Notwithstanding its unhappy contents, Ld. Minto's is a most kindly, gentle letter. The dear man says, of Gillespie's lies, that he, Ld. Minto, takes a deep and keen interest in all that concerns Tom's public trust, and his personal reputation and welfare. Alas, he then warns again what is warned also in the official dispatches: there is continuing disagreement at home over the annexation of Java to The Company's territory, and the establishment here of a permanent British settlement; Tom's land sales may be disapproved, disavowed, and annulled by the authorities in England, as they are considered a grave indiscretion.

Much will now depend on the judgement of Ld. Hastings. And him a man quite unknown to us! We ain't reassured by what the gossips say: he's thick with the Prince Regent – that booby – come to India by Prinny's favour solely to clear the debts he's run up trying to impress His Lardy Lowness. Will a spendthrift hanger-on have the wit to see that as a public servant no man c'd apply himself with more zeal and attention and honesty to the arduous duties of his office than does my Tom?

February 1814, Buitenzorg

Is anything more precious to a man than his honour? Tom says fame is nothing without it, and, in defence of his, he has written to Ld. Hastings saying he will withdraw from all interests in the coffee plantations he bought from the public domains last year, in consequence of insinuations being made prejudicial to his private character.

'Tis also decided our good, loyal friend Travers will travel first to Calcutta, and then to London, to make the authorities acquainted with a true and fair statement of the case concerning the land sales, and to meet any representations that may have been made privately by Gillespie.

Travers will stress Tom had unimpeachable motives for selling off the land: that there was particular exigency, given the urgency at the time of Java's financial situation; that he only went in as a private investor for thinking that if the Lieutenant-Governor himself were involved, the sales w'd not be repudiated by the government in Bengal, or by any future Dutch administration.

Alas, from the effects of distance it must be a year at best before Tom can know if he is exonerated. And us facing ruin for these utter nonsense charges.

March 1814, Buitenzorg

The anxiety of the accusations levelled against Tom spoiled even our wedding anniversary, which fell yesterday. Nine years! O Olivia, the dizzying speed of life! This year we had eighty people at our party, but Tom was but little amongst us, being so much engaged with the dispatches he prepares of sad necessity for Travers.

April 1814, Buitenzorg

Travers this morning quit these shores for Calcutta, carrying with him the dispatches answering Gillespie's wicked charges, which is to say he has Tom's honour in his hands, his good name, and private reputation. I was much affected by our parting, and wept at our adjoo, and he too was overcome. For all he is sometimes as stodgy as a steamed dumpling, I will miss this kind, reliable man.

May 1814, Rijswijk

I have been feeling poorly these past few days, nevertheless I have come with Tom to Batavia, to celebrate Boney's defeat at ~~Leyspig Liespick~~* – this happened last October, but here in Java we learn of it only now. 'Twas apparently the largest battle Europe has ever seen, and afterwards the field was scattered everywhere with such promiscuous heaps of the dying and the dead it took two weeks to clear it. The reports say French troops retreat to France from all over Europe, and the Dutch have thrown off Boney's yoke and declared for the Prince of Orange and their old constitution. In consequence, Batavia is everywhere festooned with orange, and banners wave saying *Oranje Boven*, which means *Orange forever*, and the Dutch are all lying drunk in the streets.

*Tom tells me I sh'd spell it *Leipzig*.

May 1814, Rijswijk

Tom and me last night threw a ball and supper here, to mark the recent events in Europe. 'Twas attended by all the bo mond of the metropolis, and our numerous guests detained me till a late hour, so I am almost too tired to write of it. I didn't dance as I did not have spirits to be gay. We sat down to a supper which combined delicacy, profusion, and luxury, but the need to chatter tired me, and for feeling poorly, I ate little and drank naught but cherry brandy.

There was an inordinate number of speeches. Naturally, Tom dwelled in his speech on the liberation of Holland, and the restoration of the House of Orange, which provoked from the

Dutch much hearty cheering.

In their own speeches, the Dutch were fulsome in their praises of Tom, one man saying the most fortunate moment Java had ever known was that on which Ld. Minto selected him as Lieutenant-Governor. Tom was modest and gracious in his reply, saying that if his administration deserved praise 'twas owing to the abilities of his advisors.

To speak the truth, Tom don't feel as celebratory as the Dutch about this battle of Leipzig, for what now? Aye, his fear of general peace in Europe has come to pass, near enough, and Java will in all likelihood soon be returned to the Hollanders. Then where will Britain have in this part of the Eastward? Where then will be the field for Tom's ambition?

June 1814, Buitenzorg

I have been extremely unwell. The sickness came on in Batavia two days after the ball to mark victory at Leipzig, at which time I was seized by a return of my usual indisposition of the liver, which fickle organ did indeed collapse. I was subsequently conveyed here to Buitenzorg, where I lie now in bed and hope to recover.

October 1814, Rijswijk

I have been ill on and off for weeks – months – and have neglected all my duties, including also those of the pen, but I have been taking regular drafts of mercury, hence my liver now slightly improves, so 'twas judged as recently as Monday that I was well enough to travel to Batavia, where now once more I find myself, and whither I *wanted* to travel, 'cause here my friends Nightingall and Florentia will tonight host me a ball. Alas, I now find I ain't looking forward to it, since I am feeling wretched.

October 1814, Rijswijk

And so I have had my ball thrown for me by Nightingall and Florentia. I wore my newest white, which hung off me my frame is now so shrunken. I was very tired all evening, tho' I managed a dance with Nightingall, to *Off She Goes*, and I trust I disguised from him I'd rather have sat out.

The supper combined elegance and plenty, but c'd not tempt me, tho' I much enjoyed the Champagne, which was excellent in quality, and abundant in quantity, and Florentia sat by me on the sofa as I drank it, and made me laugh with her nonsense.

I left early with Tom, before the dance recommenced after supper, from feeling unwell, and it occurs to me now that in my white last night I must have looked like the ghost of a ghost. I almost even think that ball must be my last, and 'tis strange to think

Deathland

These blockages in my liver ... Aye, Olivia, there are facts to be faced, and 'tis strange to think the world and time will continue without you.

October 1814, Buitenzorg

In deathland still, and I won't never now get to re-read my diary in old age, but I occupy yet a literal place and I am brought home from Rijswijk to Buitenzorg.

Buitenzorg! This home I won't never now quit, and will never see Ireland again, and no more England neither ... No, 'twill be some other woman enjoys with Tom in London the fruit of his success ... Some other woman, faceless, in Tom's bed. Is it wicked to hope she ain't a beauty? Is it wicked to hope she don't never come near defining my Tom's heart? Well, if it be wicked, then so be it, for I w'd be mourned properly; I w'd my death leaves Tom as tho' he were a discarded toy, a puppet lying in the street, broke beyond repair … And children, probably, to bring him joy.

October 1814, Buitenzorg

I can feel my skeleton rising quicker through my flesh, or else time sinking quicker through it.

I do not now stir from my bed. When Tom sits by me, and looks at me I see anguish in his eyes, and in my own eyes he must see dread, and I dared to say to him this morning that 'twas ever the lot of human creatures to yearn for a longer span of life than they were given. Tom looked stricken, no, no, he says, hush, hush, my dear, sh'd Java be early restored to the Dutch, now Boney is almost defeated, we will run home for a few years, 'cause 'tis clear the state of your health requires a change, and we must hope for many and many happy days in England at no distant date.

Well, here's pity.

November 1814, Buitenzorg

I that am doubt-rippled had long supposed I must become at the end a truly believing Christian, but still I doubt. Indeed, my doubts intensify. I remember Mother – O My Mother, when I think of Mr. Etherington reading to you that letter 'twill soon be Tom's sad duty to write – I remember Mother whispering to me when I was but a girl, of the Circassian other world, where the foggy dead linger, damp and grey. What if I go soon into that chilly, sunless world? Worse, what if I go alone soon into nothing – an eternal nothing that ain't never on the verge of becoming something, but is always nothing?

November 1814, Buitenzorg

Horror looms, and yet I live a little longer in this world of love, and I have been thinking much of Jack, and of Harriet, whose miniature I have by me always, and of Tom, and 'tis some consolation to think that when my eyes close forever on the beauty of the world, and as sight fades also from my inner eye, one of these three beloved faces must be the last face I ever see.

INTERLUDE

From the *Java Government Gazette*,
December 3, 1814

Died at Buitenzorg, on Saturday the 26 ultimo, Olivia Mariamne, *the Lady of the Honourable* Thomas Stamford Raffles, *Esq. Lieutenant Governor of this colony.*

The numerous assemblage of personages of both sexes, to assist at the mournful ceremony of paying the last duties and honour to the deceased, and the general and marked expression of unaffected grief which was there evinced, is the best proof of the respect and regard which her benevolence and manners had acquired among all classes of society in Java; and her more immediate friends will justly say that, possessed in life of a heart glowing with the most generous affections, and of a mind guided by the purest principles of friendship and kindness, she lived beloved by all who knew her, and carries to the grave the certainty of being ever remembered by them with a fond, devoted, and faithful attachment.

Her remains were interred at Batavia, by the side of the late Dr. Leyden.

Part Two

SOPHIA

July 1816, Number 349, The High Street, Cheltenham

It is often said that Cheltenham consists of widows wanting husbands, old men wanting health, and misses wanting dancing partners. I am not a widow, but I am too old to want any partner other than a husband. Thirty, and as yet unwed! For shame! But I do not despair. Tho' I am past my bloom, and tho' I know I was never even then accounted a beauty, I refuse to give up hope. Likewise Mother thinks she may still find me a match. Indeed, it was to give me the best chance of catching a husband that she persuaded Father to shift our household from Essex, to this fashionable spa of Cheltenham: in summer, thousands throng this resort, to drink its famously healthful waters, and to engage in all the gaieties that society affords; amongst those thousands, Mother and I are agreed, there is bound to be a scattering of widowers wanting wives as much as health.

August 1816, Number 349, The High Street, Cheltenham

The High Street is the principle promenade of this town, and very splendid – paved and lit at night with oil lamps. Not much further along it from our lodging house are the new Assembly Rooms, where sedan chairs come and go all day, bringing visitors to assemblies, games of cards, balls, &c.

The chief currency of the Assembly Rooms is gossip, and this past fortnight one man above all has snagged everybody's attention: Governor Raffles of Java, an island somewhere in the Eastward, since last month returned on leave to England, and come here to correct the debility that arises from living in a sultry climate, for it is the universal advice of the medical gentlemen that those recently home from the Eastward come to Cheltenham with a view to getting quit of all the lurking bile they have there accumulated by taking the efficacious waters of our wells.

Alas, Governor Raffles seems in even more need than most of taking the waters, for he is not in the pink of health, but is sapped of both flesh and colour, and appears more a sallow anatomy than a man. But it is not his health that excites most attention in the Assembly Rooms, where it is universally agreed he must in Java have given the money tree a good shaking, and where it is likewise universally noted there is no Lady Governess, for it is common knowledge that Governor Raffles is a widower.

August 1816, Number 349, The High Street, Cheltenham

This morning at the Assembly Rooms I managed to gain introduction to one Mary Ann Flint, an enchanting creature, married to a navy man who is not with her now, but away with his duties to the Admiralty. Since her husband is absent, Mary Ann lodges with her brother, who is none other than the celebrated Governor Raffles. To my pleasure, the little dear invited Mother and me to call on her tomorrow, and this after only the slightest hint from Mother.

August 1816, Number 349, The High Street, Cheltenham

Whilst he waits for his health to recover, Governor Raffles stays with his various entourage at Number 3, The Crescent. The house he has taken is a very capital one, towards one end of the gracious sweep of The Crescent. From the outside it is most pretty and neat, with a wrought iron balcony at the first floor, and a blue-painted front door.

I must say Mary Ann is a delightfully open creature, and confided in Mother and me many things we would not expect to learn on such short acquaintance: she met her Admiralty man, Flint, in the Eastward, whither she travelled with her brother, to see what she could make of herself there; Flint served under her brother in Java, but she and he returned to London last year, on account of having difficulties of a pecuniary nature they needed to resolve; she was a widow when she married, or rather, remarried, and there's a daughter by her first husband, but the child is now living in Ireland, with relatives, for Flint did not want the trouble of bringing up another man's child, a circumstance which has caused her many a sad pang, but what's to do?

Mary Ann did not talk only of herself, but also of her brother: it appears our little Cheltenham society is wrong he is Governor of Java. Mary Ann says that was his former post, but when he returns to the Eastward, probably in the course of a year, or perhaps a little longer, he is to be Governor of some other settlement we have there, Bencoolen, an obscure spot, but at any rate it is on Sumatra, an island universally judged backward, and lacking entirely in elegance or sophistication, which Mary Ann can well believe, tho' she's never been there, and no more has her brother.

Bencoolen, Java, Sumatra, I know nothing of these places except that they are so impossibly distant they may as well be east of the sun, but I would be an adventurous woman if only I had means of being, and I would not be averse to seeing them, if ever chance arose. In the meantime, I shall borrow Father's map, that I may at least discover where they are.

Alas, I did not meet Governor Raffles himself this morning, for he was out with his aide-de-camp, one Travers, and his private physician, Sir Thomas Sevestre, both of whom were with him in the Eastward, and both of whom are now of his household.

Mother has invited Mary Ann to call on us tomorrow, and we

both have great hopes of this friendship.

August 1816, Number 349, The High Street, Cheltenham

Mary Ann is now become my dearest friend, and thanks to her good offices, Mother and I today had the honour of meeting Governor Raffles.

This was my first chance to appraise the Governor closely, and it was with some emotion that I beheld him, for he is handsome, in his way. He is not a tall man – he tops me by only an inch or so – and he stoops, but with more weight on his bones his figure would be becoming since his chest is full and his waist slender; his hair I thought a most attractive chestnut, tho' Mother later dismissed it was red; his eyes, beneath thick eyebrows, are the colour of amber, and they shine with kindness, as much as with intelligence; his nose is straight, and his mouth gentle; tho' his face remains sallow from the effects of the Eastward sun, I find it easy to imagine him in high colour, and healthily plump, with a shapely leg.

Mother invited the Governor and Mary Ann to return our call, and this they will do forthwith.

August 1816, Number 349, The High Street, Cheltenham

The more I know Governor Raffles the more I come to admire him. He is generous and tactful. He is filled with family feeling, and talks kindly of his mother and his sisters – he had two more besides Mary Ann, but one died last year in childbed in the Eastwood. The other, Hannah, a spinster, now dwells with their mother in London.

Also pleasing, the Governor seems most loyal to Travers, Sir Thomas Sevestre, and the others of his intimate circle. His manners are excellent, to his servants as well as to his friends. Tho' weakened by the heat and pestilential airs of India he has an unbounded flow of spirits: he is interested in everything, interesting about everything. His conversation is never less than quick and engaging and it ranges widely, which is a delight to me for Mother and my governesses taught me only those things suitable for girls – drawing, music, embroidery – and except with him my conversation is mostly confined to gossip and matters domestic.

August 1816, Number 349, The High Street, Cheltenham

I today mentioned to Governor Raffles that music is one of the great joys of my life, and he told me he has in the collection of rarities he has shipped home from Java the instruments of a native orchestra called a gamelan, which instruments are a great variety of gongs and drums and xylophones. He said he'll show me this gamelan come the day he can get it released from customs, for he is finding it the devil of a job to get the crates and boxes he brought home from the Eastward released by the customs men.

August 1816, Number 349, The High Street, Cheltenham

Governor Raffles has quite made me his victim, and with a fitting shyness not entirely acted, I have now taken Mary Ann into my confidence. She said she was not a bit surprised what's doing, things stood as she'd all along suspected they must since she saw me first in her dear brother's presence, and she would be delighted to see him happily settled before he returns to the Eastward, because he has been sad and lonely since *Olivia* died.

Mary Ann, dear puss, spoke this name in such a way, so coy and enticing, and gave me such a look as she uttered it, that I could not resist her invitation. Olivia? I obliged. Yes, said Mary Ann, Olivia was his first wife, did you know that? I indicated the name was new to me. Ten years older than Tom, said Mary Ann, and *Circassian*, she added, meaningfully.

I cannot approve inquisitiveness or importuning, and yet I found it curious Governor Raffles had taken a wife so much older than him, and never mind that she was Circassian – Circassians are known to be a very *glamorous* kind of woman. In truth, I would have pressed for more, but, alas, Mary Ann gave me no time to pose questions. Instead she rushed to promise she'd do all she could to further my cause, adding it would be very pleasant to her to have a hand in making a match.

At this, my cheeks flared hot as glowing coals. Still, I was grateful Mary Ann would help me, for what other result did I want than this, when I revealed to her my heart's desire?

September 1816, Number 349, The High Street, Cheltenham

I did not expect to see *Somebody* this day, and yet because I have not done so, my heart is very heavy ...

September 1816, Number 349, The High Street, Cheltenham

I find myself downcast and miserable, for Governor Raffles has told me his party is to leave Cheltenham for London. He has hinted, however, that he would not object if I maintained a correspondence with Mary Ann, through which means I may tell him of my doings, and likewise learn of his.

September 1816, Number 349, The High Street, Cheltenham

Governor Raffles and all his household have quit Cheltenham, to be replaced by his mother and his spinster sister, Hannah, who are to come from London to stay for a month at Number 3, The Crescent, to complete the lease. Mary Ann and I parted with tears, and we have promised to correspond. To my shame, I know

I shall never see Mrs. Raffles and Hannah without regretting the exchange that has been made; I am sure they are very amiable and good, but they are not Somebody … I can't bear to lose sight of Somebody.

September 1816, Number 349, The High Street, Cheltenham

I must remind myself that before honour is humility: over breakfast this morning Mother suggested to Father that for reasons she need not elaborate we quit Cheltenham, and visit for a few weeks in London. Both my parents looked at me; blushing at the indignity, I dropped my eyes to my porridge. Father said he'd consider the matter, and so I am in hopes my humiliation was not in vain.

October 1816, Number 349, The High Street, Cheltenham

I have heard from Mary Ann her brother has taken a house at 23, Berners Street, in Westminster, and here they both now dwell, with a large and various household. In reply, I have written to Mary Ann telling her Mother and I now quite identify her with us as one of the family, and saying the poor postman would never reach London was he to be the bearer of all the love I am charged by my parents to send her, and that I send myself also, on my own account. I added as a post script my most important lines, which for redrafting them many times are seared into my memory: *If your brother can spare the time to accept them, I am to offer the friendliest wishes of all here, too numerous to particularise – as I must add the truest affection of yours most faithfully, Sophia Hull.*

November 1816, Number 349, The High Street, Cheltenham

I have had from Mary Ann a reply to my last, in which she says that her brother enjoys all the pleasures of London society with a zest peculiar to his vigour of mind, and to the great variety of his tastes, and he instructs her to send me his most sincere regards.

I am pleased the Governor thinks of me, and when I showed my letter to Mother, she said she'd ask Father again about visiting London.

December 1816, Number 349, The High Street, Cheltenham

Hosanna! Father has agreed we can within a week or two quit Cheltenham for London and stay there through all the Season. I have written to Mary Ann to share with her this news.

January 1817, Number 22, Soho Square

I must confess to feeling triumphant, for I am transferred to the great metropolis. Father has taken a house on Soho Square, where the brick-built houses are tall and narrow, so I spend half my days running up and down stairs. I am writing now in the drawing room, on the first floor, which has high sash windows looking over the Square – a tree-studded lawn enclosed by iron railings, and around it a road with a paved walkway for pedestrians. A farmer who must be on his way to the markets east of here is driving his cattle along the road: it is amusing to see cows lumbering past fashionable carriages, and to see a little dog, out with a boy, snapping at the beasts' hooves.

Berners Street is not far from us: I have written to Mary Ann to let her know we are arrived.

January 1817, Number 22, Soho Square

Here's glee! A boy has just brought a note from Mary Ann inviting mother and me to call on her tomorrow!!!

January 1817, Number 22, Soho Square

Somebody is grown ever dearer to me through long absence. When Mother and I arrived at Berners Street this morning, Mary Ann showed us at once into the front drawing room, and there he was, warming himself by the fire, in a polka-dotted yellow silk waistcoat with a turn-up collar and embroidered trim, and now wearing his hair in the short style favoured by the Prince Regent.

The Governor left the fire's warmth directly, and came and spoke to me, which flattered and pleased me so much I could scarcely attend to what he was saying – my heart was quite going from my happy confusion.

I must say the Governor's household is unusual. Mother and I were startled to meet two people the likes of which neither of us had hitherto imagined, and both of them in partially oriental costume. These were Papuan Dick and Raden Rana Dipura, two human curiosities Governor Raffles brought with him to England from Java

Papuan Dick, thick-lipped, flat-nosed, and with skin so glossy brown it put me in mind of a well-groomed bay, is the first individual of the woolly haired races of Eastern Asia ever to arrive on English shores – or so the Governor told me. This aboriginal, a native of the island of New Guinea, was a victim of the East Indian slave trade, stolen from his country in the course of this bad traffic. Governor Raffles got him at Bali after his ship, which was attempting to navigate the easternmost coast of Java, ran aground there. When the Governor first had him, Papuan Dick wore naught but loin cloths, feathers, and beads, and even now he is exposed to English weather he protests at being buttoned into woollens. He is thought to be somewhere between ten and twelve years old and he is learning English, tho' for his backwardness not very speedily – he must be impossibly backward, said Mother, if he cannot even speak English.

All the Governor told me, he told me in a great rush, gesturing at Papuan Dick the while, and I would not have had time to interrupt with questions, even if I'd had the inclination, which I did not, for I did not wish to reveal my ignorance, but in truth I never heard hitherto of New Guinea, and nor of Bali neither.

Meanwhile, Raden Rana Dipura is a high born Javanese – *raden* is his title – a man most sophisticated and cultivated for a native, and, said the Governor, proudly, as well able to speak English as John Bull. The Governor shows him off everywhere; he has taken him to the Royal Mint; to the opera; to fashionable Drawing Rooms; to see some experiments with electricity and galvanism – they saw a natural philosopher apply electricity to the corpse of a dog; the muscles quivered, and an eye opened. The Governor told me this opening eye made such an impression on the Raden he said he would not be at all surprised to find that in England the dead could be restored to life.

Papuan Dick and the Raden are not the only curiosities of Governor Raffles' house, for it is chuck full of oriental matters, many things, strange and magnificent, and the back drawing room is quite a museum – it is where Governor Raffles keeps the choicest of the contents of *two hundred* chests and boxes he shipped from the Eastward, *thirty tons* in weight.

I know these vast numbers because the Governor this morning told me again what he told me once before: it was only with the greatest struggle and difficulty that he got the whole of his baggage, his Eastern rarities and treasures, freed from the customs house. I can quite understand why the customs men found his things a puzzle. As well as books and manuscripts too numerous to count, he has jerky, jointed leather puppets, thin as leaves, which he says tell their tales by throwing their scenic shadows on a screen. He has grotesque masks, and wicked looking knives called krises, some of them with queer wavy-edged blades, he has bronzes, and fragments of stone statuary – heathen imagery, detached heads of the idol called the Buddha. He has bowls, pots, boxes, amulets, earrings, hair pins, nose rings. He has lengths of native cloth of all sorts. He has too that gamelan he told me of in Cheltenham, its gongs and drums ornately carved, painted, and gilded, and most Asiatic to behold.

January 1817, Number 22, Soho Square

Governor Raffles mingles much with the Great Men of Town who are eager all of them to see his collections, and to talk with him of oriental matters, and this morning I met in his back drawing room Sir Joseph Banks, who was the king's friend until the king went mad.

Sir Joseph is elderly now, but in his youth he sailed with Captain Cook to the South Seas, to be his botanist, and in spite of his advanced years he is President of the Royal Society. For the importance of his collections, and for the new information he can bring to London about all matters pertaining to the remote regions of the little-known Eastward, Governor Raffles has been lately elected to that esteemed fellowship of scholarly gentlemen. Today, Sir Joseph told me the Governor is certainly among the best informed of men, and possesses a larger stock of useful talent than any other individual of his acquaintance. With this opinion I could not disagree.

Later, the Governor told me Sir Joseph has his house in Soho Square, and when I in turn told Mother and Father they were just as satisfied as me to learn of the quality of our neighbours.

January 1817, Number 22, Soho Square

I spent yesterday a most enjoyable evening at Berners Street, where I had the honour of being introduced to the Duke and Duchess of Somerset. The Duke, a mild-mannered man said to be of charitable disposition, is a serious student of science and mathematics notwithstanding his rank; like Governor Raffles he is a Fellow of the Royal Society, and it was at a reception for said Fellows that the Governor was flattered and delighted to be first noticed by the Duke. The Duchess seemed a kind creature though she is known for being close with money.

After refreshments had been served, the Raden played upon one of the Governor's gamelan xylophones several of his national melodies, which all present agreed had a striking resemblance to the oldest music in Scotland. I then played for comparison on a more conventional instrument some Scottish airs, and later the Governor told me I am a superlative performer on the piano. Tho' I blushed at this flattery it emboldened me, and I hinted he may like to come to Soho Square to hear me play also the harp? Alas the Governor missed my hint, and began to tell me of a late Scottish poet, John Leyden, a man when living most dear to him. The Governor reminisced this Leyden had been a great lover of Scottish minstrelsy, who once walked forty miles to learn the last two verses of an ancient ballad, and returned at midnight to his cottage in the Borders, singing it all the way, no doubt, the Governor said, to the wonder and consternation of all who heard him for even his friends must admit his voice was loud, and harsh.

January 1817, Number 22, Soho Square

I did not realise our recent wars in Europe extended also to the Eastward, but Governor Raffles tells me they were fought there as well as across the Straits of Dover. And when, in '15, Napoleon was finally defeated, I did not realise either that distant places were of interest to the diplomats, but the Governor says we have, as part of the peace settlement, restored Java to the Dutch, who had it in former times – hence he is now posted to Bencoolen, which is securely ours. We rendered Java to the Dutch, I gather, because our diplomats believed if we annoyed them they could ally themselves with Prussia and her friends, which they thought at Westminster would threaten Europe's hard-won peace.

Governor Raffles cannot understand why we have got so little out of victory. He thinks probably for a thousand years there will not be such a mistake as handing Java back to the Dutch. He does not accept England's safety depends on having Holland a friendly power, but thinks that when after Waterloo our diplomats had the chance to dictate to the world, they should have stipulated we keep control of the Eastward seas. Furthermore, he thinks it was wrong in all humanity to restore Java to the Dutch, for the Hollanders are accustomed to treat the little people of the island harshly, as if they were naught but crops to line the pockets of the burghers of Amsterdam.

For wanting to show our supine government we should not have handed such a pearl as Java back to the Hollanders the Governor took the opportunity of his recent long voyage home to begin a literary work, *The History of Java,* which he now prepares to present to the public.

H of J, as the Governor calls it, is to be published soon by Mr. Murray, who has his house in Albemarle Street and who publishes also that scandalous Lord Byron, and the lady novelist Jane Austen, whom they say is witty. It promises to be a very popular work; it is to be in the nature of a compilation, woven from many strands, drawing on the work of many scholars, in many disciplines, as well as on extensive collections of Javanese literature of the Governor's own collecting. It is to include passages on natural history, political history and statistics, geography and geology, not forgetting descriptions of the Javanese. The Governor calls them a most interesting people, and says tho' they now exist in a debased state, they had before their decline a society almost as developed as the ones on Continental India, and much influenced from there. *H of J* will give accounts of their foods, ceremonies, entertainments, illnesses, agriculture, trading, &c. There will be plans of their temples, drawings of antiquities, an accurate map made principally from actual survey, tables, &c, all most splendid and interesting.

The Governor intends the political argument of his book to show the liberality and success of his administration, the mercantile argument to show Java could have brought much increase to our treasury, the strategic argument to show the power we attained by defeating Napoleon could have been made effective in the Eastward by keeping control of Java, and with it the China trade, the philanthropic argument to show the Javanese are not savages, to be treated no better than buffalo.

January 1817, Number 22, Soho Square

The Governor showed me today some proofs of his *H of J* that had just come to him from the printers. As we looked over the sheets, the Governor revealed that ever since Olivia died – *my Olivia*, he called her – ever since *his* Olivia died, he has been collecting facts for this book as a distraction from sorrow, but that he did not until recently imagine he could actually write it himself, he would rather have seen the materials worked up by an abler hand than incur the risk and responsibility of undertaking the task himself. However, no abler hand having revealed itself before he commenced the long voyage home, he at last girded himself to put pen to paper.

I said in reply there could indeed be no abler hand than his to bring *The History of Java* before the public, but as I offered this reassurance, I was, in truth, thinking less of the Governor's book than of *him*: this was the first time he had ever mentioned to me Olivia, and tho' I dared not bat her name back to him, I was moved, deeply moved, and honoured, that he did so.

For all that I think it healthier by far for Governor Raffles to think of his heart's *future*, than to dwell on its past.

January 1817, Number 22, Soho Square

I today confided in Mary Ann her brother had mentioned to me Olivia. In reply, the dear puss looked at me archly, and she told me she could say nothing – *nothing* – on the subject of dear, dead Olivia, except that she was a bewitching creature, beautiful, enchanting, kind, tho' perhaps a little *surprising* as the Lady Governess of Java, and certainly a showy, stagey person, rather pushing, and not at all like me. She then begged me – *begged* me – not to press her on what she meant.

Tho' I would not pry, I fear I could not have resisted Mary Ann's temptation to conspire, except just then her brother entered the room, and came to join us by the fire, and by his presence stilled our tongues.

I must say I did not like to hear Olivia described as bewitching, enchanting, beautiful, tho' I suppose I'm glad for Governor Raffles that she was kind.

February 1817, Number 22, Soho Square

Bless the Lord, O my soul: and all that is within me, bless his holy name ... I offer to God many thankful prayers for the great benefits He has bestowed upon me, and I shed as I write many grateful tears, for Tom – for so I must call him now – for Tom has asked me to marry him, saying he has been these past few years since Olivia died, like one that has himself long been dead, but that he thinks now I can make him very happy, for he needs a wife and this woman must be redoubtable, resourceful, and resilient on account of the challenging life she'll lead with him in the Eastward and he thinks he never met a woman as redoubtable as *me*.

Oh, what welcome, precious words, and no less gladly

received for being not very spooning. No, I would not I am sure be wooed in a silly, sentimental way – tho' I was powerless to prevent sentiment colouring my acceptance, for I told Tom, joyfully: how much *my* heart is to *your* heart as *yours* to *mine*, and then I added it is the charm of my existence to cherish those I love with all my heart and soul.

Father, much relieved at this offer to have me off his hands, at once gave his permission, and so I now bend all my thoughts and all my feelings to the ways it is possible to love a husband – not forgetting even those that are unmentionable for being carnal!!!

February 1817, Number 22, Soho Square

The Hulls are humble people and so are the Raffles. In accordance with our station, Mother and I had intended a small and seemly affair for my marriage to Tom. But Tom now says he wishes to marry quickly, and so quietly it is almost in absolute secrecy, for he says of all the actions of a man's life, his marriage least concerns other people, notwithstanding marriage is ever meddled with by all abroad. He adds he cannot tolerate that work on *The History of Java* be interrupted by confusion.

I cannot disagree it would be unfitting for there to be public interest in our nuptials, and I would not want Tom's work on his book delayed, so I must approve his decision we will marry speedily, and secretly, and I *do* approve it ~~and yet my beloved's refusal to countenance even the least extravagance makes me think he dwells too much on the truth our coming nuptials must be his final farewell to another. No doubt he harbours memories of happiness and joy, memories of hours beguiled away under Olivia's enchanting spell. This I must grant is natural and proper. But could he not tolerate just a little of the customary nonsense at our wedding? And how can I not now find myself wondering: must a dead first wife shade a living second wife as a tree shades a lawn?~~

February 1817, Number 22, Soho Square

Cleanse thou me from secret faults ... I should not be envious, jealous. I should not have written what I wrote yesterday, for to think of a dead woman as her rival belittles a living one, and if I am Tom's consolation prize so be it, I am past the age when a woman can expect to be any other sort of prize, and I never had the looks to provoke in men adoration.

February 1817, Number 22, Soho Square

As betrothal gifts each to the other Tom I am are to exchange our portraits, in miniature, and today I sat for the artist my parents have commissioned for mine, Mr. Alfred Chalon. I wore a white satin dress Mother had her seamstress make for me especially, the bodice cut low, and much decorated with pearls, and with cap sleeves of lace. For jewels – hired – I chose an elegant pearl necklace – multiple strands, dangled with sapphires set in gold – with a matching broach for my bosom. For my earrings I chose golden drops, set with rubies. On my head I wore a turban in the latest style, decorated and tasselled with yet more pearls, and enhanced also with a golden band set with sapphires and diamonds. My hair peeked out from under its adornments to make short chestnut curls about my forehead.

I have high hopes my miniature will flatter me. And I do not – *must not* – hope that once he has it, Tom will soon enough cease to contemplate any picture he carries in his head of another.

February 1817, Number 22, Soho Square

I am shocked and I scarcely know what to think: Mary Ann, now she is so soon to be my sister, has told me things of Olivia that must alarm any respectable lady. The dear puss wrung from me a promise not to tell Tom she'd been talking with me of his first wife, and then she dropped her voice to a whisper, gave me a look most meaningful, and revealed that Olivia was rumoured in her youth to have entered numerous connections with members of the male chapter. More, before she wed Tom she already had a child, a natural daughter now departed.

A ruined woman!!! What a stumbling-block to Tom's ambition – and what misguided liberality, generosity, kindness, suavity he showed in making his choice. Or else what sweet simplicity to let himself be gulled. But for all his goodness, his guilelessness, he must often have felt Olivia's history a burden, and I am now more than ever convinced it must be best for him, for his reputation and happiness, that once we are wed he forget he ever had any wife but me.

February 1817, Number 22, Soho Square

I met today at Berners Street Tom's cousin Elton, the man to whom he gives grateful credit for first nudging him, via a letter dispatched from London to Batavia, to consider the advantages attending a literary work giving an account of Java. This Elton is himself one of literature's under gardeners, or so I now gather. I confess I found the man strange and bewildering. He told me he recently inherited a tea business from his father, but he has now sacked all the workforce because they interfered with his time for writing. On being asked what he is writing, he said it is his autobiography, in which he shall share nothing less than the secret of perfecting mankind – Tom later told me this autobiography is unpublishable and Elton is frittering his time documenting himself, which indulgence leaves him much distressed for money. Be that as it may, it seems Elton bears a marked fascination for one Mrs. Barbauld, an elderly poetess whose name I never heard hitherto. This unfortunate woman's husband became insane, attacked her with a knife, and then killed himself. Elton seems to hold her responsible: he cornered me in Tom's front drawing room, and began to berate her, and tried to engage me in conversation about the best way of *putting an end to her life*, and waved his arms, until I caught Tom's eye, and he walked over, and turned the subject to statistical accounts of Javanese agriculture.

When I later asked Tom if he thought we should be alarmed for Mrs. Barbauld, he said if Elton could be distracted from talk of murder by talk of the effects of a change of taxation on the production of rice and coffee, not to worry, he never in truth had murder in mind at all.

February 1817, The Red Lion Inn, Henley-Upon-Thames

As Isaac and Rebecca lived faithfully together, so these persons may surely perform and keep the vow and covenant betwixt them made ... Which is to say I am married, and am called today Mrs. Thomas Stamford Raffles!!!

The great event took place this morning, very early, before I am usually accustomed to breakfast, at New Church, Marylebone – so new they are still building it, and a crowd of builders arrived for work as we were leaving, and cheered when they saw I was a bride.

I wore my white that Mother had me made for my sitting with Mr. Chalon. The Rev'd, ancient, tall, and commanding of person, displayed perfect urbanity and affability of manners as Tom and I spoke our vows in front of my parents, his mother, Hannah, and Mary Ann. Once we'd wed we left immediately and came here to Henley-on-Thames, where we will spend tonight and tomorrow night in this famous Red Lion Inn – the same that is much frequented by royalty, and I must say it is very handsomely appointed.

My husband – *my husband!!!* – is now engaged in writing

letters, and it is to fill the time until he can be fonder that I entrust my thoughts to my diary on this most blessed day, my wedding day.

February 1817, The Red Lion Inn, Henley-On-Thames

And so my marriage night slides into the past, and I will say nothing of it, for nothing should be said of such holy things, and never, never, never have I spent such a night!!!

I cannot now think there is any woman alive more fortunate than me, for henceforth it is my pleasure to fix my narrative firmly on Tom – to obey him and to have no fate of my own, even as Sarah obeyed Abraham, calling him Lord. Moreover, the life I'll share with my husband will have broader horizons than any I could have imagined when I went to Cheltenham to cast amongst the widowers there.

February 1817, Number 23, Berners Street

An image of The Red Lion Inn will be engraved forever on my heart, but now I am returned to London: Tom has brought me to be mistress of the household here at Berners Street so now my life as a wife properly begins. My parents have sent over my things, including my piano and my harp, and happy I am to have them.

I now learn from Mary Ann that even our good physician Sir Thomas Sevestre did not know Tom and I were to be married before the event, for she says it is quite a story in the household that he was much surprised, the morning of our wedding, to be told not to wait breakfast for Governor Raffles as he had gone out to be married. Alas, I cannot forbear from thinking this is a story she'd have been kinder to keep from telling me.

February 1817, Number 23, Berners Street

The habit of matrimony is perhaps catching? In any case, Travers now confides in me he is in want of a wife, to take with him back to the Eastward, and it is his plan to journey soon to his native Ireland, to find himself there a country bride, for he says he wants a sturdy plant, and none of your London flowers.

I thought half an hour ago Travers' decision was all the news I had, but Mary Ann came in just as I was recording it and: you remind me of Olivia she said, she too was a great one for scribbling. She kept a diary? I asked. Yes, nodded my sister. I never got a peek in it, but no doubt she wrote of me waspish, now and again. I closed my own diary with something of a snap. And then I could not help blushing as I asked: Tom has it now, I suppose? Mary Ann pursed her lips. Here's a thing, she said, I don't rightly know. I suppose he read it after her death, but come to think of it, he never told me so. As to where it is now…should we ask him?

I was taken aback. No! I said, no, we cannot encroach.

As you please, shrugged Mary Ann. Perhaps from prudence he burned it? I must think any diary penned by *her* must contain things unsafe for *him*.

I could not disagree, and yet I rebuked: if he burned it, his motive must have been honourable discretion. Alas, as I spoke, I silently regretted that even now I am Tom's wife, Olivia remains between us a subject – *the* subject – on which we cannot speak, and yet, to him, it seems she was once an open book – and one penned by her own hand, to boot.

February 1817, Number 23, Berners Street

The miniatures Tom and I sat for as gifts each to the other have now arrived, and we have exchanged our portraits, as we have lately exchanged vows, and daily exchange our feelings.

My portrait pleases me for Mr. Chalon rendered delightfully my ornate costume – the dress that later became my wedding dress – and flattered my honest looks as best as they can be flattered, and all I regret is that I sat for this portrait before I was a married woman, otherwise I would have asked Mr. Chalon to ensure my left hand – and with it my wedding ring – was prominently displayed, but as it is my left hand is not visible, and nor, for that matter, is my right, the miniature being of my head and shoulders only.

Tom says it is a pretty image, tho' thank God I am altogether more capable than my pearl be-tasselled turban would suggest. Meanwhile, his miniature he gave to me I must confess I find a little … He has been painted often, and in his more public portraits he generally looks cool, confident, at ease, often surrounded by books and a variety of his Eastern treasures, but the miniature he gave to me shows him in a green velvet coat, with thinning hair of ginger – too life like to be flattering – with the florid complexion of a drunkard, and looking slightly mad. Still, with Tom as the giver, how can I not cherish the gift?

February 1817, Number 23, Berners Street

Tho' I hold Tom dear with all my heart I am too humble to expect the same in return unless I would deserve it, and this I must judge fortunate because I overheard this morning a most disconcerting conversation between Tom and Travers – they were in the back drawing room, and I was in the front, and the folding doors between were imperfectly closed.

Says Tom: You will I doubt not approve the change I have made in my condition in again taking to myself a wife.

Says Travers: How can I not when I travel soon to Ireland to seek one myself?

Tom: I advise you to do as I did, and allow neither rank, nor fortune, nor beauty to have weight on your decision.

Travers: It is never good to marry for those shallow things.

Tom: That is why I did not seek to marry a well-connected heiress. I could have done, you know, if I'd been a calculating man.

Travers: Sophia is extremely well brought up, and possesses many amiable qualities of both head and heart.

Tom: She is turned of thirty, she is devotedly attached to me, and possesses every qualification of heart and mind calculated to render me happy – more I need not say.

I confess it: I blinked back tears to hear my husband speak of me with such causal disregard. But I have since garnered my resources, and I now remind myself: that brooding is failure to trust in God; that eavesdropping is wrong; that gallantry is for knaves. Moreover, I console myself it is true what Tom said: famous Governor Raffles, fellow of the Royal Society, a man on friendly terms with people of the first rank, could have married a woman much better able to promote his worldly interests than Sophia Hull.

I am glad Travers thinks me well brought up.

March 1817, Number 23, Berners Street

There is somewhere in the Eastward an island called *Amboyna*, and we have about us at Berners Street many such things as tea caddies and writing boxes made of a precious wood that grows there. This Amboyna wood is amber-coloured, satiny, and mottled and burred almost like polished tortoiseshell.

For its beauty Amboyna wood is much coveted, and, as Lieutenant-Governor of Java, Tom once sent to Princess Charlotte, only child of the Prince Regent, a gift of Amboyna wood furniture

– also six Javanese ponies for her phaeton she had let it be known she would be pleased to accept. These gifts were well received, and now that Tom is in England the Princess remembers him, and he enjoys her particular regard, and that too of her husband, Prince Leopold, and he dines with them often at their country house, Claremont, in Surrey.

Through Princess Charlotte, Tom has lately been presented to the Prince Regent, who was by all accounts charmed by him – I have this from the Duchess of Somerset, whose husband is on intimate terms with the Prince. Certainly, the Prince was impressed by the furniture Tom gave his daughter, saying at their meeting: I hear wonderful things of the treasures you have brought from India, and everybody is in raptures with the beautiful tables you have given to the Princess Charlotte. Tom at once offered him a pair of Amboyna wood tables he had intended for Sir Joseph Banks, which His Royal Highness graciously accepted.

Now Tom has received yet more definite and flattering proof of royal regard: there appeared at our breakfast table this morning an equerry sent by the Prince Regent, asking to taste Tom's arak from Java, which His Royal Highness had heard was remarkably good. Tom leapt up, and he himself at once rushed to the Prince's London residence, Carlton House, all the arak he had in his cellar, and he told His Royal Highness he would supply him with arak as long as he lived to drink it.

On returning home my husband told me that if Prinny drinks plentifully of this arak – which he is sure to do, such is his career of reckless indulgence – it will not be *long* he lives to drink it, for it is the strongest spirit in the world.

Later Mary Ann remarked to me she is gratified Tom is taking care to cultivate his royal connections, for they can be nothing but beneficial for his fame and prospects. Naturally, I rebuked her saying Tom's friendship with Princess Charlotte is sincere – tho' in my private thoughts I grant it's also valuable, and what's the use of the royals, except that they raise others through their patronage?

April 1817, Number 23, Berners Street

These past few weeks since we married Tom has been working as feverishly as ever on *The History Of Java* so I am amazed at his industry – every morning we have boys knocking at our door bringing packages of proofs direct from the printers, and every evening boys knocking again, to carry them away. Things go on so well toward publication Tom lately wrote to ask the Prince Regent if he may dedicate the book to him. Now we have a letter saying His Royal Highness has granted his most gracious permission, and so Tom will make the dedication, joyfully, with profound veneration and respect.

May 1817, Number 23, Berners Street

Mr. Murray has sent us advance copies of *H of J*. When he beheld these books Tom, nervous, but excited, said it was a thing very strange to see the words he wrote at his own desk printed ready for all the world to read, and he was now more than ever sensible of his incapacity to appear before the public as an author.

I reminded him there is no one possessed of more information respecting Java than himself, and, indeed *The History Of Java* is a splendid work, in two fine, heavy volumes, each calf-bound, printed on paper of the first order, and embellished with many beautiful plates, both aquatints and engravings, and the folding map is said by Tom to be the best ever compiled.

Tom, almost paternally proud, and saying he hoped this work would one day prove an imperishable monument of his fame, at once rushed to the Prince Regent at Carlton House the dedication copy. This was well received, and I think it certain His

Royal Highness will approve the dedication, for Tom was careful to make it soapy, saying, cheerful, that with the royals it is ever better to be soapy than scratching.

I myself have commenced reading the whole of *H of J*, having seen before only scattered exerts from the proofs Tom showed me.

May 1817, Number 23, Berners Street

I really cannot withhold my admiration for *H of J*. I confess I find Tom's provision of detail on such matters as civil history too ample, but here I think the fault lies with me – I have an undeveloped aptitude for persevering. The sixth and seventh chapters, which describe the characters, habits, manners, customs, and amusements of the people are indeed excellent. The beautiful coloured plates I think enchanting – excepting only the one of the *ronggeng*.

These ronggengs are the common dancing girls of Java – and I gather almost even *women of pleasure*. To my mind Tom devotes too much space to their style of dancing and singing – which he admits is rude and awkward, and distressing to Europeans – to the ornaments they weave into their jetty tresses, to their slender wrists and ankles, and to their costumes. If the aquatint is to be trusted, these costumes are nothing but lengths of cloth drawn so tightly over the bosom they must be injurious to female anatomy, and which narrow the waist, and which open beneath to reveal the leg, and are indeed an affront to female elegance.

I must say I worry *H of J* is priced too expensive to be popular – eight guineas! Even the cheaper edition, smaller, and on not such good paper as my copy, is to be six guineas.

May 1817, Number 23, Berners Street

I may as well have swallowed a swarm of bees, I am so buzzing with hope and excitement: Tom is summoned by the Prince Regent to a levee at Carlton House, and from whispers coming back to us from Princess Charlotte, via the Duke and Duchess of Somerset, we have high hopes that His Royal Highness will use the occasion to confer upon him a baronetcy!!!

May 1817, Number 23, Berners Street

My husband is a knight, and I am Lady Raffles!!!

Today we dressed ourselves in our costliest liveries, in order to attend with Princess Charlotte and Prince Leopold the Prince Regent's levee – and there, in the grandly gaudy throne room at Carlton House, all gilded and furnished in the French style, and hung about with portraits, chandeliers, girandoles, and I don't know what, His Royal Highness marked Tom out, and entered into conversation with him for a full twenty minutes, and told him he has read a great part of *The History Of Java*, which may even be true, for they say notwithstanding his laziness and debauchery he is a cultured man, and in elegant manner he most sincerely thanked him for the instruction and pleasure he had derived from the perusal of his book. He then expressed the high sense he entertained of the eminent services Tom had rendered the country in Java. Tom was invited to kneel; the Prince Regent took a sword, and dubbed him on his right shoulder, and then on his left, and thus he was knighted.

Tom will always be Tom to me, but he intends henceforth to use his middle name – to be styled in public Sir Stamford Raffles – thinking Sir Stamford has more dignity to it than Sir Thomas.

May 1817, Number 23, Berners Street

Mary Ann told me today she knows Tom is in his innermost heart disappointed he got from Prinny only a knighthood, such as even

Sir Thomas Sevestre has, and not a baronetcy, which would have been more fitting to his services in Java, but she supposed even this was better than being the Duke of Puddle Dock.

I rebuked her most sharply for this naughty observation, saying Tom never expected a baronetcy, and she wasn't to go saying he did, and a knighthood was indeed a great honour, and if here I lied, then may God forgive me but I have my pride, and so also does Tom, and tho' pride is a sin, sometimes I think it is proper.

As to the Duke of Puddle Dock, a person hitherto unknown to me, I had it from Mary Ann that when Tom was a boy he used to boast to their mother he'd be a duke before he died, and she used to twit him it would be the Duke of Puddle Dock, a wretched location in Blackfriars.

Meanwhile, Tom has put in to the College of Heralds for a coat of arms; he has requested this alludes to services he rendered in the Eastward. We are optimistic we will have our armorial bearings before we depart for Bencoolen – the event is now confirmed for October, and, in consequence, Travers has left London for Ireland, to find himself his sturdy plant to take with him as his bride when we sail.

July 1817, Number 23, Berners Street,

I have had nothing to report these past two months, but I now suspect from Certain Signs I am in the family way, tho' I have kept as yet my Suspicions intimate, to myself only, in case I am deceived.

August 1817, Number 23, Berners Street

I this morning overcame my fear of appearing a fool, and took my Suspicions to Sir Thomas Sevestre, who confirmed it probable I am That Way, and if so, then, if it pleases God, the baby will most likely come as next winter turns towards spring.

I greet the news as any woman must: with trepidation. Tho' I cannot forget marriage was ordained for the procreation of children, nor can I forget God's punishment for Eve for eating of the fruit of the tree of the knowledge of good and evil: *in sorrow shalt thou bring forth children*. Will this baby be the death of me? Tho' I would be stalwart, I cannot deny I tremble, on account of the dangers.

August 1817, Number 23, Berners Street

I have told Tom what's doing. He is worried for me, as any loving husband must worry for his wife, but he is nonetheless cautiously delighted, flattering me I am a clever thing, tho' no cleverness was needed here, and saying God willing all goes well, and he's had to wait so long for a son and heir he will dote on this one, if it lives – he says we must indeed have a gentleman, and name him Leopold, for Prince Leopold, and if by ill chance we have a young lady we must call her Charlotte, after the dear Princess.

With our customary discretion towards all that pertains to his first marriage, Tom and I have never discussed the curious blow that it was childless – doubly curious because Olivia was not barren, but bore that natural daughter Mary Ann told me of. So in Tom's *I have had to wait so long* is all the allusion I think I'll ever get to what I must assume is at best my tender husband's resigned disappointment Olivia did not give him children, and at worst a haunting distress. For his sake I am gratified that, if it pleases God, I will soon be giving him what Olivia never could: a chance to hear himself called Father. And if I am gratified too for my own sake that I will soon, God willing, better my predecessor in this matter of maternity, then I must pretend to myself I am not, for I would not be a Smug Mary.

It is fortunate I know in my heart neither the gift of God, nor the gifts of God, may be purchased with gold, because I learn now the gossips of the Assembly Rooms in Cheltenham were wrong to say Tom gave the money tree a good shaking in Java. Indeed, it seems that tho' he lives without stinting, his lavish generosity and his fashionable trappings together conspire to mislead.

The misapprehension is revealed because as my departure for the Eastward rushes closer, Mother becomes regretful that I go – the more so now I am in the family way. She made her unhappiness plain to Tom last night, when he and I dined with her and Father at Soho Square. She complained my husband enjoys in London close friendship with royalty, esteem from famous savants, affectionate acquaintance on every side, and the love of all his family. So why, she asked, why was he going out East again, to an appointment which, beg pardon, she had heard was far less in importance than Java?

Tom, not a bit discommoded, replied it was him should beg pardon, for robbing her, pro tempore, of her daughter, and, in due time, God willing, of her grandson, but it was for want of money he would take up his post in Bencoolen; he returns to the Eastward only in order to make and save enough on which to retire, and she must comfort herself it will be only a little time he's gone, and then he will be back in England again, for nothing can keep him away beyond five years, and he may be home much sooner – and with him, me.

This intelligence my parents received with narrowed eyes and silence. And then Mother called on me this morning. She sat close by me on the sofa in the front drawing room, and, after glancing round for eavesdroppers, she lowered her voice and she said she must express her sympathy my marriage was not perhaps as advantageous as at first it had seemed, for all it had brought me a title, but Father said never mind if Tom has no talent for feathering his nest, for relief I'd have any husband at all he'd have married me to him even if he'd had but a few pounds a year.

To this I replied that tho' money is a shelter, Mother should remember the fruit of the Spirit is not affluence, but love, joy, peace, longsuffering, gentleness, goodness, faith.

August 1817, Number 23, Berners Street

Now we have broached matters pecuniary, Tom has told me The Company is as stingy with its allowances as it is quick to demand repayment if it thinks it has been too generous. Apparently he has been these past few years much annoyed by a petty dispute about his allowance from before even he went to Java, when he was stationed in another place, Penang. Here he received for a time eight thousand Spanish dollars per annum, but then The Company decided he was entitled only to six thousand, and demanded he repay the difference. Was this not capricious and unjust? It is only now he is home – years later – that Tom has managed to get that false debt finally written off.

August 1817, Number 23, Berners Street

We have in London the Royal Menagerie at the Tower, which is a gloomy place, and, at Exeter Change, Edward Cross' menagerie. But Exeter Change has offices on the ground floor, and the poor animals – lions, tigers, monkeys, &c – are confined in iron cages in poky rooms on an upper floor – the roaring of the big cats can be heard on the Strand below, often scaring horses that pass by.

Now Tom has read of an airy, pleasant garden in Paris, *le Jardin des Plantes*, where there is a menagerie stocked with exotic beasts which are kept in conditions as close to their natural environments as possible, so that they can be studied, and so that they can be content in their captivity. He has now decided England should have such a delightful zoological garden, which he thinks would interest and amuse the public, as well as men of science. Accordingly, he has spoken to Sir Joseph Banks about forming a society to promote the idea, but he doubts whether anything can be done about it before our final return to these shores, from those of the Eastward, at which happy date he will give to his proposed zoological garden the full weight of his attention.

September 1817, Number 23, Berners Street

Mr. Murray printed nine hundred copies of the eight-guinea edition of *The History of Java*, of these, two hundred remain unsold. Tom is not discouraged by want of readers, and begins to make provision for a second edition. We sail so soon for the Eastward he does not think he can undertake the work himself, for the difficulty of communication between here and there, far better, he thinks, the corrections be made by a man in London, who can be in daily exchange with Mr. Murray. After much thought he has given his strange cousin Elton the task of revising his book, improving it, and making corrections; his decision makes him nervous but he hopes that by entrusting his interest, character and fame to his cousin, he will concentrate his literary talents and energies on a project more productive than his endless autobiographies, and all the profits from the second edition are to be Elton's, thus easing his embarrassment.

I have told Tom to tell Elton that henceforth the illustration of the ronggeng I decidedly think must be left out. I have also suggested the second edition should give less prominence to the heathen cults of Java than does the first, and should discuss instead the good work of our Christian missionaries to that island. Alas, Tom laughed that for their lack of efficacy the missionaries don't deserve the space, and if he'd been the preacher, he'd have converted all the Eastward by now.

I do worry my dear husband is not as zealous in his faith as for his soul's sake he ought to be.

September 1817, Number 23, Berners Street

Since October fast approaches, we commence a social whirl even busier than usual, and we are making many sad visits of farewell to our friends and to our families. Mother continues querulous that I am leaving, and is often now in tears, and complains whenever I see her she wishes I could live with Tom in Cheltenham – she and Father will return to that town as soon as I quit London. Still, she does not forget to commission from me an East Indian shawl, indeed she thinks she will have two shawls, tho' Father says this is indulgent.

Mrs. Raffles is likewise filled with sorrow to think of the coming separation from her son. Tom does what he can to ease her worries, telling her what he told Mother: it will be only a little time he's gone; as soon as he has accumulated sufficient nest egg he will be back in England; nothing can keep him away beyond five years. He reassures his mother too she need not fear pecuniary distress whilst we are away; she is accustomed to have from him four hundred pounds per annum, and this he tells her she will continue to receive as long as she lives, for her support and that of Hannah.

September 1817, Number 23, Berners Street

We are in the midst of bustle and confusion, and I am much fatigued by the exertions I have been obliged to make for our departure. Tho' I have been throwing away great quantities of rubbish, and odds and ends, the house remains chuck full of curiosities, books, oriental rarities, and where to store these things while we are in the Eastward is a puzzle. Some fragments of statuary and other relics we will deposit in the museum at India House. Some boxes we will send to family members, others the Duke and Duchess of Somerset will store for us.

Meanwhile, Tom is making arrangements to bring along a small menagerie when we sail – dogs, cats, birds – and also a nursery of plants so we can have English vegetation about us in the Eastward, if his specimens can be coaxed into growing there.

September 1817, Number 23, Berners Street

Tom says the Honourable Members of the Court of Directors were in the past little minded to treat him as a person of consequence, but now he has published his *H of J*, and has been knighted, and otherwise honoured by royalty with proofs of regard, they jump to flatter him. Thus it is The Company has named for me the newly built ship that is to take us to Bencoolen – I, Lady Raffles, will sail to the Eastward on the *Lady Raffles*!!!

I have engaged a nurse, Mary Grimes, to look after my baby when it is born – she was recommended by the Duchess of Somerset. Nurse Grimes is a plump and kindly efficient spinster of forty, and I hope she'll be to me as a comfort of home, when I am in the Eastward. The others of our party will be Travers, who is to return to us soon from Ireland, bringing with him a bride, if his plans have come to fruition, as we hope, and Raden Rana Dipura, who is eager to return to the torrid zones, now that chilly autumn again draws on – meanwhile, Papuan Dick is to become a footman in the service of the Duke of Somerset.

Sir Thomas Sevestre has decided to remain here in England, so Tom has engaged one Dr. Joseph Arnold to sail with us when we depart, to be our family physician. In addition to being a medical man this Dr. Arnold is a renowned naturalist – he and Tom were introduced by Sir Joseph Banks – and he is much excited by the prospect of botanising in Sumatra and studying the animals there.

Mary Ann must stay in England when we depart, because Flint is still tied by the Admiralty. She is much downcast at the prospect of being separated from us, and we are likewise reluctant to be parted from our dear puss. With his customary family feeling, Tom is eager to do all he can for her and Flint – the man has such a pitiable allowance Mary Ann often doesn't know what she can do. Tom has told his sister that when he reaches Bencoolen he will look out for some suitable appointment for her husband that he may quit the Admiralty for something of greater pecuniary advantage, and he will send for them both to join us as soon as he is able.

October 1817, Number 23, Berners Street

My baby has quickened, a moment of deep emotion on which I will not comment. My stranger now flutters inside me, a butterfly of hope.

October 1817, Number 23, Berners Street

Tom has got his coat of arms. He chose as his motto *Auspicium Melioris Aevi*, Omen of a better age, and the design includes a griffin crest, and beneath it a representation of an honour he had in Java from a sultan who rewarded him for kind service by making him a member of the Order of the Golden Sword. This native order is represented on Tom's coat of arms by two small, golden medallions on a chain, one written in a native script called *Jawi*, the other engraved with one of those native krises with its wavy-edged blade.

It is Tom's proud intention to have his crest now stamped, or engraved, on everything we own, from bookplates, to chessmen, to knives and forks, to my harp, which is coming with us to the

Eastward, as I cannot be without my music, and I intend to bring also a piano and quantities of sheet music.

October 1817, Number 23, Berners Street

We continue with our round of farewells, and we dined last night with Princess Charlotte and Prince Leopold at Claremont – she is much advanced in pregnancy, and is bigger even than me. Our royal hosts presented Tom with a diamond ring, as a token of their united regard, the jewel is a very fine one and the Princess requested Tom sometimes wear it for her sake.

Tom remarked to me in the carriage home he wished this leave taking were at an end; that his heart is sad, and yet we must go, and the sooner we are off the better, and he does not like it that the house is now daily filled with those who are determined to say goodbye, for seeing them makes him more than ever miserable when it requires all his fortitude to keep his spirits calm and uniform.

In all these sentiments I am as one with my husband. Our approaching departure fills me with dread, for I am going to part from those near and dear to me and I am now I estimate five months pregnant, and I am unlikely to reach Sumatra before my time comes, with all its risks to me, as well as to my baby, and I must contemplate a confinement at sea, amidst all the horrors of a voyage. It is thus a sorry thing to write to my friends to bid them farewell, for when I do so the future appears sad, and the uncertainty of this world strikes and chills me. How can I write to my friends I hope we shall meet again, that I shall again see you as last I saw you, hear you speak as last I heard you speak, for each time I write to a friend I hope we shall meet again, I think: shall we do so? That we may I will implore as a mercy from heaven – I feel cowardice stealing upon me, and the longer I stay in England, waiting to depart, I fear the less of a heroine I shall prove.

October 1817, the George Hotel, Portsmouth

After a tedious, rainy journey Tom and I and all the party to sail with us have arrived in Portsmouth, together with Mary Ann, along in the post chaise to wave us off – she always was a little dear, and now more than ever.

Travers did indeed find himself a bride in Ireland and our newlyweds are also today come to Portsmouth. Tom for some reason has begun to call them Mr. and Mrs. Tot, or the Tots, and this he thinks a great joke, and it seems to me the name will stick.

Out in the roads, the *Lady Raffles* is ready to be underway. We have written our final letters of farewell to our families – Portsmouth is the farthest I have ever been from my parents and henceforth what world am I to share with them, for tomorrow I sail into the blue, carrying with me all my memories, all my hopes.

October 1817, The Black Horse Inn, Falmouth

What a curse is seasickness. The *Lady Raffles* got underway from Portsmouth early in the morning of the 23rd. I was happy with our cabin which was large, and airy, in the roundhouse, with easy access to the cuddy and space for all Tom's birds in cages, and we had a fair wind down the Channel, so all seemed set for a comfortable beginning to our voyage. But then there blew up a pummeling south-westerly gale, which produced high seas and caused the ship to roll alarmingly. I suffered severely from the motion and refused every kind of nourishment or refreshment even to a glass of water, and after I had fainted many times there were fears for my life. For my sake, the Captain decided to put in here, at Falmouth, where from the formidable effects of tossing about I am become so feeble I doubt I can sit upright long enough to write this entry in my diary without fainting – for I remain very subject to fainting fits – and I am as pale as my bed sheets, and all suffused with fear lest the seasickness should be injurious to my baby.

November 1817, The Black Horse Inn, Falmouth

I am well again, my strength has returned, and I feel equal to a second edition of seasickness, but there does not appear to be any chance of my trying my courage for the wind is still averse, and likely to continue so. We are very quiet in our inn, and everyone is glad to be ashore in these gales, and I hope when we sail again we shall have less boisterous weather. Meanwhile, I grow as large as a mountain.

November 1817, The Black Horse Inn, Falmouth

Man that is born of a woman is of a few days, and full of trouble … On November 6, we again boarded the *Lady Raffles*, with me in good spirits, but the gales soon turned so violent, and so violently against us, that we risked being blown quite the wrong way, and we had to return to port. Here we received most shocking, sad news: our dear Princess Charlotte is dead after suffering most long and terrible travail; she died but hours after she was delivered of a stillborn son, and now all blame her incompetent doctor.

The whole country is in deepest mourning, for Princess Charlotte conjured in the people most devoted adulation. Tom is horribly distressed at the loss of his friend, and as for me, this news has intensified all my fears about my own confinement, so I dare not dwell on it.

November 1817, The Black Horse Inn, Falmouth

Mary Ann has sent me a most tactless letter, commenting on the death of the dear Princess. She writes she is sure Tom says nothing indelicate, and she grants his regard for the Princess was beyond any consideration of rank, or wealth, or honour, and yet she adds in truth he must reflect that with this death must end his hopes of royal preferment.

I have decided the best thing to do with this letter is to destroy it, and to pretend I never received it.

November 1817, the *Lady Raffles*, leaving Falmouth

My patience for a fair wind was almost exhausted, but now one blows, so once more we are off, and as we must go, God grant that it be for good, and that this fine, calm weather holds.

December 1817, the *Lady Raffles*

I have been reading daily in my *Book of Common Prayer* the forms of prayer to be used at sea, for this has been until now a dreadful voyage, terrifying, with contrary winds, howling bad weather, and such heaving seas they threatened to swamp us. I have often been unable to stand, and I shudder to remember crossing the Bay of Biscay, a roiling cauldron, a particular misery, and such tossing about and seasickness I never knew and hope never to know again – the smell of vomit still lingers in our clothes, and in our damp blankets.

But, debarring bad smells, the Lord has delivered us out of our distress: the storm has now ceased; we have caught the steadily-blowing trade winds; the sea becomes calm, the sky serene; I even begin to think a ship a very beautiful thing, when white sails billow against cloudless blue.

December 1817, the *Lady Raffles*

My appetite has returned. This morning we had Devonshire cream from the cows sailing with us, and Tom promises that tomorrow he will exert his handiwork in butter making.

December 1817, the *Lady Raffles*

I continue feeling well, and the weather continues calm, with the thermometer at seventy-six and our cabin window open. Tom's dogs, cats, birds – the latter singing in cages all around me – and his nursery of plants are all thriving beyond expectation, and so am I. Indeed, I am so much improved I am turning in earnest to my Malay grammars; Tom insists I learn the language and devotes much time to tutoring me – he is a most excellent tutor, and I think I have already enough Malay to manage my servants, tho' I never thought before I could have much of a head for oriental tongues.

In the evenings, Tom reads me favourite poems, and sometimes we sit with Dr. Arnold. The doctor and I are become firm friends; it is some comfort to me to think that to this good, kind man will fall the responsibility of delivering my baby.

Christmas Day 1817, the *Lady Raffles*

There was dancing in the cuddy today, and my baby joined in, by dancing a jig inside me, but I sat out, for being as large as a house.

December 1817, the *Lady Raffles*

Today we crossed the line. Having saluted the Southern hemisphere by the firing of guns, our crew proceeded to enact the traditional ceremonies. An experienced Old Salt directed the performance with much solemnity and decorum. He appeared as King Neptune, attired in a manner that was meant to be terribly imposing, accompanied by his consort, seated on a gun-carriage instead of a shell, drawn by some of the crew, as substitutes for Tritons. In the evening, the sailors represented a comedy of their own composition, but I was not allowed to see it, as the Captain said it was sure to be too indelicate for the female chapter.

January 1818, the *Lady Raffles*

On my account the Captain has decided not to put into the Cape of Good Hope. I suffered so much from seasickness on leaving Falmouth, and was so reduced and lowered in consequence, that rather than putting in to The Cape, and risking bad weather on resuming our voyage, he has determined on pursuing our course, for the weather now is fair, and the sea calm, and he says there is good chance of continuance of both. I cherish the hope that I may arrive at Bencoolen in time for my confinement.

January 1818, the *Lady Raffles*

As my time approaches, I grow ever more anxious. I am deeply impressed with the fear that my infant may have been injured in proportion to the seasickness I have suffered – that its life may have been endangered – and so I would dread the moment of its birth even if I were not aware that then may come the moment of my eternal judgement. If we both live, I confess I fear I shall not be able to nurse it.

February 1818, the *Lady Raffles*

Before I formed thee in the belly I knew thee; and before thou camest forth out of the womb I sanctified thee … Which is to say that not a week back I armed myself with patience and prayer and withstood as best I was able the pains that are God's punishment for Eve's sin of eating the forbidden fruit, all the while trying to

259

suppress those dreadful groans and cries which so much discourage all those who hear them, and now I am safe in bed with a baby girl. I was fortunate in the weather, with the ship very little tossing and rolling. Nurse Grimes and Dr. Arnold attended me.

It is not the easiest thing to manage a new baby on a ship – the laundry of the napkins is a most troublesome production – but Nurse Grimes has since my delivery been invaluable, everything I could wish for, active, intelligent, and careful and affectionate with my dear baby.

The passengers and crew have united in rendering every accommodation which the peculiar circumstances demand. They have thrown the whole of the roundhouse into one cabin, and this I now occupy with my dear baby, and here we have received the visits of all the party aboard. The cuddy is given over to us as an ante chamber, and that is where Tom now sleeps.

Tom, much relieved I am safe, and the babe also, is not now she has arrived displeased we got only a young lady, and says any man must be delighted by a daughter as beautiful as ours. He remarks on the coincidence he was born at sea – which interesting fact, to my somewhat aggrieved surprise, he only today revealed to me – he remarks his daughter follows him, and he says everything went so well we should perhaps arrange for our next child to likewise be born at sea? He is in some doubt whether my dear baby is an African or an Asiatic – the nearest land is Madagascar, and yet he likes to think her an Asiatic.

February 1818, the *Lady Raffles*

The Captain has christened our daughter. Tho' the dear Princess is no more, we have nonetheless named her Charlotte – her full name is Charlotte Sophia Tunjung Segara.

In the Javanese tongue *tunjung segara* means *lotus of the sea* – a lotus I'm told is a water flower of the Eastward, very beautiful, and a symbol of goodness and purity because it carries its large blooms on long stems above the surfaces of the muddy ponds where it grows, and for this rising above mud the plant is much revered by the natives, who have their little sense of godliness, notwithstanding they lack Christian Revelation.

Tunjung Segara was suggested by Raden Rana Dipura, who said that the child of a great man of Java should have a name appropriate to the circumstances of its birth. I thought the idea was too simple, and too beautiful not to be adopted, tho' I do hope my dear baby will realise it.

Tho' we are at sea, and our stocks of sugar much depleted, we had at Miss Charlotte's christening both cake and caudle – that restorative eggnog traditional for new mothers, the eggs for it provided by the barnyard of fowl sails with us.

March 1818, the *Lady Raffles*, off the coast of Sumatra

We have reached Sumatra at last, and sail along its coastline, but at such a distance from it that I can make out little of the island, a big one, a thousand miles long, says Tom. The land appears to me as a low smudge; behind the distant beaches – smears of sandy pink – there seems to be nothing but the densest forest, an endlessly spreading expanse of hazy green, rising higher in an undulating ridge where the land merges with the clouds of the sky, and Tom says this is the mountainous backbone to the island, and many of those mountains are burning – I did not know hitherto that there would be burning mountains in the vicinity of my new home.

The sun is relentless. I am now at all times hot and dripping, and I sometimes half think that, apart from her napkin, Miss Charlotte should go naked most of the time, letting the heat itself become her damply pressing swaddling, but I daren't share this thought with Nurse Grimes, because I know she'd dismiss it as dangerous nonsense.

March 1818, the *Lady Raffles*, off Bencoolen

We are anchored off Pulau Tikus, or Rat Island, about six miles off Bencoolen. It appears from the *Lady Raffles'* deep draft we can approach no closer to our destination, and it is arranged that the accommodation boats will come out early tomorrow morning to take us ashore.

I'm told Rat Island is so named because at low tide the sand dunes take on the appearance of running rodents, tho' when I saw them earlier they looked to me like any other sand dunes. The sea coming in is now so heavy that on account of the vessel's rolling I can scarcely hold my quill to write more than this.

March 1818, Jennings' house, Bencoolen

Tho' we have arrived at Bencoolen, I will not say yet what I think of the place, for not wanting to make hasty, unfair judgement. We landed this morning at about eleven o'clock, with the troops of the garrison drawn up to meet us, and guns booming in salute, which tribute I cannot pretend I did not enjoy. After the official reception we proceeded to the house of the Acting-Resident, William Jennings, who has given us accommodation as most unfortunately Government House has been much damaged by the shocks of earthquakes these past few days and it will take a little time to clear the rubble and make repairs.

I did not know hitherto that Sumatra is subject to earthquakes – nor that Bencoolen is a penal colony for Indian convicts, which fact Tom thought to tell me only this morning, as we waited on the *Lady Raffles* for the accommodation boats to bring us ashore.

March 1818, Jennings' house, Bencoolen

Tom, stalwart but dismayed, says he thinks Bencoolen must be more disregarded by The Company than any other unfortunate spot, and that tho' he had not expected it to be as splendid as Java, he had been by no means prepared for the unhappiness and poverty which now meet him – he says this is without exception the most wretched place he ever beheld.

As for me, I could never have conceived anything half so bad. Everywhere is in a miserable state of desolation. My pen cannot convey an adequate idea of the state of ruin and dilapidation, resulting from the mixed effects of the recent earthquakes, and of previous neglect, that I behold each time I venture in to town. The streets are impassable from cracks in the earth, or else overrun with rank grass, and Tom says tho' Jennings cannot be blamed for the cracks, the result of earthquakes, he is very culpable for the grass, which he ought to have ordered cleared.

Where houses still stand their mildewed walls stagger, and their roofs are tumbled. Alas, their occupants seem just as sagging as these collapsing dwellings, for the natives here have a defeated air, and trudge about dull-eyed and listless.

My own intended dwelling, Government House, is rent by cracks from top to bottom, and from the circumstance that it has been unoccupied since the last Resident left, it is now a den of ravenous dogs and polecats.

The scenery is oppressive. I write now at a desk on Jennings' verandah: the view on one side is closely confined by heavily forested hills, and on the other is nothing but the monotonous flat metallic glitter of the sea. I gather few ships pass here and all today I have seen naught on the horizon but a vast expanse of blurred blue, where blurred ocean fades to blurred sky.

The mornings can be delightfully fresh, but, on the whole, the climate here is no better than I expected, and I feel too often half simmered in my skirts, like a fish in a kettle.

March 1818, Jennings' house, Bencoolen

Tom tells me the natives now call Bencoolen *tana mati*, *dead land*, which I think a fitting name – the town is pestilential, rife with the intermittent fever, and with a variety of poxes, so I grapple at night with the knowledge there is something in the climate of the torrid zones inimical to Europeans. My dear babe! Why did I ever leave Cheltenham?

March 1818, Jennings' house, Bencoolen

The public buildings here have been allowed to go to ruin, and have no gardens at all. On asking why, Tom told me that ten years back the locals rose up against the then Resident, one Thomas Parr, murdered him, and cut his head off over some trifling disagreement about his policy on trade. The bushes and trees around government buildings were all raised at that time, so as to afford no cover to bandits.

This piece of intelligence I received in silence.

March 1818, Jennings' house, Bencoolen

I feel now sometimes fogged by heat and the strangeness of things, and this swirling fog of heat and strangeness I think cannot be dispelled except by England, parents, old friends, cold weather, cold water, strawberries, roses, newspapers ... I confess I remind myself often Tom and I will not be long in Sumatra. There is nothing to keep him in the country beyond the necessity of obtaining the means without which we cannot live in England – for to be in England without money would never do – and when I think of our future comfort, I must be satisfied the present privations are for the best.

March 1818, Government House, Bencoolen

We have moved into Government House, and tho' it is supposed to be fixed the building is in a most crazy condition, and we risk our lives with split walls and crumbling plaster, for the place is nearly a ruin. Moreover, it too often trembles with the awful visitations of earthquakes: day and night, this past week we have seldom been long without them; the hanging lamps in the hall swing wildly; bedding is tossed from the beds; books fly from the shelves. The unnatural heaving of the land is worse by far than the most monstrous heaving of the sea, and I shudder to think what damage could befall Miss Charlotte in the night, as a result of her nursery shaking, and all the things in it tumbling.

March 1818, Government House, Bencoolen

Well, it avails nothing to repine, and less to murmur against Providence. I will not be discontented; I will try to make it better at Government House, and Tom will order the replanting of the garden here, and we will make ourselves comfortable, and we will be happy as we always are, and I will remind myself I am the most blessed of earthly beings, for the Lord has granted me husband, child, a life fair set for adventure, health, and what right have I to expect so much? Indeed, I have moments which banish unhappiness entirely. I am feeding Miss Charlotte myself, and when he watches me Tom says never was there such a pair of darlings. He is besotted with his daughter – a most doting father. He says his Tunjung Segara is by far the brightest floweret of the Eastern Isles, and comments often on her blue eyes, refined features, and pretty toes. He says what a beauty she is tho' he should not say it for she is the spit of him. It is true she is more Raffles than Hull, but her eyes, as Tom remarks, are blue whereas his are amber and mine are pale brown, and here I think is outward sign that from the start of her life our daughter is her own person only, notwithstanding she got her nose from her father.

Tom and I both agree that at two months Miss Charlotte is as intelligent and large as most babies are at three times that age.

March 1818, Government House, Bencoolen

Tom says no matter that Jennings has lately been incompetent, ever since the day of Parr's murder the government of this town has evidently been very bad, for everywhere in the administration he finds a deranged state of affairs, so it is no wonder the poor Malays are impoverished, depressed, and wretched.

Still, as no better friend than Tom could have been appointed to watch over them I feel certain I shall soon see happy faces, and some appearance of industry and self-reliance – at present I see less of that than of the desolating power of slavery. Alas, tho' slave trading is now illegal, we found on our arrival that at Bencoolen endure many slaves imported in former times: Malays from various islands of their extensive maritime nation; local aboriginals; Africans. Tom says this tolerance of slavery is intolerable and he will end this dreadful evil, and the tolerance of it both.

March 1818, Government House, Bencoolen

Tom has emancipated the slaves, those poor relicts of the past, and he has set up a school for their children, the African ones in particular being in a notable state of nature, vice, and wretchedness. I have taken one little blackamoor for our treasure Nurse Grimes, to be under her a nursery maid. This bright-eyed girl I rename Jane, because the name she brought with her was nothing but a string of clicks, and quite unpronounceable.

As well as banning, in accordance with his principles and

British law, the importation into Bencoolen of slaves, Tom has ameliorated the lot of the transported Indian felons by giving them land, and encouraging them to become settlers.

Furthermore, for the good of the natives, he has also banned cockfighting – birds ripped to bloody shreds – and gaming. These measures will cost The Company, for the license holders who operate the cockpits and gambling dens pay the treasury steep taxes to do so, but Tom says he will no more govern here, than he did in Java, for bare mercantile profit alone, and both gaming and cockfighting are abhorrent to him and must be stopped.

Tom has written to the Court of Directors, to let the Honourable Members know what he has done, and he expects they will censure him for being precipitate, but he says he is inured to their censure, for being so often its recipient, and in any case they may not read his letter, for all he made it short – it is a common remark with my husband that he suspects his letters to Leadenhall St. too often remain unread, especially his longer ones.

March 1818, Government House, Bencoolen

Out of anxiety for Miss Charlotte we are determined to live in a healthier spot than this pestilential town, and we have been asking our new acquaintance here to recommend one. Now Tom has found a hill about twelve miles inland – Bukit Kabut, Hill of Mists.

No European had set foot on this Hill of Mists before Tom climbed it, but he says the summit is just the site we want: it commands a most extensive view of the surrounding country, and the temperature is lower there than here on the coast. Accordingly, he has ordered land cleared, to the extent of about three hundred acres, that he may have built for us on it a country house, and that we may there establish a plantation – coffee, nutmeg, cloves. Since our house will be built almost in the native style, of wood and the palm called atap, Tom is confident the work, once commenced, will conclude quickly.

Hill of Mists is still too much covered with forest to allow of easy access, else I'd visit it myself.

March 1818, Government House, Bencoolen

Bencoolen is in such an exhausted state it cannot even feed itself – rice must be imported from Bengal – and it is no small drain on The Company. When Tom checked the treasury accounts he found a deficit of forty thousand pounds. This deficit the settlement must now somehow repay. Tom sighs it is the story of Java all over again, for in that place too The Company's expenditure regularly exceeded by some margin its income. To save money, poor Tom has had to let go his personal bodyguard, and he is in all ways trying to reduce government expenses. To raise money is a puzzle, for Bencoolen is suffering under an annihilation of its export trade; in other parts of Sumatra they grow coffee, or mine gold, but the only product of this area is pepper, and the price of pepper is falling. Worse, the Americans are undercutting our market by buying pepper not from here, but from Acheen – this is the court, in the northern part of the island, whose sultan conferred upon Tom the Order of the Golden Sword. Acheen belongs neither to us, nor to the Dutch, and that is why the Americans, with their neutral flag, and their interloping ways, slide in and do their trading there.

March 1818, Government House, Bencoolen

Notwithstanding Bencoolen's sad want of money, and many disadvantages, Tom now wishes, for strategic reasons, to expand this settlement. Since the restitution to the Dutch of their empire in the Eastward, they wish to do again as in former times they used to do: to monopolise the China trade by absolute control of the Eastern Seas. Alas, Bencoolen is not well placed to be a spoke in the wheel of their ambitions, for being on the south-west coast of Sumatra, far from the main trading routes to China. Still, Tom, with his customary buoyancy of spirits, refuses to be pessimistic. He says tho' our diplomats were played for fools when they agreed to allow the Dutch to put their noses beyond the Cape, it is his duty to do what he can to promote both The Company's, and the country's, trading interests and in this most necessary work he must use what is to hand, and never mind if what is to hand is only Bencoolen.

Hence my husband has today sent Tot to Batavia, which is now again the Dutch capital in the Eastward, to negotiate with the government there for an extension of our British lands here in Sumatra. Negotiation is necessary because the Dutch maintain a few small posts hereabouts and on this basis they like to claim, emptily, and arrogantly, general suzerainty over the parts of the island not controlled by us. This notwithstanding there are great tracts of the interior where they've never seen a Dutchman, because like us the Hollanders cling mainly to coastal parts.

Tom in particular wishes Tot to broach with the Dutch the matter of the port of Padang. This port, north of here, we now have, but Tom, to his distress, is ordered by the Court of Directors to cede it to the Dutch, to keep them sweet in Europe. He thinks this instruction so insane he is determined to ignore it, and he wishes Tot to argue at Batavia that we should retain Padang.

Mrs. Tot is gone with her husband to Java tho' she is in the family way, and very large – she proves herself as sensible as Tot wished, for she does not draw attention to her pregnancy, or complain. Their party includes also the Raden, as he thinks it is high time he returned to his homeland.

April 1818, Government House, Bencoolen

Our first letters from Home!!!* And what welcome, precious letters – Tom was so eager to have them, I thought he would jump off the verandah to snatch them from the runner who brought them from the ship. The packet included for me letters from my parents – my mother asking how my pregnancy goes along, an echo of the past very strange to me now I nurse the baby, my father saying he has unrolled his map, to follow my progress across the globe – and for Tom a letter from Mary Ann, dated November, when we had barely left Falmouth, asking when she and Flint can come join us in the Eastward, and what Flint can do here. Tom sighs he has no choice but to reply Bencoolen is so impecunious and forlorn, he can give them little yet but eating and drinking and a broken down home, and asking they be patient a little while longer and remain in England perhaps another year until some opportunity presents itself.

*I notice I wrote the word *home* with a capital H, for I meant Old England, which remains my home, notwithstanding I dwell in Bencoolen – unless I dwell in Tom? And not forgetting I have a higher home in Our Saviour. In any case when I mean by *home* Old England, I will henceforth do as I just did, and write it *Home*.

April 1818, Government House, Bencoolen

In barely a blink, it seems, the Tots are back from Java, bringing with them one Dr. Thomas Horsfield, hitherto a stranger to me, tho' even before I met him I knew a little about him, for Tom had spoken to me once or twice of this naturalist and antiquarian he much admires.

Dr. Horsfield has now come to Bencoolen that he may again pursue his scientific studies under British, not Dutch, protection.

He is so keen for his natural history he has brought with him birds without number, beasts of every kind, and plants, seeds, &c, in abundance. Tom, who so loves company, and who complains we are a prosing domestic couple without it, is delighted he is here, and his menagerie also, and Dr. Arnold too is happy to have on hand another naturalist with whom he can converse.

Meanwhile, the Tots are full of the news they stayed a few days at Tom's former home, Buitenzorg. Mrs. Tot, now quite a mountain, reports her husband confided in her there are wonderful changes under the house's new Dutch mistress, and that it is much improved and is superbly finished, and is altogether altered, and is very much better than it was before – in short, that Olivia lacked the proper skills of household management, and was unable to maintain a comfortable home. Or so I must conclude. Moreover, Mrs. Tot brings me hints my predecessor was known to all abroad to be ... not quite *quite*. She says she should not tell me, for it is wrong both to pass on gossip, and also to speak ill of the dead, but Olivia is remembered in Java as an elderly lady, rather fantastically dressed, who claimed to be much celebrated in song – the Nona of a certain little bard, and never for one moment let Batavia forget it. Mrs. Tot even heard it whispered Olivia was too fond of a glass of brandy, and when she had taken too much of it, and got Tom's aides-de-camp about, her no modest woman could sit in her company.

I will not allow myself to comment on these various items of intelligence.

Alas, Tot made no progress at all with the Dutch, neither in the matter of their ceding lands in Sumatra to us, nor in allowing us to retain the port of Padang.

April 1818, Government House, Bencoolen

I am in some commotion, for today, when I was tidying his

papers, I found by chance on Tom's desk a hasty pen and ink sketch, poorly executed, of what, despite the artist's lack of skill, was evidently a beautiful open rotunda shading a plinth. Beneath the sketch was written a verse:

> *O thou whom ne'er my constant heart*
> *One moment hath forgot*
> *Tho' fate severe hath bid us part*
> *Yet still forget me not*

I took the drawing to Tom, and I asked him, innocent of all intent of prying: what's doing? My husband blushed, and glanced away, and then he mumbled this was a sketch Tot made for him at Buitenzorg, as a souvenir. Naturally, I asked: a souvenir of what? With evident reluctance Tom told me this was Tot's likeness of the marble monument he, Tom, had had erected to Olivia, in the garden she'd so loved. Tho' I knew he did not wish to be pressed further, I could not help myself. What of the verse? I blurted. Was it you who wrote it? No, said Tom, Olivia had written it herself some years before she died, and had herself suggested it as her epitaph, and come the sadly fateful day he'd had it engraved on the plinth, to honour her.

I must say I think Olivia's rhymes too jaunty, and her sentiments too sentimental, and for a woman to write her own epitaph I think unseemly.

April 1818, Government House, Bencoolen

Mrs. Tot is safely delivered of her child – a girl, very ugly and sickly looking. She has now entrusted the care of her baby to a native nurse, but I lent Nurse Grimes for the laying-in, and I have been looking after Mrs. Tot as tho' she were my sister.

Meanwhile, I am to wean Miss Charlotte, that I may

accompany Tom on a journey of diplomacy to the Pasemah Highlands, like the Hill of Mists before my husband trod it, this is a place where no European has ever gone before, not even the Dutch. It was bandits from Pasemah who decapitated that unfortunate Mr. Parr, for trying to interfere with their coffee trade – Pasemah is famous for its coffee. Tom now decides he must reconcile the conflicting interests which have distracted people in the region ever since that wicked event, and The Company's reprisals, which were necessarily severe – villages razed and so on, tho' Tom says quite the wrong villages, the blameworthy ones being remote miles beyond the reach of our redcoats.

Our journey will require us to penetrate the forest interior of this island. The natives say it is impossible for Europeans to survive even a day in the deepest forests, but Tom will not listen to difficulties, and I will not be separated from him merely for my own convenience. If my story ends in the forest, so be it; I grant my death would be sad for Miss Charlotte, and I would very much like to know how her story unfolds, but a good wife must ever put her husband before her child.

May 1818, Government House, Bencoolen

Dr. Arnold, who is to be of the party journeying to Pasemah, thinks I should not go. He told me this morning he knows I would accompany Sir Stamford to the world's end, and, indeed some would say I have already done so, but I should remember we know nothing of the difficulties explorers may encounter in the Sumatran interior, nor anything of the disposition of the people they may meet, except that former reports mentioned they are treacherous and murderous. I told him: no matter, I will go.

Tom now tells me Dr. Arnold has likewise tried to persuade him not to permit me to go, but that he replied he may as well say he did not permit the sun to rise. He said also that by taking me to visit with them, the people of Pasemah would be more certain of his coming with a peaceable intention, and I am happy to be thus useful to my husband.

May 1818, Government House, Bencoolen

In haste, before departing – I have given Nurse Grimes final instructions, and with a sorry heart I have kissed goodbye to Miss Charlotte. Soon I will mount my horse for the first stretch of the journey to Pasemah. As well as Tom and Dr. Arnold, our party consists of six Bugis to form our guard – the Bugis are a famously fierce nation – several guides from Pasemah, and somewhere around sixty or seventy Malay bearers carrying equipment and supplies.

Manna, a settlement we have about eighty miles along the coast, is our immediate destination.

May 1818, The Residency, Manna

For the past two days we have trotted along the coast from Bencoolen to this small outpost at Manna – myself the only one of our party sitting side-saddle – and we stayed last night in a village along the way. Tomorrow we turn inland, to follow the course of the Manna River, as it winds into the interior. We will have with us both Edward Presgrave, who is the Resident here, and also a native aristocrat, the Pangeran of Manna; both men henceforth join our party.

May 1818, a camp in the forest

I am exhausted. Yesterday, we had to send back the horses, because of the precipices and forests we began to encounter almost as soon as we left Manna. Since then we have had to proceed on foot. I walked between twelve and fifteen hours today, which Tom tells me is to be our routine.

Walking through the forest is like walking through honey, it clings so – even *clots* – not at all like walking through an English woodland, and the trees most unBritannic in their height – some of them are over two hundred feet tall. The great girth of their trunks is buttressed by prodigious roots that in places flare from the trees like fins, or sails, and in others twist across the ground like monstrous serpents. The vegetation everywhere thrusts, bursting in all places with a great exuberance of leaves, and with vines festooned in swags, and with thorny stems, and with hanging tendrils. To make a path the Malay bearers must slash at the clogging undergrowth with alarming big knives called parangs.

I breathe at all times the faint sickly scent of corruption, for where it is not matted with vegetation the forest floor is slippery and slimy with reddish mud, and rotting leaves which ooze and squelch underfoot. The air is so damp it drips all day, and it is so hot for being trapped beneath the canopy of the trees it could be steam coming from a kettle; my body is at all times so salty and glowing I may as well have been sea bathing.

Everywhere is hard going, even the flat – but hardly anywhere *is* flat. Today, where the way was especially steep and slick and narrow I had two bearers to hold my hands, one before, the other behind, pushing me, and pulling me until I attained the top of the slope.

Wherever we went, our guides seemed nervous; one, who was whistling, but not happily, broke off to tell me the forest rustles with spirits, *hantu*, that would steal men's souls and inhabit their bodies, so that they can give up their ghostly lives and live again earthly ones. He said that as I walked I must not be silent, but I must sing as I passed, so my human voice would scare off these predatory hantu. I did not like this heathen way of talking, so I said I was more worried by the thought of encountering elephants, than of encountering ghosts – we saw many signs of elephants as we struggled along.

Tho' I cannot countenance superstition, and indeed I pride myself I am a sensible woman, I must say the forest is an eerie place: cobwebs as big as bed sheets are spun between branches, and at their centres are spiders to give the bravest a fright; ceaseless unnerving noise swells all about, a symphony of chattering and screams, of whining insects, of inhuman grunts, calls, shrieks; notwithstanding the forest is breezeless, the vegetation shudders, shivers, whispers, sways; the light, filtered by the soaring mosaic of leaves, encourages alarmed fancy, dimly green, it flickers with shadows. As I pushed through the gloomy vegetation I found myself imagining tigers lurking at the edge of my vision, and I did not much like to think of venomous reptiles either.

I should note the guide and I conversed in Malay, for thanks to Tom's diligence as a teacher, and my many opportunities to practice, I am fluent now, near enough.

May 1818, a camp in the forest

There are red ants crawling in my hair, and tonight, when I took off my boots, I found them filled with blood, so many leeches had fallen into them, and fed off me, and likewise my legs under my skirts were all bloody – I wish I had with me long pantaloons to wear beneath my skirts, but I have only unmentionables of the usual length, to the knee. If only I could borrow a pair of Tom's trousers, and dress in the forest like a man, but such a thing could never do, and so I must bear with patient fortitude my skirts – to be a man would make ablutions easier too, for all our business we must do in the forest.

Disgusting leeches! I sit now in a rough hut constructed by the bearers from branches, and these slimy torments fall constantly from the leaves that shelter me from the weather, which is rainy, and the candle I write by is haloed by moths, which sometimes fly too close to the flame, and sizzle for it, and the steaming air I breathe is heavy with mosquitoes.

May 1818, a camp in the forest

Today, Dr. Arnold and a group of five or six Malays ventured some way before the rest of our party. Suddenly one of the Malays came rushing back with shining eyes, and called out to Tom: Come with me, Sir, come! A flower very large, beautiful, wonderful.

Tom, Mr. Presgrave, and I all went with him about a hundred yards into the forest. There we found Dr. Arnold, kneeling, pointing to a flower – a truly astonishing flower – growing close to the ground, under the bushes. We all agreed that this was the most extraordinary vegetable production we had ever seen, and each of us avowed that had we been alone, and had there been no witnesses, we would have been fearful of mentioning its dimensions, so much did they exceed those of every other flower any of us had ever seen or heard of, for the bloom measured across from the extremity of the petals more than a yard! The inside of the cup, something like a pitcher, was nine inches wide, and just as deep; Dr. Arnold estimated it held a gallon and a half of water. He likewise estimated the weight of the flower at about twenty pounds.

The petals of this prodigy were nowhere less than half an inch thick, and of a firm, fleshy consistency, like a mushroom – Dr. Arnold said the flower's chemical composition must be fungous. It had no roots, no leaves, no stem, but was a parasite, said Dr. Arnold, and indeed it was just seated on its host, the exposed root of a vine, with a swarm of flies buzzing over it – the flower attracted these carrion lovers because it had not a pretty scent, but stank of rotting meat.

I do not know why the Malay sent back to fetch us had called the flower *beautiful*, for in looks it was as ugly as in smell: the inside of the cup had livid hues most hideous: here an intense purple, there shades of yellow from pale to dense, with all along its walls soft flexible spines, also of yellow. The petals were brick-red, with pustular spots of white.

The bearers built a crate from wood they scavenged from the forest, and now the flower sits in that crate, packed about with moist grass, and two porters are to carry it back to Manna. Alas, Dr. Arnold is not hopeful it will keep, as he hasn't got with him sufficient spirits to preserve it, though he has done his best with what he has.

Between ourselves to be playful we call our strange flower *Daisy* – though none of us ever saw a daisy looks remotely like her.

May 1818, a camp in the forest

Tho' I do not like to take chairs at Home, as it almost engenders in me a sensation of shameful sloth at human beings slaving under my weight, my scruples are less, here in the forest. Sometimes when the way is more than ever testing I am grateful to be carried in a hammock of matting slung between two poles with a bearer at each end – indeed, without this indulgence I think I must before now have collapsed. But today, I could not be carried at all for our route was too arduous. We covered nearly thirty miles, and each of those miles a scramble over thickly forested, mountainous terrain, jutting here and there with dangerous rocks. The journey was so difficult that a number of the bearers deserted – turned their tales and fled, for which I cannot in charity condemn them.

May 1818, a camp in the forest

We did not bring with us enough food, and now subsist on rice and claret. I have neither energy nor light to write more than that, for I can barely see, the shadows gather so.

May 1818, a hut at Pagaralam, Pasemah

Let us offer the sacrifice of praise to God continually, that is, the fruit of our lips giving thanks to his name ... Which is to say we have reached the highlands of Pasemah. We were met at the boundary of their land by local chiefs to guide our way, and these men, far from seeming treacherous or murderous, were most welcoming, and expressed particular delight in meeting me, the first fair woman they had ever seen.

Our guides led us through a pretty, cool, and misty region, cultivated, so we walked on raised banks between flooded fields where the natives grow their rice, which grassy crop spread emerald all around us. It was easy going, so I could enjoy the open views towards distant mountains, and enjoy too the butterflies flitting about, here an iridescent glitter of blue, there of green, there of yellow, or red. We passed a place where I was able to take in secluded privacy a bath in hot springs, which was a most welcome indulgence. We passed too a village we could not enter, for fear of smallpox, which now rages in this region. Dr. Arnold whispered to me he has with him the things he needs to vaccinate the natives, if only they will allow it, which for fear of witchcraft they may not, for he has often encountered the native belief that the pricking of his needle brings not protection from disease, but a variety of sorcery would enslave their souls and make them his chattels, and sometimes for trying to vaccinate natives he has been chased away and even threatened with death.

Eventually we reached Pagaralam, the principal settlement of this region, where we were guests at a ceremonial feast of meats grilled on sticks, and where we now lodge in a large hut, with goats and chickens scratching outside it. The village women cannot be prevented from entering to gaze at me and they bring also their children – they all, women and children, think me a strange sight, being the first fair lady who has visited their country, and the first woman they have ever seen with hair anything but black, eyes anything but dark brown, not to mention my nose – Malay noses are broad and flat and splayed, whilst mine is retroussé. And I think they are as well astonished to see a woman wearing proper clothes, for all they wear is the rough woven skirts called *sarongs*, and nothing about the bosom but a length of cloth, and their legs often uncovered for all to see.

May 1818, a hut at Pagaralam, Pasemah

Tom has been meeting all day long with the local chiefs, and now his diplomacy is concluded. It has been most successful; the resentment simmering here, since the murder of the unfortunate Mr. Parr, and The Company's necessarily harsh, if misdirected, reprisals, has by my husband's sweet suavity been quite erased. He has made a treaty with the chiefs by which they have placed themselves under the benign protection of the British government, and the disputes and misunderstandings of the past have been quite set aside.

The local women and children continue to regard me as a great attraction. It is not only the villagers but also large numbers from the surrounding countryside who come to stare at me in my hut. When they are not chattering like birds in a flock, they gaze at me so intently it is as if they expect me at any moment to start to fade from view, as if I were not flesh and blood, but an apparition, and the intensity of their regard I find most unsettling.

May 1818, a hut at Pagaralam, Pasemah

Tom, with his insatiable curiosity and his scholarly intent, has been questioning the natives on their religion, for tho' hereabouts they are professedly Mahomedans they believe still in an ancient mythology, and make offerings to at least twenty idols, which Tom says are Hindu. Dr. Arnold has likewise made profitable use of his time in Pasemah: his fears he may be accused of witchcraft proved unfounded; with their cheerful and unworried agreement he has vaccinated many locals against the smallpox.

Tomorrow we commence our return to Manna by a different route from that which brought us here: we will for much of our journey trust to native rafts and use the Manna River as our highway back to the coast.

Mr. Presgrave assures me I have made such an impression on the local people I must be remembered by them as some very extraordinary person for having overcome such difficulties to reach here – more that for being the first fair lady to visit their country I must come to be for them a fabled creature of legend.

May 1818, The Residency, Manna

The day we left Pagaralam was the worst our party had experienced since setting off from Bencoolen: the route was imperfectly known; it poured all the time we were walking so we became drenched and dreary; the terrain, churned to mud by the deluge, was so hard going that walking was more than usually irksome. As the shadows began to lengthen, Tom and Dr. Arnold took the only guide, and hastened forward in the hope of reaching the Manna River, and preparing a fire. The remainder of the party gradually lost their way, and became dispersed. At last Mr. Presgrave and I were left entirely to ourselves, and while debating what to do, and pursuing our walk in no little anxiety, the duskiness of the oncoming night, the pouring rain, and our wet clothes not adding to our comfort, Mr. Presgrave met with an accident which nearly proved serious, and caused me some alarm:

he sunk into a large pit, and disappeared entirely, and with him sunk my spirits. He fortunately succeeded in extricating himself, and after continuing our walk some time longer we found the river, Tom, Dr. Arnold, and all. A happy night succeeded, tho' the bearers still lagged behind, and for having none others to change into I had to sleep in my wet clothes, with a smooth river stone Tom found me as my pillow.

Yesterday was much better, and much enlivened by a little girl I met in the village where we waited for the natives to build us rafts to take us down the river. I was sitting in the shade of a tree when the pretty child approached me. On being asked if she wanted anything she replied: No, but seeing you were quite alone I thought you might like to have a little chat, and so I am come to offer you some sireh, and sit beside you, for anything like you I have never seen before, and I just want to look.

The rafts the natives built us were of lengths of bamboo lashed together with vines, once these were floated, we clambered aboard, and placed our lives in the hands of native guides, who steered the rafts with poles. In some places we glided smoothly through glassy water under the welcome shade of overhanging trees, in others we must negotiate the swirling white water of rapids, and then the dashing of the raft through the current, the roaring noise, the flying spray, the momentary danger, the degree of exertion necessary to preserve a hold, and the stunned silence of each fair person, combined to create a degree of thrillingly terrifying excitement such as only the bravest of riders must feel, as their mounts hurtle at breakneck speed over iron-hard ground towards fences almost too high to jump.

At last we arrived here in Manna, and tonight I will sleep in a bed. Tomorrow, most of our party will commence the eighty-mile ride back to Bencoolen – Mr. Presgrave, the Pangeran of Manna and some of the Malay bearers will remain here.

As soon as we attained Manna Dr. Arnold opened Daisy's

crate. Alas, all that remains of one of the greatest prodigies in nature is but a small part, and two buds, each as big as Miss Charlotte's head. Daisy's petals have mostly rotted away and are now dark brown, crawling with maggots. Her remnants will be sent Home, to Sir Joseph Banks, that she may become known to men of science, and Dr. Arnold hopes soon to send also other specimens taken from the forest, and better preserved in spirits.

We learn now that the natives call our Daisy *Petimun Sikinlili*, which means *The Devil's Sireh Box*. Whatever her name, rotted she stank so much worse even than the horrid stench of her when fresh that I thought I'd faint when her crate was opened.

May 1818, a camp on the shoreline

The ride along the shore back to Bencoolen is proving trying, and was earlier almost even fatal: our cavalcade was passing a projection of rock called by the natives *tempat kematian*, *place of death*, when the tide rose so rapidly, and the surf surged so high, that the horses began to stagger, and we riders began to despair, and it was only with utmost difficulty we turned our mounts, and urged them back that we might take a longer route through the forest, where we had to contend with a great variety of insect wildlife, and I worried we would encounter tigers.

Our eventual return to the shore brought more misery, as it was by now about noon, and hot enough to shrivel hell, as my husband put it, and tho' I cannot approve this phrase, I concur in the sentiment. It makes my skin burn just to remember the vertical rays of the tropical sun striking down on us like spears, without any shade. This slicing heat, after the fatigue and exposure we had already experienced, was distressing to all, and proved fatal to one of our remaining Malay bearers. Tonight, from its effects, Dr. Arnold is running a high fever.

May 1818, Government House, Bencoolen

In seventeen days I have walked all over Sumatra, but now I am back at Government House and to my joy I am reunited with Miss Charlotte, who has grown much since last I saw her. The natives here, so convinced before we left that no European could penetrate the forest, and certainly no European woman, now look upon me as a sort of wonder for returning alive – but alive I am, and healthy, for I have escaped the forest uninjured, which was more than I had any right to expect. Tom boasts to all who will listen that I withstood the fatigue and the exposure of our adventure like a heroine, and indeed I think I did.

June 1818, Government House, Bencoolen

I have visited for the first time the Hill of Mists. Work on our bungalow progresses well, and we should be able to move there by Tom's birthday, July 6. The bungalow is simple, the main part composed of a long run of rooms arranged all in a line. The site is atop a ridge which has a fine view over a valley empty of everything but the endless forest with all its incessant noises of insects, frogs, monkeys, &c.

As we surveyed the scene, from our partly-built verandah, Tom told me the forests I could see all around bristled with tigers and with elephants. He did not forget to add one of the local villagers told him that both his father and his grandfather were carried off by tigers, and that there is scarcely a family that has not lost some of its members to them.

This was another of my husband's pieces of intelligence I received in silence.

In a most welcome, happy change we have left Government House, full of cracks and fissures, and shifted to our bungalow at the Hill of Mists; we have called it *Permattam Ballam, the abode of peace*, and if elephants and tigers keep away, then so I hope it may prove.

Our new accommodation is airy and spacious. Tom and I each have a noble bedroom, very large, and mine has a shaded verandah and doors all round. There is a drawing room and here I have installed both my harp, and my piano, so I am happy.

Tom turns his attention at once to the planting of coffee and spice gardens on the cleared land encircling the building. He intends also an avenue of clove trees to lead up to the front door – nothing can be more beautiful than an avenue of clove trees; the luxuriant fragrant foliage makes the air most charming.

It is delightful to think of Miss Charlotte becoming a great girl here, becoming my companion, coming to me with her prattle, laughing with me over this or that. Perhaps, if it pleases God, she will one day be joined in her games by a brother? A sister? Brothers and Sisters? Perhaps Tom and I will have a veritable menagerie of children tame and wild running about the garden? Against that day, and, in the here and now, for my lovely Miss Charlotte's sake, I have given the gardeners the *strictest instructions* to kill on sight any cobras de capello that slither into the compound, for this is a most deadly serpent, notwithstanding Tom calls it a beautiful one.

My husband mentioned Permattam Ballam puts him in mind of a simple rustic house he and Olivia once occupied on a hill outside the settlement of George Town, on the island of Penang. Tho' our situation is undoubtedly rural, and our house of native construction, I think Permattam Ballam is altogether so splendid it must outshine any cottage that could be described as *rustic*, or *simple*, and I trust Tom is happier in *this* house than he ever was in *that* one, for being now married to a woman who knows how to make a comfortable home, and for being now a father. In any case, he says he likes it here because it is retired, and as he advances in age retirement becomes more and more congenial to him.

July 1818, Permattam Ballam

Notwithstanding he claimed so recently to value retirement, Tom tells me we must soon be off exploring again, for he wants to put his nose in the ancient and independent kingdom of Minangkabau.

This Minangkabau is wealthy, rich in gold, and once it was powerful, too: Tom learns from his studies of Malay literature that in former times it ruled over all Sumatra, and even over some of the other islands of the Archipelago; it still receives everywhere here vestiges of homage. It lies over the mountains, in the highlands at the centre of Sumatra – another blank on the map, and one that Tom's scholarly friends in London would be interested to see filled in.

Tom thinks he can turn Minangkabau's present independence and past history to our diplomatic advantage; he dreams of seeing the ancient greatness of Minangkabau re-established, to the advantage of the local Sultan, The Company, and of Britain. It is his idea that if all Sumatra can be in future as in former times unified under the Sultan of Minangkabau, and if the Sultan is pledged to us, and not to the Dutch, then the result will be all Sumatra being unified under British influence. From this kernel he thinks could sprout an empire in the Eastward, an empire he thinks Britain *will* grow, and Britain *must* grow, to exclude not only the Dutch, but also divers other nations who may wish to have this part of the globe.

Dr. Horsfield will accompany us to Minangkabau, to collect

botanical and geological specimens, and so will Dr. Arnold, if he isn't too sickly. I haven't seen him since we moved, for he lodges in town, but Tom says he remains weak from the bout of fever he suffered on the ride along the coast from Manna.

The port of Padang is the gateway to Minangkabau – which Tom thinks is reason alone to deny it to the Dutch. But the Resident there, Charles Holloway, informs Tom by letter that the interior is quite impenetrable, and access to Minangkabau is impossible. Tom takes no notice, and writes to the Minangkabau chiefs to advise them of our coming, and to ask them to send guides to Padang.

July 1818, The Residency, Padang

With much regret Tom and I once again kissed Miss Charlotte goodbye, and left her in the care of our treasure, Nurse Grimes, at Permattam Ballam. After busying ourselves a few days at Government House, we sailed on the *Lady Raffles* up the coast to Padang, and here we now ready ourselves to journey on to Minangkabau. We do so in the teeth of the continuing objections of Charles Holloway, who remains unhelpful, and who is quite convinced we will be swallowed by the great green maw of the forest. Alas, we find this obstinate fellow in a feverish state with the flux.

Dr. Horsfield has already left for the interior – he precedes us that he may gain extra time for botanising. He set off today at first light, carried aloft on the shoulders of four natives, in a forward party of two hundred Malay bearers with their loads, a fifty-strong military escort including sepoys and Bugis, and personal servants – the whole procession walking in time to the beat of a drum. Tom laughed to see it go, saying this was a most ridiculous cavalcade.

We will follow on tomorrow, and rendezvous with Dr.

Horsfield and his party soon after. We will travel with the principal traders of Padang, and two chiefs and their followers sent from Minangkabau to be our guides. Dr. Arnold judged himself well enough to come with us from Bencoolen, but it seems to me the poor man remains so sickly I doubt he'll be able to join us on the expedition.

July 1818, The Residency, Padang

Our departure is delayed by pelting rain, violent rain, each drop a missile. Dr. Horsfield has sent back a note for Tom, warning of the conditions he is encountering in the forest, informing him there are many difficult passages, and saying he despairs for my progress, saying he doubts if even in favourable weather I could come on. Apparently, the way passes through many streams, which rapidly swell with the deluge; Dr. Horsfield reports if the rains continue the natives are positively of the opinion that progress forwards and backwards will be impeded, most especially for a lady.

I think from his caution Dr. Horsfield does not realise what manner of woman I am. For all the risks, I am determined to go with Tom, my life. To be parted from him is the only misery my soul shrinks from; to be united to him in life and death the only bright hope of my existence. Indeed, I think no good wife could be surprised at my running every personal risk to avoid a separation from my husband, were she in this climate, and witnessed the sudden illnesses, the violence and quickness of life's termination.

Alas, that drear thought reminds me that as I predicted, Dr. Arnold is too ill to travel; I am alarmed my friend is becoming gradually decayed.

August 1818, Pageruyong, Minangkabau

I sometimes think I must have a man's soul housed in my woman's body, for the exertions I have endured. We left Padang on a day of clear skies, in good spirits, and to a salute of guns from the soldiers there. At once we plunged into a rivery region of the forest. After days of struggling through stinking swamps, of being bitten, stung, sucked half to death by mosquitoes, spiders, ants, bees, leeches, of fatigue, exhaustion, of being always wet, either from rain, seemingly determined to dissolve us, or from being submerged in rivers, or from the drenching of our own skins, of sliding on mud, of being knee-deep in bogs only passable by stepping from one tree root to another, of stumbling along river beds, and scrambling over slippery rocks tumbled beside roaring cataracts, of tripping on, becoming entangled in, being pricked and scratched and grabbed by a great variety of luxuriant tropical vegetable productions, of climbing mountains not less than five -thousand feet in elevation, after all this we have finally – finally – arrived in the principle settlement of Minangkabau, Pageruyong.

It was a strange arrival. The Minangkabau people live in a prosperous country, highly cultivated, its boundaries marked by sacred fruit and coconut trees. When our party, much bedraggled, first came to their rice fields, and began to traverse the raised banks between the flooded areas where they grow the crop, we were joined by thousands of native warriors from the hills. They looked fearsome, their brown bodies almost naked, shoeless, dressed only in sarongs, and sometimes with cloths about their shoulders, or wrapped about their heads, and many with their hair hanging long and black and glossy. They had their krises tucked into their sarongs, and they were armed too with spears and staves. They shouted out with what I thought were war cries – their voices curdled my blood – but an old woman working in the fields told me they were shouting in friendly welcome, and no harm would come to me.

On seeing me, the spearmen were struck with amazement: it was clear from their faces the question was not *who* is that, but *what* is that? Tom and I agreed that to them my dress, and what must seem the extraordinary appearance of fairness linked to female nature, must be unaccountable. We supposed that, with all the wonder of ignorance, these natives immediately conceived there must be something supernatural about me, as, I think, did those other ones in Pasemah.

It was evident news I had appeared amongst them spread quickly: soon women started coming and mothers pressed about me in crowds imploring to have their children touched as a preservative from all future evil. It was in vain to protest my hands could not heal, to claim fatigue, to entreat to be excused; no one liked to lose so easy an opportunity of ensuring future good, so touch I did, and the noise, the smell of native bodies, the pressure and confusion were all very great; when one crowd was satisfied a fresh one collected, and I cannot guess the number on whom I bestowed my slight, but coveted, act of kindness.

If it were blasphemy to touch them so, to pretend to have the power of healing when I knew I did not, then may God forgive me, for I acted from charity only. And if vanity stained my charity, then may I not be pardoned, for, under such circumstances, could any human creature say any different?

Once we achieved Pageruyong we were received with the utmost hospitality, and tho' the natives' manners were sometimes rude and annoying it was impossible to misunderstand their intentions, which were most friendly. Our party was conducted to my present resting place, the best dwelling in the village, the *rumah gadang*, a sort of palace. It is extensive and well-built of wood and woven palm matting, about sixty-feet long. The wood of the shutters, columns, ridge poles, and doors is richly carved and coloured with red, white, and black. The roof is most extraordinary, with tiered, upswept gables, these, Tom tells me, are intended to mimic the horns of a buffalo. The rumah gadang is beautifully situated on the banks of a river, the Soongy Amas, or

Golden River, which must be named for gold panned from it, for its waters are muddy brown, and not yellow at all.

Awaiting us in the rumah gadang was a woman introduced to us as the *Tuan Gadis*, or *Virgin Queen*; we gather she has some role in the administration of the country, for we understand the Minangkabau women have a prominent place in their society. Indeed, it seems that in many matters the women rule over the men, which is most unnatural, and Tom will conduct his negotiations with the Sultan, not with his wives – not even with his First Wife.

Perhaps the Tuan Gadis *is* the Sultan's First Wife? I decidedly think she cannot be virgin as she claims, for she has many children running about.

August 1818, Pageruyong, Minangkabau

Our party has found at Minangkabau the wreck of the great and sovereign empire Tom told me of. Everywhere we see ancient stones inscribed with Sanskrit or carved with Hindu images, and also broken statues of heathen idols with too many arms. Tho' their profligacy of limbs puts me in mind of spiders, Tom says these relicts fill him with admiration for the faith they honour, and he is delighted to scramble amongst them. Indeed, his zeal for Hinduism is such I this morning felt it necessary to remind him it is not a faith, but a *false* faith, and we must pray the blessed light of Christianity soon spills over Asia. Alas, he laughed he is a good deal more inclined than I am to let people go to heaven in their own way, which as a response to my anxiety I thought true, but inadequate.

August 1818, Pageruyong, Minangkabau

Tom has entered into a treaty of friendship with the Sultan here, whom he has named the Lord Paramount of all the Malays. This tractable Sultan has sworn fealty to King George, to whom, at Tom's urging, he has addressed a protest about the return of the Dutch to Padang; more, he has ceded some of his coastal lands in west Sumatra to The Company. It is agreed that when we depart Minangkabau we will leave behind a Resident and a small military force as tokens of British power in central Sumatra. These diplomatic successes please Tom greatly.

While Tom was busy with political discussions, I was left in a small, planked hut with a sepoy posted at the door to keep the crowds at bay; nevertheless, I was subject to the treatment that is becoming customary in the interior: the natives gathered in such numbers that the sepoy was overwhelmed and in successive waves hundreds pushed inside the hut to look at me. Eventually, I asked them to leave so that I could retire, but they seated themselves on the floor, saying they particularly wanted to see my method of sleeping. It was only when Tom returned that they could be prevailed upon to move. Then, during the night, I saw dark faces peeping in through the nets that surround my bed, and this morning people wanted to watch me eat.

August 1818, a camp in the forest

We have set off on our return to Padang, and are plunged into the forest again, and now I understand more than ever its dangers: our party came this morning upon a tiger crouched on a forest path, ready to spring. The porters immediately stopped and addressed him in terms of supplication, assuring him they were poor people carrying the *Tuan Besar*'s – the great man's – luggage, who would be angry with them if they did not arrive in time. Therefore they implored permission to pass. The tiger got up and walked quietly into the depths of the forest, and we came on, the Malays perfectly satisfied, tho' I was trembling. Tom now tells me the Malays believe ancestral spirits dwell in tigers, and when a tiger enters a village, the people prepare rice and fruit as an offering; the tiger, touched by their well-meaning attentions, passes on.

August 1818, a camp in the forest

I have Certain Suspicions I may once more be in the family way, tho' I can't think of any of that now, for being in the forest, and certainly I must breathe nothing of my Suspicions for the consternation they would cause to all abroad. Fortunately, I remain quite well.

August 1818, The Residency, Padang

For a loss I must come to shortly I cannot exalt it, but we are returned to Padang, after walking two hundred and forty miles in fourteen days. Except for the added interest of the tiger, our return journey was just as before: another sore trial of travelling up and down mountains, and through rivers, always wet up to my knees, walking sometimes fifteen hours out of four and twenty, with scarcely any refreshment – no rest or comfort of any kind – and the way sometimes so steep, sometimes so slippery, that I was often certain I must be left behind, and always so *hot*, and always under assault from numerous ambassadors of the insect kingdom – sometimes there were ants even in my eyes – and much of this while I harboured in secret my womanly Suspicions.

Alas, I cannot now consult Dr. Arnold if I am That Way. A sad return we've had of it, for we now learn Dr. Arnold, poor man, was taken by his fever three days after we left for Minangkabau.

Oh, that my dear Dr. Arnold, he who delivered Miss Charlotte, should become yet new evidence of the constant necessity of preparation for death, and of repentance! His last day alive he spent vaccinating local children against smallpox, and this I think typical of his goodness, and I feel his loss most keenly, and weep much for him – I'd go into black, if I had the clothes with me.

Tom, too, is much affected by Dr. Arnold's death. He consoles himself our late friend has won immortality by the discovery of that prodigy of nature Daisy, or The Devil's Sireh Box, which no doubt must soon bear his name as its official, scientific one, bestowed by the men of the Linnaean Society in London.

We have also lost Charles Holloway, who in our absence undertook a short sea voyage for his health, and has now drowned at sea. I feel no need to praise overmuch the departed.

August 1818, Permattam Ballam

We are returned to our abode of peace, and I cannot express my relief to be reunited with Miss Charlotte, to find her thriving, and, indeed, greatly expanded since we left her. Alas, my joy in her is tempered by more bad news: while we were away the Tots' baby was seized by spasms, and perished. Tho' the loss of an infant scarce four months old is one of those things which in itself may soon be got over, knowing how uncertain life is at that period, Mrs. Tot is sick with grief. Tom remarked to me he supposed it were not wise of parents to suffer their affections to entwine themselves so closely round their children that is was agony to separate them, lest death require their parting. However, he added that now he is father to Charlotte he knows this wisdom of distance could never be his.

As for me, I shiver to think death is a country of the young, and hug Miss Charlotte close, and pray she grows strongly, and continues bonny.

August 1818, Permattam Ballam

Alas, we have had a most melancholy letter from Tom's mother, Mrs. Raffles in Hampstead, dated February, saying that Hannah died in that month of a tendency to generalised dropsy, and one of her nieces died in childbed, and so too did the baby. Tom, much saddened on all fronts, remarked to me it is not the adventurers who are exposed to most dangers who suffer first, but those who stayed at Home. I too weep for Hannah, and I am most alarmed by the fate of Mrs. Raffles' niece and her baby, for Nurse Grimes and I are now quite agreed I am in the family way, and I do not wish to be reminded of how soon death may my steps attend – needs must I discuss these things with Nurse, tho' I never would do such a thing in England.

August 1818, Permattam Ballam

My condition is by no means yet apparent, and I would not bring attention to it by making it a subject of general conversation, nevertheless I have confided in Tom that next spring I hope to present him with a son and heir. He blanched and said it is a good thing I have the constitution of an ox, for if I did not our baby could not have survived our expedition to Minangkabau, and nor could I. It much displeased me to be compared to an ox, notwithstanding I am grateful for the robustness of my constitution.

August 1818, Permattam Ballam

Tom has begun writing accounts of our recent journeys for the newspapers at Home. He uses such headings as *Interior of Sumatra Traversed*, and *Notes on the Kingdom of Minangkabau*, and he hopes that by these efforts with his pen our travels in central Sumatra will become widely known, which should add to his reputation, even to his fame, and hence profit him with The Company.

August 1818, Permattam Ballam

There is squabbling over Palembang, a once restive native court of this island that has control of the tin trade. In former times Palembang was ruled by the Dutch, but we had it when we ruled Java, and Tom put down insurrection there, and installed on the throne a sultan more favourable to us than the previous treacherous chief. Tom thinks we ought now to keep this court, tho' the Dutch want it back; since military action possibly impends, Tom has despatched troops to Palembang, and these he has called the Sumatran Hill Rangers.

August 1818, Permattam Ballam

Notwithstanding my condition I am soon to leave Miss Charlotte once more with our treasure Nurse Grimes. This distresses me because of the difficulty of communication, but Tom has booked us passage to Calcutta on the *Udney*, and we leave next month, and what can I do?

Tom deems our journey necessary because he considers it imperative he now meet with Lord Hastings, the Governor-General of India, to discuss with him various complexities: the value of Bencoolen as a brake on Dutch ambitions to establish a trading monopoly in the East Indies; the possibility of excluding from all influence on Sumatra those same Dutch, by exercising, through the court at Minangkabau, power over the whole island; the consequent urgency of our retention of Padang, gateway to Minangkabau; the problem of Palembang.

Alas, there have been, in the past, difficulties between Tom and Lord Hastings. The coolness between the two men was caused by false charges laid against my blameless husband by one Colonel Gillespie, now departed. This scoundrel was for a time in Java Tom's chief military man – and also his bitter rival. Indeed, he was so bitter that when Tom replaced him, for a variety of infractions, he went straight to Calcutta and began spreading vicious calumnies about both Tom's private character and his administration. Thus, through malice and misrepresentation, he poisoned Lord Hastings against Tom.

But Gillespie is no more – killed in Nepal in the war with the Ghurkhas, shot cleanly through the heart in the midst of an attack so he fell from his horse stone dead – and now he has quit the scene – and now too that Tom has been noticed by Prinny, and has been knighted – Lord Hastings is most friendly, and has written to my husband it pains him that in the course of his public duties he had in the past to express an opinion unfavourable to his measures in Java. Indeed, Lord Hastings now says he thinks in truth Tom is due praise for his anxious and unwearied exertions in ameliorating the condition of the native inhabitants under his sway, with results highly creditable to the British Government.

In short, Tom has received the most full and satisfactory conclusion to the affair of Gillespie's false charges, and he is now most hopeful his arguments will be heard in Calcutta, and that his opinions will have some weight.

On matters personal, I have it from Mrs. Tot that Tot hints darkly Olivia shot Gillespie through the heart as surely as did that Ghurkha with his musket.

September 1818, the *Udney*, Bay of Bengal

Tom and I have left Miss Charlotte at Permattam Ballam, and have set sail for Calcutta. My husband let slip he was once in the city with Olivia, back in Lord Minto's day, so I must suppose he'll remember her often while we are there, and I do not like this small brig the *Udney* which has only one cramped cabin with a single porthole and is infested with centipedes and scorpions – also ants and fleas, a source of actual torment and disgust.

Bye-the-bye, this Lord Minto, a man Tom talks of often and fondly, once his staunchest protector, is another from my husband's story now departed: he perished on his way home from Calcutta. The poor man got as far as England, but he never reached his native Scotland, where his wife was waiting for him, a latter-day Penelope, because he was gathered whilst on the road.

September 1818, the *Udney*, grounded on a sandbank

In the middle of last night, whilst in the charge of a drunken pilot, the *Udney* ran aground on a sandbank at the mouth of the Hoogly River – the river that leads up to Calcutta for the city it seems is surrounded by miles and miles of bogs and rivers. On this sandbank we remain stuck fast, grounded in a most desolate spot, with mud-coloured water all around, and illimitable mangrove swamps beyond. We now await boats to carry us to the town, and I expect to be for a few days always hot, thirsty, and plagued by mosquitoes.

September 1818, Government House, Calcutta

We are now safely arrived in Calcutta, a city I must call depraved, and Hinduism a depraved religion also, perverted, corrupt, for barely had we disembarked, to a flattering salute of guns, than our party encountered a scene so disgusting that a kind of incredulous horror of what was passing riveted us to the spot, for it was an act of *sati*, a heathen wickedness in which a widow, live, is sacrificed upon her husband's funeral pyre. The unfortunate victim was already alight, and as she began to be consumed before our outraged eyes, the tremendous and convulsive motion which her body exhibited plainly showed that sensation and life existed in the miserable wretch within, so the scene became too shocking for Christian eyes, and we hurried on.

Tom says we have banned sati in Calcutta, but the natives too often ignore our prohibition, which is proof enough they need Britannia's firmly guiding hand, and it falls to us to teach them that the burning of widows is revolting to human nature.

The sati has made me uneasy, and I think Calcutta's air is dangerous, for it smells bad, feels greasy, and has a sour taste. Meanwhile, many of the buildings look leprous they are in such a state of disrepair, and I saw today an actual leper with his face half gnawed away, the skin hanging from his cheeks in rotting strips, for there are here many lepers, and beggars.

Still, we are staying with Lord Hastings at Government House, a mansion as comfortable as it is grand and splendid, and where Olivia never stayed, for Tom tells me when she visited this city with him they lodged with their late poet friend, John Leyden, in a dwelling I gather was shabby and crumbling – Tom says its roof was supported more by stacked books, than firmly mortared bricks. I decidedly think this must have been a decadent episode, for our second evening here Tom asked me if I'd like to share a pipe of ganja, a spiced and inebriating tobacco very common in these parts. My face provided my answer, and Tom apologised this was something he and Leyden and Olivia were accustomed to do. I forbore from commenting on a lady's taking of a pipe, instead I said I did not think it fitting to the dignity of a knight to indulge in native habits, and I'd thank him to stay away from ganja now I am his wife.

Our host, the Governor-General, I must call ill-favoured in looks, and self-important in manner. He lives in a regal style, and keeps a most lavish household, surrounding himself always with the comforts of opulence and the fruits of influence. When he drives out it is in a carriage and four, an open barouche, with grooms running beside each horse, and a dozen mace bearers running in front, as well as his bodyguard and troopers. They say he came out from Home heavily in debt; for his extravagance I think he'll return the same way.

Lord Hastings has in his garden a large menagerie, to delight Tom's heart. His collection of animals includes a tapir, a creature I had never heard of hitherto, but which it transpires Tom had long wanted to see. Tom says he had been told it is an animal in every respect the model of an elephant, but that now he sees it, he thinks it more like a hog. As for me, I think it more like a cow – if an elephant, then one of diminutive size, and the most docile creature I ever met with. Tom has now made a correct drawing of it, to send to Sir Joseph Banks, that natural historians in London may come to know of it.

October 1818, Government House, Calcutta

Tom learns from Lord Hastings that for thinking Dutch friendship vital to England's future safety, there is now in London a great desire to sign with the Hollanders an Anglo-Dutch treaty, to settle once and for all how in the overseas settlements, theirs and ours, things are to be arranged now that Napoleon can no longer annoy us. Hence the Foreign Secretary directs that whilst negotiations proceed we must in the Eastward conciliate the Dutch, and do nothing to distress them.

Thus Lord Hastings says Tom must give up his idea of ruling all of Sumatra through Minangkabau; indeed, he refuses even to honour the treaty Tom has already made with the Sultan there. Nor can Lord Hastings be persuaded we should retain Padang, but orders we must hand it back to the Dutch. He likewise orders Tom must recall the Sumatran Hill Rangers, and have nothing further to do with Palembang.

Poor Tom has even been forced to promise that in all future communications with the Dutch government he shall maintain the most conciliatory and amiable spirit. Worse, he has been given to understand that for all he was under the impression he had a free hand at Bencoolen in diplomacy, he should have restricted his activities to matters of trading.

This is all most displeasing, but Tom is less cast down than he could have been: tho' Lord Hastings conceives him to have misconstrued his powers, he has agreed Tom's explanations for his military and diplomatic interventions are perfectly satisfactory, and tho' he thinks he was imprudent, he is fully persuaded Tom was influenced only by motives of unquestionable zeal for the interests of the Honourable Company, and the nation. Tom, in turn, admits, cheerful, he never was one to let his prudence outstrip his zeal.

October 1818, Government House, Calcutta

My husband cannot be without his plans and projects, and now he can no longer concern himself with Minangkabau and Palembang, he turns his attention to the Straits of Malacca, which he calls the key that unlocks the China trade, for he says whomever controls those Straits controls all the eastern Seas.

Alas, we no longer have as we used to Malacca itself, for it was rendered to the Dutch at the conclusion of the recent wars. Meanwhile, Penang, which remains ours, is too far north on the Straits to guard their southern entrance, but not far north enough to guard their northern entrance, and so possession of that settlement does not give us control of shipping sailing to and from China.

Under these difficult circumstances of politics and geography, Tom thinks we should annex to The Company a new territory, to be Britannia's trapdoor into the eastern treasure house. There are apparently many islands scattered in the seas at the southern entrance to The Straits of Malacca, and any of these he thinks may do as a base to let us get purchase on the China trade. He says as well as our fulcrum occupying a strategic position, it is equally important that the Dutch never had it, so we can make it ours. Alas, he fears by now the Dutch have hardly left us an inch of ground to stand upon – which is to say left any of the southern islands unclaimed, so that we may have them.

October 1818, Government House, Calcutta

Between his suavity, and his convincing arguments, Tom has persuaded Lord Hastings we should establish that trading base he dreams of at the southern entrance to the Straits of Malacca. More, the two men have now agreed that as soon as we have our base, we should secure a treaty with Tom's old friend the Sultan of Acheen, who controls from his kraton the Straits' northern entrance. It is their idea that if we could thus control access to the Straits from both the north and the south, this must be to our mercantile advantage, and also to our strategic advantage – all this at the expense of the Dutch. Indeed they say if we could thus pincer them, it would shatter the Hollanders' arrogant dreams of establishing a trading monopoly in all the Archipelago.

October 1818, Government House, Calcutta

For Tom's zeal, for his virtue, for his charm, and for his local knowledge, Lord Hastings now entrusts to my husband that most important and urgently essential service they have been so much discussing; he charges him with nothing less than finding a suitable southern island where we may establish a trading post from which to run the China trade, and founding there a settlement.

I would write more, but I am this instant called away to mount an elephant for an evening ride with Lord Hastings so I must put down my quill – the Governor-General's elephants have most splendid golden *howdahs,* encrusted with gems, that are indeed like tiny castles on their backs.

October 1818, Government House, Calcutta

It emerges Lord Hastings favours as our southern base for the China trade some island Rhio, which the Dutch don't have, and which he says lies exactly in the track of ships passing in or out of The Straits of Malacca. Tom's attention, however, is principally turned to another place, Singapore, an almost uninhabited island north of Rhio, which is likewise free of the Dutch, and which he thinks from its position guards the southern entrance to the Straits better than any other place.

Seven years back, when he sailed with the war fleet from Penang to Java, Tom actually saw with his own eyes this Singapore. He says the island is now merely a haunt of pirates – the local view is that piracy is an honourable profession, and not an evil of ancient date – but his friend Leyden learned from translating a work of native history, *The Malay Annals*, that it has a glorious past, and was once a busy emporium, a thriving port of call for trading vessels from near and far, and indeed nothing less than the maritime capital of the Malays. In those days it was called *Tamasek*; it acquired its new name when a prince, one Sang Nila Utama, was shipwrecked on its shores, and glimpsed in the forest a strange animal, which he took to be a lion, tho' it was more probably a tiger, and so he named the island *Singapura*, because *singa* in the ancient Hindu tongue of Sanskrit means *lion*, and *pura* means *city* – more evidence, says Tom, of East-Insular India's purely Indian past. As to why the great city Singapura declined, Tom says it was some centuries back sacked by the Javanese, and all its people at that time fled to Malacca.

My sentimental husband thinks if only he can make the erstwhile Lion City ours, and see this ancient emporium reborn as a British one, then dear Leyden's influence will shine on. More prosaically, he is in no doubt whatever must be done about our proposed new settlement, whether it be on Singapore or elsewhere, must indeed be *quickly* done, to forestall the Dutch from making every southern island theirs

November 1818, Government House, Calcutta

Tom once knew in Malacca an engineer called Farquhar, then the Resident there. Now Malacca is in the hands of the Dutch, Farquhar has shifted to Penang. Apparently, they are in Penang as convinced as Tom and Lord Hastings of the need for a new trading post south of Malacca. Indeed, Tom now learns that at the behest of the settlement's Governor, one Bannerman, Farquhar has recently made trading treaties with two islands either of which it is thought in Penang may serve as such a trading post, one that Rhio favoured by Lord Hastings, and another one called Lingga.

Tom and Lord Hastings are pleased to think they have allies in Bannerman and Farquhar, and they plan to enlist them in their scheme of founding a new settlement. More, they are united Farquhar's long experience and admirable qualifications eminently fit him to be Tom's second-in-command during the exploration of the southern islands, and then, once we have found a suitable place, for the command of the new post which it is desirable to establish there – which is to say they are agreed that once Tom, the settlement's founder, has hoisted the Union Jack, he should leave to the good engineer the local superintendence of our interests and affairs. Accordingly, Tom decides he must now sail to Penang, to consult with Farquhar.

Tho' I am now I estimate nearly six months gone with child – my baby wriggles much within me – I will travel with my husband. I will not be sorry to quit the smells and noise, the heat and dust, the lepers and beggars, the burning widows, the opium addicts, and the drunks of Calcutta, but I now doubt I can be back in Bencoolen before my time comes, and I fear I must suffer my second laying-in under circumstances almost as trying as the first – amongst strangers, with no nurse in whom to confide, and I fear no experienced medical aid.

Meanwhile, I fret about Miss Charlotte. I am now nearly three months without any news of my dear babe, Oh, what a sad and anxious separation!

November 1818, Government House, Calcutta

Tho' Bencoolen and Penang each of them now has its own governor, Tom has been pondering that for simplicity, economy, strategy, and commerce the administration of our possessions in the Eastward should be conducted all as *one*, with *one* governor as the chief, to be the *one* man in direct communication with Calcutta, and that when we acquire our new settlement in the southern isles that should become his seat, and our new capital in East-Insular India. He has now put this idea to Lord Hastings who has agreed with him that this strategy is sound. More, he has added that no man is better qualified than Tom to be the head of a new overarching government, and that on the removal or going away of Governor Bannerman, who may object he has a prior claim to the post, he will certainly recommend the measure.

December 1818, Government House, Calcutta

As respite from the frenzy of Calcutta, Tom takes me sometimes to stroll in the fine Botanic Garden – six hundred acres devoted to floral and arboreal collections, filled with useful and ornamental plants, so Tom says it is indeed a splendid living herbarium, and I say it is a tranquil park in which a woman can recover her calm.

One afternoon not long after we arrived, we were walking beneath the mango and tamarind trees which shade its grassy lawns, when Tom fell into conversation with another visitor, Dr. William Jack, a young botanist from Aberdeen, and by design they have met often since. Today Tom has engaged Dr. Jack as both our personal physician, and also as his scientific collaborator, the dual roles once fulfilled by poor, lamented Dr. Arnold.

I fret to think my laying-in will be attended by a botanist, and yet I must hope all goes on well.

December 1818, the *Nearchus*, Bay of Bengal

I face again the privations of a voyage. Tom, Dr. Jack, and I have left Calcutta for Penang, and I must be grateful our ship, the *Nearchus,* is an East Indiaman and not a small, private vessel, for my soul now sickens at the very idea of small vessels, such were the horrors of sailing on the *Udney*.

Tom carries instructions of his own drafting, to form stable connections, political and commercial, in the southern regions, in furtherance of the project of founding a new trading post beyond Malacca, such as may command the entrance to its eponymous Straits. All negotiations and arrangements are to be left to Tom's judgement and discretion; Farquhar is to accompany him to the southern islands, and is to be left in local charge of the settlement we there found, on whichever island it may be. The general management of the new settlement is to be under Tom's immediate control, as Lieutenant-Governor of Bencoolen.

Lord Hastings still favours Rhio as the island we need, but Tom will not relinquish his hunch Singapore is our most likely prospect. Wherever the new settlement is established, once he has raised the Union Jack, Tom must proceed at once to Acheen, to negotiate a treaty with the friendly Sultan there, so that we can have control of both the northern and southern ends of the Straits of Malacca.

Of necessity Lord Hastings and Tom have made their various arrangements without reference to the authorities at India House, for if they were to await the Court of Directors' approval, we could for delay lose the China trade to the Dutch. Tom is quite unworried to be acting without the Court's authority, saying they can in London never pronounce on what's best to be done in the Eastward.

December 1818, the *Nearchus*, Bay of Bengal

What's the use of second thoughts? Still, as a brisk wind blows us ever closer to Penang, I am not sure I want to go there. I think I will be uncomfortably aware on my arrival that too many of my new acquaintance must remember Olivia, who lived so long amongst them, and was not merely a visitor in George Town as she was in Calcutta. Tho' I know the Penang people cannot find me the lesser woman except in looks, I doubt I will be able to prevent myself wondering: do they compare us?

New Year's Day 1819, Government House, George Town

After a gratifyingly tedious voyage without the least hint of adventure, Tom and I arrived in Penang yesterday, the last day of 1818. Our reception was far from fulsome. Farquhar is absent visiting the Sultan of Johor, the native court at the southern tip of the Peninsula, and is not expected back for a few days. Meanwhile, Governor Bannerman seems a very stiff fellow. He greeted us with little ceremony, and with the news, delivered curtly, that Rhio has been grabbed by the Dutch. Tom is unruffled by this intelligence, and sets his sights firmly on Singapore as the likeliest location for our new settlement.

January 1819, Government House, George Town

We dined last night with several ladies and fellows in the marble hall at the private residence Governor Bannerman is renting from a member of his government, a Mr. Phillips, who was absent – Tom later told me this Phillips is an old enemy from when he lived here.

As we ate our dinner, I felt many appraising eyes upon me, and here was confirmation, I thought, that I was being compared to Olivia, which did not make me happy. There was, too, a difficult moment when the conversation turned to the absent Phillips. As sometimes happens there was a lull in the conversation, and thus my poor husband had the attention of the whole table when he remarked Phillips did not possess the capacities to set the Thames on fire. This minor and mild observation caused the general silence to deepen in a most meaningful way, and glances flew to our host, Governor Bannerman, who looked most stony. We later learned Phillips has just married Governor Bannerman's daughter.

January 1819, Government House, George Town

Governor Bannerman seems to have taken a great dislike to Tom – Tom thinks from petty rivalry because the man wants to govern the new settlement we hope soon to found in his own person, from Penang, but it is quite clear that Tom is to govern it, from Bencoolen.

January 1819, Government House, George Town

I have been forced to confront anew that my husband must be haunted here by memories of his first wife, the ghost who rubs between us. This morning, Tom and I were walking together along the North Beach Road, when he blanched, and jolted to a stop outside a long, low house, painted white, with open arcades beneath. I thought he had been taken poorly, but he said no, not ill, assaulted by the past, for this was Runnymede. Runnymede? I queried. Yes, said Tom, he'd built this house for Olivia, and they'd lived in it happily, tho' not for very long. I let a beat of silence elapse, and then another. At last, I commented on the house's balconies, which were enclosed by carved railings, and Tom agreed they were pretty. Alas I cannot call this conversation an *exchange*, for the vastness of all we left unsaid.

January 1819, Government House, George Town

It seems that here in Penang Tom is enmeshed by the past in a way that almost makes us strangers. Olivia, yes, but he steps as well into old enmities, old quarrels, old shadows of which I am only dimly aware.

Now Dr. Jack reports he has met a scoundrel called Ibbetson, who told him cool as a cucumber Sir Knight – my husband – is netting out for *himself* an empire in the Eastward, with no regard for The Company or for Britain, and then he sneered that even an empire could not satisfy Sir Knight's overweening ambition, and that it is Sir Knight's selfish conviction that the whole range of eastern subjects does not requires the talent of more than one man to rule them, and that man he desires to be.

Dr. Jack was much aggrieved by this backbiting, and reports he became heated with Ibbetson, and rebuked him: sir, I cannot express how much I am delighted by Sir Stamford, who is of the real sterling stamp, and of that active and comprehensive mind that diffuses a portion of its energy all around. He says he forbore from adding it is the lot of men such as Sir Stamford to have lesser men disparage them, but, nonetheless, he thought it.

I suppose I should pity Ibbetson his bitterness, but I don't, and Dr. Jack and I will say none of this to Tom, for all he's ever repeating what the natives say: you can't kill a horse with words.

January 1819, Government House, George Town

Farquhar has now arrived from Johor, and treats Tom coolly. Tom has heard he is proud of his own efforts towards Rhio and Lingga, and brags they are the only substantial measures which have been attempted in these seas since peace with France. Apparently, he thinks Tom's presence here diminishes the value of his previous services; worse, we hear whispers he still hopes to be made first man in this great undertaking of founding a new settlement, and to see Tom reduced to second man.

January 1819, Government House, George Town

I do not write Home of it, but it is sometimes found in the Eastward that fair men take up with native women, who then become their nonyas, which is Malay for *wife*, tho' these women are not *wives*, but the men's less reputable companions.

Farquhar has long had a connection with a nonya, which Tom had warned me of before I came to Penang, but now I am actually confronted with this woman, Nonio Clemaine, I find myself uncertain how to treat her. She knew Olivia, but it is not that disconcerts me, but the colour of her skin, which is lighter than the usual brown of India, but still a muddy coffee. She is approaching old, very fat, and very ugly, with a mouth made horrible from chewing sireh, and I cannot think it right a fair man should consort with a dusky woman, or a gentleman with a woman not a lady.

Alas, Farquhar tolerates interbreeding of races even unto the second generation. He and Nonio Clemaine have a large brood living with them here, and their adult daughter, Esther, is married – I mean church married – to one of our army men, Captain Francis Bernard. But between this pair the miscegenation is disguised: Esther's sallowness is almost fair for all her mother is dark, and this must be because of the blanching power of her father's Scottish blood.

January 1819, Light Street, George Town

For not wanting to be in the difficult atmosphere of Government House, Tom has rented us a house on Light Street. He and Dr. Jack are proceeding to turn it into a menagerie and botanic garden mixed. In the space next to the bathhouses fish, flesh, and fowl alike contribute to the collection, and above stairs our rooms are variously ornamented with branches and flowers, rendering them so many arbours.

Tom tells me we now stay two houses down from where Mary Ann once lived with her first husband, Thompson.

January 1819, Light Street, George Town

Tom learns there are some here doing what they may to spike what they see as his too rapidly revolving wheel, and claiming Farquhar should be the chief in the venture to found a new trading post.

Indeed, Tom says there seems to be abroad a prejudicial belief that he has impertinently intruded on Farquhar's turf: his enemies complain it is the very height of injustice Lord Hastings foisted on Farquhar a fresh man to reap the fruits of his labours; that Farquhar has already done all that can be done in the matter of the new trading post; that he is eminently qualified to carry through the plan entirely on his own.

My charitable husband thinks the best strategy for dealing with this resentment is to remain open and friendly; he thus includes Farquhar in all his discussions.

January 1819, Light Street, George Town

Alas, the Penang government exercises its power and influence in every possible way against the attainment of the important objects Lord Hastings entrusted to Tom. My zealous husband had planned to slip away for a few days to Acheen, but Governor Bannerman now tells him that he is not to go, and until he himself can hear personally from Lord Hastings what's doing, all Tom's various diplomatising must be suspended.

This suspension, however, does not apply to Farquhar, who is now authorised by Bannerman to proceed in a reconnaissance of the islands south of here, and to determine which may be most suitable as a base for the China trade; he is to take with him the redcoats he'll need in case he wishes to make a territorial claim.

Tom, furious, has refused to yield that Farquhar is first man in the great venture, but he *makes it appear* he has decided against sailing with him to the southern islands. He has agreed Farquhar should proceed, and has told him he must ascertain the capabilities of Singapore and its vicinity – for he still thinks Singapore the island most suited to our needs – and he adds the results being satisfactory, Farquhar should make arrangements for securing to us the important command of the new station.

However, *in truth* he has no intention of kicking his heels in Penang whilst Farquhar has all the glory, and all the adventure, and he makes secret preparations to sail to Singapore on his own ship he has requisitioned for southern exploration, the *Indiana*.

He asked me last night if I would go with him, and risk a second confinement at sea, or wait quietly here in Penang whilst he was away. I reminded him that after the birth of Miss Charlotte – we still have no news of our dear firstborn – after last time he said all had gone so smoothly he thought he might arrange for our next baby also to be born at sea, and he could not doubt I would go with him.

I think my decision must please Dr. Jack, who will now sail with us, and who is I am sure as eager for adventure as Tom, and who would have regretted being compelled to linger here on my account – which reminds me I this morning overheard the two men talking. Tom was instructing Dr. Jack he was not to pity me, or to think him hard-hearted for dragging me about in my present state, for, he said: she will not remain from me, and what can I do?

January 1819, Light Street, George Town

It is midnight, and moonless. Tom is out in secret overseeing the loading of the *Indiana* that we may be ready to sail on the same tide as Farquhar when he leaves from here, which he plans to do at dawn, if the winds are favourable.

My clever husband, ever alert to native sensibilities, is having loaded onto the *Indiana* a red carpet, that he may unroll it at Singapore, to give to the chiefs there face – to pander to their dignity – when it comes time for them to sign the treaty by which they must cede their island to us.

Later: four ante meridiem, the sky just rimmed with light like a beckoning finger, and now Tom has come in, back from the harbour. He hears from his spies Farquhar does not intend to sail for Singapore, as he was commanded, but for another island, Carimon, which he thinks may suit for our new settlement. Tom dismisses all talk of this Carimon – he thinks it too far west to be of use – and now I must sleep, or suffer for it.

January 1819, the *Indiana*, Straits of Malacca

Farquhar sailed for the southern islands at first light. We slipped off too, in stealthy pursuit – the rising sun above us like a peach, staining the sky with its juice.

Tom arranged for one of his men who sails with Farquhar to give him a note to say we are on our way, and will rendezvous with him at Carimon; he would sail direct for Singapore, were he not in need of Farquhar's redcoats, for without the threat of muskets we could never take any island.

Likewise, Tom left a message for Governor Bannerman, to be delivered once we were safely over the horizon. It is a deliberately insulting message, saying Tom thinks it prudent to exercise a more immediate and active superintendence of the object of Farquhar's mission than envisioned by the Honourable the Governor, but that he has willingly acceded to his wishes by not sailing to Acheen.

It is wrong to delight in imagining Bannerman's face when he reads this message, nonetheless, delight I do!!! And so does Dr. Jack; the two of us are quite agreed my husband's superior merit consists in acting for himself instead of asking for orders, or even going against orders if he thinks them wrong, and this from an admirable decision of character, and a confidence in his own opinion which is well justified.

January 1819, the *Indiana*, anchored off Carimon

We have rendezvoused with Farquhar and his party off Carimon. Farquhar, summoned aboard the *Indiana*, was not at all pleased Tom had refused to relinquish this expedition to him, but after a heated exchange – so heated I shudder to recall it, and such *words* I never heard, nor knew my husband knew – after much raving he had little choice but to accept my husband's authority. Likewise he has had to accept Tom's view that Singapore is the most eligible station for our purposes, tho' he insists that the island is surrounded by mud banks and will admit of no place to land.

Tom says these mud banks exist only in Farquhar's head, and he has given the command that we sail for Singapore tomorrow, it is only about fifty nautical miles and he expects to be there easily within two days.

January 1819, the *Indiana*, anchored off Singapore

Our small fleet of ships has now arrived at Singapore. As it hove into view I was most struck by its beaches, which are of sand so white they glitter in the heat like the snow-covered fields of cold winter, at Home. I have not yet been ashore, but Tom tells me there are hundreds of human skulls rolling about on the gleaming sands, some old, some new, some with the hair still sticking to them, and all of them the result of piratical activity, rampant in this vicinity, for sometimes there is wholesale slaughter among the crews when the cargo is grabbed. Tom says when Singapore is ours these skulls must be gathered up and carried far out to sea, and there thrown into the waters.

Notwithstanding the skulls, and for all that Singapore is a tiny island, mostly forest, Tom is delighted by its advantages. Not only is it in a commanding position to protect our ships as they enter or exit the Straits of Malacca, on their way from India to China, from China to India, but also it has been his good fortune to discover here one of the safest harbours that could be imagined – Farquhar was quite wrong we would not be able to land on account of mud flats. There are no Dutch on the island and never have been. This Tom knows from an *orang laut* who rowed out to meet us when we first dropped anchor – these orang laut, sea gypsies, live on ramshackle houseboats, with their dogs, cats, even hens with their chicks; they sail from place to place in search of good fishing grounds, and some of them we now find at Singapore. From curiosity they have surround the *Indiana* in their little boats – they make no attempt to molest us, except to try to sell us fruit and fish.

Now he is here, Tom is more than ever convinced he who

holds Singapore can command the China trade, and if only we can have it and keep it, then in a few years our influence over the Archipelago, as far as concerns our commerce, will be fully established, and what's more he thinks we could from here rule all the Eastward.

But will we have it? As well as orang laut, there are also living on the island Malays and some Chinamen who originally came here to trade – and all these natives much startled at our arrival. It is with the Malays that Tom must deal. They live in a village on the north bank of the island's most prominent river, under the charge of their *Temenggong*, or chief.

Tom and Farquhar landed yesterday, with stores and soldiers, and they met with the Temenggong near where the river meets the sea. Tom said his party and various Malays all sat together on a carpet in the Temenggong's hut, and he told the Temenggong we want to found a trading settlement here. The Temenggong was agreeable, but he said he has not the power to make treaties, that power lies not with him but with the Sultan.

Singapore is part of the Johor-Rhio sultanate, now under the control of one Sultan Abdul Rahman at Rhio. The Temenggong explained that only this Sultan Abdul Rahman could give the British permission to set up a trading post, but he was now under the thumb of the Dutch, who would not allow him to allow the British to occupy Singapore.

And there things might have rested, except the little Malay courts are ever riddled with intrigue and fratricidal machination, and the court of Johor-Rhio is no different. It seems Abdul Rahman is only a pretender to the throne. When his father died, his older brother, Hussein, the rightful heir, was absent from the court, getting married in another sultanate. Abdul Rahman seized power with the support of the Dutch. Hussein, bitter, now lives quietly in retirement; the Temenggong here supports his cause.

On learning of these intricacies, Tom immediately decided

he would recognise Hussein as the rightful sultan, and then obtain his permission to found a trading post here. Accordingly, the Temenggong has sent some of his men to bring Hussein to Singapore from Rhio – this to be achieved in utmost secrecy, so as not to alert the Dutch – and Tom says he must come by hook or by crook, even if he has only a shirt on his back.

February 1819, the *Indiana*, anchored off Singapore

Tom writes many letters to Calcutta and to London, all triumphantly inscribed at the top of the paper *Singapore*. When not at his correspondence, or busy with his other duties, he steals time to explore, and to his delight he finds many relicts of Singapore's past as the great Lion City of Sang Nila Utama. The lines of the old city – the ramparts that formed its defences – are still to be traced and lying here and there within them is evidence of its history as a place of trade – pots lying broken on the ground, and some of them come from China, Tom says, and some from west even of India.

The ramparts enclose a hill, *Bukit Larangan*, Forbidden Hill, said to be Sang Nila Utama's last resting place, and considered by the Malays to be very haunted and sacred. Tho' some may object we are precipitate, we have here run up the Union Jack whilst we await the arrival of Hussein, and another one flutters from a flagpole on the beach.

February 1819, the *Indiana*, anchored off Singapore

Hussein has arrived, and today came aboard the *Indiana* to confer with Tom. He is a fat man, unprepossessing, and Tom says he is terribly fearful of repercussions from the Dutch if he helps us. But his fear does not outweigh his bitterness to his brother, so he has declared he is the lawful sovereign of Singapore, wickedly cheated by his relations, and willing to sign a treaty with Tom.

Apparently, Farquhar mutters Tom's tactics, his crafty manner of acquiring Singapore, if successful, which he doubts, risk provoking a war with the Dutch. But Tom is sanguine the Dutch will protest our occupation only with words, not with troops and canon, and he says he is no more afraid of the Hollanders' bluster and bombast than of their tulips.

February 1819, the *Indiana*, anchored off Singapore

Tom has taken possession of Singapore!!! I went ashore for the first time yesterday that I might witness him signing the treaty which will enable The Company to set up a trading settlement in the southern part of the island. On any other day I think I would have caused the usual sensation amongst the natives, for the fairness of my skin, for my female nature, and for my skirts – and this even had I not been in the family way, enormously swollen. But such was the general excitement few even glanced at me.

It was a clear day, very hot, very still, and Tom put to good use the red carpet he had the foresight to bring from Penang, this was unrolled a hundred feet along the white beach, and made a splendid piece of theatre. Our redcoats lined up to either side, forming a guard, a scarlet hedge, and behind them were commanders and officers of the ships and I think probably every native from the island come to watch proceedings.

Sultan Hussein was shaded from the fierce hot sun by a yellow umbrella, a badge of royal office in these parts, but for all that he was perspiring profusely, Tom later said from nerves how the Dutch would react to us landing on Singapore, which would no doubt be with vengeful fury towards our damp sultan as much as towards him.

Tom received the Sultan and the Temenggong under a canvas awning he'd had erected, and here the great treaty was read aloud, in English and then in Malay. Next, it was signed between Sir Stamford Raffles, on behalf of the Honourable East India Company, and Sultan Hussein Mahummed Shah, Sultan of Johor, and by this signing Singapore is ours, and all the Sultan wants in return is five thousand Spanish dollars a year, and the protection of the British.

We presented gifts to the Malays – guns and scarlet wool cloth too hot for the climate. The Union Jack was run up the flagpole – tho' it had been flying a couple of days already, Tom had had it hauled down earlier, that it might be ceremoniously raised now – and volleys were fired by field guns brought onto the shore, and from the ships, which were all jauntily decked with flags.

Cold lunches were provided, and then much wine was drunk, the Malays sitting down with the English. Toast after toast was proposed, making everybody very lively. Afterwards one of the captains proposed giving Tom three cheers. After demur from Farquhar this was done with spirit by all except him, for his mouth was too grudging to give egress to cheers.

But we Britons are so few, and so far from Home, that needs must we work together or our enterprise fails. Which is to say that, notwithstanding Farquhar's resentment, Tom has issued a proclamation announcing him as Resident and Commandant here, and directing all persons to obey him accordingly. He announced too that Singapore is a dependency of Bencoolen, not of Penang, and that it has been placed under his command, not Bannerman's.

Tom has written out extensive instructions for Farquhar, touching on diplomacy, practicality, and trade. He must avoid any measures which could be construed as interfering with Dutch authority in those settlements where they hold sway, and he must exercise caution and delicacy in his dealings both with native rulers under the influence of the Dutch, and also with free and independent tribes who will no doubt come here to trade. Constructing a port and providing watering facilities for visiting ships are priorities – the watering facilities to be near the mouth of the river, where the shingle is firm for rolling the casks. Tom has said where the cantonment must be, and various other buildings and defences he directs built in other places also. He is most particular this is to be a port for free trade, and he instructs that no port duties are to be extracted from visiting vessels, neither native nor European, so as not to inhibit them from coming. Farquhar must submit to him quarterly accounts, and keep him informed of all developments in this new settlement.

Farquhar could not much object to any of this, so he objected instead that Tom asks him to live pro tempore in a house of atap, as my husband does not think himself justified in yet authorising the expense of the erection of a brick built house – for the manufacture of which bricks we'd need first to build a kiln.

Once he had finished writing proclamations, memoranda, instructions, and commands Tom took himself off botanising, and found three species of pitcher plant, as yet unknown to men of science, and each in elegance and brilliance far surpassing any other pitcher plant he has yet seen.

Last night we gave a celebratory dinner here on the *Indiana*, and Tom remarked to all the table it was a relief to him the great treaty was signed, for if it had not been he'd have had to return to Bencoolen and become a philosopher. Farquhar was not present, he remained on the island with his officers, and his sepoys.

February 1819, the *Indiana*, anchored off Singapore

The offices of the new government to be formed here begin to be assigned, and Farquhar and Tom have quarrelled over the post of Master Attendant and Marine Storekeeper, which provides the man who holds it with great opportunity to feather his nest. For his daughter Esther's sake, Farquhar wants this post for his son-in-law, Captain Bernard. Alas, Tom has had to remind him that offices are not to be created to suit individuals, or to serve the purposes of private patronage, for he wants this post for Flint.

As the outcome to this squabble, Tom has appointed Bernard to the coveted post, in an acting capacity, until Flint can relieve him. Meanwhile, he has written to Flint and Mary Ann, saying he can at last do something for them, and saying they should book passage to the Eastward.

Later today we set sail to return to Penang – Tom will drop Dr. Jack and me there before proceeding to Acheen. As I think I really must now be within a few days of my time, perhaps my second baby will indeed continue in what is becoming the family tradition, and be born at sea? In which case Tom says we must name him Oceanus.

February 1819, the *Indiana*, Straits of Malacca

The *Indiana* has just got underway. Tho' Tom now watches Singapore slip out of sight, his intention is to return after as short an absence as possible. He has written in a personal letter to Lord Hastings all that transpired after Hussein arrived, and he will now await with resigned interest the Court of Directors' reaction to the news that quite without their permission he has acquired for The Company a new territory: he thinks the Honourable Members will object to the expense of having Singapore, but will not repudiate its acquisition, because even those dullards must realise that in short order Singapore's costs must be outrun by very great profit.

As to the Dutch, Tom remains confident that by claiming Singapore from under their noses he will not spark any war except a paper one of documents exchanged between Bengal and Batavia, between London and Amsterdam, between our British ambassadors and their Dutch statesmen – in short he anticipates thousands of pages of protest and counter-protest, but no fighting.

My husband seems proud to think the Dutch will forever hate him for outwitting them, and he says, cheerful, no doubt they wish to see him entirely rubbed out.

February 1919, Light Street, George Town

We are returned to Penang, and still no new babe, so if I am blessed with a gentleman he is not to be named Oceanus after all, but, praised be God, I found waiting for me a letter from Nurse Grimes, bringing news of Miss Charlotte. My dear firstborn! I learn now the pet is well, babbling, and beginning to toddle – and barely a year old! Is Miss Charlotte not advanced?

As to public life, Tom has had a furious exchange with Governor Bannerman, who is most put out at my husband's audacity in defying him by sailing to Singapore when he'd told him not to, and by placing Singapore under the command of Bencoolen, not of Penang. According to Tom, Bannerman began his tirade by screaming Bencoolen is eight weeks sailing from Singapore, whilst from here it is but eight days, and there could be no better proof that he ought to run it. Tom coolly replied this proximity was as much reason for him to be made Governor of Penang, as it was for Bannerman to be made Governor of Singapore. At this calculated insolence Bannerman grew redder in the face, and was spurred to ever more deranged ranting, accusing Tom of personal ambition and a desire for aggrandisement, which serious faults any impartial judge must agree blot not Tom's character, but his.

February 1919, Light Street, George Town

Bannerman remains so jealous of Tom, he has refused his request to send more sepoys to Singapore, saying when – *when* – the Dutch protest our occupation of the island the settlement will have to be abandoned, so the smaller the military force to be evacuated the better.

Tom ignores this obstructiveness as much as he can and keeps himself busy arranging for tools and supplies to be sent to Farquhar, and writing yet more reports for Lord Hastings.

February 1819, Light Street, George Town

The expected Dutch protest against our occupation of Singapore has arrived from Malacca; the Hollanders say they have general suzerainty over all the southern islands, and thus it makes no odds they never set foot on Singapore, we should not have claimed it. Tom says their talk of general suzerainty is so much catchpenny claptrap, and those clodpolls know it, they are but grasping at straws.

Meanwhile, my husband has announced he will soon fulfil his diplomatic duties with respect to Acheen: he will sail to that court to sign a treaty with the friendly Sultan, to make Acheen the second in the veritable chain of ports he now envisions will break Dutch power in the Archipelago.

Governor Bannerman is almost bursting with fury Tom intends to sail to Acheen, saying he misconstrues Lord Hastings' instructions, but Tom says it is his duty to go, as he must establish on a permanent footing British influence in the Eastern Seas.

March 1819, Light Street, George Town

Tho' it cannot be much longer before nature brings to a close these last dragging days before my laying-in, Tom has this morning sailed for Acheen. He went on the *Indiana*, saying as we parted he hoped my suffering is tolerable, and reminding me since Oceanus is put aside I must name his son Leopold, for the Prince. I must confess I feel low in spirits, lonely without my husband or even a nurse, and when I remember Dr. Jack is a botanist I cannot prevent cowardice stealing upon me, notwithstanding I am sturdy, and would be courageous.

March 1819, Light Street, George Town

Make a joyful noise unto the Lord, all ye lands ... I think to his surprise, as well as to mine, Dr. Jack proved capable, and after travail no worse than to be expected, I am safe in bed with my new baby – as I hoped and trusted, a gentleman, by the grace of God. Leopold Stamford is a most endearing pretty creature, lusty, and his new-born smile like the light of the first day.

May 1819, Light Street, George Town

I have not written my diary this past six or seven weeks for being too busy with Leopold – I have no nurse, only the household servants to help me. Still, a finer babe, or one with more promise of intelligence never was beheld, and, to my joy Tom is now returned, to agree with me our baby is a wonder. He is relieved to find me well, and Leopold too, and is cock-a-hoop to have a son and heir – he says Leopold is the best of gentlemen, and the most perfect babe he ever saw, and a more winning new-born even than was Charlotte.

The tractable Sultan of Acheen signed a treaty giving us exclusively the freedom to trade in all the ports under his control, so Tom has now successfully concluded both the missions Lord Hastings entrusted to him, and we are to return to Bencoolen, via Singapore.

May 1819, a government bungalow, Singapore

My travelling hither and thither sees me once more at Singapore, brought here by the trusty *Indiana*. I did not write during the voyage for I had Leopold to fill my time, and nothing to say of any interest except to mothers, and for the dreariness of events I offer many grateful prayers.

Farquhar has achieved much in four months: more than fifteen miles of road have been laid; already a population of about five thousand souls has collected under our flag, many of them come fresh here from China, fleeing famine and other disasters, and looking for an opportunity to trade; the harbour is filled with shipping from all quarters; everyone is comfortably housed, provisions are in abundance, the troops healthy.

Tom is delighted by the progress he now sees all around him, and tells me constantly that this can be a great commercial emporium, and indeed that fulcrum he dreamed of whence we may extend our influence politically. Such is the place this settlement occupies in his heart, he calls Singapore *child of my own*.

May 1819, a government bungalow, Singapore

Since Tom anticipates it will not be long before Singapore becomes a place of magnitude and importance, he is much concerned to achieve an economical and proper allotment of the ground intended to form the site of the principle town. Accordingly, he has issued Farquhar with clear instructions about land use. He has specified such things as that the European warehouses must be in one area, that the Chinese must dwell in another, and that government buildings must be in another. He has specified too that the cantonment, in the area between the ramparts of the ancient fortifications and the Singapore River, must exclude all private dwellings except that of the Temenggong.

June 1819, a government bungalow, Singapore

Coolies clearing the forest at a rocky point near where the Singapore River meets the sea have uncovered a sandstone boulder, split in two. Ten feet high and ten feet wide, it is covered with indecipherable lettering. The script looks to me like the scratching of chickens in the sand, but Tom believes it to be some variety of Sanskrit. He thinks this stone dates from between the tenth and the thirteenth centuries, and he is much excited by such wonderful evidence of Singapore's glorious past. He is pleased, too, it was found before we'd quit here for Bencoolen, which we do within the week.

June 1819, the *Indiana*, the Eastern Seas

We left Singapore in the warm glow of its success. Tom seems almost besotted with the place, and he says all he wants now is the certainty of permanent possession, which alas depends on authorities beyond his control: the approbation and sanction of the territory by the Court of Directors; the aggrieved forbearance of the Dutch. Still, he says he cannot be wrong to persevere in his duty to promote The Company's, and the country's, interests in the Eastward on the assumption the Court will approve his actions, and the sulking Dutch will keep their hands off Singapore.

June 1819, the *Indiana*, the Eastern Seas

This voyage threatened to become too interesting. Yesterday, the *Indiana* got stuck on a sandbank off Rhio. It was feared she could not be got off, and she was only re-floated by throwing overboard all the water loaded for the voyage. We sent a boat ashore, asking to be resupplied with water, but the Dutch Resident asserted Tom went as a spy, and refused our request out of fury that we have

Singapore, and that it was Tom who won it for us. Wicked man! And Leopold but four months old!

Fortunately, a Good Samaritan appeared in the guise of one of the beautiful American vessels so numerous in these seas. The Captain generously, and at considerable risk, for the wind was strong and in his favour, stopped his course, and with great difficulty, by means of ropes, conveyed some casks of water. I do not know the Captain's name, but I will never forget this American kindness.

June 1819, the *Indiana*, the Eastern Seas

I am content, peaceful, and so is Tom. Notwithstanding Dutch howls his success at Singapore seems reasonably secure; we sail with Leopold toward Miss Charlotte, our firstborn that we haven't seen since last August – nearly a year, such a separation, and at such an interesting age. Anticipation of seeing her makes everything lovely, so I now think the seas of this Archipelago the most beautiful in all the world. When I stroll the decks, the views seem to bear witness to the goodness of their creator: the lightness of the cloud-streaked sky; the many small islands here and there clustering together; mountains of the most fanciful forms, wreathed in mist, cloaked with rich and luxuriant vegetation extending even to the beaches; silkily stippled water rippling; little native boats, often with in them only a fisherman, naked but for a loincloth, continually drifting about, wafted from shadow into sunlight, from sunlight into shade, as we humans are likewise wafted by the winds of good fortune, adversity, kind destiny, cruel fate.

August 1819, Permattam Ballam

I thank the Lord most merciful that at last – *at last* – I am home and reunited with my daughter. My dear Miss Charlotte! I have kissed every inch of her, and I offer many grateful prayers I find her in good health – radiant – shining to me as bright as a star. She had a most happy introduction to Leopold; she is quite the little mother and has cuddled him and cooed over him as much as I have cuddled her and cooed over her.

Meanwhile Nurse Grimes hugged her new charge to her hard and said ain't he a duck, and Jane, our blackamoor nursery maid, is delighted with him too, and I am most relieved I will henceforth have their help for I begin to find it tedious as well as tiring to be always at Leopold's command.

September 1819, Permattam Ballam

I am just returned from visiting town. For all Tom has been absent a year Bencoolen is much improved under his care: it no longer has that gloomy and desolate appearance which so struck me when I arrived from England; the buildings now are neat, the gardens flourishing, and the people busy and smiling.

My calls this morning included one also on Mrs. Tot, who introduced me to her second child, for while we were away she and Tot became parents again – a bonny son – and we must hope that this one lives.

For that matter I suspect *I* am once more in the family way, and Nurse Grimes agrees it is probable – one a year is it seems to be my pattern.

October 1819, Permattam Ballam

I have told Tom I suspect I will next spring present him with another son. My husband laughed I am such a good breeder he can scarcely worry for me this time, and from our lusty appetites we would have too many and must be like that old woman who lived in a shoe, except we would never whip all their bums and put them to bed, for being too much inclined to doting to use on our children a whip. Such was my husband's happiness I overlooked his various vulgarities.

September 1819, Permattam Ballam

We have had newspapers arrived from England – *The Globe, The Observer* – carrying those reports Tom wrote about our journeys to penetrate the interior of Sumatra, also many letters all reporting our exploits there have created quite a stir at Home – I could even say a sensation.

Now I learn of this I feel I am very unworthy of the attention I have excited, and which has quite astonished me. In travelling about I was influenced by only one motive: affection for my husband.

October 1819, Permattam Ballam

The brig the *Favourite* arrives, bringing news of the death from cholera of Governor Bannerman of Penang – no great loss – and so ends his dispute and rivalry with Tom over the establishment of the British garrison and colony at Singapore. We learn too that Tom's old enemy Phillips, Bannerman's dullard son-in-law, is made Acting Governor of Penang, until a permanent appointment can be made.

Tom thinks for its proximity to Singapore he should now be appointed Governor of Penang. Accordingly, he has decided to take passage on the *Favourite* when she returns to Calcutta, to press with Lord Hastings his claim. He also wishes to remind the Governor-General of what he said before: that on the removal or going away of Governor Bannerman the administration of our possessions in the Eastward should be brought under *one* government, and that he, Tom, should be its head, ruling from our new settlement to the south of Malacca.

This promise was given even before we had Singapore, but now the island is ours, assuming only approbation from London, and the agreement of the Dutch, Tom is eager to make it our capital in the Eastward, to give us command of the Archipelago, as well in peace as in war, and so that our commerce, and our principles, will be known and felt throughout. Hence he is to suggest that if he is made Governor of Penang, he should rule it – and also Bencoolen – from Singapore.

The *Favourite*, a small vessel, has but one cabin, the captain's, and Tom must share this with him. But tho' the captain says he can do no better than offer me a corner of the hold, I am determined to travel with my husband to Calcutta, notwithstanding I think that city a wen – women of pleasure flirting about in all directions – and no matter I am again in the family way.

Tom assured me we will not be away above three or four months, yet I worry this could stretch to five, six, or more and in that case my next confinement may be amongst strangers, as was my last, and perhaps at sea, as was my first, and I cannot be happy at the prospect of being separated from my children – such pretty prodigies! Leopold even excels Charlotte in beauty and expression. Still, I must wean my son, and be off, with many grateful prayers Nurse Grimes is indeed a treasure, and perhaps less grateful ones our botanist Dr. Jack will be on hand to physick him, and Charlotte too.

October 1819, the *Favourite*, Bay of Bengal

And so to sea again. The *Favourite* seems a robust vessel, but my corner of the hold is no better than to be expected: I now find myself accommodated in a cabin formed from slung canvas, in a space more usually occupied by sacks of pepper or coffee, and on all sides I am surrounded by the same. I have a chair of the workaday variety, but my bed is a hammock swinging from the ship's ribs, and my desk is a plank balanced across an old opium cask – relict of a previous cargo. Still, the coffee smells pleasant, I have a candle to write by, this voyage should take no more than a month, and today the ship but rises and sinks and does not toss about, and I feel quite well so I must tell myself I am content.

November 1819, Government House, Calcutta

The best I can say of my voyage on the *Favourite* is that now it is over, and I lodge once more in the gilded guest apartments of Government House. Lord Hastings is as ugly and extravagant as ever, and Calcutta is just as leprous and stinking; this city seems to smother me like dirty rags.

But what is grimy chaos, when set against family feeling? Which is to say, to our delight, on our arrival here Tom and I found staying with one of our government officials, awaiting only a ship to carry them east, Flint, Mary Ann, and a little stranger, that she bore last spring, and is introduced to us now as Charley Boy – a fine, lively infant, tho' he can't hold a candle to my Leopold.

Notwithstanding I have received no letter from Mary Ann since I can't remember when, she says she has written often, and, indeed, that she replied at once to that letter Tom wrote her and Flint from Singapore telling them to come to the Eastward, as he wanted Flint at our new settlement, but all her letters must have gone astray, or failed to find us on our recent wanderings. No matter, they booked passage and sailed in June, and now here they are.

What a noisy reunion we made of it!!! Tom and Mary Ann could not have been more delighted to embrace each other; I was all joyful surprise at meeting Charley Boy; Mary Ann was all unnecessary squeals to find me That Way and, indeed mother to two children, for last she heard I was still expecting Leopold. Later, when we two women were alone, she subjected me to shocking confidences of her own recent laying in, which confidences I did not enjoy, and did not return.

Tom has written to Farquhar telling him to warn Bernard, Acting Master Attendant and Marine Storekeeper, that Flint is on his way to relieve him, and directing him to give his son-in-law other work in his administration. He says he hopes Farquhar and Bernard will receive his intelligence with good temper, for all it heralds a reduction in Bernard's emoluments and perquisites.

When Tom and I return to Bencoolen Flint, Mary Ann, and Charley Boy will sail with us, to visit a while, before Flint must take up his post.

November 1819, Government House, Calcutta

Lord Hastings is out of favour with me: despite the assurances he gave Tom last time we were here, he now refuses to accept my husband's plan to consolidate our Eastern possessions into one government, and to make Singapore the capital from which we rule all the Eastward.

Poor Tom, dejected, says Lord Hastings remains in principle in favour of his idea, and nor does his Lordship doubt either that one day Dutch claims to Singapore will be relinquished, or that, come the day, The Company will then recognise the settlement, but until these things have come to pass he thinks it would be premature to fashion, even provisionally, any plans to make Singapore our first seat of government in all the Eastward.

November 1819, Government House, Calcutta

More bitter developments: tho' Tom retains the care of Singapore, he is not appointed the Governor of Penang, instead that dolt

Phillips is confirmed in the post. Notwithstanding his natural buoyancy of spirits, Tom is heavy and sick at heart at this blow to his dignity, and to his ambition, and so am I on his behalf. He says he could lie down and cry, and weep for hours together for being unhappy, thwarted, and I am only thankful I travelled with him, and that Mary Ann is here, otherwise he would be a solitary wretch in Calcutta, with no one of congenial feelings with whom he could communicate.

December 1819, Government House, Calcutta

Tom remains low from his recent reversals. He is bothered by terrible headaches which make him very ill, so he often has to stay in bed, and I worry he is afflicted by a dangerous indigestion of the brain. Even when he is up on his legs he is miserable and broods on recent developments. Moreover, he misses the children – we both do.

January 1820, the *Indiana*, Bay of Bengal

Tom was as good as his word he would not keep me from Bencoolen above three or four months. He and I – and Flint, Mary Ann, and Charley Boy – have quit Calcutta on the *Indiana*, and we breathe once again the health-inspiring breezes of the open ocean.

I am in hopes I will see my children again within the month, which makes me cheerful. Likewise, Tom, fortified by thoughts of the coming reunion, seems to have left in Calcutta some of his despondency, and his head, tho' still too often bad, is at any rate better than it was.

Flint I must confess I find *difficult*, and on account of his presence I expect *challenges* from this voyage. I now have nothing else to record, except that I enjoy the best of health, and I am growing larger and larger – what a relief that this babe, God willing, will be born at home, and not whilst I am jaunting about from here to there.

February 1820, the *Indiana*, anchored off the cannibal lands

Ocean air has effected in Tom a wonderful change so I may fairly say he is in good health and spirits, and now, from his insatiable curiosity, he has ordered the *Indiana* to pause on her journey at a place on the north coat of Sumatra where dwell the Battas people.

These Battas are cannibals, and it is Tom's plan to go ashore tomorrow to satisfy his mind most fully in everything concerning their customs – he says they are not a bad people, notwithstanding they eat one another. My condition may be delicate, yet I intend to go with him, for I would not have him devoured unless I share his fate – when I told him I would accompany him he said before I go I must write to my friends at Home to warn them if we never be heard of again they may conclude we have been eaten.

February 1820, the *Indiana*, anchored off the cannibal lands

I have survived the man eaters!!! Tom and I both remain whole, without loss to the table between us of even a single limb!!!

I did not with my own eyes see anybody eaten, for which I am thankful. Indeed I was left most of the day quite alone in a hut, whilst Tom consulted with the Battas elders, including also their witch doctor, a fearsome man, much adorned with paint and ornaments of bone – human or animal I dared not ask – and carrying to my distress a most alarming carved stick Tom said had been dipped in the blood of a sacrificed child, to give it magical power.

From his discussions Tom concludes the Battas' man-eating is no worse than European torture of two centuries ago, or even than our capital punishment. He says the Battas nation possesses codes of laws of great antiquity, and it is from regard for these laws, and a veneration for the institutions of their ancestors, that they eat each other. For certain crimes their law declares the perpetrator must be eaten ALIVE, in careful slices. Tom learned the palms of the hands and the soles of the feet are the delicacies of the epicures, their flavour enhanced by being dipped in a *sambal* – a common sauce of lime, salt, and chilli, and I shall never again see sambal without thinking how it may be used.

I ate nothing whilst I was with the Battas, for fear of what their dishes may contain, but Tom later told me I need not have worried, as human flesh is forbidden to females, tho' he was told women get a bit of it by stealth now and then.

The whole time Tom and I were consorting with the man eaters Flint and Mary Ann stayed aboard the *Indiana*, shuddering the while, or so I should imagine. Mary Ann scolded me both before I left, and also when I returned, that a woman in my condition should have more regard for her flesh, and that of her expected stranger, than to risk becoming dinner.

March 1820, Permattam Ballam

Blessed be God, which hath not turned away my prayer, nor his mercy from me ... Our voyage from the cannibal lands went without incident, except at the very last of the way we had such rough weather we were forced to disembark at a spit of rock some distance from the harbour at Bencoolen, and horses and carriages had to be sent to fetch us, but now we are three days home, and to my very great relief I find my lovely little ones in high health and spirits, both of them much grown – expanding daily. They are such winning infants, all and everything we could wish them. Indeed, my heart is in my mouth to see them, and Tom says never were parents more blessed.

Meanwhile, my proud husband has remarked to Nurse

Grimes I am now as big as the house – he, alas, from his recent sickness is as thin as a scarecrow – and Mary Ann is as satisfied with her niece and nephew as I am with Charley Boy.

March 1820, Permattam Ballam

The beauty of our abode of peace, the retirement, the quiet domestic life which we lead in this happy retreat produce in Tom continued improvement in his health, and in his mind he seems now resigned to his recent bitter reversals. He says he has now thrown politics away, and he will no longer go striding from one side of India to another, overleaping mountains, or forming new countries, he will instead tend to his garden here, planting coffee and cloves, and he will try to do the best he can with Bencoolen, and with Singapore.

March 1820, Permattam Ballam

Tot has told Tom he can no longer hazard his son's life in the torrid zones; for his little boy's sake he wants to return with his family to Ireland.

There never was such a doting father as Tom. It is a common remark with him that to follow custom and send the children Home without us is out of the question. He has now told Tot he quite approves he is another will not follow this chilly custom, and he has granted his dear friend the freedom to go.

This episode unsettles me, and Tom also. How can we not now turn our own sights to Home? How can we not confront anew the deleterious effects of heat on European children? Oh, our two dear little rogues, and the new being I have within me! In two or three years both Charlotte and Leopold will require a cold climate, for their bodies' sakes, so we are quite agreed we must take them away from here before the warm damp makes inroads on their delicate constitutions.

Moreover, we must think of Leopold's schooling. It will not be many years before Our Leo has grown beyond Tom's management, and it will be time to commence upon the rudiments of a better education than his father can give him, or than is otherwise available in the Eastward, so here is reason again to take him Home, and there find for him a school or tutor.

I must confess we long for England on our own accounts, too. Tom's headaches impress upon us that his health is delicate – he alarms me by saying he cannot last more than another two or three years in the Indies – and I pine often for my parents. Indeed we dream together we must one day soon look out for some cottage or farm not too far from London, and once we have our cows we must endeavour to sell butter and cheese to advantage, asking each other: do you think this would do?

April 1820, Permattam Ballam

Our household, our circle, and our spirits are all sadly reduced: the Tots have sailed for Calcutta, from where they'll make their way across the globe to Ireland; the Flints have left for Singapore, so that our brother can take up the appointment Tom has kept for him there.

I must regret that I will not have Mary Ann as a companion, whilst I await my next laying-in, nor to encourage me in travail – it is lonely sometimes to be so much lacking the companionship of my own fair sex. Still, for his competence at Leopold's delivery, I am at least this time less nervous of Dr. Jack than I was last, and Nurse Grimes will no doubt be able to guide him, if he becomes flustered.

We have sent with Mary Ann potatoes to plant in Singapore, and also several nutmeg trees which we hope will be the foundation of a valuable plantation for Charley Boy. With the Tots we sent a variety of song birds in cages we hope will thrive in northern climes, and three boxes of spice of our own production: nutmeg, clove, and cinnamon.

May 1820, Permattam Ballam

As it was decreed, so it has happened. After a confinement no stalwart woman could complain of, I am safe in bed with another fine boy. We have named our latest son Stamford Marsden, whom we call *Cooksey* – I knew I should have a second gentleman and am not disappointed. Tom is as relieved and delighted as if Cooksey were his first and this new son and heir has a little pocket watch face, and his blue eyes are two vessels to be filled up with memory.

I am so happy to be recuperating this time in my own bed, at home, with both nurse and nursemaid on hand to help me, that I can hardly say it.

July 1820, Permattam Ballam

I realise with some surprise I have written nothing in this diary since May; in excuse I can say only that I have been occupied with Cooksey, and the heavy demands of my growing family. Still, I feel as well at present as I ever have, and Tom says I look the best he has ever seen me. We are both delighted by our brood, our joy. Charlotte and Leopold are both running about, and are as remarkable for their uncommon intelligence, as for the sweetness of their dispositions. At two Charlotte prattles in English, Hindustani, and Malay, depending on her company; if she is sent with a message, she translates it at once into the language of the servant she meets with. Tom calls her of all creatures the most angelic he ever beheld. She has a soft heart, and is so full of mildness and gentleness that we fear she will have many trials to go through in this unfeeling world. Her brother, Leopold, however will take her part for Our Leo – the wonder of all who see him – Our Leo, all boldness, has the spirit of a lion and is absolutely beautiful. Tom calls him the handsomest and the most princely little fellow that ever lived – he struts about the house all day with an air of the most complete independence. Meanwhile, Cooksey is a docile, contented baby, and we are upon the whole as happy a family as I can well conceive.

September 1820, Permattam Ballam

This diary is proving lately a gappy thing, like lace rather than close-stitched embroidery, and this thanks to the continuing distractions of my happy domestic life. But I now pick up my pen to report that not four months after I was delivered of Cooksey, our three little darlings, the finest children that ever were seen, must soon I think make room for another: I suspect I am again in the family way. When I told Tom, he said ye gods, if we go on at this rate we shall require at least two ships to convey us Home.

November 1820, Permattam Ballam

Tho' contentment makes me lately a dilatory diarist, I today find myself with such shocking news I feel compelled to record it: the last day of last year Tom's Cousin Elton blew his brains out. This news came in a letter from Tom's mother, and she included with the package a letter Elton had left for Tom, sinfully attempting to explain away his sin of self-murder: *if anything is a man's own, it is surely his life … Go on, be as merry as you can. If you can be religious, good. But don't sink the man in the Christian.*

Tom, when he had recovered somewhat from the shock, said he never was in any danger of sinking the man in the Christian, for all Christianity is so useful for making people behave, and here was sadness, and Olivia always said Elton was insane.

I wish my husband had not remembered Olivia at this moment of high emotion. And I pray hard he may soon start to cleave to Christianity for more than its practical utility. How can he show so little concern for his salvation? So little zeal for Our Saviour? If *he* is unworried at the dangers he brings to his soul, then *I* am not.

November 1820, Permattam Ballam

Elton had all the papers for Tom's second edition of *The History of Java* – the two of them have been corresponding about plates, additions, revisions, &c, these past two years – and now his cousin is dead, my poor husband has been fretting what will happen about his book. I last night reminded him that even if he had the papers he needs, he could not shepherd a second edition through the press when he exists at such a distance from Mr. Murray's house in Albemarle Street, and thus I advised him to postpone all thought of a second edition until we are back in England, when he can give it his full attention. To my considerable surprise, Tom agreed this was wise counsel, and claimed he would follow it.

December 1820, Permattam Ballam

Another death. Tom counted amongst the Great Men he was honoured to entertain at Berners St. Sir Humphrey Davy, inventor of that ingenious lamp which forestalls death by fire-damp and choke-damp down the mines, and now Sir Humphrey and Tom are correspondents. My husband had from him today a letter, dated last June, giving the news of a sad loss to science: Sir Joseph Banks died that month, some good few years after he'd run through his threescore years and ten.

We cannot call it faint compensation, but Sir Humphrey also wrote that before he died Sir Joseph discussed with him

Tom's idea that London should have an establishment similar to *le Jardin des Plantes* in Paris, where animals, kept in parkland, could be studied at leisure both for the amusement of the public, and also to further scientific understanding. He reports he and Sir Joseph resolved to form soon a zoological society to support the foundation of such a garden, and that tho' his friend is gone, this resolution he now intends to bring to fruition.

Tom, enthused, at once sat down to reply he wished to be kept informed of the progress of this society, and adding it is his ambition that once there is established in London a zoological garden, then this should have the most extensive collection of animals in the world.

Now, my husband announces he must send to Sir Humphry a shipment of skins and skeletons of various quadrupeds, and stuffed versions of the same.

New Year's Day 1821, Permattam Ballam

A new year, and from our current content and satisfaction I dare to hope it will be a happy one.

Politically, Tom feels he has done much that is necessary for the good of his country, and in our private life, we acknowledge with grateful thankfulness that every wish of our hearts is gratified. Uninterrupted health has prevailed in our family, and our children, our pride and delight, imbibe from us already those tastes it is our pleasure to cultivate – in gardening, in natural history, in music – not forgetting, if it pleases God, there is another coming, to bring us joy sometime next summer.

Meanwhile, our days follow a placid pattern. Tom interests himself much in the agricultural affairs of the settlement. He rises early, and delights in driving into the local native villages, inspecting the plantations, and encouraging the industry of the people. Later, he writes and reads, studies natural history, chemistry, and geology, or superintends the native draftsmen of whom he has five or six constantly employed on the verandah, making for him a collection of natural history paintings more comprehensive than any other in the Eastward. He has often Charlotte with him, or Leo toddling along, as he goes from one pursuit to another, visiting his beautiful and extensive aviary, as well as the extraordinary collection of animals which he is always domesticating in the house. When the children, the older two, are not with him, they are just as often with me, my shadows as I attend to domestic affairs; Tom and I are quite agreed they are the best of companions.

Our evenings we spend in reading, music, and conversation; before retiring we walk in the garden, in order to enjoy the delicious, scented-coolness of the night breezes, and, if there are no clouds, a tropical moon, the most beautiful lantern of all the heavens, and crowded around her all the candles of the stars.

January 1821, Permattam Ballam

On re-reading my diary entry for yesterday I realise I mentioned only in passing the extraordinary collection of animals Tom is always domesticating in the house, which was poor tribute to my husband's zeal for all God's creatures. He is particularly fond of tigers, and he is now raising two young cubs, quite tame and playful at present, which he feeds on vegetables and milk only. His other favourite is his bear, a local sun bear, which he allows to dine at our table, where it shows a preference for Champagne, a taste Tom indulges when it is ill. We also have about the property a baby elephant, a gibbon, and two deer, so our house is a perfect animal kingdom. It is a rather curious scene to see the children, the bear, the tiger cubs, a blue mountain parrot, and a cat all playing together, the parrot's beak being the only object of awe to all the party.

January 1821, Permattam Ballam

I think Tom must have found this diary, and read it, as I know he sometimes does, and I will not complain at that, for what is it, if not my love letter to him? But my husband feels, perhaps, that I am inviting disaster by relishing so much our happiness? Certainly, he warns me of hubris, and says our scene is too sunny to continue unclouded, and tells me not to expect to retain all the blessings God in his bounty has heaped upon us, but to feel that such happiness, once enjoyed, ought to shed a bright ray over the future, however dark and trying it may become.

February 1821, Permattam Ballam

Tom has had another letter from Sir Humphrey Davy, this one dated August, and reporting that the Linnaean Society in London has named that prodigious flower poor Dr. Arnold found in the forest back in '18 *Rafflesia arnoldii*. Tom is greatly flattered, but disconcerted, for the discovery of this wonder of the vegetable kingdom was Dr. Arnold's so by rights its name should be *Arnoldia rafflesii*. Alas, there's now nothing to be done about this business of the naming, except to hope Dr. Arnold's ghost forgives it.

Sir Humphrey gave no news of the proposed zoological society, so Tom has written to ask how it goes along, and to say if only a London zoological garden can be established, he will send it a pair of tapirs, as well as divers other creatures of the Eastward. He now makes arrangements to send to Sir Humphrey a consignment of serpents preserved in spirits.

March 1821, Permattam Ballam

There is discontent in Singapore. We have had a letter from Mary Ann saying Bernard is behaving most truculent for being displaced from his post of Master Attendant and Marine Storekeeper: he openly protests against the reduction in his perquisites, and complains often to Farquhar he has been treated unfairly. Farquhar takes his part, and Mary Ann says he makes life as difficult as possible for Flint.

Meanwhile, The Company does not allow its men to engage in private trade, for wanting no competition with its own business and profit, but Mary Ann reports Farquhar allows Bernard to export rice to Rhio, as a private gentleman. She says her husband has protested to Farquhar of the irregularity, and that this quarrel has worsened the rift between them.

Tom regrets Farquhar is not more particular, but he fears Flint has not the tact to sooth other people's ruffled feathers. He has decided he must now write to Flint, reminding him whatever the provocations he must keep his temper, for if he loses it he could too easily place himself in the wrong – he can be a hot tempered fellow. He is to include a chit for Mary Ann advising her that she and Flint should keep to themselves, and must not engage in disputes.

April 1821, Permattam Ballam

A deathly sickness stalks Bencoolen, a variety of flux. As a precaution, I have had Dr. Jack vaccinate the children against bowel complaints, and Tom and I reconfirm we must remove them from this bad climate, and take them Home as soon as we are able – we think in about three or four years. Dr. Jack has also vaccinated Tom, but not me, for fear his medicine could be just as dangerous for the new being I have kicking inside me, as could the flux itself – I try not to be too afraid, but I must wish my new babe were coming at a healthier time.

May 1821, Permattam Ballam

Exactly a year to the day after I gave birth to Cooksey, I was again brought safely to bed with suffering only such as I'd have been ashamed to scream at. This time I did not have the luck to get a gentleman, but a second young lady, Ella Sophia – now four born within as many years!!! And each as luminous with the future as the last – this one when she is not swaddled wafts her little limbs as tho' they were seaweed.

I make a good recovery under the care of Nurse Grimes and my plantsman, Dr. Jack, and Tom teased me last night I seem so milky and contented in motherhood he is almost afraid there has been a miracle, and there is another on the stocks, immaculately conceived, and yet God forbid! I must say I did not like this tease, on various counts.

June 1821, Permattam Ballam

O almighty God, and merciful Father, to whom alone belong the issues of life and death; look down from heaven we humbly beseech thee, with the eyes of mercy upon this child now lying upon the bed of sickness … We hear that the cholera morbus has latterly committed dreadful ravages at Acheen. There is abroad great apprehension, dread, for Bencoolen, and at this very moment of alarm it happens Leopold falls poorly. Dr. Jack says it is not the cholera, but the common flux he vaccinated him against, and I must try to be reassured. What can I do but pray to the Great Author of all Events it shall be His good pleasure to restore Leopold to his former health, that he may lead his life in fear of Him, and to His glory.

June 1821, Permattam Ballam

Leopold has been unwell for the past fortnight and is a good deal pulled down, but we think he is getting better.

November 1821, Permatt ... Abode of peace? I cannot continue.

November 1821, Permattam Ballam (for so I suppose I must still call my house)

A letter came from Mother last week, dated January, a letter to add anguish to my anguish, so when I first read it, it fell from my hand, for it is her reply to mine telling her of the birth of Cooksey, and when she has asked after him, she asks after Charlotte and Leopold too, saying she particularly wishes to know how Our Leo gets along, for it fills her heart with joy to think of this little gentleman flourishing in the tropics. And now I must pick up a pen, and write to tell her – I who have been unable to hold a pen since I wrote to her *before* of the birth of Ella – of all my children to take the best – how can I bear to see it in cold ink? It does not seem real – and yet too real – I remain as one stunned.

November 1821, Permattam Ballam

And God so loved him He took him to Himself and it is blessed to be the mother of an angel ... I must acquiesce in this privation as the all-wise purpose of my Almighty Father, working for His own glory, which, though mysterious to the limits of my understanding, must be clearly known to me in the hereafter.

November 1821, Permattam Ballam

I knew the risk Death may require him to leave me, and yet I could not deny myself the rashly exquisite pleasure of making him my favourite child. My little son – his brightness, and his beauty – I long to have him back again, to hold him again, if only for a moment. I cannot contemplate him in his present blessedness, sheltered on the bosom of Our Saviour. I see nothing but his earthly form bouncing through our rooms, hear nothing but his laughing and singing, unless it is his constant gentle call of Mother, Mother.

November 1821, Permattam Ballam

To see your child perish in all the bloom of health and beauty – to see its thread of life cut short – to hear it call upon you – feel it cling to you – and have no power to save it – those scenes I cannot, dare not dwell upon.

November 1821, Permattam Ballam

This rambling will not do. I must summon courage, and coherence. I must steel myself to write to Mother, it is my filial duty. And it is as well my maternal duty, to Leopold, to make a record of his death in this diary that is I now judge the fullest record of his life, tho' I did not realise I was acting as his record-keeper when yet he lived.

On June 27, the very day fixed for Ella's Christening, we lost our dear darling Leopold; after a short illness, it pleased God to deprive us of the finest by far of our children; he died of a flux that tore through his body like a tiger through a chicken.

That dreadful night. I remember running wild with Tom to the nursery, bending over my little son's bed, finding him tossing, his eyes dull, seeming suspended between wakefulness and sleeping. I remember lifting him into my arms, clasping him against my breast, and then carrying him back to my own bedroom, Tom by my side. We took off his nightshirt, which was soiled and wringing, and wrapped him instead in one of Tom's long nightshirts, then we laid him on my bed. We lay down beside him. At the last between him and me was no tender embrace, but a desperate clutching, and my parting kiss to him was violent in its hopelessness. And, hopeless, Tom and I could only watch as Leo's spirit ascended to his Creator, and we left were bereft. Then began my tears, and shrieking.

At his funeral one of our missionaries spoke with deep and reverent devotion of the resurrection of the body, and said Leopold had left us only for a little time: that Tom and I would again meet him in the same body, bearing the same appearance as when he played before us, and we would know him as our son, and he would know us as his father and mother, but even here I could find no consolation, so for a while I thought I could not pray – and if I could not pray, what then? Indeed, I think for a time my wits were lost. By night I stalked the house from room to room carrying a lantern, sobbing: where is Leopold? By day I shrank even from those I love: I took to my couch in a darkened room, and overwhelmed with grief I could not even bear the sight of my other children, who seemed nothing to me in the scale to my dear Leopold. I remained in this numb torpor many days, weeks, months, until Jane, my blackamoor nursery maid, reprimanded me: I am come because you have been here so long shut up in a dark room, and no one dares to come near you. Are you not ashamed to grieve in this manner, when you ought to be thanking God for having given you the most beautiful child that was ever seen? Were you not the envy of everybody? Did anyone ever see him, or speak of him, without admiring him; and instead of letting this child continue in this world 'til he should be worn out with trouble and sorrow, has not God taken him to heaven in all his beauty? What would you have more? For shame, leave off weeping and let me open a window.

And so I roused myself. I reminded myself Leo is not gone, but gone to God. I remembered what the missionary said: that Leopold had left me only for a little time: that I would meet him again in the same body, bearing the same appearance as when he played before me, and I would know him again, and he would know me as his mother.

Here, at last, I find consolation – I *do* find consolation – and if it pleases God to afflict me, I remember this visitation is not His angry judgement, but His loving, paternal lesson: I was perhaps too proud; I hoped too much; I needed to be humbled. I *am* humbled. And in my humility, I acquiesce: God's will be done. But, oh, when I look over Leo's little wardrobe, his little gowns, his little socks.

December 1821, Permattam Ballam

After our house of joy became a house of mourning it became also a hospital. A complete hospital. We have maintained but a crazy existence this past half year, and we have all been ill. Tom – his whole soul was wrapped up in Leopold and his heart is ready to break – Tom has been desperately ill, with at one time his legs and his feet swollen from the knees down, and increasingly plagued with his head. My poor husband, wretched, is at this moment salivating under the operation of mercury, tho' he is getting better from his latest bout and says he does not mean to die from it.

Now, I comfort myself my remaining children at least begin to revive. The inevitable loss of my milk, from the anguish of bereavement, proved really serious for Ella – poor little thing – so that for a time they hardly knew whether she would live or die, tho' I could not concern myself much for her then, for being forlorn and mourning Leopold. But she recovered, and Tom calls her now one of the finest and most lovely children that was ever seen. Cooksey, a generally happy child, has been most cross grained and feverish with his teeth, but today his forehead is cool. Charlotte, our Tunjung Segara, is becoming ever more delightful as her petals unfold.

December 1821, Permattam Ballam

I am almost exhausted, with continual watching, night and day: Charlotte has been suddenly seized by a violent attack of the bowels, in the same manner as my darling Leopold – my daughter, my firstborn, she writhes as the flux sears her innards, and her agony is also mine, so I struggle to acquiesce this is God's visitation. She is suffering too under her illness' treatment: Dr. Jack knocked out one of her front teeth, in giving her a dose of lunar caustic, which accident has destroyed her infant beauty – and how my hand shakes as I write this, and makes my words spiders on the page.

December 1821, Permattam Ballam

In everything give thanks: for this is the will of God in Christ Jesus concerning you ... My Merciful Father has amply rewarded my reliance on Him; by His Grace Charlotte lives still, tho' I often feared for her life, and tho' too she remains terribly pulled down and altered – no one would know her to be the same child she was in November.

December 1821, Permattam Ballam

Tho' neither Tom nor I could countenance it before, the gravity of our loss of Leopold, and our recent fears for Charlotte, have together persuaded us to put aside our belief that to send the children Home without us is out of the question. Indeed, we are now so thoroughly convinced a change of climate is absolutely necessary for our dear little ones, our three remaining blessings, we are determined to send them Home without us as soon as we can, that they should not suffer in Bencoolen the ravages of sickness and disease, but may instead grow robust beneath grey skies in a cool, northern clime.

January 1822, Permattam Ballam

A small private licensed ship, the *Borneo*, is now called at Bencoolen, and Tom has engaged the Captain to take our darlings back to England. She is set to sail in February or March; I have perhaps only a month longer to enjoy my children's company. It is agony for me to think of parting from them, to contemplate the separation soon to be betwixt us, but a wife must ever prefer her husband above all creatures, so what can I do. Tom likewise dreads the coming separation, but there can be no life without sacrifice, and we tell each other often we should not be justified in keeping our darlings here longer at such risk merely for our own gratification.

Nurse Grimes will take charge of the trio on the voyage. I am desperately anxious to let them go without a doctor, and in such a small private vessel as the *Borneo*, without the suitable accommodation of an East Indiaman, but she is the only opportunity that offers.

My beautiful Ella is as bright as the morning star, Cooksey is still annoyed with his teeth, but is otherwise healthy, poor Charlotte still suffers much from the effects of her recent illness, but she is wonderfully improving.

March 1822, Permattam Ballam

Trust in the Lord with all thine heart; and lean not into thine own understanding.

March 1822, Permattam Ballam

But the other day we were alarmed lest we should have too many.

March 1822, Permattam Ballam

Death, jealous, saw their beauty ... Cooksey, Charlotte, two more blessings withdrawn, their two pairs of eyes, blue and blue, limitless sky, limitless ocean, now closed forever.

March 1822, Permattam Ballam

My Tunjung Segara ... my innocent flowers, bidden to the garden of God, ever to be spared the sin and misfortune of adulthood. *The Lord gave, and the Lord hath taken away; blessed be the name of the Lord.*

March 1822, Permattam Ballam

Both our angels gone – sent to the grave by ravening inflammation of the bowels. Cooksey had seemed better from a flux had seized him; we left him his last evening in the world in an apparently tranquil and reviving sleep, but Nurse Grimes soon called us back to the nursery, and with pitiless haste, in less than half an hour, he was a corpse, soon laid in his coffin.

Charlotte languished some time delirious in a parching fever, then was for a few days more a perfect skeleton without life and spirits and scarcely knew anyone, and then she too was snatched from us.

Two coffins sliding down. I dare not close my eyes, for when I do, I see them sliding down again. Or else I see Charlotte, sitting with a lap full of shells, singing to herself as she sorts them, or else Cooksey trying to run on wobbly legs barely yet used to walking.

I feel now I am untethered, drifting through a life that doesn't feel like mine, so many of the bonds of affection that anchored me to me, to my own self, have been severed. And yet: God's will be done; I must be reconciled for only the foolish would protest the secret things of omniscience. *I will not ask, neither will I tempt the Lord.* I will instead re-read of David's lesson in faith, the loss of his son. I will cultivate the humble conviction, in my hour of agony, that such misery would not have been decreed for me if it had not been necessary – these trials to prove my faith – my whole aim in life is now acquiescence, I can have no other.

March 1822, Permattam Ballam

Severe as the dispensation is, we still have reason to thank God: we have still one little one left to us. Our dear baby Ella. We have now seized the first opportunity of sending her to a safer climate. Tomorrow we will bundle her aboard the *Borneo*, in the care of Nurse Grimes, who is charged with seeing her safely to my parents in Cheltenham, for it is with them that they must both reside, until Tom and I can return to England, to reclaim our daughter – at most only another two years, we hope. Yes, Tom and I have decided we must get Home as soon as can be arranged, and tho' I did not write it then, for being too sad to hold a quill, or to notice anything but my own sorrow, at the end of January, the cruel month that seemed to rip us from our lives, Tom wrote to London to tender his resignation from The Company, on account of his disappointment – his thwarted ambition in the matter of the Governorship of Penang – his grief, despair, extreme ill-health, and he requested to be relieved of his duties in the Eastward at the close of next year.

Until I can embrace them again, Nurse Grimes is charged, too, with telling my parents what's doing, and will take with her my letters for them, giving news of our latest sad losses, and theirs. I am desolate to think of Mother mourning her grandchildren she never met. I am desolate to remember it was our intention the *Borneo* should take home *three* of her grandchildren.

March 1822, Permattam Ballam

The *Borneo* left on the evening tide. This little ship carries with her my only hope, and Tom's – all our hopes. We wept in each other's arms as she pulled away from the roads. But we console ourselves Our Ella left us in excellent health, and by the strong measure we have taken of sending her away, we pray that we may be spared this *one* comfort to solace and enliven our declining days – what a waste of waters now lies between us, and yet the distance daily widens, and will widen until half the world divides us.

May 1822, Permattam Ballam

We are ransacked parents in a ransacked house – without Nurse Grimes and the children – never was there such a change – we wander from room to room, solitary and dejected; but God's will be done, and we must be content.

June 1822, Permattam Ballam

I suffer now at all times an unearthly feeling as if I am wandering in regions of desolation and woe with no friends or companions but the shades of dear departed spirits.

July 1822, Permattam Ballam

My soul is numb, and my body too is miserably reduced and lowered by my losses – the same as well for Tom, my hollowed husband, his eyes like holes. We are both ravaged by the inflammations of the bowels that robbed us of our children, and we are suffering too under the mercury treatments that should cure us – tho' we drool we do not improve. Indeed, Tom has repeated attacks of brain fever, cruel, crushing headaches which confine him to bed and almost make him mad, and for these Dr. Jack scarcely knows how to treat him, so I pray it is the will of God that my husband continues even as he is.

We both yearn for Ella, and for Home. We cannot expect for months yet any reply from India House, to Tom's letter of resignation, nonetheless, he assumes his resignation will be accepted, and proceeds accordingly. Thus, he commences now putting everything in order for his departure.

August 1822, Permattam Ballam

Singapore must be Tom's most important legacy in the Eastward, and he feels that before returning to Old England he is honour bound to visit once more this base he founded, not only to instruct Farquhar in its future management, but also to establish for it a constitution, the principles of which he hopes will ensure its prosperity. The utmost possible freedom of trade and equal rights to all with protection of property and person are the objects he wishes obtained, and he says he shall do his duty to the best of his ability, and that he shall spare no pains to establish such laws and regulations as may be most conducive to them.

For all that he thinks duty dictates a last visit to Singapore, Tom has no heart for it. Indeed, he says that on account of all his sadness the time has passed when he could take much interest in it.

There can be no question that I will accompany my husband when he goes to bid farewell to Singapore, now more than ever my life is only him.

September 1822, Permattam Ballam

It is fixed we will sail to Singapore on the *Minto* – named for Tom's late patron – which is expected in the harbour shortly. We plan to stay six months, and then come back here, to Bencoolen, for the purpose of packing up our things and winding up our affairs, for what else is there for us to do before we return to England?

At some moments I dread leaving Permattam Ballam, this house where I endured such dreadful misery that I, the mother, feel orphaned, where two of my children were born, where all lived, where three died, where I embraced them, which was the setting for their every infant achievement – sitting up, walking, talking – this house where they prattled, smiled, frowned, laughed, suffered tantrums, cried over trifles, cut their knees, engaged in games, engaged in quarrels … Yet, at other moments I welcome my coming removal from this scene as temporary deliverance from heartache. Dread and the anticipation of relief, I feel them both for but one reason: here in this house I am ambushed daily by memories that make me weep; I see my children everywhere; it seems to me their butterfly spirits flit through every room – and, oh, to imagine them as they would be now, tomorrow, growing up.

September 1822, the *Minto*, the Eastern Seas

Before we quit Bencoolen it pleased God to instruct us again we must live every moment in His good graces, lest our time comes to be gathered: Dr. Jack is gone. My dear Dr. Jack, my companion in Penang, he who delivered three of my babies, and who physicked me in my grief, is called to the harvest-home of heaven. His lungs collapsed without warning, and he died most suddenly when we were already aboard the *Minto*, on the very eve of our departure for Singapore. I feel his loss almost as that of a brother, and how many more tears must I shed?

September 1822, the *Minto*, the Eastern Seas

The beauty of the Eastern Seas still bears witness to their creator, but now it seems to me this beauty is a lament. Still, the ever increasing distance from Bencoolen, and the ever decreasing distance to Singapore, do together at least remind me that the change of coming, or going, from here to there, must soon force me to mingle again with my fellow beings – I who have been so much retired these last ten months, so much set apart from the living race – and for this coming communion I must be thankful.

October 1822, Mary Ann's house, Singapore

Tom and I have arrived in Singapore, which is a scene of the greatest energy and excitement – here at least all is life and activity.

We are lodging with Mary Ann and Flint who have a wood and atap bungalow in the European part of town. Our reunion was a sad affair; Mary Ann wept for her niece, her nephews, and Tom wept too, and so did I. I confess it is disconcerting to be once more in a household with a child, to be confronted hourly with the ordinarily miraculous happiness of an unravaged family, but it is too a comfort to be reunited with my sister, and Charley Boy is impressively grown – a spirited little boy, fearless, and when I see him I do try not to be bitter, envious, nor to make comparisons with Leopold.

October 1822, Mary Ann's house, Singapore

Alas, Tom and I now find we have landed in a load of trouble between Flint and Farquhar. Farquhar recently imported nine chests of opium from Calcutta, to sell for profit, as a private trader, which role the Resident and Commandant should not fulfil, and Flint protests to Tom he is profiteering from the poppy that has struck so deep into the habits of the people, and has extended its malignant influence to their morals, and in all ways degrades their character, and enervates their energies. Meanwhile Farquhar protests Flint is quarrelsome, lackadaisical in his duties, and disordered in keeping his books.

Tho' Tom regards opium as a detestable drug, its exchange a trade in lives as bad as slavery, he is displeased with his brother that he has not managed to keep things with Farquhar friendly, and he has reprimanded him for a tactlessness he judges so great it risks barring and neutralising his intentions for Singapore. Her brother's rebuke of her husband has in turn displeased Mary Ann, so there was yesterday something of a pall over our family dinner.

Notwithstanding these exasperations, Tom is already much revived by being here, tho' Singapore, that he once called *child of my own*, he now calls, through saddest circumstance, *my almost only child*. As for our *actual* only child, my heart aches to report we still have no news whether Ella is safely arrived in England, and until we know she is there, Tom's hopes for Singapore must sustain us both.

October 1822, Mary Ann's house, Singapore

Tom told me last night the coldest and most disinterested fellow could not land here without surprise and emotion. In little more than three years Singapore has risen from an insignificant fishing village to a large and prosperous town, containing at least ten thousand inhabitants of all nations, actively involved in commercial pursuits, which afford to each and all a handsome livelihood and abundant profit. The roads are packed with square-rigged ships, and native vessels from all over the Archipelago call constantly here to trade. Along the wharves all is hustling – goods loaded, goods unloaded. This busyness gladdens Tom's heart, and reconfirms to him the correctness of his decision to establish Singapore as a free port, the trade thereof open to ships and vessels of every nation, free of duty, equally and to all alike.

After all the risks and dangers of its earliest infancy, to find Singapore grown and advanced beyond measure – beyond even his warmest anticipations and expectations – fills my husband with a new life and vigour, and makes him feel differently than he did in Bencoolen: he says that for seeing his settlement he cannot understand he ever thought the time had passed when he could take much interest in it.

October 1822, Mary Ann's house, Singapore

To my surprise, I now learn none of the merchant vessels that visit here is English. So as not to antagonise the Dutch, no English ships have yet been allowed to trade at Singapore, and will not be allowed to do so until the paper war is resolved – for the diplomatic skirmishes Tom sparked in '19 rustle on in a great mass of verbiage. Still, my husband thinks it most unlikely Singapore will ever now be handed to the Dutch, for he cannot think The Company, or the government at Westminster, could be such a set of fools they'd let another nation have this place. It has generated thus far eight million Spanish dollars, and this year the value of the trade here Tom thinks will exceed that of Penang and Malacca put together. No, Singapore's commercial success is not in doubt. Indeed, Tom says it would be difficult to name any place on the globe with brighter prospects than this roaring Lion City – or one giving more present satisfaction.

October 1822, Mary Ann's house, Singapore

There last night arrived here at Mary Ann's house an unannounced Malay guest, come to visit Tom – when asked how he knew where my husband was staying he replied a great man is easy found, when no one knows a poor one. It transpired this guest, Munshi Abdullah, a man in his mid-to-late-twenties, had once been of Tom's secretariat in Malacca. He has now a wife and children in that town, but he came alone to Singapore two years back, to teach Malay to Europeans, and to act as a translator for them. He wept at his reunion with Tom, and my husband too was almost overcome.

October 1822, Mary Ann's house, Singapore

I have heard it said that to the natives we Europeans all look much the same, and perhaps it is true, for the Munshi Abdullah, who is now our frequent visitor, seems quite unable to distinguish me from Olivia, and speaks to me often of times past in Malacca, and however much I remind him I never knew those times past, which he spent in the company of the *first* Mrs. Raffles, whereas I, Lady Raffles, am Tom's *second* wife, he persists in this oddly blind behaviour.

There was a time when to be confused with Olivia I would have thought a great affront, but I find the anguish, losses, and despair of the past year have sapped me of the energy for petty jealousy of my predecessor – and here I think is some variety of grace?

October 1822, Mary Ann's house, Singapore

Farquhar has by now shipped to Singapore Nonio Clemaine, and their six children – including Esther, Bernard's wife. I suppose from long familiarity with it, Tom continues less disconcerted by the mingling of races that is Farquhar's connection than I think he ought to be. Nevertheless it worries him that through his nonya, the Resident is open to pressure from her numerous relations, for they have followed him here in a great waddling, chattering mass, eager for the boons he can bestow, and Tom says their extortions lead Farquhar towards favouritism, irregularities, and partiality where he ought to be impartial.

Indeed, Tom thinks Farquhar's connection with his nonya is leading him generally into an abhorrent laxness and pragmatism towards traditional Malay vices. The man has quite failed to stamp out gaming and cock-fighting – even slavery he tolerates. Tho' Tom banned slave-trading here, and tho' it is a felony for any British subject anywhere, slaves are being sold openly in a market on the Singapore River near Farquhar's house. When Tom challenged Farquhar how he could allow this, the Resident replied indifferently that circumstances accounted for the irregularity.

My upstanding husband worries he has so little time to set things right in the settlement, but in the short time available, he intends to see to it his own principles prevail. Accordingly, he has today announced measures prohibiting all gaming houses and cockpits as being highly destructive to the morals and happiness of the people, and likewise prohibiting slave trading. He has decreed all slaves in Singapore are henceforth entitled to claim their freedom, excepting only those belonging to the Sultan or to the Temenggong, out of deference to their authority, and to their native ways.

October 1822, Mary Ann's house, Singapore

It is with irritation I must report Tom has been pulled into a long-running disagreement between Flint and Bernard about a shipment of flooring tiles. Bernard accuses Flint, in his capacity of Marine Storekeeper, of negligence in the matter of these tiles, some of which have gone missing, but Flint blames Bernard for the shortfall, which he says arose during the period of his charge. Tom in public takes Flint's part, and Farquhar Bernard's, and the atmosphere between all four of them is most difficult, even poisonous.

In private, Tom censures Flint and tells him the amount short of the stated consignment of tiles will necessarily stand as his debt until explained, and to me he says Flint is more than unreliable, he is becoming an embarrassment, tho' for Mary Ann's sake he must tolerate him.

I have tried to suggest to Mary Ann she should intervene to moderate her husband's behaviour, but she takes his part, and presses his case, and will hear not a word against him, so I suppose he will continue to act in his own interests, without regard for Tom.

October 1822, Mary Ann's house, Singapore

Tom now disagrees violently with Farquhar over land allocation, and it is my husband's intention to issue new regulations concerning the registration of land, to control unauthorised building development – in short, to develop a town plan for Singapore, for which purpose he has convened a Town Planning Committee.

The new regulations are necessary because Farquhar has flagrantly disregarded the instructions which Tom left him in '19, and has allowed haphazard development, which cannot promote communal harmony, or efficiency, or good sanitation, and he has even built his own house, and allowed others to build theirs, on land set aside for the cantonment.

Tom has now ruled that all structures erected in the wrong places must be demolished, and that there should be clear demarcation between races and professions. The European merchants' warehouses are to be moved to land set aside on one bank of the Singapore River for commercial and mercantile purposes – this area is swampy, and Tom will oversee its drainage. The Chinese now living there are to be moved inland. These Chinese are numerous, and Tom thinks they will henceforth always form by far the largest portion of the community in Singapore, but he does not neglect the Malays, or other races. He has granted two hundred acres to the Temenggong, and arranged for new villages to be established for the Bugis, the Arabs, and the Indians resident here. These villages are to be sited with care for the religious sensibilities of the Mahomedans, and the Hindus. Moreover, Tom plans also a police station, a new market, a marine yard, a bridge over The River, a church, &c, for he foresees Singapore becoming one day a great city.

Bernard is one of those who built a house in a place not authorised by Tom, and which in consequence he is now required to demolish. Tom suspects that with Farquhar's encouragement Bernard will try to claim inflated compensation for rebuilding this house, but he says the man may as well kiss his petticoat – an expression I cannot approve, but what's to do?

November 1822, Mary Ann's house, Singapore

Farquhar, with his strangely native notions, is dismissive of Tom's Town Planning Committee, saying he considers the land of Singapore to be vested in the Sultan, and the Temenggong, and the port to be a native port – extraordinary ideas, in Tom's view, and in mine. Then again, tho' Tom is prepared to overlook Farquhar's minor defects, he has had occasion to reprimand him over his dress, which he calls most mischievous, provoking toggery: when Farquhar is not engaged in any official duty he dispenses with his Commandant's uniform and dons a sarong, an eccentric departure, not fitting to British authority, or dignity – we must ever be formal, even in the heat.

November 1822, Mary Ann's house, Singapore

Tom has had another attack of the brain fever; my poor husband had to take to his bed almost a fortnight with blinding headaches. Now he is recovered under my care, and he is most gratifyingly loving. He says often now he is so much opposed in all he wants to do by Farquhar and other local interests that I am become his principal, his only, counsellor, and if he does live to see Old England again it must be entirely owing to my love and affection, without which he should have been cast away long ago. For his kind words I love him more than ever – the consciousness that his feeling for me has deepened over time is delightful – and for his pessimism I rebuke him, saying God forbid he should not see Old England again.

November 1822, Mary Ann's house, Singapore

Flint so exasperates Tom, and this so much affects our domestic pleasure, that my husband has ordered Chinese carpenters build us a modest bungalow on that hill which was once called *Forbidden Hill*, but is now renamed *Government Hill*.

Tom chose the specific site by the simple expedient of tossing a stone in the general area he had selected. Our bungalow is to be designed by an Irish architect resident here, one George Coleman, whom Tom thinks a capital fellow, very skilled at his craft.

Coleman is also advising Tom on the grid of the central streets of Singapore, these streets to be lined by buildings to accommodate shops or small businesses on the ground floor, with living space above, which shop-houses will be the width of the standard length of timbers cut from forest trees – twenty feet – and will have open verandahs forming a covered walk-way, five-foot wide, in front of them to protect passers-by from both sun and rain.

November 1822, Mary Ann's house, Singapore

There is called here this week one John Crawfurd, a Scot, who is on his way back to Bengal, after acting as Lord Hastings' trade envoy to Siam, and to Cochin-China. It seems to me he is a cold dour fellow, and Tom does not disagree, but he says he knew Crawfurd in Java, where for all his sternness he was a safe pair of hands as Resident at a troublesome native court.

Crawfurd is fluent in Malay, and, like Tom, he has a great interest in oriental people, languages, customs, and religions – indeed he published a little while back *The History of the Indian Archipelago*, making him and my husband rivals in the matter of their books – and Crawfurd's the more ambitious in scope, which rankles Tom. Still, they spend much time in each other's company: together they have inspected that ancient stone written all over with Indian script that was discovered near where the Singapore River meets the sea; together they have tramped the lines of the ancient city of Singapura, and likewise they have tramped all over Government Hill – where the coolies have already cleared the site for our bungalow, and make speedy progress on the building.

November 1822, Mary Ann's house, Singapore

Tom quite loses confidence in Farquhar, saying that tho' he fulfilled his duties well enough in Malacca, a drowsing, dreaming backwater, he is totally unequal to a charge so peculiar and important as Singapore has now become. Meanwhile he says he will let neither literary rivalry nor Crawfurd's curmudgeonly nature cloud his judgement, the man is a talented, conscientious, and efficient administrator.

In short, Tom thinks Crawfurd would be much better able than Farquhar to bring to fruition the ideas he has for Singapore, to secure its growth, and to promote it as a place for free trade, and so he has talked to him, circumspectly and in private, about taking over from Farquhar as Resident here, if only Farquhar could be inveigled into leaving. Crawfurd has indicated, discretely, and not in so many words, that he would not refuse The Residency, should a new man soon be required to fill the post. Both conspirators, if such I may call them, are agreed no word of their discussions should be allowed to be whispered abroad; Tom confides in none but me, and Crawfurd, we assume, confides in nobody.

December 1822, Mary Ann's house, Singapore

Tom has had a headache so violent the doctor warned him he should hurry off to England by the next ship that sails, but my stubborn husband says happen what will, he cannot move from Singapore until some new man be found to have charge of it, if it should be his fate to leave his bones below ground here they would at least have the honour of mixing with the ashes of Malayan kings, whereas if he died at sea he must become food for fishes, which sort of talk frightened me so I chided him for being alarming.

December 1822, Government Hill, Singapore

We have moved into our bungalow on Government Hill, which is of wood and atap, and feels to me most insubstantial, as if it may at any moment be swept away by the wind. It is not large, being but two rooms, and two wings for bedrooms, with narrow verandahs to the front and back, but it is tolerably comfortable, and well-shaded, tho' the interior walls are nothing but rough planks.

The carpenters are still at work around us, finishing off the construction, so I can hear as I write sawing and hammering, all accompanied by a sing-song chatter of their impenetrable Mandareen. Still, it is good to be away from Flint's tantrums, and Tom and I both feel immediately the beneficial effects of the cooler air and the breezes that come with being atop a hill.

The views from our verandahs could not be more beautiful, or more interesting. From where I write now, on the front verandah, I can see it the foreground soaring trees, and beyond them, curving away from the base of the Hill, the busy, bustling High Street thronged with horses, carriages, sedan chairs, and beyond that the colourful harbour alive with vessels, both native and European. Tom says it will give him great satisfaction to remember this view when we are returned Home, and to imagine how it must change as his Lion City prowls into the future.

Flint now requests that because Tom and I stayed in his house whilst we were waiting for this bungalow to be ready, and Tom had his office there, his rent for the period should be paid by the government. Tom is minded to grant this request, for Mary Ann's sake, tho' he says Farquhar will no doubt demur, which I must grant probable. Indeed, I anticipate this matter of Flint's rent will cause more crossness between my husband and The Resident.

December 1822, Government Hill, Singapore

Tom has been presented with one of the monkeys called orang utan, or men of the forest, a little one, not much above two feet high. We call him Mr. Sylvio and he is the most beautiful of his kind that can be conceived – his face is jet black, and his features most expressive. Tom dresses him in a coat, trousers, and a hat, and we give him the run of the house. I think he understands human language: he just now came up to my writing desk and slowly took up my quill. When I said to put it down, down he put it. Indeed, he is in his disposition and habits the kindest most correct creature. He always walks erect, and Tom says he is sure he must become a favourite in Park Lane.

January 1823, Government Hill, Singapore

We have at last a reply from India House to Tom's resignation letter written about this time last year. The Court of Directors accepts his resignation in words of conventional regret, and faint praise: tho' the Honourable Members mention he should not have founded Singapore without first asking them, and note its continued possession is by no means certain, they remark themselves disposed to acknowledge its use, and also to commend Tom's integrity, zeal, and ability.

Tom says it is better the Honourable Members had accepted his resignation than not, but had they not, it would have made no difference to his plans, as the rice is already porridge – as for me, I dream anew of that farm outside London where we may make butter and cheese.

January 1823, Government Hill, Singapore

More problems! Tom has moved Bernard to the police department, and this has infuriated Farquhar, who has written him a letter so ill-tempered Tom says it must have been dashed off in haste and under misconception, and he has replied saying he trusts Farquhar will see the propriety of reviewing it.

What Farquhar writes is that he cannot but consider the expression *Head Constable*, which Tom applied to Bernard, must have been intended as a premeditated insult and affront to his whole family, as no one with the slightest pretension to rank as a gentleman in society would ever be so degraded as to be called a *police constable*.

Tom, exasperated, continues to go on in his public duties as steadily and quietly as possible.

January 1823, Government Hill, Singapore

Nobody could doubt my husband's generosity, or patience, and yet he has by now such little confidence in Farquhar, he has written to Calcutta suggesting he should be replaced here by Crawfurd. He has likewise written to Crawfurd saying he has recommended him for the relief of Farquhar. Under the necessity of circumstance, all these arrangements he has made without hinting to Farquhar what's doing.

February 1823, Government Hill, Singapore

Mary Ann, made anxious by our losses of Leopold, Cooksey, and Charlotte, has asked that when we return to Bencoolen, and from there to Old England, we take with us Charley Boy, and bring him up for a time with Ella – still no news – that he may be spared the dangers of the east, and grow robust with his cousin, in the safer northern clime of Home.

I am not unhappy to have this charge; I anticipate Charley Boy will provide me with much amusement and comfort in the coming months, and already I love him almost as my own – tho' he'll never be my Leopold, and never mind that every time I look at him I catch glimpses of what my lost son could have become, so I have to remind myself: *A sound heart is the life of the flesh: but envy the rottenness of the bones.*

February 1823, Government Hill, Singapore

Let Israel hope in the Lord: for with the Lord there is mercy, and with him is plenteous redemption … I hardly dare even to think it, but there are Signs of another baby forthcoming in about seven or eight months … This jewelled hope … If only I am right, and if only the infant lives … I will say nothing to Tom until I am surer the Signs do not deceive me.

March 1823, Government Hill, Singapore

There is a type of criminal madness known only amongst the

Malays and called *amok*, which means running through a busy place slashing at people at random with a knife, usually one of their krises or parangs. Yesterday, Farquhar was slashed by a Malay running amok: he suffered much loss of blood, but there was no risk to his life; the Malay was killed. Tom could not allow such an outrageous affront on British authority in the person of The Resident to go unremarked, and so this morning he had the Malay's corpse drummed round town in a bullock cart. He then had it prominently displayed suspended from a gibbet in an iron cage he commissioned last night from the blacksmiths. But he was warned this humiliation might inflame all the Malays against the Europeans, so after seeking the counsel of the Sultan and the Temenggong, he has agreed the body should be taken down and released to the Sultan, for burial with Mahomedan lustration and prayers.

March 1823, Government Hill, Singapore

I am now sure I am once again in the family way, and I have told Tom, who received my news sombrely and said God willing this one will be in England before the climate and pestilential airs of the Eastward can steal it, and we are both in hopes it may be a gentleman, but we fear we shall never have another like our Leopold.

March 1823, Government Hill, Singapore

I have taken Mary Ann into my confidence – and so it seems has Tom. In any case, after I had revealed, as I thought, my secret, she told me he had said to her I am always at my healthiest when coming into bearing and showing fruit. She then added, as her own original contribution to the discussion, that I am so productive a breeder I should offer my counsel to Mrs. X, an Englishwoman here of our acquaintance who has apparently, and I must think unwisely, confided in Mary Ann she wishes to be with child. The pain I felt at being called a productive breeder was nothing to the pain of remembering that I've lost most of the children I've bred. Still, I replied mildly enough that if any woman asked me, I should tell her these things come of course if only people would have patience and perseverance, and nothing is gained by being in too great a hurry.

It is true, in the past, all my bodily complaints seemed to be absorbed as my pregnancies advanced, and so I hope it shall be this time also.

April 1823, Government Hill, Singapore

Tom is determined we may one day see Singapore not only a centre of commerce, but a centre of civilisation also. Hence he is now to found here a native college, to be called The Singapore Institution, the object of which will be to diffuse light and knowledge to all around.

The Institution is to educate the sons of the higher order of natives and others – including Europeans who wish their sons to learn native languages. It is to comprise a literary and moral department for the Chinese, and another for Malays, and a scientific department to serve both. There will even be a class for girls, a thing unthought-of amongst the Malays.

Funds are being raised by subscription. Tom has put in two thousand Spanish dollars, and I have put in two hundred. Tom has also put in two thousand Spanish dollars on behalf of The Company; he knows he has no authority to commit The Company in this way, but he is sanguine the Court of Directors will honour it.

When funds can afford it, the scientific department is to be furnished with an observatory, and an astronomical clock. It will offer natural philosophy, natural history, chemistry, and the elements of anatomy and medical science. The language of instruction will be English, but Tom specifies professors must pay attention to native languages and where possible translate scientific books. Meanwhile, the literary and moral departments will collect the scattered literature and traditions of the Eastward, and publish and circulate the most important. To this end the Institution will in time be provided with a printing press, and a variety of fonts – the Indian islands are very fertile in alphabets.

The Institution's motto is to be our own, *Auspicium Melioris Aevi*, Omen of a better age. Tom has decreed it should be the duty of the professors to cherish at all times a paternal feeling of kindness to the students, and to set an example of patience, moderation, good temper, and assiduity. The forms of Protestant worship will be observed, and the European masters must be Protestants, but the native masters may or may not be Christians, but they shall be correct moral men, according to the opinion of their own nation. Pagans, Christians, Hindus, and Mahomedans will all be admissible as students. Neither native students nor native masters will be compelled to attend Christian worship.

I am not sure I like this tolerance, but when I tried to protest Tom should be as strict in his zeal for Christianity as he is in his zeal for learning, he said this worry for his soul was kindly maritorious, but he'd rather bring to the natives chemistry than Christianity.

April 1823, Government Hill, Singapore

Singapore is in uproar. Yesterday Farquhar, that odd, whimsical man, attended a government reception dressed in a sarong. My long-suffering husband, saying this shedding of English dress was almost a shedding of Englishness itself, was goaded by Farquhar's disgraceful toggery into relieving him at last of the performance of all his duties as the Resident. He has written to Calcutta, informing Lord Hastings what he's done, and saying he will take upon himself the direct exercise of all Farquhar's civil duties until he can be relieved, he assumes by Crawfurd, tho' he has had as yet no reply to his letter of January. He's written too to Crawfurd, directing him to come here at once. As to what will happen if Lord Hastings does not confirm Crawfurd as the new Resident? Tom says he never in his life crossed a bridge before he came to it.

On account of the winds, we are anxious to get away from here by June, but Tom says he will not quit Singapore except in the knowledge it is governed by a capable man.

April 1823, Government Hill, Singapore

Farquhar, mortified and humiliated, does not speak to Tom, but all day messengers arrive here carrying agitated letters from him, and then run back down the Hill with my husband's replies. He wrote yesterday demanding to know again on what authority Tom is removing him from his office, and asking to see a copy of any letter from the government in Bengal relieving him as Resident at Singapore. Tom replied that he has supplied already the information required. Farquhar has now written back that he will appeal Tom's decision to the Highest Tribunal in India, under the confident hope that ample redress will sooner or later be afforded him for all the severity and injustice he has received at Tom's hands.

Tom accepts both that he has acted under his own authority only, and also that Farquhar will appeal, but he is confident the government in Bengal will support his decision, for it is in The Company's interests, and in Britain's, that Singapore is well governed.

May 1823, Government Hill, Singapore

Tom has not yet told Farquhar he plans for Crawfurd to replace him, but now he has learned of it in any case, and we hear he says it was perfidious of Tom to plot and make arrangements behind his back. For his part, Tom says there was neither plotting nor perfidy here, only his urgent desire that Singapore should succeed, and that this, his almost only child, should be spared the sad effects of Farquhar's continuing misrule.

May 1823, Government Hill, Singapore

As Tom anticipated, a letter now comes from Calcutta saying the government there supports his removal of Farquhar, and telling him to expect Crawfurd shortly on the *Hero of Malown*, for Lord Hastings is resolved this competent Scot must relieve his incompetent countryman post haste.

Now that he has the proper authority, Tom has directed Farquhar that as soon as Crawfurd arrives he must give up the Resident's bungalow so that the new man in the post can straight away move into it. He has further instructed that on Crawfurd's arrival, Farquhar must, as a public duty and mark of respect, be present at his vacated bungalow to welcome its new occupant.

Farquhar is insulted and outraged. He accuses it was not necessary for Tom to point out to him the necessity of a public duty, or of showing respect and courtesy to Mr. Crawfurd on his landing here. He protests he built the bungalow at his own expense, and asks where else is he to keep his wild animals, for he has an extensive menagerie in his garden.

Tom, unmoved, says the bungalow is government property, and Farquhar must relinquish it, and that he will be recompensed the present value of the building.

Alas, I hear whispers some call my husband's treatment of Farquhar harsh. Indeed, I must in conscience confess it is difficult to call it otherwise, and it worries me Tom's enemies may twist his ungenerosity in this particular instance to paint in general a black picture of him. But when I tried to tell him I fear what his rough touch may do for his reputation he brushed me aside, saying *his* only fear is for Singapore's future. He said he did his best to prevent a rupture with Farquhar, but now it has taken place he naturally prosecutes his cause with vigour and effect – only a fool would not do so – and tho' he is resigned Farquhar must go complaining abroad he has been sharp in his dealings with him, he is hopeful he will soon come round to his opinions on things generally. He says it was never – could never be – his wish or interest to annoy Farquhar, or Farquhar's to annoy him, they both have a great interest in the prosperity of Singapore, but he could not allow the government of the place to collapse into confusion because of the incompetence of the chief. Indeed, he said such was his concern for Singapore that had he judged a brother opposed to her interests, he must have acted towards him as he did towards Farquhar.

I wish Tom's detractors would remember he has been feeling lately often unwell, being bothered so much by his head that pain may sometimes sway his judgement from impartiality.

May 1823, Government Hill, Singapore

Crawfurd has arrived on the *Hero of Malown*, looking morose and grim. Since I am in the family way, Tom had written to him to bring me from Calcutta a bottle of ether – a new sort of vapour said to ease the pain of confinement by causing the woman breathing it to fall unconscious – and so now I have such in my possession.

May 1823, Government Hill, Singapore

I offer many grateful prayers, because we have at too long last a letter from Mother telling us Ella and Nurse Grimes are arrived safe in Cheltenham, and both of them in good health. My patience to hear this news had almost given out; I should have trusted better in the Lord. And to think my Ella is now nearly two, and must be running around, prattling.

June 1823, Government Hill, Singapore

Tom this morning laid the foundation stone for his Institution, and in his speech he expressed the hopes it will for generations light up lives in the Eastward with the fire that is education, and that through its alumni it will become a way of civilising and bettering the conditions of millions now and in the future, and a long way beyond Singapore.

All the elite of all races were present, Chinese, European, and Malay, everybody except for Farquhar and Bernard. Since Crawfurd arrived, those two skulk all day in Bernard's bungalow, no doubt cursing Tom.

Bye-the-bye, now Farquhar has been relieved as Resident, he has from bitterness resigned his commission as the garrison's Commandant. Accordingly, he must in due course quit this settlement, tho' whether he will sail for England, for Penang, or for India even the servants do not know – to stoop to have gossip from the servants is to let them encroach, but pragmatism demands now and again a swishing aside of the curtain.

June 1823, Government Hill, Singapore

Last night I attended with Tom a reception at Residency House – the disputed bungalow now Crawfurd's – where my husband received from the merchants of this town a most touching farewell address, saying it is to his unwearied zeal, his vigilance, his comprehensive views they owe the foundation and maintenance of this settlement of Singapore, a place unparalleled for the liberality of the principles on which it has been established. They noted that what was so recently the haunt of pirates has become the abode of enterprise, security, and opulence, and did not forget either what Tom has done here in the cause of humanity and civilisation, mentioning in particular his Institution, and his measures against slavery. They begged him to accept the expression of their sincere respect and esteem, without distinction of tribe or nation.

My modest husband remarked in the carriage home that here was panegyric, with which opinion I told him I decidedly cannot agree.

June 1823, Government Hill, Singapore

We have said our private farewells to the munshi Abdullah and to Mr. Sylvio both, for we have given one into the care of the other. Abdullah said Mr. Sylvio ever reminds him of Baba, a man of the forest Tom once had in Malacca, which was the first I ever knew of this Baba.

Mr. Sylvio showed little distress at our parting; not so Abdullah. He assured Tom, through copious tears, that his courtesy and understanding are pre-eminent, and that he has a noble nature unparalleled in its ability to win the affection of others. At the conclusion of this pretty speech I gave him twenty-five Spanish dollars, for his children in Malacca, and he clasped my hands, and thanked me profusely, and wept even harder than before. With a flourish, he then pulled from the sleeve of his baju a decorative, gilded sheet of paper, upon which he'd written us a verse, in the Jawi script. Through sobs, he explained it compares Tom and me to a country lane grown all about with brambles, tho' which of us he intended as the lane, and which the prickly bramble I could not determine. Nonetheless, I would have been much pleased to hear Abdullah make between myself and Tom this comparison, except I suspected he intended it to compliment *Olivia*, not me.

And so we have left Singapore, and in our charge we have Charley Boy to keep me company when Tom cannot, and a sad parting Flint and Mary Ann had from their son, and we from her.

After our last breakfast at our bungalow, a most melancholy meal, we went to Government House, and Tom formally transferred the charge of Singapore to Crawfurd, and specified it is no longer to be considered a dependency of Bencoolen, but of Bengal, and thus placed in direct communication with the supreme government there.

We were given a fine send off at the beach. On shore were crowds, redcoats, the booming of canon fired in dignified salute, and the crackle and rackety snap of firecrackers let fly by the Chinese who are mad for these flashy noisy things. Then, as the pinnace conveyed us across the choppy waters to the ship riding in the roads, we were accompanied by hundreds of people of all races in sampans and barges, as well as by the clatter of musketry fired from merchant ships, native and European.

Once we had ascended the ship's side, and the crew were raising the anchor, I left Tom alone in our cabin, and as I stepped from the door, I turned and saw him standing at the window, raising his hand in farewell to Singapore; his face was flushed, as if he were fighting tears. I am sure he stood there until he saw Singapore slip further from view, and further, further, until, with a last glitter of its snow-white beaches, this dot of land slipped quite under the distant, fading horizon, and disappeared.

Later, Tom told me he trusts that one day better luck may happen to his almost only child than anybody now dreams of, and he is not deserting it, and never will, for all he must henceforth both follow, and promote, its progress always from a very great distance. As for his exasperation with Flint, and bitter disagreements with Farquhar, he said however annoyed he has sometimes been these past few months, how dreadfully harassed and fagged, the close of his administration has been just what he wished, as things have mostly been ordered as he wanted them, and it is with a sense of satisfaction he now quits the scene.

June 1823, the *Hero of Malown*, the Eastern Seas

Tom talks incessantly of Singapore, and says all he did there he was looking a century or two ahead so as to provide for what his almost only child may one day become. He repeats often all he wishes for it now is unarguable, undisputed confirmation that it is to be ours forever, and not tossed to the Dutch, and that this is the *unum necessarium*, the one necessary, for the future of his city, and hence also of any British empire in the Eastward.

Writing of the Dutch reminds me we will soon stop off at Java, as the Captain has goods to land there. Tom says the Dutch, who think he is the very devil, will be a little astonished at his presence, but what's to be done.

June 1823, the *Hero of Malown*, the Eastern Seas

I am confined to my couch, stricken by seasickness, and too ill to write anything but that.

June 1823, McQuoid's house, Batavia

The day before yesterday we put in at Batavia to land the captain's cargo and to re-water. This was the first time Tom had set eyes on his beloved Java since he quit here in '16, and he was curious to see how it progressed under the rough handling of the Dutch, but I am sorry to say our reception has been very *Dutch* indeed. As soon as we arrived Tom wrote to the Governor to say we were in the roads, and that I was with child, and very ill with seasickness and it would be a relief if I could get ashore for a day or two. The reply was in the Governor's own hand – that it was exceedingly *disagreeable* we had come, nothing could be more so – that he would have no further communication of any kind with Tom – tho' his humanity would not allow him to refuse permission for the ship to remain a few days, and for me to come ashore. I really never read so ungentlemanly a production.

Tom insisted on my being brought on shore, so here I, Charley Boy, and a couple of servants have been these past two days in the house of one of the few Britons still resident here, whilst my husband remains aboard the *Hero of Malown*.

Tho' I was very much reduced when we arrived, I already feel rejuvenated, and I am anxious to get on board again, and be off.

July 1822, Government House, Bencoolen

To my relief, we are once again on firm ground in Bencoolen: we had a most uncomfortable voyage between Java and Sumatra, against violent winds all the way. I became exhausted from seasickness, and this morning, when we were conveyed ashore, I had to lie in the bottom of the boat, reclining on a mattress. We rest here tonight, and will drive to Permattam Ballam tomorrow, and I anticipate a melancholy satisfaction in being once more in the house where my gossamer children lived and died, where are the things their fingers once touched, their cups and spoons, and servants who knew them.

July 1822, Permattam Ballam

How greatly my heart has been torn ... The memories of my children ... To see Charley Boy running around ...

And yet I must not despair. I must remember that God, merciful, has not only left me one blessing, Ella, but has also granted me new hope tho', in truth, I have scarcely had time to think of my expected stranger, except to acquire two glass sucking bottles for infants, as we will be sailing with it to England when it is still very young, and at sea I think I must bring it up by bottle. In the meantime, the basket is to be prepared and things sent to the *dhob*y – the washerwoman – when we are more settled.

It is a relief to me this is another one will be born at Permattam Ballam, and not while I am shifting from pillar to post, but how I now regret anew the absence, through death, of Dr. Jack, and through distance of Nurse Grimes. Still, the new doctor in Bencoolen is indeed a medical man, and not a botanist, and I will have Jane to care for my new babe – she's been working in the kitchen since we shut up the nursery, and was hitherto only ever nursery maid, not nurse, but no matter.

July 1822, Permattam Ballam

Tom commences writing a memoir of the founding of Singapore, apart from that, he says, he has nothing to do but prepare for Old England.

July 1822, Permattam Ballam

On studying our accounts, Tom finds we have less money than we thought to take with us to England – and to be in England without money is a contingency not to be looked upon without dread. It is thus with the utmost urgency he is looking to make a collection of handsome tortoiseshells, of the best quality, and wishes he may soon fall in with a lot of cheap diamonds, for these things – tortoiseshell, diamonds – are easy to transport, and altogether an excellent way of carrying money Home.

Notwithstanding we share the general hope to live comfortably, we were never very covetous of affluence, and since our children died riches are of less value to us than ever.

September 1822, Permattam Ballam

I will extol thee, my God, O king: and I will bless thy name for ever and ever ... A week ago, after a tolerable confinement made more tolerable still by ether – what a wonder! – there arrived in this world our third daughter, Miss Flora – and a month before I calculated but the doctor says the young lady had been quite her proper time. I had only made my nest the day she appeared, and the doctor happened to be out here, attending Tom who is going through a course of medicine for his headaches. I was determined to have a young gentleman, so I would not at first believe I had made a mistake. But tho' Flora is merely a young lady, she is nonetheless more welcome than I can express. I had wanted to call her Hope, but Tom said no, he liked Flora better, and so she is another little floweret of the Eastward, and we must pray she is hardier than our beloved Tunjung Segara. Tom says there is special magic in any beginning, but in hers especially so, coming as it does so hard upon ending, ending, ending.

Holding Flora makes me long more than ever to hold again my other remaining child. Oh, would that Ella were not so far away from her new sister, and from me!

October 1822, Permattam Ballam

My dear baby was a fortnight old yesterday and has not yet cried night or day or tasted even a bit of magnesia, even soap and water does not rouse her ire. I nurse her entirely myself, and intend to go on till she is six weeks old, and then put her to suck on a bottle, hoping to get her strong before I take her out to sea for the Homeward voyage. She is as fat as a little pig, tho' not so pretty as Charlotte, or Ella.

October 1822, Permattam Ballam

We have been anxious to hear of a ship to take us back to England, for the sake of Flora's health, and Charley Boy's, but we could find none available. Now news comes from Bengal that The Company has chartered a ship, the *Fame*, to take us Home, and she should arrive in early December, which news cheers me greatly.

October 1822, Permattam Ballam

I am entirely recovered from my confinement, but I begin to feel poorly today. To my relief my dear baby remains well – our little Flora expands daily.

November 1822, Permattam Ballam

I have been attacked this past fortnight with a severe inflammatory fever, and for several days my life was in the balance, I remain in a very delicate state, and it was only last night, that Tom was forced to apply to my back thirty leeches, and I must have recourse to warm baths and laudanum to keep down inflammation.

Tom too has been ill with the same brain fever which so often and so suddenly overwhelmed him at Singapore.

November 1822, Permattam Ballam

My fever is down, and I am in better health, but I am still confined to my couch and the loss of my milk has turned Miss Flora that was as fat as a little pig into a creature less beautiful, for being too skinny, and most unwilling to suck on the bottle.

December 1823, Permattam Ballam

Their fragility, these little ones I grew within me ... Whatever I read, whatever I write, whatever I speak, whatever is spoken to me, I see and I hear and I form only the two words of the lament *if only*.

If only we had got her away.

December 1823, Permattam Ballam

Behold, he taketh away, who can hinder him? Who will say unto him, What doest thou? ... I must bear it, and if I cannot bear it I must in any case endure. And if in weak and wicked moments I sometimes wish I need not endure, then I must remember it is a sin to reject any of God's blessings: blessings He so generously bestows on all His creatures moment by precious moment. And Tom, when he despairs, I must tell the same.

December 1823, Permattam Ballam

Again, I must write the worst of news: at the end of November Miss Flora, who had hitherto been most promising and thriving, died – carried off in a few hours by one of our dreadful fevers that are the scourge of this land.

I am heartshredded, and so is Tom. This loss of our fifth and only remaining child in India – our dear baby, so glowing with health and strength – has revived all our former afflictions, and been almost too much for us, so we are almost indifferent to anything but our own suffering, and our attendant illnesses – we are both now more like the shadows of earthly beings than anything possessing life. Tom is tormented by his headaches, and I have been so ill I hardly expected to get over it - the leeches that have of necessity been applied to me, and the mercury I've swallowed have saved me, tho' they have much reduced my system

Charley Boy remains healthy – a robust little gentleman.

December 1823, Permattam Ballam

We are most anxious to get away from such a charnel-house as this, but here we are detained until the arrival of the *Fame*. We write chits daily to Bencoolen, asking our friends there to scan the sea for her. Tom says either he must go to England, or by remaining in India die – we are both certain that in the case we do reach England alive, no inducement shall ever lead us to revisit India.

January 1824, Permattam Ballam

Where is the *Fame*? I remain ill and every day I spend here in this feverish place and horrid climate is a danger to me; Tom expresses the hope that she may still arrive in time to save our lives, tho' he has little confidence that this will be the case.

January 1824, Permattam Ballam

The *Borneo*, the same ship that carried Ella to safer climes, has now put into Bencoolen, once again on her way to England. She is not a commodious vessel and her accommodation is wretched, but we are now inclined to cut and run at all costs, and so we have booked passage. Well, we've sailed in worse.

Tho' I would to God we were Home, and out of these enervating regions, now the time so soon approaches when I must go for good, I find I cannot think of quitting Permattam Ballam with an easy heart: here the spirits of my dear departed children seem to be hovering just out of sight, blooming and smiling as if in life, and I feel that if only I could stretch my fingertips further, just a little further, they would brush against the butterfly wings of my infants' infant ghosts.

January 1824, Permattam Ballam

I have commenced packing for our Homeward voyage, and tho' it is harassing, it is at least an activity so exceedingly busy it allows little time to brood.

Tom must take with us when we sail all his books – he has at least three hundred bound volumes – his many unbound manuscripts, his scrolls, his texts written on leaves and bark. These literary things I direct the servants to wrap in waxed cloths and pack into leather cases. I also direct as they pack assorted rarities – various eastern curiosities – and his natural history collections – hundreds of stuffed animals, birds and reptiles, insects preserved in spirits, geological specimens, &c. I think in Old England Tom can stock a whole museum from his collections – this without all the things we have stored there, and haven't seen at all these past seven years, and as well the things we've sent back in the meantime.

Nor does Tom forget his plants, nor his tigers, bears, monkeys, &c, of which he has no small family; his living collections, as well as his others, he plans to take to England. Indeed, he says we shall have as we sail a second Noah's Ark, and it pleases him there will be scarcely an interesting animal, bird, beast, fish, or plant which we will not have on board: a tapir; a new species of tiger; splendid pheasants domesticated for the voyage. He has written to Sir Humphrey Davy that he may expect him to arrive in London with sufficient menagerie to stock the entire zoological garden, if that plan progresses, for his news of it is less than scanty.

January 1824, Government House, Bencoolen

We have left Permattam Ballam for the last time – Jane and all the servants weeping – and at this departure I felt as if I were saying goodbye to my children all over again, and Tom too was missing them this morning, for tho' he did not say so, and no more did I, his eyes were dark with love, anguish, memory, full to overflowing with his children.

January 1824, Government House, Bencoolen

Tom's collections fill a hundred and thirty-five good wooden crates and boxes, each one stamped with his name, and then all his plants in pots, and animals in coops and cages. He spent the last few days supervising the loading of this precious cargo into the hold of the *Borneo*. It took twenty barges to ferry the greater part of his things from the beach, to the ship, and then just as everything except the animals was loaded, the *Fame* finally hove into view, and soon enough she was riding in the roads. Notwithstanding her calamitous tardiness, she is a nice little ship, very commodious, with excellent accommodation, so we now order all our things manhandled off the *Borneo* and onto her. We are told there is room for all Tom's plants, and also for his menagerie.

January 1824, Government House, Bencoolen

Our crates will take up most of the *Fame's* hold, but where there is space, I learn it is to be filled with saltpetre, the essential compound in gunpowder, and long an important item in the India trade. I do not like to think of sailing on a powder keg, but sail on a powder keg I must.

February 1824, the *Fame*, the Eastern Seas

Oh, to be in England! We set sail this morning, with a fair following wind, on our way Home at last, after all our blessings, and all our trials. In my heart, skimming airily over the surface of muddier, more troubling feelings, is joy at the prospect of reunion with Ella.

Charley Boy is wildly excited to be at sea. I bought him for the voyage a fur cap and a blue cloth jacket trimmed with lace and ornamented with gilt buttons, and a pair of trousers, and in this outfit he looks a most splendid little sailor.

The sea being so calm, we have every prospect of a quiet and comfortable voyage, so Tom and I are indulging ourselves in anticipation of future peace. Our relief at being off and quitting India is such that were we not leaving here the spirits of our children, we must regard this as one of the happiest days of our married life.

February 1824, Permattam Ballam

If thou faint in the day of adversity thy strength is small ... Oh, what melancholy destruction. We are destitute of everything, for it has pleased God to visit on us another calamity: the *Fame* is lost, consumed by fire our first night at sea, so I am now once again at Permattam Ballam, and I must face again my children's ghosts.

We are here virtually without resources – the house half-empty, echoing, and our clothes all lost. I had not even a pair of stockings on when we abandoned ship, nor shoes, only my pelisse to wrap me. Oh, my dresses! No finery now, we are fitted out with all sorts of odd garments through the compassion of our friends - Tom says we must be glad to get hopsacks to cover our nakedness, and indeed I am grateful I have now coverings, if clothes I cannot call them.

The *Fame* was about fifty miles off Bencoolen when the alarm was raised at about half past eight. I had just retired for the night – just laid my head down on my pillow – and Tom was in his little dressing cabin when the cry of *Fire! Fire* roused us from our calm content. I rushed to the cabin door; outside, I saw a man spring up the hatchway covered with flame. Tom flew to the cuddy to see what could be done – which was little. Cries of *fire, water, water* resounded through the ship, which was all in flames.

Tom returned to say it was all over, we must perish, and I fancy I called aloud Ella's name, for certainly I was thinking I may never see her again – my last little prattler! And then the cry rang out: Lady Raffles, to the boats! I had only time to throw on my pelisse, and get Charley Boy – whose cabin was in flames when I dragged him out of bed – and wrap him in a shawl and we got into a boat.

Flames were bursting all about us – bursting through windows – as the boat was lowered into the water, descending tight by the ship's side – the *Fame* was by now a sheet of flame, one grand mass of fire, and the masts and rigging all falling about, ashes drifting in my hair, cinders catching in my pelisse, the roaring noise stupefying, crushing, and the choking air an acrid stink.

The Great Author of all Events showed forbearance of our sins, and ensured there were enough places in the boats – two of them, that stayed together through all the long night – and in ten minutes every soul had quitted the fiery *Fame*, tho' the birds and animals could not be saved – oh, that poor tapir, that tiger roasting meat. We went so quickly there was not even time to get a drop of water or refreshment of any kind before we were launched bobbing upon the ocean.

Fortunately, even amidst the chaos, our Captain had the presence of mind to seize the *Fame's* compass, before he quit her, and this was everything to us, enabling us to determine the direction of Sumatra, and the crew rowed manfully that way. The night was very dark – the cold beauty of the stars – but very calm, and the sea was smooth and we hoped and prayed for continuance of fine weather.

The *Fame* blazed on as we pulled away from her; she was rocking in the water, from the force of the burning, so she looked as if she were dancing a demented jig. At about midnight, she exploded and sent up one of the most brilliant flames that ever was seen, illuminating the horizon in every direction, and casting over us an unearthly blue light most horrible. We lost sight of her as she went down in a cloud of smoke.

Tom had escaped in his coat, and the tails of that, plus a pocket handkerchief, served to keep my feet warm. I had snatched Charley Boy from his bed without even breeches, but we made him a pair from some of the men's neckcloths, and he slept soundly all through the night, oblivious of our peril.

As the morning approached, our anxiety increased: where were we? Had we managed to row against the current? Or had we been carried to the southward, into that immense ocean that laps, eventually, on the frozen shores of those new found lands they say lie at the Southern pole of the earth? If so we had no hope of life, but must die in those cold, endless, endlessly empty seas. If not, we in any case had no food, no water, and we were all perfectly convinced we were unable to undergo starvation and exposure to sun and weather many days. But the light increased, and we beheld Pulau Tikus – Rat Island – but six miles off Bencoolen.

The men behaved nobly and renewed their exertions with the oars, but they were much fatigued, and we began to fear we should not make the port. By noon I was nearly exhausted, and fainting continually, for we had nothing to shelter us from that pitiless blade, the sun.

To our unbounded relief, we were spotted by a ship lying in the roads of Bencoolen, and the Captain brought her near us, and we were most thankful to get on board. We were back on land by two o'clock yesterday, and Tom said if any proof had been wanting, that his administration had been satisfactory, he had it unequivocally from all who gathered to greet us: there was not a dry eye ...

We were driven straight back here, to Permattam Ballam, which I thought never to see again, and were in bed within an hour of landing, and slept through until this morning.

Had this dreadful accident occurred a day later, or had the smallest of the many favourable circumstances a merciful God combined for our preservation been wanting we should have perished the most dreadful of deaths. The shock has been a great one – my hand shakes even now, as I write my account – but I must be thankful there was no loss of any man's life among us, but of only the ship; I must cling to that faith and hope which has enabled me to bear so much.

February 1824, Permattam Ballam

We now learn the fire broke out in the store-room below our cabin, where a careless steward with a naked light went to draw off brandy from a cask, which caught, and leapt at once to a general conflagration.

The loss has been for us a ruinous one. All Tom's collections of maps, dictionaries, vocabularies, grammars, histories, and books are lost. All his irreplaceable manuscripts of the literature of the Malayan nation, and of other natives, are lost. All his papers are lost – correspondence, notes, narratives, memoranda – relating to his administrations in Java, Bencoolen, and Singapore alike. His memoir of the founding of Singapore he was writing – lost. He has lost all his beautiful natural history drawings – upwards of two thousand in number. The cream and best of everything he had collected these past few years – gone – all is gone. The silver plate given him by the inhabitants of Java when he quit that island went down with the *Fame*, and all our gold work too, and our diamonds, and our tortoiseshells by which we hoped to transport Home considerable money. Tom lost even the diamond ring Princess Charlotte gave him the last time they met, and we have lost also the miniatures we exchanged as betrothal gifts.

As for me, I have lost as well as that sentimental keepsake, my clothes and all my personal possessions, including my harp, my piano, and all my sheet music. I have lost all my jewellery – pieces given me by my parents, and by Tom. Indeed, this diary is now almost my only possession, excepting only my wedding ring, and a golden bracelet hung with lockets containing curls of my children's hair, treasures I wear on my person always.

My precious diary! I deduce from where I found it, joined with the evidence I write in it now, that I must have slipped it into the pocket of my pelisse, after I wrote on the *Fame* of anticipating a calm voyage, tho' I have no memory of doing so. Its calf binding now is all stained with seawater, the ink of my writing here and there runs and bleeds into the paper from getting wet, and the damp pages release as they are turned a slight smell of smoke. Still, it is a blessing it survived, for it has become a remembrance of my children, and to think of their commemoration sinking to the seabed, there to disintegrate in a sodden mass of paper, makes my heart ache, notwithstanding it didn't happen.

February 1824, Permattam Ballam

From nerves Charley Boy is now suffering from hesitations of speech. I have written to Mary Ann to say her son is safe; I only hope my letter reaches her before news the *Fame* went down, unless that news includes also the intelligence none were lost – and when I think she entrusted Charley Boy to us, to preserve him from danger …

February 1824, Permattam Ballam

More things we have lost: embroideries and cloths, ivories, shawls, muslins, table linens, wines to be drunk on the voyage. I shall jot down other things as I think of them.

February 1824, Permattam Ballam

The loss of the fruits of the labours of so much of his life would have broken most men, and indeed Tom has suffered a great deal – we are both very weak, and have both had recourse to salivation. But as we have been so long afflicted by misfortune, it perhaps falls more lightly on us now than it otherwise would have done? What are these new losses, compared to the loss of our children? Tom is in any case stoical. He has submitted to his fate with the most wonderful patience and good spirits – without a single murmur against Providence. Indeed, it is now a common remark with him that the lot of man is a mixture of good and evil, and we must be content with it, and at all events we know that all worketh for good in the end.

This I think most commendable fortitude, and, today, I really could not withhold my admiration on seeing my husband sit down with his usual energy and pleasure and recommence his memoir of Singapore, and then later send for the native draftsmen, and set them to work as he used to do, all as if nothing had happened.

His Chinese artists have already produced for him a drawing of the branch of a cashew nut tree, and another of a vile-smelling local fruit called a durian, these to be the beginning of a new collection of natural history drawings – how the loss of Tom's old one must cause men of science to weep, and how orientalists must likewise weep at the loss of his Malay manuscripts.

Our writing cases, my fans, all the furniture we provided for our cabins, Charley Boy's trunk and everything in it.

March 1824, Permattam Ballam

It is now arranged that we will sail for England on the *Mariner*, a small Botany Bay ship – she will also convey Home all the officers from the ill-fated *Fame*. We will depart in early April, and I commence praying already for a trouble-free voyage.

My sewing box, my bobbins and thimble, silver forks and spoons – it may be I placed too high a value on, or was too much attached to, the things of this world, and needed to be taught anew to value above all the things of the spirit.

March 1824, Permattam Ballam

Mrs. Raffles has lived now near enough her threescore years and ten, and, alas, we have had letters from Home giving melancholy accounts of her. Tom, ever a loving son, is much distressed, and he weeps he can hardly expect to see his mother again alive, tho' he hopes and prays he may be wrong.

April 1824, Permattam Ballam

If the winds oblige we depart tomorrow. I am desperate to be Home, but, oh, the horror with which I think of the coming voyage, and the dread I have of going to sea again – such a scene as that we witnessed aboard the *Fame* can never be forgotten – the flaming ship shuddering as tho' it were a living creature, and imagining Tom's animals, the tapir, the tiger, trapped, terrified, burning.

July 1824, Plantation House, St. Helena

It seems even my soul has been reeling to and fro, and staggering like a drunken man, and I have been at my wit's end for we have had a miserable time aboard the *Mariner* – the ship nearly torn to pieces and ourselves nearly worn out with terror, and seasickness, for off the Cape of Good Hope it was our misfortune to encounter one of the severest storm seasons ever known. The gales were so fierce that I had to be tied into my bed at night, to prevent me being tossed out, and they blew with unabated fury for three weeks during which whole time the ship pitched and heaved, and seemed to me a wreck upon the water, with the topmasts down, and a single storm sail set, and even that was eventually carried away by the sea breaking over the roundhouse and all the time the roar of the wind was such that we could not hear each other speak, and the sea poured often through the deck into our cabin, so we wallowed in brine, and we resigned ourselves to finding that our pilgrimage in this world was soon to close.

Still, the Lord preserved us, and we are now safe at St. Helena, Britain's isolated island that was Napoleon's final place of detention, and has ever been a favoured watering place for ships Homebound from India. The Governor here, Governor Walker, and his wife are putting us up at The Residency, Plantation House. We will remain on land about two weeks, recuperating, whilst the *Mariner* is repaired, re-watered, and re-loaded.

July 1824, Plantation House, St. Helena

Governor Walker tells us we almost overlapped as his guest with Farquhar, whom we learn from him is now also sailing back to England – Governor Walker says still much disgruntled with Tom, and sick to his liver it is my husband, not him, who is credited with the founding of Singapore. Farquhar's ship had put in here a few days before we arrived, but when he heard Tom was approaching on the *Mariner*, the poor, disappointed man directed her captain to prepare to depart post haste. He quit here the night before we arrived, such was his desire to avoid my husband.

According to the Governor, Farquhar plans to travel to Scotland immediately after he lands at Home. This, Tom says to me privately, is a great relief, and here I think is all the admission my husband will ever make that he was ungenerous to Farquhar, or that the older man could have caused him a load of mischief if from ill-temper he'd chosen to linger some time in London, and to vent his spleen at India House.

Meanwhile, Farquhar's domestic arrangements provoke gossip far-and-wide, and I have it from the Lady Governess that he sails Home without Nonio Clemaine and their mixed breed children, for this dusky family he has left in Singapore, including also Bernard and Esther. Lady Walker invited me to speculate how long it will be before Farquhar weds a proper bride, a fair girl in her bloom to replace old Nonio Clemaine and to provide him with respectable heirs, but I refused to conspire, tho' I cannot think it will be very long.

July 1824, Plantation House, St. Helena

St. Helena offers little diversion; there is nothing to see except Longwood House, the estate that was the scene of Napoleon's captivity. How I wish I could call on the tyrant! Tom saw him once, for my husband disembarked here in '16, when he sailed from Java to England for his Home leave. He met the famous despot when they were both walking in the garden at Longwood. Tom says Boney was a heavy, clumsy-looking man, small, moving with an awkward, strutting gait, and he found him just as bad as his reputation – which is very bad, for the ignorant say it was his custom to eat children. Tho' Tom was intrigued by his fame, and compassioned his situation, and had expected to admire him as strategist and tactician, he says by the time they separated, he disdained him. Boney, arrogant, apparently hogged the conversation, and Tom says it was little compensation for his haughty selfishness that he later had the honour of receiving refreshments off the imperial silver.

Still, for all Tom says he thought Boney a monster he regrets as much as me there's no seeing him on St. Helena now, since the dictator that would have ruled all mankind is now three years dead.

July 1824, Plantation House, St. Helena

News reaches us here of the death of Tom's mother, heaven rest her soul! She went on February 8, before even we received the letter saying she was ill. Tom has a heavy heart, and I think his health and spirits will not admit of him dwelling on this latest loss, which is a sad stroke as he had been allowing himself to consider the possibility of once more embracing his mother. When he talks of her his eyes are blinded by tears, and he shakes from nervous sadness. Indeed, he has been made quite ill by misery, and is in constant agony from his headaches, and is debilitated, and subject to bilious attacks.

July 1824, Plantation House, St. Helena

Tom is somewhat better, and tomorrow we board the *Mariner* once more, for the final haul to England, so our conversation turns often now, with a seriousness becoming the gravity of the subject, to what articles of food we shall indulge in, on our first arrival at Home – Tom looks forward to cheddar cheese, and I am in hopes of strawberries.

I am pleased to say Charley Boy has recovered from his hesitations of speech, brought on by the shock of the *Fame* going down, and he is indeed now quite naughty.

August 1824, the *Mariner*, off the Cornish Coast

And, behold, I am with thee, and will keep thee in all places whither thou goest, and will bring thee again into this land ... I have had my first sight of Home for nigh on seven years. Tho' in the Eastward Old England sometimes seemed to me unreal, like a dream of Home, and not a literal place on the globe, Cornwall is now crouched in the angry sea to our starboard, and is just as real as sharp granite rocks will allow.

I hardly know how to say how I've changed since last I saw England. I sometimes feel so disunited from that Lady Raffles who sailed Eastward on the *Lady Raffles* I can scarce think we are the same person – I cannot recall her, it sometimes seems, and must judge she was mistaken to think she ever could return Home. More, I scarcely know how to say who I am now, what I am, what manner of person?

As for Tom, now turned of forty, lit now only by shadows of his youthful fires, he says he feels just as wearily jumbled as me, just as uncertain how to begin to make sense of all that has happened these past seven years, if indeed any sense can be made of our lives at all, and he says it is a puzzle to know whether his two sojourns in the Eastwood enabled him to put on, at various times, a new self, as a man may put on a new coat, or if, while in foreign climes, he became more than ever the man who first left, and now returns, to Old England.

August 1824, The Bell Inn, Plymouth

We are landed at Plymouth, and what it is to breathe in a cool summer smell of mown grass, and to luxuriate in a soft, lingering twilight, which is a thing unknown in the Eastward, where night swoops down like an owl on the day, and to see again the ashy greens of English trees, and to be pattered by rain that does not feel like water warmed on a fire.

Tonight we lodge at an inn called The Bell. Tom tells me nearly twenty years ago he and Olivia lodged in this same Bell the night before they sailed for Penang, and I think perhaps there is some meaning for me here, but I cannot uncover it. In any case, we have ordered the best dinner procurable in the place, including also cheese for Tom, to be got ready as soon as possible, so I anticipate a most enjoyable evening, tho' we are too late in the season for strawberries, and I must wait almost another year until I can taste them.

News of the sinking of the *Fame* precedes us. Details of the ship's misfortune were printed in all the newspapers, and caused a sensation, and everyone we have met at The Bell has demanded we tell them of that terrible night. Tom now plans to write his own account of the disaster for publication.

We found waiting for us here a heap, a happy heap, of letters from our friends and families, one from Mother reporting Ella is well, for which I am indeed as grateful to the Lord as I ought to be, and another from Father to let us know the *Borneo* reached England safely in May. On learning this Tom and I looked at each other a long moment, and his look could have meant a hundred things, and so, I suppose, could mine, and neither of us spoke a word.

There was less perplexing news in another letter, an official one from India House: whilst we were trapped in Bencoolen, after the sinking of the *Fame*, the British signed with the Dutch the treaty that has been four years in the making – the one intended to bind them to us as allies in Europe, and to that end deciding how we will arrange between us our possessions in the Eastward, now Napoleon cannot put his nose into our plans.

Here's the rub: the Dutch have withdrawn all opposition to our occupation of Singapore. Tom, gratified, satisfied, vindicated, says here begins in earnest the glory of the settlement he founded, and as well this decision must be to the future splendour of that British empire in the Eastward he so keenly anticipates.

Moreover, the Foreign Secretary has endorsed Tom's plan, long-dormant, now revived, that all our possessions in the Eastward should be brought under *one* administration, headed by *one* governor, and that this governor should rule from Singapore, which will henceforth be our capital east of Bengal.

Notwithstanding these personal triumphs, and tho' we both relish his success, Tom is much reduced and exceedingly weak, and admits to a sad headache from the effects of landing. I feel quite well, I think from joy, excitement, at the prospect of being reunited with my family: tomorrow morning we leave The Bell, and take a post-chaise to Cheltenham, to my parents, and to Ella. Oh, my little girl! She is three years old, she can walk and run. She can call mama and tell me what her doll says, and my patience to hear her prattling has almost given out.

August 1824, The Swan Inn, between Plymouth and Bath

Our misfortunes being so widely known from the newspapers, we are receiving the most gratifying reception from all classes of people as we journey to Cheltenham. Indeed it seems a pleasure for the people to look at us, in some places along the way they crowd round the carriage quite like the natives of Pasemah and Minangkabau, and the inn keeper here at the Swan told us that out of sympathy for our plight he would tonight accept no payment for the tavern bill.

August 1824, Bath

Our progress has been delayed by the traffic of assizes, horse races, air balloons, and other festivities of the summer season, but now we are at Bath, and tomorrow we will set out for Cheltenham with a vengeance, and I shall make the post-boys drive the post-chaise so fast the wheels will catch fire, such is my impatience to see my little one … And, oh, when I think of my other little ones, left on that distant shore.

August 1824, Number 349, the High Street, Cheltenham

Let everything that have breath praise the Lord … I am reunited with Ella. My Ella Bella! To say her name is singing to me, and the sound itself is a song, and my child is all that my fondest wishes could have desired – pretty as the most perfect regular features can make her, and possessing as well the most intelligent of expressions, with a gentle nature as sweet as honey, and her speech for her age notably advanced, tho' unlike Charlotte the only language she speaks is English. In looks she takes after her father, with straight chestnut hair, but not a very fair skin – she retains even now some slight sallowness of the Eastward.

Oh, would that this child of mine, precious wreck of my family fallen sacrifice to India's pestilential airs, grows to adulthood, and has many fine children of her own – I must watch she does not now collapse under the weight of *all* my hopes.

August 1824, Number 349, the High Street, Cheltenham

From being so absorbed by Ella I forgot to write yesterday of my parents, and of dear Nurse Grimes. They are all well. Mother and I both wept at our reunion, our tears a comingling of joy, and regret. Father said Tom has done the country proud for securing for us Singapore. Nurse Grimes is as comforting here as in the Eastward, and she cossets me as tho' I were another infant charge.

August 1824, Number 349, the High Street, Cheltenham

Ella and Charley Boy play together happily, which is a great pleasure for me to see. I intend to commission a drawing of Charley Boy, to send to Mary Ann – and I when next I write I must remember to pass on that Mother says her son is the spit of her.

August 1824, Number 349, the High Street, Cheltenham

I have been talking with Mother of Charlotte, Leopold, Cooksey, and Flora. She told me I should not berate myself I could not keep my children safe for no mother could, in the Eastward. Thus she made me more than ever sensible I lost my children, I judge, through my own deficiencies of mothering, if only in keeping my darlings so long in that dangerous climate. I reminded her, more tartly than I intended, we must beware not to murmur against the ways of Providence, but must console ourselves that as Divine Justice will never fail, and full compensation seeming to be wanting on this side of the grave, the deficiency will be amply filled up in another state, where life, bliss, and happiness will be everlasting.

August 1824, Number 349, the High Street, Cheltenham

Tom says he thought when we came Home he would be like a fish who'd found water, but not at all, even England seems foreign to him now. As for me, I feel sometimes as if, from my long years away, and my bitter experience, I am not now part of life in Cheltenham, but am viewing it through thick, distorting glass. Still, we both trust we are merely suffering from a transient mood of gloom, no doubt common to those returned from travels, and in any case we will soon have the busyness of moving from my parents' to distract us: Tom has rented us a snug little house, at Number 2, Wellington Place. Here we will collect about us a few of the things that make life easy, to replace our lost ones and no doubt we'll soon feel comfortable and settled.

August 1824, Number 2, Wellington Place, Cheltenham

We are established in our new lodgings. The children are happy with the nursery, as is Nurse Grimes, and Tom and I are feeling steadier than we have of late. We intend to live here a generally retired existence, seeing no one but members of the family, and endeavouring to gain a little health and strength to see us through the coming winter – our first cold season for seven years. Tom's headaches are now very slight, and he is putting on some weight, even getting fat. It pleases me to see some flesh upon my husband's bones.

September 1824, Number 2, Wellington Place, Cheltenham

The Court of Directors has asked that Tom prepare a statement of services for the Honourable Members, to be presented at India House. He is to draw out a brief review of his public administration during the last twelve years in Java, Bencoolen, and Singapore, and to include also an account of the lost documentation of his activities in the Eastern Isles, the ashes of which documents now feed the fishes at the bottom of the sea.

With his characteristic stoicism, Tom has decided the loss of all his records renders compiling this statement of services all the more interesting, and he went to his desk this morning with relish, and he has been absorbed in his writing now above two hours.

September 1824, Number 2, Wellington Place, Cheltenham

We calculate we lost on the *Fame* goods to the value of between twenty and thirty thousand pounds, and none of our things insured. Hence Tom is resolved that when he presents his statement of services to the Court of Directors he will take the opportunity to remind the Honourable Members of our recent pecuniary losses, and also to argue they should compensate us for those losses – this in addition to any pension the Honourable Members grant him.

This matter of a pension is a vexed one: Johnny Company grants an annuity to most of its servants of long standing, but as favour, not as right. For himself, Tom *does* expect a pension, and he has written to the Honourable Members pleading with them to be generous, as they have the power to ensure he is able to end his days in honourable retirement, and not in destitution.

Tom says these various matters of ensuring he is treated fairly in a pecuniary point of view are to be Our Winter Campaign. He has warned that such are the ways of India House this campaign must be enervating, and must require all my fortitude, and I must be stalwart as I always am.

October 1824, Piccadilly

Tom and I have come to London that he may make his statement of services to the Court of Directors, and that he may in person plead our case for compensation, and a pension. We have left Ella and Charley Boy in Cheltenham with Mother and Nurse Grimes. I do not wish to be long-separated from my daughter, so we will remain in Town no longer than ten days

How London has changed since last I saw it! New buildings everywhere, and such shops as I had almost forgotten existed: milliners and haberdashers, and stationers, and pastry shops, and shops for boots and shoes, and drapers and tailors all with their displays most tempting, so I could dash about all day and buy replacements for all the necessities I lost on the *Fame*, and also I think any frivolous luxury in the world, if only I had the money.

Even in this town of so many diversions and distractions, the fate of the *Fame* caused a sensation, and on account of it we have received the kindest reception from the people. When I gave my name, Lady Raffles, to one of the shopkeepers he said: Lord, Ma'am, you ain't the lady that was burnt on the *Fame*? Come here Bessy and see them!

We are staying in rooms on Piccadilly – such a fashionable address – just around the corner from Mr. Murray in Albemarle St. Despite this closeness, Tom has made no mention of calling on his publisher, so I hope he has put aside all thought of a second edition of *The History of Java*, which pleases me, for I fear the effects of too much literary exertion on his constitution.

October 1824, Piccadilly

Tom has met up again with Sir Humphrey Davy who has been able to give him most pleasing news: his plan to form a zoological society, to promote the idea to found in this city a scientific zoological garden, has come to fruition. More than this, barely a month ago, at a meeting in July, the society's members appointed Tom in his absence their chairman, in anticipation of his return.

Tho' I worry it may be too demanding, this I think a most fitting honour for my husband. Tom himself is much flattered, and delighted to serve. He teases that if his zoological garden comes to pass, as indeed it must, then after he is dead its trustees must feel obliged to place a bust of him in the lion house, for which gloomy sort of gallows humour I rebuke him most soundly.

October 1824, Piccadilly

I today accompanied Tom to India House, so I could hear him present his statement of services to the Court of Directors; in consequence I am now in a state of decided agitation.

India House is a most grandiose, imposing edifice, with more columns along its façade than any building has need of. Inside is a grand hall, where, from above, kind Britannia watches proceedings below, for on the ceiling is a picture of the East making tribute to her of its riches – the East represented by a dusky Indian woman offering her pearls, and a Chinese woman offering her a vase. The Court itself sits in a grand panelled room of double doors and doubtful acoustics. It is nearly filled by a huge horseshoe-shaped table, its wood polished to such a high gloss it seemed to me it gleamed as much as some of the balder Honourable Members' pates.

Tom delivered his statement fluently, confidently, and loud enough so I could clearly hear him where I sat at the back – this in contrast to one or two of the Honourable Members who addressed the Court in inaudible mumbles.

Once Tom had finished, there followed much discussion of Singapore, which the Court called a political venture that had turned out well, tho' it might not have: even now the Honourable Members refused to condone the way Tom acted without their previous sanction; they praised him for his zeal and ability in bringing to the country this new settlement, which all agreed was rightly by Britain preserved; they censured him for doing so in a way which might have caused a war with the Dutch.

Grudging recognition of his success was only so much as we had expected from the Honourable Members. But once they'd done doling out their critical praise, they truly shocked and horrified us, for the discussion turned to the matter of recompense for our losses in the sinking of the *Fame*, and far from giving Tom fair or favourable hearing, the Honourable Members said they would not recompense him: his losses were due to mischance; The Court could only ignore such an extravagant claim, and Tom must put aside all idea of it, and think only of compensation through his pension.

The Honourable Members then dealt a blow worse even than this; they ordered Tom to refund his allowance from '16 to '18, the period when he was last in England, or sailing back from here to the Eastward, as they said he wasn't working for them then, but on leave, and a hence for the duration a private gentleman, so he should never have claimed or received his allowance in the first place. They added they would withhold any pension they may in future feel inclined to grant him, until he has cleared with them this supposed debt, the sum amounting, they say, to some six thousand pounds.

I feel dizzy with the distress of it, and Tom now rages on all fronts. About Singapore he protested to me that nothing could ever be done in the Eastward by a man unprepared to exceed his remit, and by God he'd never again found by himself for The Company a settlement, by God he wouldn't, which taking of the Lord's name in vain I did not like, tho' from tact I did not rebuke him.

October 1824, Piccadilly

Tom, angry but resigned, has written to his business agent in Calcutta making arrangements for his disallowed salary to be paid from the Bengal Treasury to India House out of government securities he has there in his name. He has likewise written to the Court of Directors informing them of these arrangements, and asking that they may now release his pension. We remind ourselves often we have had far worse in life to face than the miserliness and meanness of the Honourable Members.

October 1824, Number 2, Wellington Place, Cheltenham

For worrying about our pecuniary troubles, I became ill in London, and spent much of the latter part of our visit in bed, but my health is improving now we have returned to Cheltenham – my Ella Bella is better tonic, and sweeter, than any medicine – tho' I must complain of loss of weight. Tom too has lost the little fat which briefly clothed his bones, and, alas, he is much annoyed with his headaches, tho' they are *bilious* not *nervous*, which I think reassures me.

October 1824, Number 2, Wellington Place, Cheltenham

Tom has had a relapse, with his head tormenting him to a sad degree. His bilious headaches turn once more nervous, and the pain, sharp, lancing, throbbing, maddening, crushing – his descriptions vary – confines him to his bed. I cannot pretend I am not alarmed.

November 1824, Number 2, Wellington Place, Cheltenham

To my very great relief, Tom is at last up on his legs, but he will not rest, instead he continues to think of Our Winter Campaign. In order that we may better prosecute it, he insists we remove our household to London, so we have purchased from Sir Humphrey Davy the lease on Number 23, Lower Grosvenor Street, in Mayfair.

In an attempt to reassure me Tom claims that once we are in town whenever he is not scheming, flattering, cajoling, and blustering at India House he will fall to idling and playing the fool with his time, this in order to save his health. I wish I could believe him, but I doubt a nature as impatient as his will manage such a squandering, for his restless frame and mind want ever occupation.

November 1824, Number 23, Lower Grosvenor Street

Lower Grosvenor Street is on a fine square, laid out with expensive taste, and our house, on the east side, suits us exactly. We are much enjoying being in London, everything is so new, varied, and important, after so long an absence in the woods and wilds of the East. Tom says that, like the bee, he wanders from flower to flower, drinking in delicious nutriment from the numerous intellectual and aesthetic sources which surround him.

For all that, we both suffer greatly from the damp and cold, and however much we wrap up in worsteds and woollens we never seem to be warm, and our bones ache, so we tell each other we sometimes miss even the searing noonday sun of the Eastward, tho' when we lived there we did all we could to avoid it.

December 1824, Number 23, Lower Grosvenor Street

Tom has been busy petitioning many of the most important men in The Company on our pecuniary behalf, and with some success, for he now hears from his friends at India House that the feeling seems to move very much his way, and the matter of his pension will soon be settled in our favour. He says we can surely expect to hear good news by Christmas, and he'll be a director of The Company yet.

I would be as happy as my husband, except seldom a day passes when he does not have an engagement for dinner, and all the time we have been in London he has scarcely been able to command an hour's leisure. I wish he would bear in mind that if he yields to the many flattering invitations his friends press upon him, he must not expect to renovate a constitution much shaken by long residence and arduous labours in the enervating clime of the Eastward. Indeed, I have had to warn him to remember this is his first season since our change of climate, and he must take care not to over tax himself, or his constitution could be forever undermined.

December 1824, Number 23, Lower Grosvenor Street

From being too fagged and harassed Tom is again afflicted with his head. Alas, he seems settled into a pattern which sees him suffer terrible headaches, then appear to recover, then suffer a little while later a relapse.

When poorly he is a mostly uncomplaining patient. When well he appears his usual self. Is his composure acted? If so, for his sake, I try to go along with his pretence but I am uncomfortable in my mind. In truth, I think he needs a change of air, and I have begun to look in earnest for a country house where we can be quiet, and retired. We seek a permanent home in the surrounding country of London, to retreat to in the summer, when everybody of first rank is forced from Town by the heat of the season, indeed it is our plan now to find that farm we dreamed of in the Eastward – about two hundred acres thinks Farmer Tom.

Christmas Eve 1824, Number 23, Lower Grosvenor Street

So much for hearing good news by Christmas. There is still no word on our pension. Tom is cast down, and reflects Our Winter Campaign goes badly. He says, gloomily, that what Johnny Company will do is ever uncertain, but if the Court of Directors' liberality keeps pace with their delay, he ought to expect for his pension something handsome.

January 1825, Number 23, Lower Grosvenor Street

Speculation, peculation, London has gone mad for money, and people are making fortunes through investing in this expanding company, or in that enlarging scheme, or in the other enriching stock.

Alas, for our scarcity of funds, this luck of money conjuring from itself yet more money cannot now fall to us, and for anxiety we'll miss our chance, Tom has written to his agents in the Eastward, asking them to remit all the monies left with them as soon as they can, as he is anxious not only to settle his supposed debt to The Company, and to buy a farm, but also to invest what little fortune he has remaining to him as early as possible.

February 1825, Number 23, Lower Grosvenor Street

It seems I was wrong ever to think Tom had put aside all thought of a second edition of *The History of Java*, for yesterday he collected his papers from his Aunt Elizabeth, his late Cousin Elton's mother, and now he has visited with Mr. Murray, to talk about both his second edition, and also his memoir of Singapore – notwithstanding all our distractions he continues to work at that, when time allows. He said that in the front upstairs drawing room at Mr. Murray's house he encountered a scene somewhere between a salon, with great pictures on the walls, and literary gentlemen exchanging gossip by the fire, and a country lawyer's office on the day the tithes are paid, for everywhere there were papers heaped about, and more people arriving with manuscripts all the time – as to his own projects, Mr. Murray quite approved them.

April 1825, Number 23, Lower Grosvenor Street

I have had little to report these past few weeks, but Tom last night attended the first General Meeting of his zoological society. He gave the opening address, and he explained that tho' he looks to country gentlemen of independent means for funds for the proposed menagerie, he is clear that the character of the institution must depend on the proportion of serious men of science that it contains.

For all Prinny, as was, is now elevated to the throne, he retains an interest in Tom. Hence it was by monarchal favour my husband was able last night to read out a letter from the Commissioners of His Majesty's Woods, Forests, and Land Revenues agreeing to lease the society five acres of Regent's Park, the Commissioners being at liberty to require the removal of any of the society's animals which may be deemed likely to become a nuisance or objectionable in the neighbourhood – a most understandable caveat, says Tom, for Regent's Park has shooting up around its perimeter numberless elegant new houses and it is a well-known fact fashionables don't like to be disturbed in their doings by animals may eat them.

April 1825, Number 23, Lower Grosvenor Street

We have found a farm near Hendon, in Middlesex, and Tom is negotiating for us to buy it. Highwood is just the place to ruralise – neither too close to Town, nor too far – and it has with it a hundred and eleven acres, mostly laid down to grass, well stocked with sheep, pigs, and cows and with ample stabling for the horses. The house, a modern edifice, stuccoed, of two stories, has a pretty façade, with on the ground floor two rounded bay windows flanking a central portico, and inside the hall a sweeping staircase, curving, and most delightful to behold.

The property sits atop a hill, and looks down over green slopes and fine groups of trees, upon a broad and fertile expanse of wood and cultivated ground – the views are most extensive and the mingling of hill and dale, wood and lawn could not be more harmonious.

May 1825, Number 23, Lower Grosvenor Street

Highwood is ours. The negotiations were so troublesome we

almost thought to give up on them, but Tom persevered, and once more we have a hill, tho' not this time a hill of Eastern mists, but one of good, homely English views. We paid eighteen thousand pounds for the property, our monies remitted from the Eastward, and anticipate spending two thousand more on improvements – we will move there as soon as some work we commission is finished. Tom is assured he has not paid too much for it, and he thinks the money we get from the produce of the farm will much exceed the profit we could have had from renting out the land. We have bought the standing crop of hay.

June 1825, Highwood

Hosanna! We have fulfilled the dream that sustained us in the Eastward, and moved to our farm where we may make butter and cheese. I am enchanted by Highwood, tho' we are nowhere near straight. When he's not at his desk, Tom takes great delight in the estate, and says it is better by far to look on his own land in England, than the same in the Eastward, and he has already derived incalculable benefit to his health from the air and exercise ruralising has given him. We are in the midst of a heatwave, so I am too hot to write more than this, for all I have tolerated the fierce sun of the Eastward.

July 1825, Highwood

I am surrounded by crates and boxes and the people unpacking them, and more arriving all the time, for the wreck of Tom's collections – the things we put in storage when we left England for Bencoolen, or shipped back since – are now returned to us. Tom says he must have his gamelan in the hall, and one of our main rooms is to be turned into a museum for his remaining natural history specimens. Already we have unpacked an extensive series of stuffed quadrupeds, birds, reptiles, insects, and the skin and skeleton of an orang utan.

July 1825, Highwood

Our parish church, St. Mary's, Hendon, gives but one cause of dissatisfaction: I do not like to speak ill of men of the cloth, but I must say Our Vicar is of a very peculiar character – a most difficult, peppery gentleman. He is dour to everybody, but he has taken a particular dislike to Tom. This antipathy, we learn, is on account of Tom's well-known opposition to the slave trade, for Our Vicar's family has plantations in Jamaica, and their money came from slaving, hence he deplores the abolition of the slave trade.

With his single curmudgeonly exception, the local people all acknowledge Tom's zeal, civility, and many virtues; our neighbours urge him to become a magistrate, and he has decided to put himself forward. Notwithstanding his willingness to serve, he fears that tho' he has spent his life directing others how to execute similar offices, he may himself be deficient in the details.

August 1825, Highwood

We live here an idyllic life with Ella, Charley Boy, and dear Nurse Grimes. My children – for I now quite count Charley Boy as my own – my children are delightfully well, working in the garden all day. I take charge of the poultry and the pigs and milk the cows – what a delightful pretty dairy I have – and Tom takes care of the sheep and tends the bullocks. We brew our own beer, and bake our own bread, and lead an entire country life. We are in most things self-sufficient, wine and fish are all I have to buy in – and I do not mean to say I milk the cows myself, I have dairymaids to do it, and likewise Tom has a cow boy for the bullocks.

November 1825, Highwood

Where has the time gone? I realise now I have not picked up my quill since high summer, and now it is winter, both in actual fact, and in the nation's spirits: the bubble that has been expanding people's purses is burst; for reasons none seem able to fathom the country has been plunged into a financial panic; we are being devoured, apparently, by a monstrous national debt; there is great scarcity of money; trade is stagnant; banks are failing up and down the country; property values are falling; wages the same; stocks are being sold for farthings; prices are rising; taxes are soaring.

Some say the Bank of England is to blame, for irresponsible lending, and the bankers must be punished because they are wicked, crafty men who would fleece simple, honest people, and others say greedy debtors are to blame, for grasping, irresponsible borrowing. Whatever the truth of it, fortunes are being lost, many are going under, many face ruin, and Tom says money is turning to toilet paper in people's hands.

Christmas Day, 1825

Our Vicar this morning cut Tom after communion, and this I think a most uncharitable thing to do, and today of all days, but when I protested of it to Tom he laughed and said he should think less of himself if he didn't now and then rouse to ire a lukewarm clergyman, which remark upset me greatly.

January 1826, Highwood

The financial panic is not abating, and indeed it is a fast-growing hydra-headed thing that seems to know no geographic bounds, and is rampaging still through many lives – including ours. Alas,

Tom learns now that our resources are alarmingly diminished: following a run set off by rumours and false reports, his bank in Java last year failed, with a consequent loss to him of sixteen thousand pounds.

I must remember: *He that loveth silver shall not be satisfied with silver; nor he that loveth abundance with increase: this is also vanity.*

January 1826, Highwood

We are in some confusion whether our agents in the Eastward ever received Tom's instruction to release our funds from the Bengal treasury to India House, for certainly the transfer has not yet been completed. Nonetheless, Tom has written to the Court of Directors asking the Honourable Members to commence as soon as possible payment of his pension, which, more than a year after he first asked for it, has still not been forthcoming, and if we ever see this pension I will be most surprised, tho' I do not say so to Tom, who remains optimistic.

February 1826, Highwood

My recent pessimism over matters pecuniary has received the best of rebukes: Tom now hears from his friends at India House that the Court of Directors has had laid before it his recent letter, and they tell him to anticipate good news from The Company. Tom is happy, tho' he fears his pension will be very moderate and five hundred pounds a year is the largest amount he hears of.

February 1826, Number 23, Lower Grosvenor Street

We have closed up Highwood – carpets being taken up, &c – and returned to Lower Grosvenor Street for the London Season, and

Tom has again all his Great Men about him, and all he needs now, to complete his satisfaction, is confirmation from The Company that he can have his pension.

April 1826, Number 23, Lower Grosvenor Street

I am dazed by anger and sorrow mixed: Tom has received a most shocking letter from the Court of Directors: instead of granting him his pension of five hundred pounds per annum, the Honourable Members have demanded from him the preposterous sum of twenty-two thousand two hundred and seventy-two pounds.

Notwithstanding they know full well Tom is trying to remit to them the alleged debt they claim, they demand again repayment of the disputed principal, and also interest on that amount.

But this is not the end of it: the so-called *Honourable* Members demand now that Tom repay commission he claimed on exports when he engaged in some petty private trading at Bencoolen, for which trading he had received permission from Bengal.

Worse – incredible – they have the gall to demand Tom repay nearly five thousand pounds for contingent charges he incurred in the founding of Singapore – this settlement that is expected to bring them this year perhaps ten million Spanish dollars – which expenses he is now told he should never have authorised.

I tell myself this is a worldly affair, and that it must not affect our happiness.

April 1826, Number 23, Lower Grosvenor Street

Tom, dignified, has written to the Court of Directors reminding the Honourable Members he expects soon the disallowed salary to be paid from the Bengal Treasury, and explaining the commission on exports he made as a private trader was sanctioned by the Bengal government. As to the charges he incurred in founding Singapore, he has felt obliged to point out that they amount to but a trifling sum, when set against the profit the settlement has brought to their pockets, and to those of The Company's shareholders.

In the case they are not persuaded to fairness, Tom has had to explain to the Honourable Members that because of the failure of our bankers in the Eastward he is unable at the present moment to meet their demands, and he requests he be given time to order his accounts.

April 1826, Number 23, Lower Grosvenor Street

We mean to go abroad next year, everything here is in such a dreadful state – the financial panic – people starving, people made homeless, labourers idle, beggars on every street corner, many children amongst them, merchants failing, bankers ruined, austerity, meanness, misery, severity, in short, nothing can be more melancholy – we thought ourselves so comfortably settled, and now we shall be obliged to dispose of Highwood to meet the losses we have incurred in the Eastward, and the debts The Company claims we have accrued.

Tom worries long over our accounts, and I worry long for his health for I fear our pecuniary disaster would be enough to endanger a man of far more robust constitution.

May 1826, Number 23, Lower Grosvenor Street

I have been re-reading, as I have too often been called upon to do, in my *Book of Common Prayer* the order for the visitation of the sick, for Tom today suffered an attack most sudden and unexpected: he collapsed in Portland Place, where he had been visiting a friend. He was brought home by the servants, accompanied by a doctor who happened to be passing when he fainted. He was unconscious for an hour, but now, after bleeding with leeches, he is up and about again, tho' still weak and nervous, and his head not quite what it should be.

May 1826, Number 23, Lower Grosvenor Street

Tom reassures me his recent attack was not apoplectic, and I call his honest seizure a fainting fit, and yet I think we are both afraid. Certainly, something has changed in my husband since his collapse. Tho' his spirit and animation are great, his speech is at times heavy, thick, even inarticulate.

June 1826, Number 23, Lower Grosvenor Street

I am uneasy, filled with disquiet, for Tom told me today he remembered his Olivia saying, during her last illness, that it was ever the lot of men to yearn for a longer span of life than they were granted, and, to his shame, he'd hushed her when she'd said it. My heart clenched as it always does when Tom talks of Olivia, but now more than ever, and I felt my skin prickle with dread. I fixed my husband with my beadiest eye, and I told him here was no shame at all, because our span of life is determined by The Great Author of all Events, and to yearn against His plan for us is indeed a failure of faith. Tom glanced away. When he glanced back, he took my hand, and he said he was glad for me my own faith was such a solace.

June 1826, Number 23, Lower Grosvenor Street

Debarring his slurred speech, Tom is much recovered, and he seems to have put aside his recent morbid melancholy – so much so, he once again mingles with all the Great Men of Town, and he is again busy with his plans and projects. I am grateful for his improving health, and for his buoyancy of spirits, but his resumed activity worries me.

June 1826, Number 23, Lower Grosvenor Street

Tho' I urged him not to, for his health's sake, Tom has attended the second council meeting of his zoological society. He presented a sketch of the plan for laying out the grounds of the zoological garden in Regent's Park, and a thousand pounds was voted for proceedings.

Tom also reported a proposal from Edward Cross, owner of the Exeter Change Menagerie, offering his services in the management of the society's animals, plus his own present collection. The council declined. Last February an elephant in Cross' menagerie rampaged. The poor beast was crazed by pain from a poisoned tusk; soldiers had to be summoned from Somerset House and it took more than a hundred musket balls, and a thrust from a sabre, to bring him down. The council felt this undermined confidence in Cross's abilities as an animal handler.

June 1826, Highwood

The Season continues a little longer in brilliance and gaiety, and yet I have insisted we return early to Highwood, to escape from Town in this heat of summer – people call it oppressive, tho' it is cooler than a spring morning in the Eastward. Still, it raises in Town many stinks I do not like to breathe, and I *do* like to see my children running about the garden at Highwood, and above all I want to cajole Tom into resting, that he may recuperate fully from his fainting fit. I try to command he be lazy, tho' he wants to be all day at his literary projects, or at his farming, and when I protest he asks me: what is existence without occupation?

June 1826, Highwood

Why would Tom not listen when I asked him to rest? I have snatched a moment from my duties in the sickroom to record that my husband has exhausted himself, and he is now suffering from a bilious attack, accompanied by much vomiting.

New Year's Day 1827, Highwood

A new year, and I must make something of it, notwithstanding it is a beginning I must face alone; my years as a wife are over; I am wedded to my husband now not through union but through separation – a widow grieving deep in deepest black.

How I yearn for Tom. To think of him overcome with dizziness at the head of the stairs, grabbing for the handrail, missing, glancing down and seeing a well shaft where the stairwell should have been, a dark, dank hole, and at its base not water, but a swirling pool of ghosts, stretching their arms towards him, yearning, willing him to join them ... it is too horrible, I must stop this imagining, or go mad.

January 1827, Highwood

For as in Adam all die, even so in Christ shall all be made alive ... God has done great things for me, and been very tender. I can still trust Him. I must not be less resigned because my sense of suffering is acute. I must not question. And yet, even after six months, my thoughts remain so wild and sad it is only with effort I can remember my bright and beloved husband is surrounded now by Charlotte, Leo, Cooksey, and Flora, the father and his children enjoying their happy home, tho' longing to have me with them, as I would long to be with them as well, were it not for Ella.

But is Olivia also there, reunited with Tom? (This is a

question I must not ask, for fear of filling my head with ruinous ruminations.)

January 1827, Highwood

Be ye also ready, for the Son of man cometh at an hour when ye think not ... It was July 5, the day before Tom's 45th birthday, when I found him dead at the bottom of the sweeping staircase here at Highwood – how I shake at the memory. He had retired to rest on the Tuesday evening, between ten and eleven o'clock. Notwithstanding many ominous signs, I failed to apprehend the fateful hour was so near. Oh, the shock! The following morning, I was wakened before dawn by a feeling that made the hairs on the nape of my neck stand on end. Alarmed, I rushed to Tom's room: empty. Had he been driven from it by pain? By foreboding? In any case, after some moments of panicked searching I found my husband lying cold and insensible on the hall floor. Medical help was procured, and every means resorted to, to restore animation, but the vital spark had fled. Tom died alone – I was not there – which thought must ever now torment me, notwithstanding he was crossing from darkness into light.

It was his brain fever, or indigestion of the head, that killed him. This I know for sure because I asked a surgeon to open his body the same day he died – a strange thing to do, perhaps, and perhaps not very Christian, but a kind of madness enveloped me in the first hours of my widowhood, and from within its mist, I thought discovering the cause of Tom's death was a way to honour his uncommon curiosity, his interest in science, the love of the natural world that had so enriched his life, whilst humbly leaving to God the question *why*?

The surgeon discovered many irregularities of Tom's cranium, and of his brain, which was in many places a swollen tangle of blood vessels, and in one place he found a coagulum of blood the size of a pullet's egg.

This horrid pullet's egg of clotted blood killed me as surely as it killed my husband. I mean to say that with Tom's death, the recollection of past happiness at once became, for me, the only happiness of the present moment, and my life as something vivid ceased to exist, for Tom was my life, and now my life is over.

As to my beloved's funeral, I arranged for Tom's remains to be interred at St. Mary's, but owing to the peculiar character of Our Vicar no memorial tablets were permitted to be set up, so I now record my husband's unmarked remains lie in peace in *a vault beneath the south chapel*, for I cannot allow Tom's final resting place to be forgotten, any more than I can his name. Indeed, beyond ensuring I raise Ella to adulthood, and keep Charley Boy safe until Mary Ann can reclaim him, I have no purpose now except to ignite a flame will keep Tom's memory blazing long into the future.

January 1827, Highwood

Some may say Ella, our last earthly treasure, is the flame will keep Tom's memory alive. But this forgets she is merely his daughter, so if it pleases God she lives to be married then she will one day take her husband's name, which is a poor sort of honouring for her late father, and if she has the ill-luck to remain a spinster, then the name *Raffles* will die with her.

January 1827, Highwood

Singapore, I suppose, will be Tom's memorial? A monument to his patriotism, sagacity, and fervid spirit. But Tom's almost only child is half the world away from anywhere that matters. And beyond India House, Westminster, London how many even of his countrymen know of its existence? Then again, its name is

Singapore, not *Raffles Town*, and how shall *this* name keep *Tom's* name in view?

February 1827, Highwood

In settlement of Tom's alleged debt, the Honourable Members of the Court of Directors have taken all my little investments, so I now face a life of embarrassment – alas, I must soon sell Highwood, and when I do I shall shift to the continent, where all the costs are less than here.

But what is financial distress, or sacrifice, compared to my duty to memorialise my husband – he who is still my first object in this world? Notwithstanding the littleness of my fortune I have commissioned from the sculptor Mr. Chantrey a life-size statue of Tom seated, in white marble, for erection in Westminster Abbey. Through Mr. Chantrey's good offices I am promised that when the work is completed this statue will be placed in the north choir aisle of the Abbey – a splendid, visible position.

February 1827, Highwood

I have been meditating on the literary projects Tom left unexecuted – the second edition of *The History of Java*, his memoir of Singapore – oh, the pity of these ambitions left unfulfilled, of all Tom's plans that never came to fruition! I have been thinking, too, that words can perhaps make a more enduring memorial to a man than can a statue, however skilfully it is sculpted, and however prominently it is placed. In short, I have been thinking I should commission some willing friend to write a memoir of Tom.

April 1827, Highwood

I remember Tom telling me once, of *The History of Java*, that before he began it, he did not imagine he could actually write it himself, he would rather have seen the materials worked up by an abler hand than incur the risk and responsibility of undertaking the task himself. However, no abler hand having revealed itself, he began working on his history. And so it is with my proposed memoir of him: after six weeks of searching, I find it difficult to enthuse any friend to take on the weighty task, for they plead with one voice they cannot make sense of Tom's life without the documents lost on the *Fame*, and thus I think I must write it myself. And yet I am so completely ignorant of book making that I really do not know how to set about this, and widows are not expected to take up their pens in duty to their dead husbands.

April 1827, Highwood

This diary, this memory of my husband, will be a most substantial help when it comes to writing my book, so, were circumstances not so sad, I could almost commend myself on anticipatory prudence in keeping it. But what of the years when I did not share Tom's life? How shall I know what to say of the period before he went to India? And yet something ought to be said. And I am too quite at a loss regarding all the period in Penang, and in Java – how can I fill up the gaps? And not forgetting Olivia remains to me a perfect *blank*.

April 1827, Highwood

My object with my memoir must be a record of Tom's *public* achievements more than a popular reading volume to satisfy gossips. Discretion shall preserve me; I shall say nothing of a *personal* nature. As to my marriage, I shall not draw aside too far the veil from that domestic altar, which, to all who have been admitted to its highest and holiest duties, is very sacred. And as to Olivia I will decidedly say nothing of her, for what can I say of a *blank*?

Moreover, I shall not allow my voice to intrude on Tom's: I shall be his papers' *editor* only, so that when my memoir is published Tom shall be on the whole his own biographer, for he can speak for himself better than I ever could. And who could have any interest in my opinions, in my voice, in me, were it not for him?

May 1827, Highwood

If it pleases God that I live to complete it, I intend to place my memoir in the hands of Mr. Murray – tho' perhaps it is wrong to think of handing my manuscript to a publisher before even I have begun it?

Still, I imagine my book as a quarto vol, in a red cloth binding, and if it is erected by the time of publication, I think an engraving of Tom's statue in Westminster Abbey would do very well for a frontispiece. I have settled, too, on a title: *Memoir of the Life and Public Services of Sir Thomas Stamford Raffles*. This has, I think, a dignified, weighty ring. My *Memoir* must have a portrait of Tom – his bust – a map, and four or five plates. Notwithstanding I do not intend a popular reading volume, Mr. Murray must make it as cheap as possible

May 1827, Highwood

Tho' I feel quite bewildered and unequal to my task and refuge – a melancholy pleasure that causes both my head and my heart to ache – I have commenced editing those of my husband's papers not lost on the *Fame*: his remaining reports, despatches, speeches, minutes, memoranda, letters, and other ephemera, but how to order his documents and statements is a puzzle – the division into chapters, how is this to be done?

In any case, all will be done under such a sense of prayer for God's guidance and blessing that I cannot think I shall greatly err. And however harassing the necessary editorial work, this is my promise to Tom: through my *Memoir*, I, your widow, will assure for you an historical reputation, and one of greatness. Tom, my beloved, through my efforts I will assure you for one of your heart's desires: fame, enduring fame.

EPILOGUE

Excerpt from the introduction to *Memoir of the Life and Public Services of Sir Thomas Stamford Raffles*, by his widow.

The following Memoir of Sir Stamford Raffles, it is hoped, will afford an outline of the public life of one who was placed in situations of no common responsibility, and filled them with no common firmness, talent, and success. His exertions to promote the honour of his country, the happiness of the people committed to his charge, and, therefore, the best interests of his employers, can only be duly estimated by a knowledge of the peculiar difficulties with which he had to contend ...

... The loss of all the papers with which, after his last government, he was returning to England, and which were destroyed in the calamitous burning of the ship, has added much to the difficulty of the task of recording the details of his public life. It is owing, indeed, to this misfortune, that the undertaking has fallen upon the present Editor, who would otherwise have gladly availed herself of the abilities of those better qualified to perform the task. The wreck of Sir Stamford's papers ... it was found could only be fully made use of by one well acquainted with the events of his life. From peculiar circumstances, the Editor had the happiness to participate in almost all the scenes described during his last administration in India, and also to become generally acquainted with the events of his former government.

... The Editor cannot conclude without expressing her

hope that the motives which induce her to compile this memoir, (a desire to do justice to her husband's memory, and possibly, in some degree, contribute to the information of the public on topics of great national importance,) will justify the attempt, and procure for her the indulgence of which she stands so much in need.

Author's Note

I wanted wherever possible to incorporate words, phrases, snatches, sentences and fragments from letters, diaries, and other documents written by Olivia, Sophia, Raffles, and their contemporaries, British, Dutch, and Malay. I used these sources without acknowledgement within the text, but I do now want to stress my indebtedness to the dead, my unwitting ghost writers.

In particular, Sophia's memoir of her husband preserves many of his letters, letters sent to him, and other documents, sometimes linked by passages she wrote herself. Given the wealth of material, in some sections of Part Two I have almost taken on the role Sophia assigned herself: that of editor, if an intrusive one. Hence, in some entries of Sophia's fictionalised diary, words presented as written by her, or anyway versions of them, were indeed written by her.

Passages reliant on the memoir include: Sophia's descriptions of Mr. Presgrave falling in a pit; of seeing the tiger in the forest; of domestic life at Permattam Ballam.

Lines from personal letters are scattered throughout, especially in Part Two. Sophia and Raffles both allow us glimpses of their children, and of their feelings on their deaths, in letters to friends and family. As an example of how I incorporated others' words into this novel, and to stand as a tribute to all the other quotations I wove in, I should like to acknowledge that one sentence in particular was not written by me, but by Raffles, in a letter to Mary Ann. With hindsight it is a wrenching sentence:

'Leopold has been unwell for the past fortnight and is a good deal pulled down, but we think he is getting better.'

The description of the sinking of the *Fame* is based on Raffles' own account in a pamphlet he published in London. The description of the discovery of *Rafflesia arnoldii* is based on a description given by Dr. Arnold in a letter found after his death, quoted in *Raffles and the Golden Opportunity* by Victoria Glendinning.

I am not an historian. I treated history as a first draft for a novel, hence I took many liberties which would horrify historians. Where the facts, or versions of them, are known, I sometimes ignored them, and generally I bent them. The politics behind the British conquest of Java, and the founding of Singapore, were to say the least complicated. I simplified, and then simplified my simplifications, and then simplified again. I fiddled with the dates of many private events – the problem with lives, I found, is that too much happens at once, or else nothing much happens for ages. I changed people's names – from my point of view, there were too many women, in Raffles' day, called 'Harriet'. I failed to acknowledge when people changed their rank or title. In Part One I referred to the man now known as 'the Duke of Wellington' as 'Wellington', even though he had not yet been granted his dukedom. I amalgamated people's roles. I chopped people from the story. I here and there misattributed a few words. I sent Olivia and Sophia along with Raffles on journeys he took without them. I made things up.

I hesitate to describe the background reading I did as 'research.' I used and abused numerous websites, and the following books. I recommend them all to anybody wanting to find out about Raffles, his wives, and the history somewhat precariously underpinning this novel.

Antiques of the Orient *Sir Thomas Stamford Raffles, book of days*

Barley, Nigel *In the Footsteps of Stamford Raffles*

Bastin, John *Olivia Raffles / Sophia Raffles* (two separate books)

Collis, Maurice *Raffles the Definitive Biography*

Glendinning, Victoria *Raffles and the Golden Opportunity*

Hannigan, Tim *Raffles and the British Invasion of Java*

Key, John *The Honourable Company: a History of the English East India Company*

Ministry of Education, Singapore *Understanding Our Past: Singapore from Colony to Nation*

Raffles, Sir Thomas Stamford *History of Java*

Raffles, Sophia *Memoir of the Life and Public Services of Sir Thomas Stamford Raffles*

Uglow, Jenny *In These Times: living in Britain through Napoleon's wars*

Yule, Henry and A.C. Burnell *Hobson-Jobson: The Anglo-Indian Dictionary*

Acknowledgements to the Living

Thanks to you, Dear Reader, if you've got this far, for spending however many hours with Olivia and Sophia. Thanks, Fran, for being so enthusiastic when I first mentioned I was thinking of writing about Raffles' wives. Thanks, Kelly, for your invaluable criticism of early drafts. Thanks, Philip, for liking this novel enough to publish it. Thanks, Sujatha, for your copy-editing skills. A, J and M, just thanks.